Savage Run

E. J. Squires

This is a work of fiction.
Any characters, organizations,
and events portrayed in this novel
are either the products of the author's
imagination or are used fictitiously.

First Edition Dec. 10, 2014

ISBN-13: 978-1505406375
ISBN-10: 1505406374
Copyright © 2014 E. J. Squires

All rights reserved.

Other books Available by E. J. Squires:

Wraithsong
Desirable Creatures Series, Book I
(Now available)

Blufire
Desirable Creatures Series, Book II
(Now Available)

Winter Solstice Winter
A Viking Blood Saga, Book I
(Now available)

Summer Solstice Summer
A Viking Blood Saga, Book II
(Now available)

Midgard Fall
A Viking Blood Saga, Book III
(Coming Soon)

Trepidation
White Witch Black Warlock Series, Book I
(Coming Soon)

For more information, go to:
http://ejsquires.com

For my children.
May freedom and love
be the inspiration behind
every choice.

Part 1

The Escape

Chapter 1

Biking up the same mile-and-a-half long asphalt hill is so much harder when I know that at the end of the journey I'll either be an outlaw, or I'll be dead.

Rippling wind tugs at my black uniform as I push the pedals on my bike, one after another. The rhythm of the squeaky, swooshing sound is as familiar as the fragrance of the seemingly never-ending lavender field to my right—the purple meadow that divides the Masters' estates from the Laborers' slum: the slum where I was born, the slum where I live, the slum I hope to escape from soon.

I glance down at the prescription bag lying in the rusty basket attached to the steering wheel. The bag is supposed to hide my father's kitchen knife, but it has shifted and catches the sunlight, winking at me from the bottom. After a quick scan of my surroundings to confirm that no one is watching, I reach down and readjust the bag over the blade. And just in case, I glance over my shoulder to make sure the change of clothes is still attached to the back railing of my bike. It is.

Zooming up the wide, cracked road, I pass countless Laborers—nameless, faceless shadows—scurrying to their

Masters in the mountains or toward the factories and fields. The muted, gray line of men, women, and children winds toward Mount Zalo, and will eventually disintegrate as each person disappears into the white, gated estates they are assigned to. This long walk is the extent of a Laborer's freedom. Most are forbidden to go anywhere without their Masters—unless they are traveling to or from work, before dawn—after sunset.

I pass a few young men, guys I thought for sure would have signed up for the Savage Run, a grueling, new obstacle course program that for the first time in history, allows inferior class teenage boys to demonstrate their worthiness to become Masters.

As I continue to bike ahead, I see my best friend's mother, Ruth. Since Gemma left last year, Ruth has diminished into a walking skeleton. Not that she ever had any extra weight on her anyway. All Laborers pretty much have the same build with sunken cheeks and concave bellies grumbling on and on because the measly amount of food we're rationed could never be enough. But unlike all the other Laborer women, Ruth's hair is still short—even after a year—an indication that she's been in trouble with the law. Normally I welcome any meeting with her, but because of where I'm headed, and because of what I'm about to do, not so much today. Yet gliding right past her and pretending not to see her is just not right, no matter what. Not after what she's done for me.

I slow my bike as I approach her and say, "Nice day for a walk."

"Ah, good morning, Heidi. You already running deliveries?"

I eye the bag in the basket to make sure the blade isn't showing again. "Yes, I'm on my fifth one."

"Where are you headed?" Ruth smiles, and the sides of her brown eyes crease like the wrinkles on a scrunched up paper bag.

Should I lie to save her feelings? I decide on the truth. "To Master Douglas."

"Ah..." The edges of her lips rise upward a little, but the rest of her face is like a dry ocean.

I should have lied.

"Tell Gemma I say...hello." Her words carry the weight of our late-night conversations. But rehashing how her only daughter serves a Master who is rumored to have beaten two of his Laborers to death won't help. I wish I could tell Ruth what I'm really doing—what I've been obsessing about for months. And I would if I knew I could pull it off. If I could look her in the eyes and promise her nothing would happen to her Gemma. But I can't.

"I will." Then I quickly change the subject. "So, did you see anyone heading toward Culmination this morning?" President Volkov decreed today to be Savage Run registration day, a day off for male Laborers and Advisors ages thirteen through seventeen. "To give the least of us a chance at liberty." I thought for sure every Laborer who fit into those categories would jump on the opportunity. As I left, I didn't see a single soul do anything other than depart their squat, aluminum trailers and join in the march.

"No. Trusting President Volkov's words is like digging your grave with three sticks of dynamite."

My stomach sinks. A lot. "Well, I should get going so I won't be late."

6

"It was good to see you, Heidi."

On my way to the mountains, I pass the tail end of the Laborers' sector. In front of our sector there are light waves that everyone calls "the veil." They hide our less than aesthetically pleasing buildings from the Master side of town. It would be a shame to ruin their view. I can't see it from here because of the veil, but each ten by twenty, squat aluminum trailer is stashed on top of another, three high, and side-by-side, fifteen long. When they built our housing, each trailer was intended to house one family. Now, two families occupy most trailers, though a few of us are lucky and don't have to share. Outside of work we spend our free time around campfires preparing lackluster meals or doing laundry. If we once in a while manage to have a few moments for ourselves, we huddle together around bonfires or visit with neighbors.

I approach downtown and ride by the Colosseum where many of the national sporting events are held. The cultural hub of Newland, Culmination is one of the country's most esteemed towns and is the home of the Porto Tower—the tallest building in the world. It's a town brimming with sculptures, mosaics, paintings, museums, and art academies, and it's even rumored that the ancient statue of David and the Mona Lisa are kept beneath the Culmination Historical Museum. In Newland's early years, many world-renowned architects and artists settled in Culmination, drawn here by President Volkov's offer of immediate Master status by President Volkov Sr., and the dramatic countryside. Now a little Rome, Culmination is the place to send your Master kid for an education in art.

As I let my bike roll to a stop a generous distance away from Master Douglas's gate, the wind whistles through the trees, sprinkling some of the leftover raindrops on my hands and face. I've been here hundreds of times before to deliver medicine, but I have to admit that my hands have never shaken so much that I had to white-knuckle the handlebars just to steady them. Dare I go through with my plan?

Lifting my gaze, I see the ivory stonewall that encases the white, oval mansion. The abode itself is at least fifty times larger than the trailer my father and I share, with six thick marble columns and more floor-to-ceiling windows than I would ever want to clean. Poor Gemma.

Most girls my age are already stuck inside a mansion similar to this one—cleaning, cooking, serving, or washing clothes. But since my father worked the majority of his life as a pastor at Culmination Hospital, he submitted my name, hoping I would qualify as one of their prescription couriers. And I did. I quite enjoy my work. Although, I don't like being under my father's scrutinizing eye. He reminds me almost daily that I should abstain from all appearances of evil. Whatever that means. As Laborers, my father and I are fortunate to have such great jobs since working in the oil rigs off the coasts, sorting trash, harvesting fruits and vegetables, or laboring in sweatshops are the norm.

Venturing into the woods with my rusty three-speed, my feet sink into the damp forest floor. The scent of the sodden, musty earth rises into my nostrils, and the earthy fragrance reminds me of when Gemma and I used to hang out in the woods behind our lane, commiserating about how unfair life is for Laborers. Her spontaneous laughter would vibrate off the sidings and bring life to all of the rusty trailers on our street. It's been almost a year since Gemma received her vocation, since I heard her laughter—that free and careless sound. Now, whenever I see her, her eyes are like dead stars.

I never truly questioned my obligation to submit myself into the service of a Master—it's a Laborer's place, my God-given contribution to society. My father has pounded this fact into me before I can remember. However, when I came here a couple of months ago and saw Gemma's eye crusted with blood and swollen shut, everything I so blindly believed, lived, and trusted—the entire framework of our society—all came tumbling down at once.

I sneak around the towering wall and all the way to the back of the Douglas household. Carefully, I slip my sandals in my bike's basket for easy access just in case I have to make a run for it. And before I proceed, I glimpse at the knife and the tan plastic bag to ensure they are still there. They are.

Grabbing onto the lowest branch, I press my feet against the trunk, hoist myself up, and climb high enough that I can glimpse into the backyard. I see Master Douglas sitting outside on a garden couch, wearing a black silk robe over red silk pajamas. He's drinking beer and reading the newspaper. The man is well known and highly respected in Culmination, and from his charm and charisma, and the fact that his name is on the majority of art museum contributor plaques, it's not hard to see why. But even without considering the rumors I've heard, there's just something about being around him—or even just thinking about him—that makes my skin crawl.

I find a wide spot on one of the thick, lower branches and straddle it. Still keeping Master Douglas within eyesight, I see him tearing out a Savage Run advertisement from the newspaper. He rips it to shreds and scatters the pieces so they fall to the white marble floor. I've talked to a few Masters about the Savage Run program and it's funny how all of them insisted that the survival of our nation depended upon individuals remaining in their class of birth. They couldn't understand what President Volkov was thinking creating a program that made it possible for inferior class citizens to receive Master status.

My chest squeezes when I see Gemma come out with a silver tray filled with all sorts of heavenly pastries. She's wearing a ruffled, peach, above-the-knee length dress that has a low neck, showing off her cleavage. Riding around town, I see more and more Laborers wearing fine clothing. And it's funny how in the past few years, it has almost become a competition among Masters to see who can have the prettiest and most well-dressed Laborer. A Laborer doesn't get to keep the clothing, but changes into it when arriving at their Master's and leaves it when they head home. Some Laborers, like Gemma, are forced to live with their Master and wear whatever they're told whenever they're told.

Gemma approaches Master Douglas with slumped shoulders and her gaze is down, as if she can't take a breath. Seeing how she has turned into one of these nameless, faceless shadows makes me want to scream at the man.

"What took you so long?" Master Douglas yells. She opens her mouth to answer, but a gust of wind rustles the leaves above my head, overpowering her reply. He hits the tray out of her hands so it lands on the ground with a crash.

My stomach clenches with anger.

He demands that she clean it up and tells her to go get another platter with the crumpets. Gemma apologizes, cleans up the mess, and scurries back inside the mansion, her face as ashen as the scattered clouds above.

Back when Gemma found out who she was being sent to work for, we joked that if things got too bad, we'd run away and somehow miraculously gain our freedom. I never dreamed that one day I'd actually find a way to make it happen.

It's not only Gemma who needs to get away, though. This morning my father woke me, shouting from the living area, asking where his lazy good-for-nothing daughter was. As I served him breakfast, he continued to lecture me about how it's not like I can skip a day's worth of work and sign up for the Savage Run or anything. I'm just a girl—the wrong gender. And besides, the hospital needed me to make an "emergency" prescription delivery to Master Douglas by 7:00 a.m. Yelling after me as I left, he said he'd pray that I'd swiftly repent of my irresponsible ways.

Like my father, Gemma has no clue about my plan, and I'm not even sure she'll go for it—it's kind of like jumping from the lion's den into the valley of death. However, being dead can't possibly be worse than enduring the life I'm living now, or the life I'll soon be forced to live. When I turn eighteen next week, I'll be assigned to my own Master. My father says he'll miss me, though he won't miss having another mouth to feed. What he'll soon realize is that he doesn't even have to wait until next week to be rid of me. I should be well on my way when he finds the note I left under my pillow, explaining that I won't be returning home.

Birds sing freely around me as I wait for Master Douglas to finish pigging out on the sausages. I peruse the forest, making sure no one's around. If caught straying from my responsibilities, I'd receive a harsh punishment like solitary confinement or beatings. Though these types of reprimands are fairly common, they're still dreaded among Laborers. Not to mention degrading. But occasionally there's a Laborer who for whatever reason openly defies their Master or tries to run away. In those instances, the retribution is much worse. It's always a heavy day when we're forced to Skull Hill to watch a beheading.

Sitting here is awkward and my leg is starting to tingle. I shift a little to get comfortable and to prevent it from going completely numb. I peer over the wall again, but still no Gemma. What could possibly be taking her so long? Doesn't she know that Master Douglas will ream her out again if she doesn't hurry? And the longer she takes, the more likely it is that my plan will fall completely apart. Finally, Gemma comes out with a new tray overflowing with pastries and crumpets and sets it on the marble table. How much breakfast does the man need? Even for a Master, he has an exquisite taste for gluttony.

From studying Master Douglas' routine, I've figured that the best time to get Gemma and make a run for it is right after he leaves for his hour-long walk. Around that time, the front gates will be left open for about ten minutes to let in a shipment of goods. The Unifer guarding the gates will be busy with the delivery and will take time to chat with the delivery driver. With a little luck, Gemma and I will slip behind the truck unnoticed.

I lean my head back onto the tree trunk, and let out a soundless sigh. This is taking way too long. Then suddenly, a lighthearted laugh catches my attention. I peek into the courtyard and see Master Douglas' seven-year-old daughter hopping onto his lap and planting a kiss on his pudgy cheek. She's always smiling and laughing, especially around him.

"Hi, sweetheart." His black, round eyes fill with adoring love for the child. "Will you be coming with me this morning to go horseback riding?"

"Not today, Dada," she says, hanging on his neck and stroking his graying hair. "I want to go swimming."

"Swimming?"

"It's so hot, and Gemma promised she'd take me."

"She did, did she?" He twirls her golden braid around his finger, while staring at Gemma. "I'll make sure I tell Gemma that she needs to take extra good care of you."

"See you later, Dada." She slides off his lap, and skips back into the house.

Master Douglas gulps the rest of his beer, pushes his palms against the armrests, and rises to his feet. He flicks his wrist toward Gemma. "Get lost!"

Gemma bends her head lower, and without a sound, she shuffles back into the house.

Heading inside, Master Douglas lets out a loud belch. I'm not quite sure, but I almost think I can smell his beer breath from all the way over here. I cover my nose with my hand and feel pressure rising at the back of my throat. Well—at least he's on the move.

I hop down from the tree and shove my feet into my cold, wet sandals. When I arrive at my bike, my whole body is shaking. This is it.

* * *

I once heard that if I run toward my fears as fast as I can, my fear will transform into courage—and courage will lead me to freedom. But as I sit down and wait with my bike behind the thick hedge in front of Master Douglas' property, my whole body is quivering. Where is the courage now?

I have a heightened awareness about everything—from the soft rushing sound of the leaves to the squirrel in the tree chewing on a chestnut, to the damp spot on the back of my legs. The pit in my gut is growing wider by the second, festering like an untreated ulcer. Is this a ridiculously bad idea? After all, it isn't called Savage Run for nothing. I shouldn't even be considering signing up. If I'm discovered, as a female Laborer—the lowest ranking citizen in our nation—I'll immediately be taken to Skull Hill.

No. I can't second-guess myself now.

Hearing the whirring sound of an aircraft above, I look up. It roars loudly as it makes its final descent into Culmination. Red, yellow and white stripes—the official colors of the Savage Run—decorate the tail. My father says billions of newkos have been spent on the Savage Run program and it disgusts him. Although I'm sure that if he had a son who could honor him by becoming a Master Citizen, he'd think differently.

Suddenly, I hear the gates creak open and my arms clasp my chest, just above my racing heart. Master Douglas jogs past me in a green jumpsuit and continues down the road. I undo my ponytail and pull back my black, wiry hair, looping the elastic band around so tightly that it tugs at the edges of my already slightly slanted eyes. I wait until he disappears around the bend, and when I'm sure he's gone, I push my bike out onto the road. Grabbing the concealed knife from the basket—just in case I need it—I slide it up my sleeve and head straight for the gates.

A transporter zooms by me, and I pretend that I'm just doing my job as usual, delivering medicine. This transport is one of the newer models, shiny blue, oval-shaped and with three wheels. Not only can it drive up to three hundred miles per hour, it can also with just the press of a button fly you anywhere in the world. I stop at the entrance feigning to pant, as if I just climbed the long hill, and nod toward the heavily armed Unifer. Recognizing me, he punches in the code and the tall steel gates open. Clutching my arm against my abdomen to keep the knife in place, I walk the bike across the courtyard and rest it against a fountain. I pick up the prescription bag from the basket and step up to the stained-glass-encased silver door. I ring the golden doorbell. A few moments later, the door swings open. I'm ready to greet Gemma with a warm smile, but when I see that the entire left side of her face is red and bruised, I gasp.

She quickly lowers her eyes.

"What happened?" I whisper, barely able to speak.

She shakes her head. When I reach out to touch her, she takes a step back and wraps her arms around her abdomen.

"You can't stay here anymore," I say.

Gemma's bottom lip trembles, and her brows draw heavily over her eyes. "Go—before he comes back." She holds a pale hand out to receive the medication.

"No, listen."

Her eyes cautiously flick to mine.

"When the truck comes...follow me; I have a plan and I can explain on the way." But standing in front of her now, I somehow know she'll object.

She shakes her head again, her blue eyes wide and fearful. "He'll hunt you down and kill you," she whispers.

I step closer to her, eyeing the Unifer behind me. He's talking on the phone. "If we make it downtown, we'll be safe. I promise."

She closes her eyes, and a tear rolls down her cheek. "Please—just go."

"No—come."

Opening her eyes, they wander side to side like they always do when she's thinking. Just as she opens her mouth to speak, her gaze focuses behind me. Gasping, she brings her hand to her lips.

"Heidi," Master Douglas' voice trills.

The hair on the back of my neck spikes as I slowly swivel around to face him. I notice the sweat beads on his tall forehead, and a patch of moisture on his chest. Instantly, I lower my eyes, and as my inferior class dictates, I wait to speak until he invites me to.

"How are you, dear?" he asks.

"Well—thank you." My vocal cords feel like sealed clams. "Did you go...running this morning?"

"Yes, well, normally I go for much longer, but this morning I seem to have a bit of indigestion." He shoots Gemma an accusing glare as his beer breath hits my face.

"This is for you," I say, handing him the prescription bag. I hope he doesn't notice how my arm shakes.

Master Douglas steps into the doorway, shoving Gemma behind him like she's nothing but a rag doll. "Thank you for coming on such short notice." He signs the flap on the bag, tears it off, and hands it back to me. "But I ran out of a very important medicine, and I simply can't live without it. It's life or death."

I eye the green label, which means the content in the bag is a supplement, not a prescription.

"It was no problem." I nod, looking for Gemma, but she's vanished back into the house. He takes my hand in his and strokes it, and my skin feels like it has a hundred slithering snakes crawling beneath the surface. All I want to do is rip my hand away, but infuriating him would be dangerous.

"I just thought I'd let you know that I've considered the possibility of you coming to work for me when you turn eighteen—next week, right?" He touches my cheek with the back of his lotion-scented, smooth hand, his fingernails immaculately manicured.

I close my eyes and try not to let the revulsion show on my face.

"I wanted to let you know that, Heidi."

I nod and smile, although my smile probably looks more like a frown.

"You are at liberty to leave." Then right before he closes the door, he adds, "Oh, and say hello to your father for me. He's such a wonderful man—righteous. Honorable and God-fearing. It was his idea that you come and work for me. Brilliant. Absolutely brilliant." He slams the door in my face.

I blink. This isn't what was supposed to happen. Gemma was supposed to come with me...and...and...we were supposed to...and my father? What is he thinking? Doesn't he see through Master Douglas? Maybe he does and that's exactly why he recommended I come here—to punish me. Get the devil out of me. For a moment, it feels like my heart is sinking into a bottomless pit, and I am unable to take a breath. I should leave now—I delivered the medicine—but my feet feel as if they're fused to the cobblestones beneath.

The Unifer grunts at me, startling me back to reality. Forcing my feet to move, I drag myself away from Gemma, swallowing again and again, stuffing the tears deep down. I pick up my bike, and passing the Unifer, I nod to show respect. Even though there is none. Just as I exit the gates, the delivery truck pulls up and parks in the middle of the driveway.

Chapter 2

Pausing outside the gates, my eyes sweep across our deep valley, the soaring mountains surrounding it, and the glistening river that I've swum in countless times. It must have been an amazing country when it was free.

After the S1-P1 virus killed ninety percent of our inhabitants, an army of Unifers arrived in their blue and green uniforms. Unifers, as everyone knew, were soldiers from the Eastern Republic, a super nation comprised of most of Asia, Russia, and Europe—a society built around goodwill, liberty, and peace. However, the Eastern Republic didn't send the soldiers; these soldiers were a rogue Unifer army led by the power-hungry General Volkov, looking for a land to make their own. Finding us in a defenseless state, they immediately seized control. General Volkov Sr. was elected president, our nation was renamed "Newland," and citizens were categorized into three classes: Laborers, Advisors, and Masters. That was sixty-six years ago, and now, President Volkov Sr.'s son, President Volkov Jr., rules the nation.

I discreetly place the knife back into the basket, reenter the woods, and return to the same spot I was earlier. After I park my bike by a tree, I kick the trunk a couple of times.

Plan B.

I lean my back against the rough, damp bark, and stare at the pale wall. Climbing over it and getting into Master Douglas' property won't be a problem. Not getting noticed will. Suddenly, I hear Master Douglas yelling obscenities from the other side of the barrier. I grab the knife, quickly climb the tree, and carefully peek my head over the edge of the wall. My blood boils when I see Master Douglas hauling Gemma outside. By her hair.

"I've told you before, you little tramp. I don't want you talking to anyone who comes to the door. What do I have to say to make you understand?" He lets go of her hair, but grips her arms instead, shaking her so roughly that her head bobs. "I'll kill you, you little rat, and I'll get another one just like you who is smart enough to comprehend and follow my rules!"

"I'm sorry, I was just..." Gemma says.

Master Douglas' daughter comes outside wearing her swimsuit. "Dada, I want to go swimming now."

"Hi sweetheart. Go back inside while I punish Gemma," Master Douglas says, his hands still clasping Gemma's arms, his tone of voice like the purr of a cat.

She pouts. "But I want to go now."

"Do as I say, child. Gemma needs to learn her lesson, even if I have to beat it into her."

Master Douglas' daughter stomps back inside and slams the door shut. I can't get over how indifferent she seems to how her father is treating Gemma, though I hardly should expect anything different from the offspring of such a man.

"You don't deserve to work here." He tears Gemma's shirt open, exposing her shoulders and breasts, and then he throws her to the ground so she lands face down. When she lifts her head, blood flows from her mouth and she's crying. The white floor has spots of red. He undoes his belt buckle, draws his belt out of his pants and strikes Gemma with it. The belt makes a sharp cracking sound as it hits the skin on her upper back.

"Please, please," she pleads, lifting her arms to cover her face. But he keeps whipping her.

Something snaps inside of me. Without really thinking, I hop the fence, and charge toward Master Douglas. What I'm about to do goes completely against the laws in our society where Laborers must at all times—even in life or death situations—maintain respect and remember their inferiority to their superiors.

I don't care.

He doesn't see me coming until the knife is already raised above my head. But before I stab him, I hesitate. I don't want to kill him, just injure him enough so I have time to take Gemma with me. I jab the knife into his shoulder, and quickly pull it out. But it's not enough. He grabs me by the shoulder and slams me to the ground, my head hitting against the marble surface. I drop the knife.

"Heidi," Gemma says, her mouth gaping open.

Master Douglas clamps his hand around my neck and squeezes tightly so I can't breathe. I kick my arms and legs, trying to free myself, but he only pushes harder. I start to see stars in front of my eyes.

Suddenly, I hear a thump, and the next thing I know Master Douglas falls on top of me. I gasp a few times to catch my breath, and then with all my might I push his lifeless body off me. There stands Gemma with a rock in her right hand.

"Is he...dead?" she says.

He moans.

Still feeling the pressure from his hands around my neck, I stagger to my feet and pick up the knife. "Let's go." I grab Gemma's hand and pull her with me toward the wall. But there's no tree to climb up on this side. I head for the mansion instead—desperately hoping the delivery truck hasn't left yet. If it has, then the gates are closed. "The front door—now."

We sprint through the sliding doors, across the living room, and into the foyer with the marble floors. Frantically, I open the front door. Outside, the truck driver is talking to the Unifer, waving his hands and laughing.

Clutching the bloody knife, my eyes steal to the gates. Relief washes over me when I see them wide open. I take Gemma's cold hand in mine and we slip behind the truck. The truck's door slams shut and the engine starts with a roar. Exhaust spews out in front of me just as we pass the back end and out the gates. Once outside, I curse myself for leaving my bike behind the house. But even though it will take an extra minute to get it—and those few extra minutes might be what will make or break my plan—we need the bike to have any chance of escaping.

I pull Gemma behind the hedge, the leaves scratching my arms. "Wait here." Tearing into the forest, I get my bike and throw the knife in the basket. Before I know it, I'm pedaling hard, zigzagging my way among the trees, adrenaline coursing through me like a fiend, my body rising into a frenzy.

Gemma steps out from behind the hedge with fresh tears on her cheeks. She's gripping the front of her dress, gathering the material where Master Douglas ripped it apart. The right side of her mouth is even more red and swollen than before, but it's not as bad as the despairing expression in her eyes. I help her get on to the back rack of the bike, and within seconds, I'm in my seat and we're flying down the hillside, the wind straining against my body. Only a few moments later, I hear a dog barking.

"He has dogs?" My throat is dry—parched. I've never heard them before, despite having been there hundreds of times.

"Two!" Gemma yells.

The Rottweiler catches up quickly, running alongside us, barking and snarling. Its gums are peeled back from his teeth. I pedal faster, and Gemma's thin arms clutch harder around my waist.

Suddenly she lets out a loud shriek.

"What?"

"The dog bit me!"

The dog snaps its teeth at me, and I swerve quickly in an attempt to get away from it. The sudden shift in direction feels unnatural with the extra weight of Gemma. When I hit a thick branch—the road still slick from the rain—I lose control and crash into the ditch. I feel sharp pain several places on my body. I have no time to really feel it because the Rottweiler dives toward me. I kick the animal in the snout, but just as soon as it falls to the ground, it springs back onto its feet. My father's kitchen knife lies on the ground right next to my foot, and just as the dog charges toward me, I pick up the knife and stab it in the chest. It keeps growling, so I pull the blade out and stab it in the chest again. And again.

Finally, it whimpers and retreats down the road, falling lifeless to the ground.

There's blood smeared across my hand and my whole body is quaking. Still clutching the knife, I notice that my palm stings. I open my hand, letting the bloody knife fall to the ground, and when I look at my palm, I see blood and grime compressed beneath my skin. My right knee hurts, too, and the hole in my pants has blood around the edges. There's no time to sit here and cry.

"You okay?" I ask Gemma. She's still on the ground and has twigs tangled in her blonde hair and dirt on her white dress.

She doesn't answer.

I help her to her feet, and we hop onto the bike again.

"Come back here! Or I'll send my Unifers to shoot you dead!" Master Douglas bellows. He must really think I'm an idiot if he believes I'll do as he says. I start pedaling.

Speeding forward, all the way down the hill, I keep looking behind me, afraid that Master Douglas will come after us in one of his fancy transporters.

* * *

The shortest distance to Sergio's is of course straight through downtown Culmination. I'll take my chances. Riding by the lavender field, we come to the fresh food market that borders on downtown—canopy tents with tables lined up along Main Street. These shops are owned and operated by Advisors, like so many other small businesses in town. The main differences between Advisors and Masters are that they can't vote, they can't hold political positions, and they can't own property. Most Advisors run businesses like these, become teachers, or work in the service or hospitality industry.

Riding past the Culmination Justice Building—a structure built to emulate the Parthenon, but constructed entirely of glass—I see Savage Run protesters camped out on the stairs. I recognize several of them—Masters I have delivered medication to at one time or another.

Laborers shadow their Masters, carrying groceries or their Masters' personal items. Just as we approach Michelangelo Street, we bike past a Master beating her Laborer with a Palka—a short, flexible iron rod commonly used to remind us of our place. Another Master Douglas. I feel the iron against the palms of my hands, but like everyone else passing by, I don't interfere.

I steer down a dark side alley: our first safe place. I can hear glass breaking beneath my tires, but it's difficult to avoid. The overhang darkens the whole passageway. We pass an abandoned transporter, and I jump when I think I see a rat scuttling deeper into the darkness. The closer we get to the dumpsters, the stronger the smell of rotten fish and moldy bread becomes, and the harder it is to see even the large pieces of trash in my way.

Gemma's muffled sobs echo against the gray concrete walls. Once I reach the dumpsters, there's a narrow ray of light shining from above. I stop the bike and hop off.

"Your hands," Gemma gasps, climbing off the bike. "And your leg." I look down and the bottom half of my black pant leg is saturated with blood.

"I'm fine." I stoop down beside her to look at her wound. The dog bite isn't too deep; I've seen much worse than this one at the hospital. From the looks of it, she probably won't need stitches. Not that we'd be able to find a doctor for her anyway. "We just need to clean it, or it could become infected. Are you hurt anywhere else?"

She shakes her head as she wipes a tear from her bruised cheek.

"We'll be fine," I say with a thin smile.

"No, he'll kill us." She buries her face in her hands and moans.

I wrap my arms around her, noticing that she's a mere ghost compared to before, so thin, so fragile, so weak. When Gemma lived at home with her mother, she was sturdier and wore a constant smile on her face. Her hair was thick and golden, but now it's thin and matted and her cheeks are sunken—pallid. "The worst is behind us." But I get a sinking feeling that we've only seen the first of many evils.

I open my mouth to tell her what I have planned but words fail me. Gemma has always been the type of person who knows exactly what to say—just like how she knew what to say when we first met.

That day I had been delivering medicine for my father. I was ten, and new to the job. And I didn't really understand all the crazy long codes or colors or different types of bags. Although my Pharmaceutical Scantron did help a lot. Don't get me wrong, the training was extremely thorough—a Master would never send out anyone to another Master without it being up to standards. Impossibly high standards. Keeping up with all the biking and never receiving enough food to have the strength when I needed it, I felt like I was falling farther and farther behind. Yet, there was simply no choice other than to keep moving and hope—pray—for the best. If I asked too many questions, I'd receive an angry reprimand from my supervisor. If I, heaven forbid, was late for a delivery and my father heard about it, he'd bring out his Palka the second I walked in the door and use it on me, the iron stick thrashing against my ten-year-old palms. He would deliberately hit the insides of my hands so that no one else would see. "Can't be looking like that delivering to our superiors, now, can we?"

On the day I met Gemma, I had been working at the hospital for six days. It was in the dead of winter, and the snow was coming down like a solid white curtain. Biking around kept me from freezing to death, but my knuckles and toes were numb. I had just finished dropping off thirty-one deliveries—the most I'd ever had. I returned to the hospital well after dark. The snow was coming down hard, my legs felt like overstretched elastics, and all I wanted was to sink myself into bed and get warm. But just as I was leaving to go home, an emergency delivery came in on my Pharmaceutical Scantron for Mistress Johansen—the chief surgeon's mother. Of course I couldn't go home, but I wanted to, oh, I wanted to. Dragging my feet to the pharmacy, my PS stopped working—I think the battery ran out. I told the apothecary I was there to pick up the prescription for Mrs. Johnson. Coincidentally, there was a prescription there for that very person. Since the names were so similar, and I was exhausted and hadn't had anything to eat since breakfast, I didn't notice that I had pronounced the name wrong.

The apothecary said she knew about the delivery, and she handed me the prescription. I rode all the way to the very uppermost house on Mount Zalo, delivered the medicine, and returned to the hospital with the old lady's signature. When I came back, there was a different apothecary. He noticed the mistake almost before I had walked through the door, and contacted Mrs. Johansen right away.

Thankfully, she hadn't taken the drugs yet. Not that it mattered. It would only have knocked her out for the night with no damage done. The apothecary was nice enough about it, letting me off with only a few harsh words.

I hopped on my bike and headed home. But the closer I got to the Laborer sector, the stronger the nervous gnawing feeling grew in my gut. I knew that my father would find out sooner or later, if he hadn't already. I waited outside the entrance to our sector, tall steel gates guarded by Unifers twenty four seven.

I couldn't go home because I knew what was in store for me, and I thought it might be better to stay outside and die than to face what was coming. But a Unifer noticed me hiding behind the bush and fired a couple of shots in my direction so I'd come out. He didn't hit me, but it scared me half to death. Grabbing me by the arm, he escorted me home.

Walking through the narrow mud-packed streets to our trailer, I passed a woman I had never seen. She smiled at me with an encouraging and warm expression before vanishing into a trailer close to ours. Approaching home, I saw my father waiting at the front door, beating the Palka in his hand. He thanked the Unifer and apologized profusely on my behalf for being such a defiant, ignorant child. I still remember watching as the Unifer walked away, and wishing that I could go with him. Instead, I forced myself to walk inside, terror coursing through my veins. Had I just had some strength left in my legs, I would have run away, but my legs didn't have an ounce of strength left in them.

The physical punishment wasn't as bad as I imagined, an angry fist in my face and a few dozen Palka lashes in my palms. But there are some punishments that last so much longer than physical pain. With each whip, my father repeated over and over, how all these years, he wanted a boy, but he only had me. A girl who had murdered the love between him, and the woman he loved. Murderer! Murderer! He shouted again and again as the lashes slowly drew out the blood from my palms.

At age ten, I wasn't mature enough to realize that I didn't murder my mother. That the circumstances that led up to her being dragged away by the Unifers weren't my fault. Nothing was. All I knew was that he believed it was true, so I did too. I didn't have the wisdom to see the lie he was telling me. And himself. I couldn't see how much he was hurting, and that the only way he could find relief was to put the blame on others. After that night, my father threw the Palka away—I think he felt bad about what he did, though not so bad that he didn't get another one later.

After lying in my bed awake for hours, pressing my cheek against the expanding wet spot on my pillow, I decided to run away. I climbed out of my window, found a secluded spot in the woods, and tried to figure out a plan. When Gemma walked by, it was well past midnight. My fingers and toes had frozen stiff, and I had grown weary of watching the white vapors of breath rising from my mouth. The first thing she said was that she liked to walk outside at night to watch the stars—it made her feel connected, as if everything had purpose. Her comment took me off guard. Purpose? There was no purpose to this. She asked me if it was all right if she sat down next to me, and I nodded. Sitting so close she studied my face for a moment. I know she saw the bruise on my cheek, and by the way her face warmed with compassion, I even think she had her suspicions about what had transpired between my father and me. But she didn't prod—just stated that she was so glad she'd found someone to talk to.

She explained that she and her mother had just moved to our street that day from another Laborer sector right off the East Coast. Several had been relocated because there was simply no more room. The Unifers went through the city and handpicked the women and children to be sent to Culmination. The oil rigs don't need pretty faces, they had told them, but the cultural hub of Newland does. When they arrived, the Unifers crammed her and her mother in with the Porter family. They were nice enough—a little too involved in the neighborhood gossip, but decent folks.

After telling her story, Gemma invited me over to her home, and her mother offered me a cup of peppermint tea and a bowl of rice and lentils. Ruth was the same woman I had passed on the streets earlier, and I wondered if she had sent Gemma out to me after witnessing my father waiting for me with his Palka. This made me feel embarrassed, but they didn't bring it up at all. Not once. Sitting up until three a.m., we exchanged stories about our lives and laughed until my cheeks cramped. At the end of the night, Ruth said she would be my substitute mother since I didn't have one, and ever since that night, she would ask how my day was and how things were at home. It was that night of kindness that made me think that maybe, just maybe, there's some purpose to this crazy life after all. That it might be worth living for a few rare moments of bliss. Although my father never found out about that first night, he did catch me sneaking out a few months later. That's when he barb-wired my window. But even though he had taken so many things from me and continued to do so over the years, he could never touch the part of me that holds my most cherished memories.

But I am not Gemma and I don't have a velvet touch when it comes to difficult conversations. I just lay it all out in one clear, unapologetic statement.

Just as I'm about to tell her my plan, she points at my bike. "You have a flat tire."

My heart misses a beat. In all my planning, I hadn't planned for this. I look her straight in the eyes. "I don't have time to fix it. We're going to register for the Savage Run." My lungs constrict as I wait for her reply.

Gemma's eyes widen. "This isn't the time to joke around."

"Sergio can get us fake IDs."

"Who?"

"Never mind, it's a long story. Will you do it?" I ask.

"Wait—you're serious?"

I pause a moment before I answer. "Completely."

"But they're not going to let us register."

"If we get new IDs from Sergio, they will," I say impatiently.

She shakes her head and her hand hits her temple. "This is so bad. Totally illegal. If they discover us, we'll be outlaws. Or they'll take us to Skull Hill."

"Well, we kind of already are," I remind her.

She gives me an annoyed look. "And—what—we're supposed to pretend to be guys?"

"Yes."

"But...we'll just...die in the Savage Run. Haven't you heard that the obstacles are deadly?"

"Well, they estimate that around seventy-five to eighty percent of the participants will make it."

She pauses as if to think. "I can't do it."

"We'll die if we stay here." My pulse quickens. Surely, she must see that?

"Was this your plan all along?" Her tone is accusatory.

"Yes."

"But it's crazy." She breathes erratically and paces back and forth. "I should just go back to Master Douglas and beg for his forgiveness before he kills me."

"This plan is way better than returning to Master Douglas. This way we have a chance to be free."

Her body goes rigid and she glares at me. "Don't you remember the time you convinced me to climb a tree and I fell and broke my arm?"

I do and I felt really guilty for pressuring her into doing it. But she's older now and must be at least a little stronger. "You were twelve."

"All those dangerous obstacle courses—I don't have a chance."

"You do have a chance, and besides, wouldn't you rather die trying than...just die?"

"I don't know, Heidi. I remember we joked about something like this before, but I didn't think we'd actually be considering it."

I groan and let my head fall back. "Well, do you have a better plan? If we go back to your mother or my father, Master Douglas will find us."

"What about living in the mountains? I could fish and pick berries."

"Where would we live? In the trees?"

"I don't know. But we could work it out."

"Gemma..."

"We could just move to another country where everyone is free."

I had thought about it, but in all reality, where would we get the money to travel? Or eat? We would still need fake IDs to get out of the country, and what would we do once we arrived somewhere else, unfamiliar with the language? I figured the chances of making it were much greater if we sign up for Savage Run.

"I don't want to die." Her hands flail for a moment before she buries her face in her palms, sinking to the ground, her back against the dumpster.

The ground is covered in trash and is damp from the rain, but still, I sit down next to her.

Her hands drop into her lap and she exhales at length. "Isn't there any other way? There has to be."

"Listen, I don't want to rush your decision, but we have to get going if we're going to make it. The registration ends at noon."

She takes a deep breath and remains still for a long time, chewing on her bottom lip.

"We'll do it together," I say. "I'll help you. You'll help me."

She pauses for so long that I think I might rip my hair out. Sitting up a little straighter, she says, "Fine. I'll agree to do it if you promise you'll stay by my side the entire time."

"Promise." Pressing my lips together, I notice that my shoulders relax a little. "Let's go to Sergio's." I grab the bag of clothes from the back rack of my bike, and we're off.

Chapter 3

Sergio's place presses up against the back side of a massive abandoned factory and is situated across from a transporter scrapyard. The wooden shack has tinted windows and a slanted aluminum roof—a perfect place for unlawful dealings.

I hand the bag of clothes to Gemma and knock with a leaden hand. Closing my eyes, I touch my locket, asking for some help with just this one thing. I listen for movement inside, but all I hear is the sound of metal clanking from the scrapyard. Pressing my hands against the filthy, water-stained window, I glimpse inside, but other than the shadows, it's completely dark.

It was an accident how I found out about Sergio. A few months ago, I had been ordered to deliver prescription medication to him, but when I arrived, no matter how many times I knocked, no one answered. Knowing I couldn't return to the hospital without a signature confirming the delivery, I stepped inside. To my surprise, I found an open trap door in the floor. Stressing about making my other deliveries before time ran out, I decided to risk descending the stairs. The light bulbs along the stairwell were lit—even though it was well past seven o'clock in the morning. We Laborers have electricity rationed to us from five to seven a.m. daily, and the government is infallible at keeping the electricity shut off the rest of the day. When I reached the bottom of the staircase, I overheard someone talking about counterfeit IDs.

And that's when it all came together and the idea of registering for the Savage Run first came to me.

I stopped breathing at that point and quickly decided to make the other deliveries first. When I came back to Sergio's place, I found him eating lunch. I've made two deliveries to him since then, and each time I brought a bottle of my father's beer and smiled as I listened to him complaining about his ex-wife. I never brought the whole fake ID thing up to him, but he's definitely some type of underground rebel, which is just the type of man I need.

I knock again—harder and longer this time.

Be home, please be home, I plead quietly to myself.

Suddenly the door flings open. Sergio's dark blond, curly hair is messy and he has bags under his green puppy-dog eyes. "I did not order medication," he says in a thick Eastern accent, a frown on his lips. He's holding a beer bottle and smells like he hasn't showered or changed in weeks.

Although I had this entire refined speech memorized, I can't remember a single word of it. Instead, I just blurt out, "I'm not here for that. We're here for fake IDs." I inhale and hold it.

His right eyebrow twitches once. He grabs my elbow, pulls us inside, and slams the door shut. The room is a dark, stuffy, beer-smelling cave.

Pointing his index finger right in my face, he says, "I don't know what you talking about, but talking like that is trouble for you and me both. Now get out of here."

"No! I rescued my friend Gemma from a cruel Master. He said he was going to kill her, and he'll kill me, too. The only way to get out of this mess is if we join the Savage Run. And for that I need my ID card to say that I'm a guy."

He runs his hands through his hair before studying me for a moment. "I don't know what you even talking about. I don't have such fake IDs." His tone is more nonchalant than before, flippant even.

I take a step toward him, my heart like a drum. "I know what you do. You have a trap door below that rug there." I point and continue to say, "And if you don't help us, I'll notify the authorities."

He frowns. "You do not have any proofs, little pteetsa."

Pteetsa? "Then I'm sure you won't mind if the Unifers search your house." I grab the rusty doorknob, silently praying he'll buy my bluff.

"Wait," he says, hitting my hand away from the doorknob. "Ah, stupid girl. How you pay me?"

I repress a smile. "Your payment is that I won't give you away." I expect him to go ballistic on me, knock me unconscious or pull out a gun to get me to leave. He seems like the type of guy who doesn't take any crap from anyone, especially a young Laborer girl without money or influence. "And if I survive, I'll...remember you and send you money. And more beer."

He starts to laugh, softly at first, increasingly louder until his round shoulders roll. "You survive Savage Run? You never will survive and I never will get pay."

"But at least I'll go to my grave with your secret."

He pinches his upper lip, huffing loudly. Then, his eyes fall upon the locket around my neck and his eyes narrow.

"You give me necklace, I give you IDs."

I reach up and curl my fingers around the smooth golden surface. My mother's locket? Just thinking about giving it up makes me feel as if I'm parting with a piece of myself. But there is no time to waste and it has to be done. Ignoring the ache in my chest, I yank the chain from around my neck and hand it to Sergio.

"You are stupid girl for doing this. In few days when you die, I shed no tear."

"Then you will have lost nothing." My voice is dull.

Sergio bolts the lock on the front door, and then peels the rug back, exposing the trap door. Gemma grabs my arm when she sees it. "Come, my little pteetsas." He lifts the circular latch and pulls the trap door open.

"What does pteetsa mean?" I ask when I pass him.

"It mean...'bird.'"

I step down the metallic spiral staircase, steadying myself on the wobbly rail. I'm not particularly fond of dark, confined spaces—as a matter of fact, I hate them—but having Gemma here helps put me at ease. The room's walls are made of rock, and the floor is an uneven slab of concrete. I get the distinct feeling that I'm in a forbidden place where hundreds of illegal transactions have taken place over the years. Oddly enough, it doesn't bother me at all.

Sergio presses the button on the old laptop and sits down on a creaky wooden chair. He drums his fingers on the desk while he waits for the computer to warm up.

"How is it that you have electricity right now?" I ask.

He stares at me for a second, his eyes as icy as his frown, and I prepare for a lecture on how I should shut up and just be grateful that he's helping us. "Have you heard of generator?" He cocks his head to the side and slumps back into his chair.

"Yes," I say, having seen gigantic ones at the hospital. We used them whenever there was a power outage.

He nods toward a small beat up machine in the corner, its hum so low that I hadn't noticed it.

"I build it with my bare hands." He lifts his beefy, oil-stained fingers so we can see them.

"And you're from the Eastern Republic, right?" Gemma asks.

"You dead soon so I tell you story. I kill a man in government because he kill my sister. He murder her in front of my old mother's eyes. The government coming after me after I stab the man dead, so I get on boat and come here. If you tell anyone, I kill you."

"Oh," is the only sound I manage to produce for a second. "We need the IDs today."

"Fine, but it take me few hours to hack into system to add your new IDs to list."

"No, you need to do it sooner than that!" I yell, my hands flailing. "The Savage Run registration ends at noon, and we have to be in the governments database by then."

He looks at me like I'm growing a third eye. "If I rush, it won't work."

"If you don't rush, we'll die," I reply.

"Well, I already tell you, I don't care if you die." He slumps back in his seat and lights a cigarette, inhaling deeply and blowing the white smoke out by the side of his mouth.

"I don't care that you don't care. We need to get into Savage Run," I say.

"I not sacrifice my whole operation so you can die."

"Well, if you don't, I guarantee that you'll be caught." I feel kind of guilty for blackmailing him, but at this point, if I don't, my entire plan will crumble to pieces and Gemma's and my fate will be in the hands of Master Douglas.

"You worse than Masters," he says with anger crinkling his heavy eyebrows.

I've pushed him to the limit, but I'm banking on him not killing us because deep down, I think he has a soft spot for outlaws. Why else would he be in this business? "You'll never hear from me again after this—I promise."

"Finally, one thing I looking forward to," he says as he types something into his computer. "Okay, okay, I make it happen. I need to take picture of you and you." He studies us both for a while. "We must make you look like boys."

"I brought clothes," I say, lifting the bag from where Gemma placed it on the floor beside the desk. "And a pair of scissors to cut our hair."

Gemma immediately wraps her hands around her long, blonde braid.

I lift the scissors out of the bag. "I'll go first." Pulling the elastic out, my thick black hair cascades down my back. I hand the scissors to Gemma and sit down in a brown, leather chair. I can't explain why the thought of cutting my hair brings a tear to my eye—it's only dead protein. It's not like I'm nervous Gemma will do a bad job. And even if she does, who cares?

"Ready?" Gemma says.

40

I nod. When I hear the scissors snap and feel the tickling of my roots as Gemma slices off the first chunk, I don't cry. But I do ache.

"Have you pick out name?" Sergio asks. His eyes are glued on the screen.

I think for a moment and settle on my father's least favorite person from the Bible. "Joseph." My father says he was an unrealistic, arrogant, self-righteous man who thought too highly of himself. But in the end, as I recall, Joseph triumphed over everything. And everyone.

"You, other girl?" Sergio draws a deep look at Gemma.

"How about George?" she says, still cutting away at my hair. "It's not perfect—a little too long and shaggy around the edges. It will just look like you haven't had a cut in a few weeks."

"There's mirror upstairs in bathroom. With different clothes and make-up you look like pre-puberty boy." He smiles grimly at me. "What is word? Sissy boy?" He laughs dryly.

I narrow my eyes at him, letting him know that I don't appreciate the sarcasm. And with that, I stand up and head upstairs with a change of clothes in hand.

At first, when I enter the tiny bathroom, I avoid looking at my reflection in the mirror. I head straight for the faucet and slide my palms beneath the running water. The water stings my raw flesh and turns the sink red. I stifle a cry and pant instead. I grab a washcloth from the cabinet, wet it, and wipe the blood off my knee and leg. The gashes aren't too deep, but they sting like crazy. Rifling through the bag for my shirt, I catch a glimpse of myself in the cloudy, cracked mirror. The short haircut accentuates my pointy chin and pouty lips, and my slightly slanted, dark brown eyes look huge, as if I'm trying to make out something in the dark. There are plenty of young men with those features, aren't there? However, my neck looks way too thin to be a guy's. My hand touches the place where my mother's locket used to hang. I feel so bare, so exposed without it. But despite how difficult it was handing it over to Sergio, using it to get the IDs was the right thing to do.

I make a few serious faces and furrow my brows in an attempt to look like a fierce competitor. I release a sharp breath. It's useless. They'll never let me sign up, and even if they do, I'm sure the other participants will suspect.

What am I doing? I must have lost my mind. I can't fathom why I thought this was a good idea; clearly, I hadn't thought this through. Because if I had, I would have...I don't know. I feel so lost. So many changes in a few hours, and it's all coming down on me at once. I realize there's no turning back now, but am I a complete idiot for having done this?

No.

I can't start to believe that about myself now. But, what if my father is right? He has told me countless times that I'm a good-for-nothing, weak-minded, and irrational being. What if my sanity has withered away after having angry, hateful words directed at me for so many years? What if I have lost my ability to think straight? What if I never had the ability to think straight? Only a crazy person would do this, right? Or a desperate one. One desperate enough to voluntarily register for a life-threatening obstacle course. Yet, what if I make it? What if I actually win my freedom? Goosebumps tingle my neck and arms. If I register, at least there's a chance. At least I'm living life on my own terms and not being forced to be a

Laborer without any choices. Better to be dead than a coward fearing my dreams.

I wrap my chest tightly with gauze and change into the black t-shirt and faded jeans I stole from my father. With the last piece of gauze, I loop it through the belt holes and double-knot it. Once I get back downstairs, Gemma's hair is already cut, thanks to Sergio.

"Computer thinking," he says as if to justify why he cut Gemma's hair, instead of letting me do the honor.

The short hair brings out Gemma's heart-shaped, rose-red lips and high cheekbones. Her eyelashes reach all the way to her light eyebrows and her small, thin nose sits like a button in the middle of her face. This will never work.

"Do I look bad?" Gemma asks.

"No, I'm just...worried..." I let my voice trail off.

"Me too," she says.

After Gemma changes into her clothes—a gray long-sleeved shirt and hunter green cargo pants—Sergio takes our pictures. While he continues to work on the computer, he says there's water upstairs. Parched, I climb the stairs and head to the kitchen. Gemma excuses herself saying she needs to use the restroom. When she doesn't return after I finish a whole glass of water, I press my ear against the bathroom door. I hear her silent sobs.

"Gemma...?"

Pause. "Just a minute."

I hear her blow her nose and flush the toilet. She opens the door—her eyes red. "I just want to go home to my mother."

The word 'mother' makes me immediately reach for my chest where my necklace used to hang. Instead I find nothing but bare skin.

I suppose I would want to go home, too, if Ruth were my mother. She's the type of person who makes sure you've had enough to eat, asks you how you're feeling, and really listens to you when you speak, never asking anything in return. In fact, she's the closest thing I have to a mother since mine vanished sometime shortly after I was born.

"Just think, if we make it through the course, you can visit her anytime you want."

The left side of her mouth rises a little—it almost looks like the beginning of a smile. "That would be nice." She sits down on the edge of the tub. "I just want to thank you for risking your life to help me. I'm sure he would have finished me off if you hadn't intervened. He kept saying it every time he would become angry with me—that one day he'd get so angry that he'd kill me."

"Of course I couldn't just leave you there." I sit down next to her.

She takes a deep breath. "Master Douglas is a horrible, horrible person."

Dare I ask her about what she's been through? I decide that it might help her to talk about it. "What did he do?"

She glances at me briefly before looking away, seemingly ashamed and not sure whether or not to tell me.

"You know I would never judge you. What happened isn't your fault."

Gemma bites her bottom lip and heavy tears tumble down her cheeks. "He drugged me...and beat me...and...locked me up..." Her voice fades lower and lower

44

as she speaks until it's barely even a whisper. "Raped me..." She buries her face in her arms, uncontrollable sobbing juddering her body.

"Shhh..." I don't really know if she wants me to stroke her back, but it's the only thing I can think to do. "I'm so sorry. It will never happen again, you hear?"

I listen to her cry for a while, and all I can think is that I should have done something sooner. Much sooner.

Gemma sniffles, lifts her head, and wipes her nose with her forearm. "I think I would have killed myself sooner or later if I had to stay there."

"Oh, Gemma..."All this time I made deliveries to Master Douglas, at least once a week for the past year, I saw her eyes deaden a little more each time. I suspected he was being cruel, but raping her? Drugging her?

"You didn't know." She puts a hand on my shoulder. "Just promise me we'll do this together."

I nod. "Every step—all the way."

Sergio enters the room and hands us our new IDs. They look identical to the ones the government issues—electronic chips, 3-D Newland emblems and all. My name is Joseph Wood and Gemma's is George Washington.

"Seriously?" Gemma says after reading her new last name.

"You don't like?" Sergio asks with a wry smile.

"Well, don't you think that it's a little too obvious?" she says.

"It popular to name sons after former president of the home of the brave." Sergio nods. "And when you think of name during obstacles, you remember, you are brave."

I don't know whether he's being a complete jerk or if he's being sincere. My guess is a little bit of both and definitely a smartass. I notice he changed my birth year to two years later than my actual birth year without me having to tell him to do it. I smile. If there's anyone who knows how to trick the system, it's Sergio.

There's little time, so we head out into the living area to say our goodbyes.

"Just—don't die right away, okay?" Sergio says as I open the door.

"I'll do my best. Thank you Sergio." I hold my hand out and he takes it. We shake.

He smiles a little and then crosses his arms in front of his chest. "Now get, get."

Chapter 4

"Life," my father would always lecture me, "isn't meant to be lived in the shadows of timidity. Man has a spirit of hope and faith." I'm sure he would vehemently disagree with how I've interpreted his statement.

Gemma and I elbow our way through the crowded streets toward the registration booth, clenching our fake IDs in our fists. The wind blows through my short hair, and the sun warms the back of my neck where my ponytail used to fall. It's a few minutes before noon, the time the registration will close, but we should be able to make it just fine.

Soon I see Pavlova Yard. The square cobblestone-paved area is enclosed by a large wrought iron fence, and dozens of Unifers stand at attention guarding the premise. There's a canopy and above it waves a red flag with an abstract, yellow saber-toothed tiger head. There are two registrars that I can see. The woman—maybe in her forties—looks like she's from the East, with slanted eyes and black hair. She has wide shoulders, strong legs, and a flat chest. From the look on her stern face, I can only imagine that she's had to fight her way to every promotion in this male-dominated field.

The other registrar, a young man—probably in his late teens or early twenties—has tan skin and chestnut hair. He wears an expression of serenity, and I get the feeling that I've met him before. School? No. I'd remember him from there. Maybe I made a delivery to him at some point.

Three sturdy boys—undoubtedly the last of many here today—stand in the registration line, ready to gamble their lives for a chance at a better future. They're handing the registrars their ID cards and signing something appearing to be a waiver or contract. I wonder what circumstances drove the boys to come here today—and if any of them are as desperate as I am.

Then I notice—at the end of the line stands Arthor, a boy from my primary school class. He still has the fiery red hair, but now it's longer and curlier. Why did he have to be here?

Then I realize why. Several years back, Tristan, Arthor's older brother and an extraordinarily strong Laborer, competed in a regional Laborer obstacle course in hopes of winning food rations for his family. Every Laborer in our city cheered for Tristan, whose presence in the race somehow brought hope that good things could still happen to the subordinates of Newland. But he didn't make it. Tristan drowned after falling from a hundred-foot cliff. His family was devastated—as were we all. Right after finishing school, when we still kept in touch, Arthor used to tell me how one day, he'd find a way to honor his brother's memory.

This is very bad for us. If he sees me, then he'll blow my cover.

"What?" Gemma asks when I don't move forward.

"Arthor," I whisper.

She gazes into the yard. "Oh, no."

"The only way around it is to wait until he leaves."

She nods.

Once in a while, by passers stop to see what's going on inside Pavlova Yard. A few haven't moved from the fence since we got here. Looking closer, I recognize one of the lingerers as Arthor's mother. She's clenching the iron rods, pressing her face between the gaps in the fence, her red, swollen eyes fixed on her only living son.

Eventually Arthor signs the paper and starts to walk away from the registration booth. Behind us, a throng of protesters enters the streets, waving their anti-Savage Run signs and chanting: "No, no to Savage Run! Keep the classes separate!"

Taking advantage of the distraction, I say to Gemma, "Let's go." Walking toward the gates, I reach up to touch my locket, but when my hand is halfway up, I remember how it's no longer there. I lower my hand.

We approach the Unifer guarding the gate and hand him our ID cards. My heart beats so hard that I think he might hear it. Looking at us with haughty eyes, he hands us the cards back and tells us to proceed. Moving ahead, I glance at Gemma. But instead of a confident façade, her face is fallen and ashy and she's white knuckling her ID. With no time to spare, we pick up our pace and run toward the booth.

Out of nowhere, a Unifer pummels me to the ground and presses himself on top of me so I can't breathe. The attack is so sudden that I don't even register a single thought before I react. I scream, and somehow manage to wiggle my leg free, kicking the Unifer in the groin. He rolls over, moaning and grabbing his crotch, his face contorting in pain. As quick as a cat, I hop back onto my feet and look for Gemma. To my dread, I find her pinned beneath two of Master Douglas's Unifers, and they're holding her at gunpoint.

"Gemma!" I shriek, my heart jumping into my mouth.

"Heidi, run!" she yells.

The Unifers look up at me and my initial thought is to flee the scene—abandon my mission. Save myself. One of the Unifers points at me and commands the other one to get me. In a split second, a moment so condensed I feel like the bubble of time might burst, I have to make a decision. Do I continue to run toward the booth and save myself, and maybe Gemma, too, by declaring that we both want to register? Or do I turn back and try to help her? The Unifers are so large, and they carry firearms, so I have absolutely no chance against them. But I can't desert Gemma! Although if I continue toward the booth, I might be able to save her also by announcing she wants to register. If I try to help her, we'll both be taken into custody and back to Master Douglas. Some seconds are so decisive that they have eternal repercussions.

"Heidi, run!" Gemma yells.

I spin around, hoping amnesty sets in the moment I declare that we want to register, desperate that I made the right choice. Instead of sprinting forward, I run into someone's chest, and that someone grabs my shoulders.

"What's going on here?" a deep, direct voice says.

I look up into his face and see that it's the male registrar. Our eyes lock for a split second, but I look down quickly, afraid he might be able to tell that I'm a girl, disguised as a guy, trying to register for the Savage Run. A split second is long enough to recognize that he carries an aura of confidence and power—this is a man used to taking charge and staying in control. He's built like an athlete: tall and muscular. Then, it hits me like a brick from the sky. The registrar is President Volkov's son—Nicholas. I'm so done for.

"I...we're...we...we came to register for Savage Run," I stutter.

"Sorry—the registration just closed," he says.

I take a step back and look into his eyes again, pleading. "Please...just let us join. I know we're a few minutes late, but this is a matter of life and death." I glance over my shoulder and see the Unifer making his way toward me, and Gemma struggling against the others.

"First of all, a scrawny guy like you shouldn't be in this obstacle course. A stiff breeze would knock you over," he says.

I try not to grimace. If he only knew. "My friend and I, we have to join the program and you have to let us—it's the law."

"Mai, come here," he says.

The female registrar makes her way over to Nicholas, her eyebrows lifted, and her lips frowning. She's wearing plenty of makeup and smells heavily of roses.

"No, no, no," she says, her dark brown, slanted eyes looking at me like I'm a lost kitten.

"No, we have to register today." I hear Gemma's screams behind me and Nicholas looks in her direction.

"What's happening over there?" he asks.

Unexpectedly, Arthor steps up beside me. I can tell he recognizes me by the way his eyes nearly pop out of their sockets. "Hey, what are you doing here?" His smile reaches all the way up to his green eyes, a touch of confusion in his brows.

I feel like I've been punched in the stomach, but somehow I manage to give him an angry look, hoping he'll know not to reveal who I am.

"You're coming with me," I hear a raspy voice behind me say, as a strong hand grips my wrist. "You're under arrest." The Unifer grabs both of my arms and starts to haul me off.

I turn to Nicholas, and in a last-ditch effort, I plead with him. "Please..." His blue eyes flicker for a split second, and then he squints. I know I've already lost, and now I'll be handed back to Master Douglas.

"Wait," Nicholas says. "This young man has declared that he wants to register for the Savage Run."

The female registrar's eyes flinch as her pouty mouth drops open, but no sooner than she loses her composure does she have it back.

Master Douglas marches toward me with another Unifer in tow. I stop breathing.

"She's mine," Master Douglas growls. Bypassers stop and stare and the crowd outside the fence is growing larger by the second.

A piercing blast rings through the air. I jump at the loud bang, and try to wring myself free to look for Gemma, but I can't budge free. "What was that?" Master Douglas' lips bend into a devious smile, confirming my deepest fear.

"Murderer!" I yell—my arms and legs thrashing—and the noise that escapes my lips sounds like the cry of a wounded animal. Everything I've worked so hard for doesn't matter anymore. Not if Gemma's dead.

"He's signing up for the program," Nicholas says.

Tears spill out of my eyes and in a daze, I say that I am, though the words don't seem to be my own, only someone else speaking for me. "And my friend—"

"This girl is under my jurisdiction," Master Douglas says.

"He's not a girl," Arthor says. "He's a friend of mine from primary school."

"And he's here to register," Nicholas says. "Plus, his identification clearly confirms it." He grabs the card from my clenched fist and flashes it toward Master Douglas. "With all due respect, sir, you're making a mistake."

"Don't play me for a fool," Master Douglas spews. "This girl is my housekeeper's friend—she stole my housekeeper from me just earlier—I saw it—and she's coming with me. You know the laws of the land, don't you?"

"Every last one," Nicholas says through gritted teeth, his blue eyes turning black. He grabs my arm and pulls me toward him, away from the Unifer.

"The laws clearly state that once..." Mai interjects.

"I know the laws," Master Douglas says, grabbing my other arm and pulling it hard. "Obviously you don't know the laws pertaining to the Savage Run because you're about to sign up a girl. And even if she were a boy, he hasn't signed up yet."

"Once a Laborer has declared that he wants to register, he's considered the property of the Army of Newland." Nicholas' face turns red and he jerks me behind him so Master Douglas loses his grip. My arms hurt.

Master Douglas' eyes go livid, but Nicholas steps between the Unifer and me. "We have a reporter from the Daily Republic over there who's taking pictures of today's events." He nods toward the photographer leaning up against one of the flagpoles, snapping shots of our interaction. "All the images will be going back to my father. I know you used to work for him and were dishonorably discharged. If I have to report to him that you caused problems for one of our participants, making a scene at a Savage Run registration, it might not be such a fortunate thing for you."

Master Douglas scowls as he glares at me.

"Don't think you can threaten me, boy," Master Douglas says, reaching for his handgun, strapped around his waist. "Just because you're President Volkov's son doesn't mean anything when it comes to the finite laws of this country."

"Rory, I need security here immediately," Nicholas says into a small device clipped onto his shirt collar.

Half of the Unifers guarding the fence run toward us and surround the registration booth, pointing their machine guns directly at Master Douglas and his Unifers.

"I'll be sure to tell my father what you said," Nicholas says sarcastically.

Master Douglas balks. "The second I get home I'm going to notify President Volkov of your illegal actions and I'll have you discharged from your position as registrar faster than you can say mercy. Mark my words." He storms off with the two Unifers in tow.

When I see them walk away, and that Gemma has vanished, I start to walk toward where I last saw her. My hands shake uncontrollably. "But my friend. He wanted to register, too. They took him." I turn to Nicholas, my mouth hot and dry, my tongue sticking to the roof of it. "They took him, and—"

"Your friend is dead." Nicholas places the registration papers into boxes.

54

Did he see her get shot? "We don't know that for sure."

"I do. Now what do you want to do? Register or leave, it's up to you."

"Then I'm out," I declare.

He looks up at me, his dark eyebrows scrunching in the center, but not angry. "I wish you the best."

"But my friend—"

He interrupts me. "Dead."

His words sink deep down into that part of me where there's no return. It's where the hope of my mother being alive lives and where Gemma's and my friendship lives.

"Where did you get this?" Nicholas asks, examining my ID.

"From the government." My voice is as hollow as my chest. "I think I want to sign up anyway."

"I don't think you should." He looks at me and raises his eyebrows.

"I'm signing up, okay?"

"Then you're in," Mai says. She grabs a stack of papers and waves for me to follow her.

"We'll talk later," Nicholas says to me. It sounds more like a threat than a suggestion.

Arthor places his hand on my shoulder and gives me a sympathetic nod. "I'm heading to the airport."

"Thanks for vouching for me," I say.

"Yeah, what are friends for?" He waves as he walks away. Outside of the gates he embraces his mother. All the way from here, I can see her entire body shaking.

I look back to the spot I last saw Gemma, and there's a red splotch of blood on the flat gray rocks. I'm a horrible friend. If I hadn't convinced Gemma to come with me she would still be alive. If I hadn't chosen to run toward the booth instead of toward her, she might still be...

Mai tells me to come and sit down by the table. Without really wanting to, I walk over and take my seat in front of her.

"I'm Mai, and both Nicholas and I will be your representatives from now on." She holds out the contract with page upon page of fine print. She doesn't read it, only explains that if in the very unlikely event I complete the obstacles in Savage Run (she sighs heavily when she says it), I will be considered a Class-1 Master citizen of Newland, with all the rights and privileges as outlined in the Master Citizen Handbook, and I will be considered a free citizen until the day I die of natural causes or relinquish my rights to them, whichever comes first. There are three ways out of the obstacle course, period. The first one is by dying, which a few of the participants most likely will, maybe even up to fifty percent.

I interrupt her. "Fifty percent? They said in the paper that only twenty to twenty-five percent might die."

"The obstacles are a little harder than initially publicized. Only the strongest individuals will be allowed into the Master Class." She continues to tell me that the second way out of the course is by quitting, in which case I will be brought back to my city of residence and expected to live out my days as a Class-3 Laborer citizen. And the last one is by completing the obstacle courses in their entirety.

"Raise your right hand," she says. I do. "Do you consent to joining the Savage Run of your own free will and do you understand all the risks involved?"

"Yes."

"And do you understand that your family has no right to any compensation on your behalf?"

"Yes."

She explains something about the top three contenders, but I hardly hear a word she says because I start to think about where they took Gemma.

Mai taps me on the arm, waking me up from my reverie. "Do you have any immediate family?" she asks.

I look over at Nicholas who seems to be listening in on our conversation. "No."

"Well, as a male Laborer, I suppose if you don't have family, you don't have much to live for," she says.

I nod and think of Gemma, the tears pressing. "Something like that."

"Any questions?" she asks.

"No."

"And you are certain that you understand the dangers and still want to proceed with signing up for the Savage Run?"

"I said yes."

"Very well." Mai's eyebrows rise. "Sign here, here, and here." She points her hot pink nails to the lines and I sign. "This is your uniform. Extra Small. It will probably be more than baggy on you." She hands me a shiny, black box with a golden Savage Run logo on it. "You have to be at Culmination airport in thirty minutes. You can go change in there." She points to a row of white stalls.

How will I get there? The airport is at least an hour and a half biking distance. And walking? I lock myself in one of the booths and open the Savage Run box. Inside lies a neatly folded, black Savage Run uniform identical to the one Nicholas and Mai are wearing. The only difference is that mine has a gray collar and doesn't have the registrar badge with my name on it. The shoes are sleek, black, and lightweight, and when I slip them on it's as if I'm not wearing anything at all.

I wash my hands in the sink and try to remove some more of the gravel that's embedded beneath my skin. My father makes me wash my hands at least ten times a day before I leave the house in the morning, between each delivery, and the second I walk in the door at home. After what I've done to my father, it's strange how I feel no sense of loss. No sadness. No guilt. No regret whatsoever. I'm abandoning him. All I'm worried about is what my father will think when he reads my letter. Surely, he'll go raging mad and believe I need to repent from this ungodly, lunatic behavior at once. I can already hear him saying that a woman must know her place in the sight of God and in her community, and that she's required to submit willingly. Maybe he'll think I've turned to cross-dressing—now that would drive him completely over the edge. The ridiculous thought makes me chuckle, but my laugh is more of a desperate attempt to drown out the feeling of panic rising in my chest than an expression of humor. What will he really do when he finds and reads my letter? Will he turn around and reveal my identity to everyone? Probably not—that would mean he'd be putting his own life and reputation in jeopardy, which is something he would never, ever do.

I throw my clothes in the trash and head outside. Should I go back to the booth? Try to find a way to get to the airport by myself?

Noticing that I'm still hanging around, Nicholas says, "You need a ride?"

"Uh...yes," I say.

Nicholas bobs his head to the side and I trail after him. Immediately, two Unifers follow after us. We arrive at the red, yellow, and white Savage Run transporter, and they get into the vehicle behind us. My door opens automatically and I get inside. This is a brand spanking new model, and probably has more bells and whistles than the other newer models. The dashboard has illuminated blue, yellow, and white buttons.

Nicholas enters on the other side. Sitting so close to him, I notice his strong jawline and dimples. He's not stunningly handsome, but I can see why other girls might find him attractive with those blue eyes, chestnut hair and well-defined lips—not to mention his broad shoulders beneath the black, silky Savage Run shirt. I've seen him in the papers quite a few times—always with a different girl on his arm. Whatever. The heavy gold chain around his neck and wrist catches my eye. In the back of my mind, my father's words echo: "The root of all evil."

"Why did you do something so stupid?" he growls.

His sudden change in mood makes me tense up.

"Do your parents have any idea about what you've done?"

I look down at my fingers in my lap, hoping he doesn't notice how my dirty, scraped-up hands can't seem to find a comfortable place to rest. "No."

"Do you really think you're serving them by doing this?" His voice is harsh.

"No, and in fact, I'm sure my father will hate me for it." There's no use in trying to explain any of this to him because he wouldn't understand. "Please, don't..."

"And your mother?"

More uncomfortable questions. My father explained it like this: When my mother went into labor, she hid in the Lavender fields from the Unifers sent to exterminate the elderly and female infants. The "cleansing" was a method President Volkov Sr. used to control the Laborer population to prevent them from becoming so numerous they could overpower the Masters. The Unifers seized the babies and threw them in the icy Culmination River, and the aged were burned in gigantic furnaces right outside each city. My father said he went to notify her that the Unifers were gone. She informed him he had a son. I can imagine my father was proud. Three days later, when her maternity leave ran out, my mother vanished without a word, leaving me—a good-for-nothing girl—with my father.

But what I say is, "My mother left when I was a baby."

"Listen," he huffs, "I didn't want to blow your cover in front of everyone back there, so I let Mai sign you up. But I can't let this madness continue. I don't know where you got your fake ID or the idea to dress up as a guy and sign up for the Savage Run, but I need to put a stop to this."

"Fake...ID?" I try to laugh, but no sound comes out.

"I know about Sergio, and listen, I know a girl when I see one."

He probably does. Images of all those girls in the newspapers pop into my mind. "I'm a boy."

"I'm not stupid. And even if everyone else believes you, which may or may not be the case, there's no way you'll ever make it past the first phase. These obstacle courses are deadly. In fact, I think we should just delete your registration and..."

60

I sit up straighter, my back like an erect board. "No."

"Listen." He leans in a little, and I hold my breath, finding his presence overwhelming. "I want to help you because I don't think it's right that you should be the victim of a man like Master Douglas. When he used to work for my father as his deputy advisor, I saw him destroy girls like you. But I have to tell you, to continue on this path is suicide."

"You don't know what I'm capable of." I stare boldly back at him—I won't be treated like a subservient any longer.

"It doesn't matter; I know what the obstacles are made of." He runs a hand through his thick, dark hair and his cologne stirs into the air. A privileged individual like him would never understand the desperate circumstances that forced me to do something like this. He breathes heavily for a moment, and when he speaks again, his voice is low. "How did you get in trouble?"

I might as well tell him everything. "It was like Master Douglas said. I helped Gemma escape because he was beating her up...I couldn't just leave her there."

He pauses for a moment, and it feels like his deep eyes see right through me. "Of course you couldn't."

He agrees with me? I'm not used to someone validating me and don't quite know how to respond, so I look out the window.

"There must be some..." he starts.

I place my hand on his arm, and it's as if the tension in the air surrenders. "I'm not asking you to help me. All I'm asking is that you keep my secret."

His gaze goes from my hand to my eyes. "You don't know what you're getting yourself into."

"I'll take my chances," I say, although having learned that the obstacles are more dangerous than I initially thought, I'm not as confident as I was just a few hours ago. And with Gemma dead...I stop myself from finishing that thought. Nothing good will come of it.

"Fine, I'll let you continue. And I'll keep your secret. I just hate to see you give up your life so easily."

So easily? He doesn't know me—how exhaustingly obstinate I can be once I put my mind to something. "Thanks."

"Maybe I can help coach you a little, and..." He shakes his head without completing the thought and commands the transporter to the airport.

Chapter 5

The airport runway is crawling with reporters and curious citizens. The protesters are here, chanting that same chant as loudly as ever. I'm surprised President Volkov hasn't had them arrested yet.

I wipe my hands on my silky pants and close my eyes, trying to think of something that might calm me. When no such thought emerges, I reopen my eyes. The vehicle slows down and forces its way through the crowd. People plaster their faces against the transporter's windows as we pass.

Mai stands on a platform in front of the red, white, and yellow Savage Run aircraft. Is it the same one I saw earlier today up at Master Douglas' house? I wonder how Mai managed to get here before us because when we left Pavlova Yard, she was still packing up all the registration forms.

Eighteen participants are lined up behind Mai. Seeing how some of their necks are as thick as tree trunks, their arms as broad as my waist, it causes me to shrink in my seat. Arthor is one of the strongest Laborers I've met, but he looks like a wiry twig next to some of these guys. I don't even want to imagine what I'll look like beside one of them. Other than

Arthor and me, the rest of the participants look like they're Advisors—a Laborer would never receive enough food to grow those kinds of muscles.

At first thought, it doesn't make sense to me why a Class-2 Advisor would risk death when his life is already pretty good. I suppose if I were an Advisor, I'd still feel trapped by not being able to own land, vote, or run for office.

One second. That's exactly how long it takes the reporters to swivel around after Nicholas has stepped out of the transporter. But he doesn't even blink an eye, just walks calmly around the vehicle and waits for me to get out. The two Unifers that followed us here—I'm now convinced they're his bodyguards—walk on either side of us up to the podium.

Mai reaches her arms out to greet me and pulls my ear to her lips. "My, don't you look like you need some happy pills..." she whispers. "Cheer up; this event is for champions and you certainly don't look it." She places me at the end of the line, next to the tallest, most muscular guy here, and gives me a stern look. I pull my shoulders back and try to fit in.

Nicholas steps up to the stand, and the gathering—even the protesters—calms into a low simmer. "Welcome citizens of Culmination to the very first Savage Run," he says. "I'd like to share with you a silly story, if you would be so kind to indulge me. As many of you know, I spent a few summers on a ranch right outside of Culmination. My favorite thing to do was to play outside—to swim in the lake beside our home and play in the woods, chasing after squirrels and harassing hedgehogs."

The gathering laughs.

He continues. "But my favorite memory from there happened one spring morning when I was ten. My father had sold the ranch and it was the last day before we moved to Asolo. Before my father could tell me no, I headed to the lake to swim."

I smile a little.

"There was a chickadee that lived in the oak tree right outside of our door. She was constantly feeding her youngsters, their hungry beaks opening and closing, accepting the nourishment from their mother. That day, one of her chicks had fallen out of the nest. I saw the poor little creature abandoned on the ground, chirping, and left to die from starvation or to be eaten alive by a predator, anticipating life to end in the most excruciating way. Not thinking much of it, I helped the bird back into its nest. Later that day, I saw the bird I had helped fly away." He pauses and grips the side of the podium. "That's what these young men must feel like now—like that little bird must have felt. Waiting. Waiting for someone to help them. For someone...to pick them up and give them wings to fly."

The gathering cheers.

"As you know, this Master class recruitment program is closed to the media and the public. However, I will personally inform you of the results after each of the three phases directly following the completion of each phase. Now without further delay, we must bring these savages to Volkov Village. Thank you."

The gathering claps and Nicholas steps away from the podium.

One by one the participants climb the stairway that leads up to the aircraft. Nicholas stands at the bottom of the stairs waiting for me, the last contender to board. Just as my foot touches the first step, I hear someone yell my name.

"Heidi!"

My heart plummets into my stomach when I recognize my father's voice. My hand twitches and almost reaches for my locket. But I'm on my own now.

"Heidi, don't do this!" he yells.

I've never heard him this desperate. A lump forms in my throat. I shouldn't turn around, but since everyone else is doing it, they probably won't suspect that I'm the one he's calling for. My father is tripping over his legs to get to me and some of the people in the crowd shove him and laugh as he stumbles to the ground.

"Heidi, don't leave. I'm sorry I messed up!" He climbs back onto his feet, his gray hair sticking to his sweaty forehead.

Seeing what's happening, Nicholas sends a couple of Unifers in my father's direction. Once they arrive, they pull their clubs out and beat my father against his head and abdomen until he collapses to the ground. With every blow, I feel the pain deep in my stomach. My father covers his head to protect himself from the assaults. I want to yell out for the Unifers not to hurt him, but I hold back, too afraid it will give me away. Maybe more afraid that my father might think I care.

"Do you know that guy?" Mai asks me.

My eyes are glued on my father, and pity overwhelms me when I see blood coming from his nose. To me, he seemed to be the strongest man alive. Now, with the Unifers pounding down on him, he appears weak and helpless, not even a man. "No, I don't know him." One last time, I look back at the person I have called father my entire life and feel like I'm betraying him by pretending he's a stranger. But he has betrayed me countless times by treating me the way he has. I owe him nothing.

I turn my back to him. Each step toward the plane is another step away from my former life and the former me. Trying to fit into his mold never worked. And it never will. I clutch onto the handrail and run up the stairs.

Chapter 6

The cabin hostess waits by the open door and smiles at me as if I'm the most important person in the world. Entering the aircraft, I see the other participants pausing to size me up. Some of them laugh. A few nods greet me with sincere expressions, but most frown and scoff, rolling their eyes as I squeeze by them.

"Welcome aboard, young man. Let me show you to your seat." The cabin hostess beams and guides me to one of four black, inward-facing, leather chairs. Mai is already sitting in one of them, holding a small mirror, and applying red lipstick. Next to her sits a black-haired muscle head. He stares at me as I sit down. Each seat has its own set of buttons to select movies or listen to music, and the cabin hostess proceeds to show me which button to push to make the chair open up into a full-length bed. "And if you need anything at all, press this button." She gestures to a red knob above my seat.

I thank her, and she walks to the back of the aircraft.

"Just get me out of this godforsaken place," Mai grumbles to herself more than to us.

I'm about to ask her why she would call Culmination a godforsaken place, but the guy sitting across from me says, "Couldn't get a job shoveling manure?"

I squint my eyes. "What?"

"You think you have a chance against all of us out there?" He pops a grape into his mouth, the juice squirting out as he bites down on it.

Mai rolls her eyes, but remains silent.

"No, I just..."

"Good, then we agree." He pops another grape in and chomps on it with his mouth open, the smacking sound unbearably irritating.

Nicholas takes the seat next to mine and nods to the grape guy. "Johnny, this is Joseph. Joseph, Johnny. I trust we'll be able to have a pleasant flight together?" His eyebrows rise.

"Doubtful," Johnny says at exactly the same time I say, "Of course." I sink in my seat.

"The flight to Volkov Village is just over two hours. Let's make it a pleasant one." Nicholas straps himself in, and seeing that I have problems figuring out how to fasten my seatbelt, he reaches across my lap and secures the buckle. His forearm brushes mine, and his skin is surprisingly warm. The captain announces that we'll be taking off shortly, and before I know it, the aircraft speeds down the runway. I dig my nails into the armrests, my stomach tightening as we lift off the ground. I feel dizzy. As the bumpy ascent calms, my grip loosens a little.

"The numbers are in, and there are two thousand and thirty-nine contenders in the Savage Run," Mai says, reading a report on an electronic device. She glances at me, I think with pity. "Well, I'm exhausted." She puts a cheetah-print sleeping mask on and pulls a blanket up to her shoulders. Johnny extends his seat into a bed and shuts his eyes.

I rest my forehead against the window and look outside. I can't see anything at all, only bright whiteness. I wonder what happened to my father, if the Unifers imprisoned him or let him go. I don't really know why he came after me; I was always in the way—eating too much or not doing enough. Lazy. Ungrateful. But, he wasn't all bad. Occasionally, he would compliment me about how well I was doing my job or tell me I had exceeded his expectations. I savored those words because pleasing him used to be everything. In time I came to learn that whenever he was friendly, he wanted me to do something for him—give him a back rub, or fetch him something across town, or deliver a message to one of the people he counseled. Praise was never just given for its own sake. There was always a long string attached.

Nicholas nudges me with his knee. "You should get some sleep, too."

I'm tired, but I don't think it will be possible for me to sleep—too many memories are creeping to the surface. I sit in silence for a while, but what I really need is something to distract myself from my thoughts. I try to think of something to ask Nicholas. I don't want to give the impression that I want special treatment, so I stick to safe personal questions. "So, does anyone ever call you Nick?"

"No."

What a conversationalist he is. "So...have you ever participated in an obstacle course?"

70

He glares at me for a moment. "I'm sorry, but I'm not here to be your friend."

I feel a flush of blood rise to my cheeks.

"Besides, you really should get some rest. There won't be much time for that once the obstacles have begun." His lips squeeze into a thin smile.

"Fine." I nod as I turn toward the window, hoping he won't notice my red face. But then I catch myself. I'm just acting as my old Laborer self: a mindless, obedient sheep. I sit up straight, search through the side pocket of my seat and find a magazine, leafing through it without really paying attention.

After a minute, Nicholas looks over at me. "What in the world are you doing?"

"Reading." I keep turning the pages.

He puffs. "Let me clarify. Why aren't you sleeping? You really should be..."

I interrupt him. "I can't, so instead, I'm distracting myself while reading about..." I hold up the page that I landed on and see the red lingerie on the model, pouting her glossy red lips, standing in a very uncomfortable pose.

Nicholas' eyes widen for a split second, but then a hearty laugh escapes his lips. "Joseph, I didn't know you liked that kind of girl."

I quickly close the magazine and return it to its holder, my face hot. "Not really, but I hear that you do." I say accusingly, as a desperate attempt to have something to say. Stupid.

"Yeah, that's what most people believe." The playfulness in his eyes turns solemn.

"I've seen you in the papers, you know." I need to stop talking now.

"Oh you have, have you?" His eyes stare me down, but they're not angry, only confrontational.

"Yes, with different girls..."

"And...your point is?" His voice is flat and stern, but he smiles like he doesn't care. "Not many people know me, and since I'm the president's son, everyone has their own opinion of me. You included, it would seem."

I hate to be lumped together with everyone else.

"I'm going to take a nap now." He leans in closer and whispers, "Heidi." Sitting up straight again, he says, "And if you'd like, you can do the same. Or not. It's completely up to you." He presses the button on the armrest, transforming his seat to a bed.

I pull the blanket close up to my head. I don't want anyone to notice how flushed my face has become.

* * *

It takes me some time, but I'm finally able to relax. Somewhere between sleep and consciousness, I hear the captain announce that we're on our final descent into Volkov Village. I bring my seat back up and stretch my arms above my head, yawning.

"Good nap?" Nicholas asks, already awake.

I force a smile, not quite sure how to act toward him after I offended him.

Mai pulls out her toiletries and freshens up her make-up again.

"Why didn't you just stay home, Imp?" Johnny stares at me from his seat.

"Imp?"

"Yeah, you're imp...eding us from focusing on what's really important about the program," he snarls, and then proceeds to snort a laugh.

"And what is that, exactly?" I ask.

Johnny scoffs. "Honor and might—the motto of the Savage Run." He rolls his eyes.

"I'm curious to know, how is he impeding that?" Nicholas asks.

"Thanks to him, the program has become about something else entirely: giving allowances to the weak. Problem is, Petunia, who will they love once you've died three minutes into the first obstacle? The answer is someone who is strong and exemplifies what the Savage Run and the Master class are all about. Someone who entered for honorable reasons." Johnny picks his teeth with a toothpick.

"And what honorable reasons are those?" Mai asks, powdering her forehead.

"Well, I don't know why anyone else entered, but I entered so that I could support my sickly grandmother—provide her with a better life these last few years she's alive," Johnny says.

"Honorable indeed, but everyone is an equal participant with equal rights." Mai's voice is monotone.

Johnny huffs. "That's not true. He's detracting from the integrity of the event."

"What is your problem, exactly?" Mai snaps.

"My problem?" He unbuckles his seatbelt, stands up and yells, "Am I the only one who takes this seriously? Am I the only one who sees how this cream puff is making Savage Run into a gag show?" Johnny points at me.

It turns so quiet that I hear nothing but the hum of plane engines.

"Sit down at once or I will..." Mai starts, but Nicholas places a hand on her lap.

"If you feel that threatened by Joseph, then how can you expect to do well compared to the other participants?" Nicholas asks.

Johnny gets a sour expression on his face. "I'm not threatened; I'm sickened. And I'm just speaking what everyone else is thinking."

"I wasn't thinking that, were you?" Nicholas asks me.

I can't help smiling a little. "No."

"Me neither," Arthor says behind me, squeezing his face between Nicholas' and my seats.

Johnny huffs loudly and turns to Nicholas. "Just because you and that bitch Mai don't see what's going on doesn't..."

He can't finish his sentence before Mai shoots to her feet, wrings Johnny's arm behind his back so it makes a cracking sound, and pins him to the floor with her foot on the back of his neck.

"Awww..." he wails.

"Rule number one," Nicholas says bending down toward Johnny. "Never, never, never upset Mai."

"Say you're sorry," Mai insists, pulling his arm back harder. "Say it." Many participants are out of their seats, their eyes glued to the scene.

"Sorry...sorry," Johnny's barely able to whimper.

Mai flings his arm to the ground, gets back in her seat and proceeds to apply make-up as if nothing ever happened.

Without a word, Johnny climbs to his feet, walks down the aisle, and locks himself in the bathroom stall.

While everyone else starts to laugh and talk amongst themselves, Nicholas leans over and whispers, "Once you get out into the obstacle fields, stay away from him."

"He's not allowed to hurt me, is he?" I whisper back.

"Out there, there will be no telling whether you died from one of the obstacles or at the hands of another. It's survival of the fittest—and meanest—and Johnny fits into both of those categories."

Arthor pokes his head between our seats again, his red, unruly hair clinging to the fabric. "I'll help you, Imp," he whispers.

Although I don't approve of his comment, it immediately puts me at ease. "Seriously? You're going to call me names, too?" I turn toward him and produce a generous frown.

"No, sorry. That was a bad joke," Arthor says, his eyebrows crinkling.

"Good, because if you're not careful, I can come up with some pretty crazy nicknames for you, too."

"Oh, really? Like what?" he asks.

"Farty Arty." I grin.

He grumbles at the unwelcome reminder of the primary school nickname. "I see how it is. Tit for tat."

"Gotta stand up for myself." Peering out the window, I see Volkov Village. From what I've read in the Daily Republic, the floating city will house the participants in Savage Run and travel around to different continents where the obstacle courses will be taking place. The perfectly round oceanic city used to be gray, with oil stains around the edges and on the docks, and made up of squat, iron buildings. It was the very city that brought General Volkov and his Unifers to our country sixty-six years ago. A few years later, after President Volkov Sr. had completely restructured our society, it was turned into a cargo ship carrying crude oil, goods, and Laborers to different parts of the world. When the rest of the world rejected the notion of tiered societies shortly after, they put pressure on President Volkov Sr. to conform. He flat out refused and immediately made it illegal to trade or do business with any other nation. President Volkov Sr. had structured Newland to be one hundred percent self-sufficient, so it didn't affect us. And when President Volkov Jr. took over, he continued on as his father had done before him. However, the leaders of the other nations were dependent on Newland's supply of oil—the only known oil left on the planet—and asked him to reconsider. He told them to go to hell.

Now, the city is quite changed from what it used to be, with skyscrapers in the middle and shiny metal buildings gradually shrinking the closer they get to the outer edge. In fact, it looks like an upside-down spinning-top.

But there's something I hadn't expected to see around the city on the water. Barges and tankers—ships that carry crude oil—are leaving the docks. "Where are the ships heading?" I look at Nicholas.

"Thanks to Savage Run, the hosting countries will have their share of oil for an entire year."

"Why did he create the Savage Run, exactly?

Mai interrupts and points. "Volkov Park, named after...I'll give you one guess."

I wonder if her intrusion was intentional. Do they think I'm asking too many questions? I look at a bare steel area at the edge of the city. In the center of the park, there's a statue of a man holding his right arm out in front of him. The statue must be gigantic, since I can see it all the way from here.

The aircraft flies past the city and does a U-turn, after which it descends rapidly and lands on the water. After the plane touches down, it glides for a while before arriving at the front of a dock. The captain turns off the seatbelt sign. I take a deep breath and try to ignore the butterflies attacking my stomach.

Part 2

Survival

Chapter 7

The moment we step off the aircraft, I climb into one of four oversized transporters, making sure I don't get into the same one as Johnny. It's a quick drive to the gated facility where we are to spend the night. A long row of Unifers stands at attention outside the walls, gripping their firearms, and they all carry the same hateful expression, like everyone around them is an enemy, a suspect to ward off.

We drive in through shiny steel gates with a "V" on one gate and a "V" on the other. Am I entering another prison? Another world in which President Volkov can control me? What will really happen if I survive this program? Ruth said that trusting him is like digging your grave with three sticks of dynamite. What did she really mean by that?

Passing through the middle of two long rows of Unifers, I see a huge banner above:

Those who trade in essential freedom for fleeting security deserve neither freedom nor security. Welcome, Savages!

We drive by a few office buildings, and a cafeteria. My stomach rumbles—I haven't eaten since this morning and I feel weak. Will they be providing us with food? The transporter stops in front of a huge roundabout. The place is already crawling with participants and their representatives. Busses zoom past us, their exteriors plastered with red, yellow and white saber-toothed tiger heads. Being here feels all wrong because Gemma should have been here with me. The plan was that we make it together. Now who will I have at the end of all this? Who will be there if I succeed? Ruth is still alive, unless Master Douglas has gotten to her, too. My chest tightens. A Laborer can never be safe. Never. Even if she's alive and I do make it, then she'll want nothing to do with me when she discovers that I killed her Gemma. She'll be able to read in my eyes that I made the choice to run. To abandon her daughter. And if she can't, then I won't be able to stop myself from telling her. I rub my hands over my eyes to make it look like I'm trying to force the sleepiness out of them—not stop the tears that are threatening to come. I can't start to cry now. They'd all have yet another reason to think I'm a weakling and a Laborer who should never be a Master. Who doesn't deserve to be a Master. Quick, focus on something else. Anything!

When I open my eyes, I see that I'm alone in the transporter. This helps me to redirect my thoughts. I climb out of the vehicle, counting the steps on my way out to keep my mind off Gemma.

Once outside, we stand in a group and wait for Mai and Nicholas to exit their transporter. To keep my mind busy, I scan Volkov Village and let each detail soak in. But what catches my eye isn't inside the village, it's right outside of it. Beyond the fence is a large, blue and green glass structure with a bar, a band, and a dance floor inside. I've biked by dance clubs in Culmination many times, my eyes lingering on couples entwined as one. I've often wondered what it feels like to be in love, as the Masters call it. Just once, I would like to feel that magic, as they call it. Once before I die. I always knew that it was never for me. Laborers are required to accept the mate their Master chooses for them.

Standing here so close to the rest of the participants, it's glaringly obvious how much smaller I am than them. The shortest guy besides Arthor stands a whole head taller and must have at least seventy-five pounds on me. And it's not just that. They have this aura of confidence—fearlessness—that a Laborer never would have. Advisors are taught that they're important, almost as important as the Masters, and it's drilled into them from the time they're born. They're not the scum of the earth like Laborers, but free individuals who can own businesses and create the lives they desire. Just the way their eyes don't lower to the floor when spoken to—that alone sets them miles apart from us. And they know it. Many Advisors I have come in contact with are worse than the Masters—more arrogant, more proud. I have a theory about it. I think deep down inside their souls they know they're not completely free, and it eats away at them. They fight hard to keep up the façade, proving to the world how much they matter. Well, at least I'm fast, and I have developed pretty good endurance riding around the mountains and hillsides of Culmination all these years. At least I have that.

When Mai comes out, her eyebrows are gathered low over her eyes, and as she walks by me, she glances at me, like I'm her archenemy. "They're coming for you," she whispers in a voice so low that I'm sure no one else could hear.

My stomach feels as if I just swallowed a gallon of poison. Coming for me? Who? Wait, does she know I'm a girl? Did she tell them, whomever it is that's coming? I look around to see if they're here—the Unifers. It has to be Unifers, I'm sure of it. But before I have time to locate my pursuers a Savage Run bus pulls up in front of us.

"This is our bus," Nicholas says.

I quickly elbow my way to the front of the line so I can get on first. Not that I think it will matter much having someone after me. I'm sure they'll find me no matter where I am.

"Easy there," the guy with the shaved head and eagle tattoo on the back of his neck says. "What's the hurry?" He laughs a little. "So you're Joseph?"

I don't want to talk to someone at the moment, but since I'm stuck here in front of the closed door, I answer. "Yes. Hi. You?" I glance over my shoulder and around the front of the bus to see if anyone's coming. My mouth is so dry that my tongue sticks to the roof of it.

"Danny. Pleased to meet you." He holds out a hand.

I bang on the door a couple of times, and when it opens, I get on at once. I run to the back and sit down, slumping in my seat and leaning against the window, looking out. From the corner of my eye I see others get on the bus and find their seats.

"May I sit here?"

I look up and am relieved when I see Arthor. "Sure." I start to chew on my nails.

"Nervous?" he asks. The bus starts to drive off.

I lower my fingers from my teeth and look down at the floor. I'm not going to tell him someone's after me. "Bad habit—I know." It's one of the reasons my father makes me wash my hands so often. Scrub the impurity from them.

"It's okay." He looks out the window. "We're all afraid. Some of us just hide it better than others. Some of us pick on unsuspecting imps." He nudges me.

His comment almost makes me smile. "Johnny?"

"Yeah." We curve around the compound to the back, passing Unifers marching in perfect synchronized rhythms. None of them appear to be after me.

A little more relaxed, but still gawking out the window, I ask, "So, why are you here?"

His brows furrow. "It would make my parents proud of me and give them something to look forward to."

"So they supported you in coming?"

He hesitates. "They don't really support...much about me. Well, my mother does, but not my father."

I remember how his mother had waited for him outside the fence when he was registering, how despairing her eyes were and how white her knuckles were, clutching the fence.

"But hey, it's boring talking about me. Why are you here?" His eyes widen.

I glance around nervously. "Maybe not right here..."

He nods.

Shortly after the bus stops in front of a blue and green Nissen hut—Unifer housing composed of sheets of metal bent into half a cylinder. They're identical to the ones I've seen in newspaper articles about Unifer training camps with a garage door for the entrance and tiny barred windows on the sides. I didn't think housing could get any uglier than our trailers back home, but these take the cake.

Before stepping off the bus, I thoroughly inspect the area. A huge Culmination flag waves in front of the structures, and the gold and red bee mascot looks fierce against the black background. There's still no sign of anyone who looks like they might be after me. Was Mai just messing with me? She doesn't seem to be concerned at all, but then again, maybe she was the one who ratted me out. But how did she know? Nicholas.

Like the others, I huddle around Nicholas and Mai.

"Tonight each of you will sleep in your own room," Nicholas says. "In your room you will find a bed, a sink, a hole in the floor to do your business, and a Savage Run uniform for tomorrow. Dinner will be delivered to your room at 8:00 p.m. sharp and breakfast will be delivered at 6:00 a.m. tomorrow morning. Speaking with or communicating with any other participant is prohibited. Leaving your room is prohibited, and if discovered, you will be disqualified from the program and sent home. Strict obedience is required at all times."

Mai takes over. "Later tonight, Nicholas and I will visit briefly with each of you, so don't go to sleep until we've stopped by." She reads off a list, stating what room number each participant will be sleeping in. She doesn't read my name.

"Everyone is to meet back here at seven a.m. sharp tomorrow morning, dressed in your Savage Run uniform, after which Nicholas and I will escort you to the Conference Center for the Opening Ceremonies. If I hear of any...any disturbances tonight, you'll be crying for your mammas to come get you. You are all free to go."

Nicholas pushes a button on the outside of the hut causing the garage door to slowly screech open.

"Wait here with me," Mai says. I do as I'm told.

Once everyone enters the hut, Nicholas closes the garage door. "You got this?" he says to Mai. Mai nods and he looks at me. "I'll be back soon." He starts down the road.

"Come." She heads across the street to a townhome and I follow after her. We walk up the stairs to the second floor. When she arrives at the top, she inserts a keycard into a slot. The door vanishes, leaving an open rectangle for us to enter through. Knowing that Nicholas also knows something about what's going on makes this whole situation a little less scary, though my stomach still feels like it's been wrung over.

Stepping inside, I see that there's a simple kitchen, two bedrooms, a small bathroom with a shower, a living room, and an entertainment room with a screen embedded into the wall. Everything is tight and small—compact, but clean and modern. I remove my sandals, place them in the barely-there entranceway, and step onto the cold tile floor.

Even before I get past the entrance, Mai says, "It was stupid of you to come here. It's a fool's quest—one that will destroy you from the inside."

I'm so stunned that I can't speak. Did Nicholas tell her about me or didn't he?

"You think you've come for freedom, but you will only find your fears. And death. Take Nicholas' offer and go home. Don't waste your life on this...mirage."

I scramble to find something to say. "Living as a Laborer isn't living at all," I squeak. I don't know why, but for some reason I don't feel like I can speak freely around Mai. Maybe it's because of what happened between her and Johnny on the aircraft. Maybe it's because she's a woman and I'm not used to answering to women or for a woman to be anything other than soft-spoken and demure.

Mai's phone rings and she vanishes out onto the balcony. I make my way over to the window. Tall buildings are everywhere, and since it is dark, most of them beam rays of different-colored light into the sky. It's nothing like back home in Culmination, where once the night has fallen in the Laborer section, it becomes pitch black. The difference is, at home I can see every single star in the sky. Here, only the moon is visible, and it's not pure and white like back home. It's an orangey-yellow.

Before Gemma was sent to work for Master Douglas, we used to go stargazing at least a couple of times a week. I'd sneak out of my father's trailer, and we'd climb the small, grassy hill next to our subdivision and lie down in the open field. We'd gaze for hours and talk about things like freedom and what it would feel like to fall in love with a guy. I look up into the sky in search of a star. But there are none. I reach for my mother's locket, but just like Gemma, it's gone.

Mai slides the glass door open and steps inside.

"That was President Volkov again. The reason he's been calling is because Master Douglas called him."

I feel all the blood leave my face. "Oh..." My arms suddenly feel like they weigh a hundred pounds each.

"He says there's a problem with your ID."

"W...what?" I try to act surprised, but it's hard to act surprised when I feel terrified.

"He's sending a couple of his Unifers to confirm your identity."

Confirm my identity? What does that mean? "When?"

"Right now."

I run my hands through my short hair and begin to pace; back and forth, back and forth.

"Heidi," Mai says, grabbing me by the shoulders.

It takes a second for me to register she used my real name, but when I do, my first thought is that she's going to maul me like she did Johnny.

"Fortunately, Nicholas already talked to me. About you." She looks at me, her eyes softening just enough for me to notice. Then she chuckles. "I'm sorry I'm laughing. There's nothing funny about this, but...I was so relieved because I'd never in my life seen such a hopeless case." She looks around the room as if searching for something, and then she stares at me for a moment. Wrapping her arms around me, she squeezes me so tightly that it becomes difficult to breathe. As if trying to contain herself, she takes a step back and looks up into the ceiling, her hands on her narrow hips. Then, she buries her hands in her face and lets out a long moan.

The way she's acting, I think she's having a nervous breakdown. "What did President Volkov say?"

Her hands drop to her sides. "Don't worry. You'll be just fine, I promise. Nicholas is seeing to it at this very moment."

But my shoulders refuse to relax. Unifers are on their way over here right now. For me. What am I supposed to do if they want to see me naked? I mean, it would be the easiest and quickest way to verify my gender, right?

"Nicholas told me about your friend, too. I'm so sorry."

All of a sudden I can't take a breath. Gemma. Unifers. The way Mai is acting. I reach for my pendant, but it isn't there. In order to keep breathing, I dash out onto the small balcony and grip the railing. My hands hurt from when I fell down helping Gemma escape, but I squeeze the railing harder so I can feel that instead of the fear tearing through me. Gemma. My throat swells and even out here, the air feels thick and unyieldingly harsh. It's like the past and the present are colliding, and I can't manage to keep them inside of me and still exist.

Mai comes out and leans her hip against the railing, facing me. Her voice is gentle, cautious, like Ruth's. "Sometimes, no matter how hard one tries to forget...about losing someone, it's impossible. I'm sorry. It wasn't professional of me to mention your friend."

I produce a few shallow breaths, and finally my lungs open and I can breathe again.

She places a hand on my shoulder. "Listen, I can't tell you what to do. If I were in your shoes, I'd probably do the same. But you should know what you're up against. These obstacles are meant to kill. They're much more brutal than I think you realize. Than any of the participants realize."

"I just...I can't go back."

Looking across the valley, she says, "I suppose I'll have to respect your wishes. Now, back to the phone call. I told

President Volkov that your ID looked authentic so don't worry. I'm not going to rat you out."

My eyes question her comment.

"I have my own reasons. I'm sure you can, with a little discernment, figure out what some of those reasons are."

The first reason that comes to mind is that she's a woman and would like to see more women doing what she does.

"Besides, Nicholas made me promise. And I never break a promise."

"So, do you think President Volkov suspects?" I ask.

"Not really. Sending the Unifers here is just a precautionary measure."

Nicholas comes in through the door holding a cup of black coffee. "Did you tell her?"

"Yes."

He turns to me, his eyes intense. "Listen very carefully, Heidi. I passed the Unifers on my way here. Whatever you do, don't panic. When they arrive, just listen and answer their questions in as few words as possible, understood?"

"Okay." I feel my pulse in my forehead. Someone bangs at the door and when Nicholas opens it, two Unifers stand there, gripping their firearms.

88

Chapter 8

The Unifers are polar opposites, one as pale as the moon over Culmination and the other as dark as night. I feel like I'm in a nightmare where I'm trying to get away from my assassin, but instead of moving, I'm shackled—immobilized—by some unseen force.

"Good evening, Sir, Ma'am," the pale one says, and both salute Nicholas and Mai by lifting their right fists up to their right eyebrows.

Without any further niceties, they step toward me. I half expect them to rip off my clothes to verify that I'm a guy, and it takes every last ounce of resolve not to retreat to the balcony or bring my arms up to my chest.

"Are you Joseph Wood?"

"I am," I say in the deepest voice I can muster.

"By command of President Volkov, I need to see your government-issued ID," the dark-skinned Unifer says.

Nicholas hands him my ID card and steps back, briefly glancing my way.

The Unifer holds up a small hand-held device with a bunch of buttons and a green light on the bottom. He inserts my card into the feeder, but as it comes out on the other side, the machine beeps and the lit button turns red. "Looks like this ID is illegitimate..." He gives me an accusing glare.

"Try it again," Nicholas says flatly.

I clamp my jaw so tight that my teeth hurt.

The Unifer gives Nicholas an irritated look, but does as he is told. This time when he runs my ID through the reader, the light turns green. "Strange..." he remarks, looking puzzled by the blip.

Wanting to get them out of here as quickly as possible, I say, "Will there be anything else?" I can't believe I'm talking to a Unifer like that, my eyes not dropping to the floor.

"No, that will be all. Thank you for your cooperation." He bows his head a tad and they're both out the door. The second they leave, it's as if the oxygen in the air suddenly returns.

"They think they're so high and mighty," Mai says, scoffing.

I'm surprised by her blatant aversion toward them, especially in front of me.

"But I can't believe you fooled them. Unifers are trained to spot deception. But with that haircut and those clothes, your chest flattened to nothing...you really do look like a boy," Mai says. "You had me fooled all along. What do you think, Nicholas?"

I touch my hair, not really feeling like a guy, yet no longer a girl. It's strange how I have come to associate with my gender so much, and how pretending to be the opposite one makes me feel like I am no longer me.

He glances at me for a moment. "I still think she looks like a girl."

90

I look down. I don't like them talking about me as if I'm not even here; it makes me feel like a child.

"What makes you say that?" Mai presses.

"She just has that natural, feminine...glow to her, I suppose." His eyes linger on me for a moment, and heat rises in my cheeks. Why am I reacting to him this way? It really bothers me.

"Heidi, I'm not supposed to give you any advice, but, oh well. When you're in the fields, try not to stand out from the rest of the group. President Volkov already thinks that Master Douglas is a nutcase, and if there aren't any more accusations or events that draw attention to you, then the allegations will dissipate into thin air." She takes a few deep breaths and then faces Nicholas. "You got this? I want to catch up on what's going on in the world."

"Let's go," Nicholas says, tilting his head to the side for me to follow him. I do as he says, but just as we're about to exit the door, I hear a news reporter say my name. I walk back inside and into the entertainment room and see a close-up of my face on the screen. My cheeks fill with blood.

"So why is this young, unqualified, pre-adolescent boy in the Savage Run?" the reporter questions, and adds, "Have the standards of the elite stooped too low?" The image shifts to a newsroom, and another reporter takes over. "Now onto the Savage Run Survival Pole. Citizens of Newland have nominated Johnny Poltinger from Culmination as the most likely to place in the top three in Savage Run." A diagram of the top ten participants appears on the screen, and Johnny's name is at the top, followed by someone named Cory, and a guy named Jared. "And here is the list of the least likely to complete any of the obstacles. I'm sure it comes as no surprise that Joseph Wood is the last man—or shall we say boy—on the list."

Whatever speck of confidence I had from being in shape riding around on my bike all these years vanishes. I mean, who am I kidding? Now I see nothing but a stupid girl who doesn't even know her own limits.

"Don't watch that trash," Nicholas says.

Mai mutes the TV and crosses her arms in front of her chest. "You're an easy target, Heidi. The media will go after you, but you have to ignore them. Besides, they don't know anything."

"How do they even know about me?" I ask.

"Drones," Nicholas says.

That's what the media uses to get the pictures they want.

"And there's not much we can do about it. Not even during the obstacle courses themselves, I'm afraid. Anyway, let's get you settled, shall we?"

At the Nissen hut, he opens the garage and we step inside the hallway. The garage door closes in a clangor behind us, making me jump. On either side of it is a long row of doors without handles, and blue tube lights hang in the ceiling, stretching all the way to the end. It makes Nicholas' face look pasty. The corridor is completely quiet, so much so that I wonder if anyone is here at all. When we get to door number nineteen, Nicholas pauses for a moment.

"Listen," he states, "just because you're small, doesn't mean you don't have a chance." He peers down at me and gives me half a smile. "And I can imagine biking around Culmination all these years has made your legs strong."

Did I tell him what my work is? I can't remember at the moment. "Thanks," I say, for a lack of anything else to say. And for some reason, my heart beats a little faster.

He inserts the keycard into the slot. Nothing happens. He flips it over and tries again. Still nothing. He keeps trying, in every possible direction, but no matter which way he puts the card in, it doesn't work. "Let's go down to the office and get a new key."

We exit the hut and walk side by side toward the office. The cool breeze plays against my cheek as the moon shadows us down the path. Passing Unifers, every one of them salutes Nicholas. I can't imagine what it would be like to command so much veneration or power. And it's strange to be treated with regard by someone who does. Is it all part of his plan to get me to trust him so I am in his debt? Of course it's a ridiculous thought because there's not a thing he would need from me, is there? Yet, why is he acting so kind toward me, almost friend-like, if it isn't to get something from me? Use me in some way? There can't be any other explanation.

Walking down the hill, we pass other participants along the way. I want to sink into the ground when they whisper and shoot me disapproving glances.

"Just ignore them," Nicholas says.

I didn't realize he noticed how uncomfortable their looks make me feel, but at least it confirms that I'm not crazy and making things up.

"So tell me again why you decided to break the law and then break the law again by signing up for the most dangerous obstacle course known to mankind," he says.

"Well...I...uh."

"You don't need to hide anything from me, Heidi. What we talk about is between us."

Precisely what a Master would say to make me open up, and later use what I say against me. Does he really believe that I'll trust him just like that? Besides, it's not like I even know what trust is; I've never lived around it or seen it in action, only fear and anger, and blame. Always the blame. Well, that's not completely true. Ruth and Gemma I could trust, yes, but to think I could get to that level of trust with President Volkov's son is outright ludicrous. Trusting a superior is something foreign—a mythical concept that doesn't exist. A dangerous road riddled with pain.

When I look at him, I see that his eyes are trained on my face.

"Did I say something wrong?" he asks.

"No."

"I'm President Volkov's son again, aren't I?"

I feel a tinge of guilt like when we were on the aircraft. I brace my arms in front of my chest.

"When I become president, I plan to restructure our entire society. No more hierarchical classes." He studies my face as if trying to read my reaction. Is he just saying that to hook me, to trick me into trusting him? What does he want in return? If I'm not careful, I might fall for it—he seems so genuine. "That's...great. Rather ambitious going completely against your father and grandfather like that."

"Ambitious. Now there's one thing my father did right; he raised me to believe I can get whatever I want. I suppose I'm rather exhausting that way."

"That explains a lot." The words just jump out before I can think. Nicholas seems to have that effect on me—

making me speak my mind even when I don't mean to. It's both terrifying and exhilarating at the same time. But mostly terrifying. "I mean..."

He starts to laugh. "Most people try to impress me or get something out of me. It would seem that neither of those are on your agenda."

I don't hear any anger in his voice, but it doesn't mean it isn't there. "I'm sorry. I should be more respectful."

He stops walking. "Don't change. Your candor is one of the things I appreciate most about you. Dealing with politicians these days, you never know where anyone really stands. But you're not like that."

My father took most of my comments as insults although I rarely intended them that way. "Maybe if I were free like a politician, I'd be different."

"Freedom doesn't change a person—only makes them more of who they already are."

I wish I were free.

"You know the first thing the Unifers bombed when they started taking over your country?"

"No." We didn't learn much about our country's usurpation in primary school.

"The Statue of Liberty."

"What's that?"

He smiles a little. "It was a statue of a robed female figure—an icon of freedom."

"Oh." Of course it would be the first thing to go.

"Freedom, I have found, is an illusion. Once you think you have it, you'll realize that you're still not completely free; no one is. It's a perfect ideal never to be had."

I shake my head. "I think freedom is a gift, and what you choose to do with that freedom is what makes us completely free."

He shakes his head. "It's okay—you don't understand."

All of a sudden, I get the feeling I'm back around Master Douglas with his haughty demeanor. "Just because I'm a Laborer doesn't mean I can't figure things out."

"That's not at all what I meant."

"Then what?"

"That you're still so pure and unspoiled from all the politics and corruption that soils our society. All I'm saying is that sometimes, it's better to not have a choice—all that responsibility," he says.

Something occurs to me. He must feel the pressures of being the next in line for president. "Are you saying you're afraid of responsibility?"

"Sometimes. Sometimes the burden is so great..." He pauses and glances at me, then exhales before continuing. "...and when mistakes inevitably are made, the one at the top is the one to blame."

"But it's so much better to at least be free to make those mistakes."

"Perhaps to some extent." The muscles in his jaw tighten.

If he knew anything about a Laborer's circumstances, then he wouldn't be saying that. Is he completely ignorant to the way a Laborer lives? To how we have absolutely no say in our lives? Before I can say anything further, we've reached the office. The front doors part as we approach them, and Nicholas walks in ahead of me. After we get a new key, a Unifer drives us back to the Nissen Hut and Nicholas opens my door without a hitch.

He stands aside. "Mai and I will be back later to brief you about tomorrow."

I step inside the room, and the first thing I notice is the wooden bed—completely bare except for the thin pillow. Where's the mattress? Even at home I have one. Not a very comfortable one; I can just imagine the feel of the boards pressing against my back before sleep takes me. And the toilet—a hole in the floor just like Nicholas said. Back home I have a toilet. The room stinks of urine and it's cold. Goosebumps appear on my arms. I hadn't expected my living standards to decrease when I signed up for this.

"I know the accommodations aren't exactly ideal."

"I'll be fine." I'm already shivering.

"There's a blanket under the bed. Mai and I will be back in a couple of hours for the briefing." He closes the door and I'm left to myself.

I should try to get some sleep. I lie down on the bed and squeeze my eyes shut, the boards cold and rigid against my back. My hands move to my chest, and I imagine my mother's locket being there. If it were, then I'd caress the smooth surface, and it would send me to sleep. A few minutes pass and my mind is processing like a high performing computer. The thought of the computer reminds me of Sergio—stupid Sergio. Now I can't get his Eastern Republic accent out of my head. Pteetsa. If only I were a bird, I could fly away. I wonder why he agreed to make those IDs for Gemma and me when he could easily have kicked us out and been done with it.

Gemma. From the very innermost part of me, I wish I could go back to that moment, the very moment when I made my decision to run—the moment that killed her. I hear her voice screaming for me to run. Run, Heidi, run! I wipe a tear that runs down the side of my head toward my ear. I shouldn't have run. There, I finally can admit it. A faint cry escapes my lips. She always sacrificed herself so I could get what I wanted. I knew that. Innately. And this time was no different. Just like the time she fell out of the tree and broke her arm. She was terrified to even get up in the tree. I could see it in her eyes and in the way her fingers trembled.

But for some reason I had to have her climb with me. It was always this way—me needing her more than she needed me. To do things with me—the one who gave me courage—meaning. And in the end she was the one who gave the most—not me. I selfishly just took it. Until there was no more to take. I feel another tear trail down from my eye. I made the wrong choice. I made the wrong choice! Why did it have to turn out this way? Why did I have to make that decision?

I sit up. I can't think about her right now; I need to remain emotionally stable—strong—the strongest I've ever been, like Ruth always told me. Never tire, she would say. If you tire, you die. But she doesn't know what I've done. I'm sure she wouldn't give me that advice now. I fall to the hard bed, pound my fists into the wood, and scream into my pillow.

I can't lie here anymore, driving myself crazy like this.

I stand up and start to pace around the small room. I continue on with the mindless pacing for hours—I think. I can't really tell, and I don't bother to check the clock. At some point the door opens and someone slides a plate in, but I don't eat it. I know I should, but I can't. Instead, I try to figure out what I could have done differently. There must have been some way I could have saved Gemma and me both. But the conclusion is always the same. If I die, she dies. If she dies, I live.

When Nicholas opens the door, my eyelids feel thick—swollen. I turn away so he won't see me like this.

"I'm here to brief you about tomorrow." He closes the door and the room smells faintly of cologne. "Heidi."

I swivel halfway toward him.

"Is everything okay?" His voice is low, a hint of concern in his tone—or maybe it's disgust.

"I'm fine."

"You don't look fine."

"Where's Mai?" I ask, wanting the attention off me.

"We ran late and President Volkov needed to meet with her."

I sit down on the bed, my eyes lowered, my hands stuffed between the wood and the back of my thighs. "So what's it like, exactly, to be President Volkov's son?"

He seems to acknowledge that I need something—anything—to distract myself with. "What's it like?" He moves deeper into the room and pockets the key card. "No one has ever asked me that before." He gazes out into the air and his face goes stiff. "It's always a power struggle. And I never feel like I'm truly free. Restricting."

What? I never thought being a Master would be restricting. And it sounds completely ridiculous when he states he's not free. Our eyes connect for a moment, but I quickly avert mine.

He continues. "It would be so freeing if I didn't have to play by his rules anymore. But being his son, there's no escape." He sits down next to me on the bed. "What's it like being a Laborer?"

"No one's ever asked me that before." When he smiles, I smile. "It's restrictive, too. Way more restrictive than it is to be a Master. I just feel...I mean...you know, don't you?"

"I have yet to visit a Laborer compound or associate with your class. You're actually, believe it or not, the first Laborer I've spoken with—like this."

"You don't have Laborers working for you?" I ask.

"They're all Advisors or Masters. Only the secondary Masters have Laborers working for them. Once one reaches a certain level, one only associates with Advisors and Masters."

I had no idea there were lower class Masters.

"Well, Mai and my father are waiting for me. So I need to brief you about the obstacle courses. Each obstacle has a shortcut or a safe zone, and if you uncover it, the obstacle will become much easier. Some of the shortcuts are easy to find, others nearly impossible. But I can't stress this enough for you, Heidi. Find those shortcuts."

"What specifically am I looking for?"

He exhales. "These obstacles are created to evaluate you in three areas; intelligence, physical aptness and emotional endurance." He sounds like he's reciting a memorized message. "These obstacles are meant to kill—that's why I didn't want you to join. I hardly think even half of the contestants will survive. If you can manage the physical aspect of the obstacles, Heidi, I don't think you'll have any problem qualifying for Master Status."

If...that's all I have? A great big 'if?' And aren't the physical aspects of the obstacles like ninety percent of it? All

I can think is how unfair this is—completely misrepresented. I should have scrutinized the Savage Run rules before I set out on my journey. Before I risked my life. And took Gemma's.

Nicholas stops by the door before he exits. "When you become free, what's the first thing you want to do?"

I noticed he said 'when.' Right now, it doesn't feel like 'when.' It feels like 'never.' But even so, my mind wanders toward the possibility. The opportunities would be endless, at least compared to the possibilities I had before as a Laborer. And it's kind of scary, like there's no safety net holding me back. I'll be able to experience my first kiss, and have children if I want, and even have my heart broken—not that I'd ever allow any guy to get close enough to break it. "I've always wanted to...go dancing."

The right side of his lip twitches. "Well, good night then." He closes the door.

After I get back in bed, I lie awake, my mind churning with the question Nicholas asked before he left. What will I do first? And to that, I fall asleep.

Chapter 9

It takes me a moment to register that there's an alarm clock going off. Opening my eyes to a dark room, I turn my head toward the sound and see red symbols reading 6:30 a.m. Where am I? My body feels sore and I'm lying on a hard surface. Slowly, it starts to come back to me. I registered for the Savage Run, Sergio took my locket, my father was furious...Nicholas...Arthor...and...Gemma. Remembering that she was shot makes me gasp and I feel like I'm going to be sick. Was it real? Is she dead? I desperately yearn for it all to just be a nightmare. But it isn't.

I close my eyes and sit for a long while, finally coming to the conclusion that I have to find a way to control my emotions. The only way I know how to do this is to pretend I don't care. Like I've done so many times with my father. Gemma didn't really mean anything to me. She was just another person who I brushed shoulders with, and I can live just fine without her. I stuff the pain down, deeper and deeper and tell myself that Gemma was a good friend, yes, but I'll be just fine like I was before I met her. The only person I need to care about is myself. I can't let one friendship lost ruin my life. I have to be rock solid; stronger than anyone, and the only person that can make it happen is me.

Once I feel like I have a hold on my emotions, I sit up. My new Savage Run uniform is lying on the floor. I pick it up and place it back on the bed. I undress, retie the gauze tightly around my chest, and then slip into the uniform. The pattern is the same as the one the Unifers wear, but the suit is tight fitting and made of stretchy material. A few minutes pass. The door opens and a plate of scrambled eggs and toast is slid into the room, next to the untouched one from last night. I pick the plate up, stuff the eggs into the toast, and eat it.

At a quarter to seven, my door opens. I step into the hallway and trail after the others all the way to the outside.

When I come outside, I see Nicholas, Arthor, and—ugh—Johnny standing together and conversing. I don't go over to them. Hundreds of participants are making their way to the Conference Center for the Opening Ceremonies. Some guys are walking with their heads down, avoiding eye contact with anyone. Some are running down the street with their city's flag, screaming at the top of their lungs. Others are speaking loudly, the excitement in their voices over-exaggerated.

Mai approaches me and studies my face for a while before saying, "You know, life doesn't always end up the way one imagines."

"Good morning," Arthor says with a grin, patting me on the back.

"Hi, good morning," I say. "Nice outfit." His matches mine exactly, though he fills out his suit much better than I do.

"Sleep well?" Johnny asks.

He must have followed Arthor over here. Is he talking to me—actually being civil? "Uh...yes." I wait for his next sarcastic remark. But it doesn't come. I remember Arthor's comment yesterday, how he said that 'everyone's afraid.' Maybe Johnny is afraid, too, and he becomes nice when he is fearful. That knowledge could be very useful during the obstacles.

A guy with bleached white hair struts past us and pumps his fists into the air. He's chanting, "I'm a savage. I'm a savage." He moves in a jittery way, like he's downed one too many coffees or something. Maybe nerves—might be his way of dealing with what's about to transpire.

Another registrar walks up to Nicholas and I step a little closer to listen in on their conversation.

"I have some pretty ambitious participants. You?" the registrar says.

"A few."

"What about that Joseph of yours?"

"He's a good guy."

"But how come you let him register, I mean...you don't really think he'll make it, do you? All you can do is feel sorry for the little guy."

Nicholas catches me looking at him, but he doesn't break eye contact. "He may be little, but he's smart. And he knows that all the things he needs to succeed are within the obstacles themselves."

I should look away, but there's something about looking into his eyes that makes me not want to.

"Well, smarts will only get you so far," the registrar refutes. "That's Cory, an Advisor from Asolo." He points to the guy with the white hair. "Cory's Master father fell in love with an Advisor and they had him. He wants to make his father proud and complete the Savage Run so he'll be a Master, too, and after this he's planning on running for office and working for President Volkov."

"Interesting. Excuse me," Nicholas says to the registrar and walks toward Mai. "Mai, will you escort everyone to the Conference Center? I'll be right there with Joseph." Mai nods, and they start walking down the road, merging with all the other participants. We start to walk after the others, but at a much slower pace. "Mai insisted I tell you that during the first obstacle—the marathon—the landmines are rigged to go off at one hundred and fifty pounds. She thought it might help you feel better about everything."

"Mai said that?"

"Yes."

It's strange that she'd insist on that. But then again, she is a woman. "Taking orders from her now?" I tease.

"Not usually. But I thought it would be a good thing for you to know," he says.

I weigh one hundred and five pounds, and he must know this from my fake ID card. It was one of the things Sergio didn't change. So why is he telling me...oh. If I team up with anyone else, I could be blown to bits if the other participant steps on a landmine. Most likely, I'm the only one here who weighs less than a hundred and fifty pounds. If I run alone, I'm pretty much guaranteed that I'll make the first obstacle.

I tuck an imaginary stray hair behind my ear. "I don't think it's fair that you're telling me this."

"Nothing in life is fair. You are free to use the information anyway you want. I know it may not be completely fair, but things are complicated." He opens his mouth to speak, but closes it again. Then he opens his mouth again. "I don't like anything about Savage Run or the creators of it. My father sells it as an opportunity for freedom, when in reality, it's just another way to gain control."

Whoa, what does that mean? I slow down a little. His comment almost makes me think that he's planning against his father. Should I believe him? "So why did you choose to work as one of the registrars if you're so opposed to it?"

He exhales at length. "It's the only way I can help."

"Help?"

"My father wanted me to be the venture manager, but I would have shown my disgust for the program too openly, so I declined and told him I'd rather work in the trenches getting to know the participants—the lower classes."

Either he's really great at lying or he's actually telling the truth.

We stop in front of the Conference Center, a huge white, glittering dome. Hundreds of participants and their representatives are making their way in through different doors.

Nicholas' eyes turn intense. "Listen, I...I think you just might have a chance to make it through the first phase. The way that it's set up, one doesn't have to be strong to survive—only smart. Strength will only get you so far; intelligence will get you all the way."

He thinks I'm smart?

"And stay away from Johnny if you can help it. I don't trust him," he says flatly, his eyes scanning the crowd.

Yeah, he hates my guts.

Once we enter the dome, Nicholas and I press through the crowd of young men until we catch up with the others. The dome ceiling looks as tall as the heavens, and hundreds of voices echo off the walls. I decide it's safest to walk next to Arthor, and he smiles at me when he sees me. Passing other participants, I'm certain a few of them look at me with disdain, but I throw the thought from my mind. I'm just being overly paranoid. I'm hardly important enough that they would be thinking about me right now; they're probably just stressed about the long days ahead.

"I get the feeling imps receive extra perks," Johnny sneers, appearing out of nowhere. He walks uncomfortably close to me, shoving me just enough so I lose my balance and stumble.

He does have a point. Nicholas did give me unfair information.

"Why are you trying so hard to make yourself look stronger and superior?" Arthor asks Johnny.

"I'm not trying to make myself look stronger and superior. I am stronger and superior. Thing is, it makes me angry when another participant gets an unfair advantage over me," Johnny says, shoving me a little harder so I go tumbling toward the ground. Fortunately, Arthor catches me.

"Come on, man," Arthor says, helping me find my balance. "Give him some slack."

"Slack? Are you serious? Are you on the imp's side? Don't you see that Joseph is receiving preferential treatment?"

"Just drop it," Arthor says.

"Hey, I'm just speaking up for everyone," Johnny says. "This is ridiculous. Seriously..." He huffs, but thankfully he shuts up and walks ahead to the front of our group.

We take our seats in the tenth row, with me sitting between Arthor and Nicholas. There are ten chairs on the stage and a stand where I'm sure President Volkov will speak from. The hall fills up quickly as participants funnel in from every direction, their voices so loud I can't hear what Mai is trying to say to me even though she sits right next to Nicholas.

When the clock on the wall reads 7:30 a.m., a trumpet march blasts through the speakers. I almost swallow my tongue. I recognize the upbeat melody as the one they played before each Savage Run pre-event newscast. The apothecaries would be glued to the radio whenever I came to pick up medicine.

My father wouldn't be caught dead listening to it or reading about it in the paper. But I do wonder if he's watching now, cursing my name, or if he's rotting away in some prison, cursing my name. Surely he must hate me so much more after what I did to him. I never did anything to deserve his contempt more. And I'm to blame, of course.

The music fades and a representative with silver hair and an athletic build walks onto the stage, taking his place behind the stand. "Welcome to the Savage Run," he says. "My name is Otto Jensen, or O.J., and I am the official host of the Savage Run. On this premier day of this event, we have put together a small audiovisual of the ten most memorable moments in Newland obstacle course history that inspired the obstacles in the Savage Run. I hope it will motivate all you participants here today. Enjoy."

The lights fade and a projection pops up right in front of my eyes, accompanied by a dangerous tune. The first contender, a fierce-looking golden-haired boy, appears on my screen. Screaming, he wrestles an alligator to the ground with his bare hands. Finally with one snap, the boy cracks the alligator's jaw open, splitting it in two. The image melts into the next one. A boy with black hair and skin appears on my screen. The boy is one of many, clinging onto a tightrope above a glacier, inching himself forward. Bodies lie frozen below, their lifeless, blue faces staring up into the heavens. I close my eyes to escape the image, feeling my stomach churn with nausea. The images continue, each one more disturbing than the next and I have a hard time keeping my eyes on the screen. The ninth image is of a grossly muscular boy, nothing like I've ever seen. The boy runs alongside other competitors in a jungle. But then the boy does something unexpected. He finds a sharp stick and starts stabbing the others in the stomach with it, their blood running down their abdomens and legs. Tigers attack out of nowhere, drawn to the scent of fresh blood. Fast-forward and the muscle-bound boy runs ahead and crosses the finish line first, his arms raised in victory.

Is this the kind of thing I'll be up against? That I'll have to revert to so I can stay alive? I look over at Nicholas who isn't even watching the screen directly in front of his face. Instead he's looking down at his hands in his lap.

The final top ten episode appears on the screen and I immediately recognize Tristan, Arthor's brother, as the boy climbing a snow-covered cliff. I glance over at Arthor again whose lips draw to a line and he looks away from the screen. He knows what's coming. This is the moment his brother died. I look back to the screen, not really wanting to watch, but unable to tear my eyes away.

Climbing the steep cliff, Tristan finally arrives at the top with the Culmination flag in his hand. A redheaded participant makes it to the top, and seeing Tristan, he immediately lunges for him, punching him again and again until blood flows from his mouth and nose. Why would he be doing this and why is this clip being shown? I close my eyes for a second and when I open them, somehow Tristan has flipped the boy onto his back, straddling him. The boy kicks his feet against the back of Tristan's head and they roll to the edge of the mountainside, the redheaded boy ending up dangling over the edge, above the icy water one hundred and fifty feet below. The boy screams, and for a moment, Tristan hesitates. Then he reaches his hand out to help the boy and hauls him up, but this act of kindness, of complete selflessness, costs him everything as the boy pushes Tristan off the cliff into the water below, sending him to his death.

My screen closes and the lights in the hall turn on. I look over at Arthor again and he has his eyes closed. Instinctively, I reach for his hand, but before I touch him, I withdraw it. I'm not sure if he sees it, but his eyes open.

"Savage Run was designed with these events in mind and to challenge both the body and the mind so participants are adequately tested, proving that they are suitable to join the superior Class-1 Master race. I believe every single participant here today has the seeds of greatness deep within him. It is the responsibility of each of you to bring that greatness out in yourself. Just remember, we created this program because we believe in you. And now, finally, for the moment you have all been waiting for," O.J. says. "Please welcome President Volkov and the representatives of the official participating countries, the generous benefactors of the Savage Run."

The crowd erupts into applause and I clap along with them, but not because I'm excited. My thoughts are still on Tristan and how with one decision, his life was over. Hopefully, I don't meet his fate, too. I want to say to Arthor that his brother did the honorable thing, and that that's what was most important. But he's dead. Is doing the honorable thing really the most important? Or is doing whatever it takes to stay alive?

President Volkov strides onto the stage, his bald head catching the light of the follow spots. He welcomes us brave souls, telling us we should be so proud to be the few who still believe in the ideal of liberty and strength. This opportunity, he says, was made for us and for anyone who ever had a dream in their hearts.

I look over at Nicholas and when his eyes find mine, they are full of quiet bitterness. Seeing him in such close proximity to his father, it becomes obvious to me that he wasn't lying about how he feels. I can see it in the way his whole body tenses and in the way his eyes smolder. To anyone else, he might just look tough and proud—it's easy to miss the subtle contempt in his eyes. But it's there. Very much so.

"Before I reveal in which nations the obstacles will be taking place," President Volkov says. "I'd like to personally thank the leaders who voted in favor of hosting my program. Most politicians know that sporting events rarely produce a financial gain, which is unfortunate. However, when a country becomes involved in supporting an event such as this one, research shows that there is a measurable increase in happiness among the nation's citizens. The excitement and partying will infuse fun into the otherwise dreary, day-to-day routine. And who isn't looking for more happiness in life?" He pauses and ambles across the stage.

And oil, is all I can think.

"Most people don't really want true freedom because it requires a hundred times more than living in bondage. But you Savages, you know what freedom costs, and you aren't afraid to embrace it. And now for the grand reveal."

The moment of truth. When all will be revealed to me. But there's someone missing, and I feel weak without her. Afraid. Alone. Gemma should have been here with me now—she deserved it more than anyone. Why do some lose it all? I chew the inside of my mouth until I can taste blood—anything to keep my thoughts from going back to Gemma.

Chapter 10

I don't know how in the blink of an eye my throat got so dry and how extremely difficult it has become to sit still and not fidget. The entire room has become so quiet. If I closed my eyes and didn't know where I was, I would think that I was alone.

"The first phase of the Savage Run will be held in the Nation of Normark," President Volkov announces. The spectators burst into applause—the rest of the participants from Culmination and myself also clapping dutifully—but I sense that some of the enthusiasm displayed by the other participants is more to drown out their fears than from any real excitement. Three women and one man enter the stage carrying Normark's flag—a green flag with a white and blue cross through it. They eventually make it to their seats and sit down.

President Volkov continues. "Normark, as you all know, has never been part of any republic or united order. They could be labeled loners." He laughs, and the gathering joins in. "As an independent nation, they have done very well, and we salute their leaders for holding to the traditions of the old world. Normark is, in short, famous for its beautiful soaring mountains and gorging fjords, and it is in this dramatic environment that you will begin your journey to freedom. In the first round of phase one, you will run a marathon—twenty-six point two miles—across a landmine-speckled field. In the second round of phase one, you will swim ten miles in e-conda infested waters—a genetically altered anaconda that is capable of generating one thousand volts of electricity."

I've never been a good swimmer, or a fan of any type of water predator, but President Volkov continues to talk before my mind comes up with all the scenarios in which I'll drown.

"Last, but not least, in the third round of the first phase, you will climb Devil's Cliff, and complete phase one by jumping into the fjord two hundred feet below. For those of you who don't know, Devil's Cliff is the deadliest cliff known to man."

I look over at Arthor, wondering how he feels about jumping off the cliff. Arthor's face is composed—ashen—making me think there's a storm brewing inside.

"Is it even possible to survive a two hundred foot fall?" I whisper. No one answers.

"The second phase will be held in the Republic of South Newland," President Volkov announces. Two men and two women step onto the stage, parading around with smiles on their faces, waving the Republic of South Newland's flag in the air. Finally, they make their way to their seats and smile, nodding to the leaders of Normark.

"The Republic of South Newland has a plethora of caves and waters." President Volkov greets each of the leaders with a handshake, his smile coming across as a forced grin. After they sit down, he continues speaking. "During the first round of phase two, you will find yourselves balancing across floating disks, high above Black Valley. During the second round, you will literally be elevated to new heights, and during the third round, you will encounter a surprise obstacle course. Finally, the third and last phase will be held in..." he waits for the crowd to grow anxious. "Do you want to know?"

"Is he seriously asking us that?" Arthor whispers. I stymie a despairing laugh by clasping my hand over my mouth. I'm so nervous that my hands feel like icicles and they're trembling.

"I can't hear you. Do you want to know?" We cheer, though we are far from enthusiastic.

"The O-Region. And the Eastern Republic will be benefitting this program." Murmurings go through the crowd while the final four leaders—all men—parade the stage with the Eastern Republic flag waving above their heads. Like me, many of the Laborers in Newland still consider the super nation traitors because they didn't send help when the rogue Unifer army usurped our country. I don't understand why the Eastern Republic didn't stop the rogue Unifers, but my father says it was because the rogue army had grown so big that the Eastern Republic was just glad to be rid of the threat of attack.

"The Outer Region?" Arthor says, his mouth dropping open.

Eastern Republic scientists were commissioned to recreate extinct beasts like the saber-toothed tiger and some of the more fearsome dinosaurs. When that succeeded, it was rumored that the scientists had also begun to create new creatures based on old mythologies, like dragons and sea monsters.

After President Volkov greets the four men, he continues. "During this part of the event, you will cross Magma Island, find your way through the Caves of Choice, and finally encounter Savage Jungle, where the most vicious beasts—not known to the average man—live."

Johnny must have seen my worried expression because he leans over and says, "Don't worry; you won't make it that far."

"Don't worry, neither will you," Arthor says without looking at him.

Johnny scoffs, but sits back in his seat.

"Now, let me talk about prizes. Participants who complete the Savage Run in its entirety, and score high enough in the appropriate areas, will be granted Class-1 Master citizenship. But the top three fastest will receive extra perks. The third fastest participant will receive one million Newkos."

The gathering gasps. One million Newkos is enough money to maintain a very comfortable lifestyle for many years.

President Volkov continues. "The second fastest participant will receive five million Newkos."

I feel the energy build in the room.

"And the fastest participant, the ultimate Savage of all, will receive ten million Newkos." He pauses, letting it all sink in.

"And now, for our very special guest. A jewel so rare he stands out like a solitary star on a black night. A boy braver than any other here—a dreamer in his own right. A young man who possesses all the Savage Run was founded upon—the courage to have faith even when all the odds are against him. Please welcome to the stage, Joseph Wood."

It takes me a moment to grasp that President Volkov invited me to join him on the stage; I'm not quite used to responding to my new name. I look over at Nicholas, who looks just as surprised as I probably do, and then I catch a quick glimpse of Johnny—whose face has turned beet red.

"Don't be afraid, young man," President Volkov says. "I heard how horrible the press has been toward you and I wanted to reward your valor publicly, among the bravest. While they may see you as foolish, I see you as a young man destined for great things." He reaches his palm toward me.

Somehow I manage to stand up and Mai takes my arm and escorts me to the stage. If only my knees would stop knocking and I could breathe I might be able to make a good first impression. He could have my head if he wanted to so I had better figure a way to keep my wits about me.

Once up the stairs, I join President Volkov at the stand. From this distance, I see all the wrinkles that line his face—the grooves of an angry man.

"What a handsome fellow." He takes my hand and raises it up with his, high into the air. About a third of the audience cheers, so my guess is that many of them aren't very glad that I'm here. Or they feel so sorry for me that they can't muster the strength to cheer for such a sad scene. By the time President Volkov lowers my hand, all the energy has been sucked out of the room, but it doesn't deter President Volkov at all. He doesn't seem to be a man who cares what others think.

117

President Volkov wishes me good luck and tells me to go sit back down again. On the way down the steps, I trip, almost landing on my face. Now everyone will think I'm a klutz, which I'm not usually, of course, just when thousands of people are watching me.

The ceremony continues and each of the representatives of the hosting countries take the stand for a few minutes, speaking of how privileged they are to be part of something so grand. Even though the countries backing the Savage Run don't subscribe to our hierarchical society, they seem happy enough to support it. And of course they can when they're receiving oil in exchange.

O. J. takes over from there. He says that phase one is not about how fast one completes the obstacles. If you survive it, you move onto phase two. If you quit, you're sent back home and if you die, well, no need explaining that.

"But it gets harder," O. J. says. "To move on beyond phase two, participants must be in the fastest fifty percent. The slowest fifty percent will be sent packing. Everyone who completes the third phase and qualifies according to Master standards will be granted Class-1 Master citizenship." Of course he doesn't mention what those qualifications are, and I have a feeling I will never know. He continues, "No one is allowed to kill or harm anyone."

Strange. During the highlights, they showed several participants who did exactly that.

"Once the first phase is completed, the survivors will be brought back to Trollheim, the capital of Normark, for a benefit gala to raise funds for the survivors of the Savage Run." Then he goes over the penalties. "Participants who veer off any course will be disqualified and participants who start ahead of the clock will receive the severest of penalties. Other warning signs and prompts will be given along the way."

Does this mean they'll be imprisoned? Killed? I sure don't want to find out.

"I wish you all the very best, my friends, and may your strength last you all the way to the end, and may honor and might be with you every step, every stroke, and every decision," O. J. says. "Now the time has come for the first obstacle course to begin. Registrars, remind your participants about the shortcuts. Participants say farewell to your registrars and exit through these doors." O. J. points behind him to the right of the stage to the gigantic steel double door. "Registrars, please wait until your participants leave, and then proceed to exit through the doors you came in." The Savage Run anthem blares through the speakers again.

"You ready?" Arthor asks me.

"No," I say. And I'm not—not even close, but I still stand up. Mai comes over to me.

"Did Nicholas tell you?" she asks, her eyes demanding.

"Yes."

"Good. I'll see you on the other side." She turns away from me, but not before I notice how she closes her eyes and exhales.

Nicholas finishes saying farewell to the others, and then he approaches me.

"Remember what I told you," he says. "Just look for the shortcuts and safe zones; they're everywhere. But if you don't find them, just keep moving. Not all rounds have short cuts or safe zones." He turns to the rest of the participants from Culmination. "For the last jump, make sure you jump feet first, no interlocking of the fingers, close your eyes and plug your nose." He hugs me like he did Arthor before me, patting me on the back and whispers in my ear, "When you get back, maybe we'll see about that dancing."

Suddenly my ears feel hot and I find myself not wanting to let go. I don't understand why. Maybe it's because he's been kind to me or maybe it's because I've started to feel safe around him. And safety is what I need right now since I feel like that little chickadee, fallen out of my nest, waiting for the end. Waiting for the predator.

Except...there's no one who will come and save me. I'm completely and utterly alone in this. If I am to survive, I have to save myself. I have to trust my every instinct.

Yet, unlike the bird, I have the ability to get up and run. And I'm the one charging toward the predator, hunting it down, challenging it to do its worst

Chapter 11

I step onto the Savage Run bus with Arthor, making sure Johnny is nowhere in sight. Making my way to the back of the bus, I inhale. The hot air sticks to the insides of my nostrils, and it reeks of sweat and exhaust fumes. Most of the participants appear clean, but after sitting through the Opening Ceremony, watching how others were slaughtered—and how they're likely to be slaughtered, too—undoubtedly, most of them have produced buckets of perspiration.

Arthor finds us an empty row in the back and we sit down. "Stay with me and you'll be safe," he whispers.

He wants us to run together so he can protect me. I want to tell him I'll be safe no matter what during the marathon; I don't weigh enough to make the landmines go off. But if I tell him, he'd probably only get upset due to my huge advantage. How do I explain that I don't want to be around him if he sets a landmine off? I know it's a horrible thing to think, but I need to stay alive.

Twenty or so minutes later, the bus drops us off by an underground autobahn—a thermal-protected titanium capsule that moves through a tunnel with the assistance of a vacuum. Cramming into a twelve-man capsule with Arthor, I get into my leather seat and strap on the five-point harness. I've heard that riding in a capsule in the autobahn feels like being ejected into space in a rocket. Obviously, I've never been ejected into space, so I don't have anything to compare it to. All I know is that this is probably the easiest part of the Savage Run, and I can't understand why my insides turn to liquid.

"Doors closing," a female voice says over the speakers. The capsule starts to vibrate and hum. "Prepare for departure," the female voice says.

The moment the capsule takes off, it's as if I'm falling from the sky. My stomach does a series of summersaults and my brain feels like it's whirling inside my head. I close my eyes. My hand is getting used to not reaching for my locket. My head spins for a moment longer before it finally stabilizes enough to where I can open my eyes. I look over at the other guys in the capsule and their faces appear just as relaxed as before we took off.

"Have you ridden in one of these before?" I ask Arthor, who also seems unaffected.

"No, but Tristan wrote to me and told me how much he would love it if I could experience it someday," Arthor says.

The boy sitting on the other side of me groans loudly and hurls into a bag. He's a lot smaller than some participants—maybe just a little larger than Arthor's size, which makes me think that he's a Laborer, too.

"Come on, man. That's gross," one of the guys says.

"I can't help it if I get motion sickness," the boy defends himself.

"I never get motion sick, but I do get nauseous when I'm nervous...or afraid," I say, trying to help him feel better.

He reaches out his hand. "I'm Clark, pleased to meet you Joseph."

He must remember me from the embarrassing moment when President Volkov had me come up on stage. I lift my hand and wave, pretending the reach is too far. Does he really expect me to shake his hand that has slime on it? "So is this your first obstacle course?" I ask.

"I've completed three other national obstacle runs, but they were much shorter than this one. You?" Clark says, wiping some leftover saliva onto his sleeve.

I force myself not to squirm in my seat. "I have to admit that this is my first one."

His right eyebrow rises. "President Volkov is right. You are brave."

"Or stupid," I mumble.

Arthor nudges me. "Brave."

I hear a guy snickering at the end of the capsule, and when I look at him, he's staring at me. Obviously he disagrees with the last comment. Then it dawns on me: maybe he suspects I'm a girl? My eyes scan the capsule and as I look at each person, they look away. They're all gawking at me. Do they know? I forget about having wrapped my chest and I briefly look down, just to make sure the gauze hasn't moved out of place, which it hasn't. My chest is still as flat as a board.

As the capsule projects forward, there's not much as far as a conversation goes. Although I'm not tired, I close my eyes, pretending to be sleeping in order to ignore all the questioning faces and prying eyes.

It seems like forever, but finally, after a forty-five minute ride, the female announcer says, "Approaching the country of Normark." The capsule slows gradually until it eases into a complete stop. "Please disembark with caution and welcome to the land of the midnight sun."

Exiting the capsule, I file out into a white underground tunnel and follow the flashing arrows that point to the left. When I get on the revolving stairs, they're already packed with hundreds of young men. I feel like a piece of krill in the midst of whales, just hoping to go unnoticed. There are no visible lamps in the tunnel, but the walls themselves give off light, making it easy to see everyone's tense faces.

Once at the top, I exit the tunnel and continue to follow the hordes of teenage boys making their way over to the start line.

When I notice that Arthor is nowhere to be seen, my chest tightens. I don't want to run with him, but I'm not prepared to be separated yet, either. I turn around and scan the masses. The current of participants continues onward, one participant after another shoving me backward as their shoulders collide with mine. When I see Johnny approaching, I quickly swivel around. Arthor probably thought that it was best for us to run separately, too. Losing each other in the crowd is the best way to avoid any awkward conversations.

Moments later, I arrive at the start line—a red tape strung from one post to another, roughly the length of the aircraft that brought me to Volkov Village. Ahead of me is a wide dirt path and on either side of the path stands a ridge of mountains that continue into the distance, far beyond what I can see.

The sky is overcast and gray—perfect for running a marathon—and the mountains remind me of the ones that enclose Culmination, specifically the very one's by Master Douglas' mansion. They also remind me of Gemma, and in an instant, my chest feels like it's going to collapse. If I had turned back for her she might be here with me now instead of buried in some unmarked grave outside Culmination. It was a spineless choice; I was such a coward. I deserted her and left her in the hands of a monster who had no intention of letting her live. I close my eyes and dig my fingernails into my palms.

No, I can't think like that.

In reality, she probably would have been a huge burden. It's not like she would have been able to handle these obstacles, and I was an idiot to think so in the first place when I came up with my plan. Gemma was always the dainty, feminine one, the one who would get hurt and complain if things became too difficult. It's best this way so that I can focus on saving my own skin and not have to look out for her. I take a deep breath and brush a tear from my cheek. I'm such a liar.

"There you are."

I open my eyes and turn around. "Oh...I thought I lost you," I say flatly when I see Arthor.

"Never. We'll run together, okay?"

I haven't had time to come up with the right words to say about how I think we should run separately. "I...uh...we shouldn't...don't you think..."

"Don't worry. I'll help you."

"No, I..." Someone shoves me from the ground so I fall forward onto my hands and knees.

"That's where you belong, Imp."

"Leave him alone, Johnny," Arthor says, shoving Johnny backward.

Another guy steps in between them. I recognize him from our group. He's the tall, blonde one. "Dude, totally not worth it. Johnny, if you continue, you'll have two to fight against."

"Yeah, sure," Johnny says. A Unifer walks by and Johnny moves farther down the line.

"Thanks, Timothy," Arthor says. They clasp hands and bump their chests together. "Good luck out there."

"Yeah, you too man. See you Joseph."

"Yeah." I stand up and brush the dirt off my pants and palms. Maybe I can wait just a tad before I separate from Arthor. We line up with the other participants and my pulse accelerates. I wonder if any of the guys here are nervous, or if any of them think they'll make it, or if the ones who will die somehow know. I certainly can't tell if it will be me who will lose my life today.

I see Clark at the end of the line and his face is like a stone. Above his head is a large electronic clock, presenting the countdown in red numbers, and it shows we have thirty seconds to go. I wipe my sweaty hands on my pants. For every second that passes, the tension grows thicker and I can feel the other participants' nervous energy like it's a part of me.

Then, from the corner of my eye, I see one of the young men slip underneath the red tape and sprint out onto the pathway. Does he actually think they'll let him get a head start? Wasn't he listening when O.J. said that there would be severe penalties to anyone who did such a thing? Before long, the young man stops running. He arches his back, and his hands flail out from his sides. I hear no gunshots going off, but he's moving like he's being pumped full of lead. He falls lifeless to the ground. My hand cups my mouth, stifling a cry—the first casualty of the Savage Run.

"A sniper," Arthor says, his eyes glued on the young man.

I look around, trying to see if I can locate the shooter, but he's too well hidden. They must be all over the place ready to shoot anyone who doesn't follow the rules.

"They weren't kidding when they said severe," he says through his teeth.

A hovercraft flies over the dead body and sends out a cone-shaped ray, disintegrating the young man's remains faster than my frazzled brain can register. This all happens so hastily; there's still five seconds left on the clock. The marathon is continuing on as if nothing happened, as if some young man wasn't just shot down—murdered.

"Tread lightly," Arthor says to me, and with that, the piercing sound of the start pistol being fired rings through the valley.

Chapter 12

The sound of the start pistol brings me right back to that moment when Gemma was shot. And suddenly all I can see is her lifeless body lying there, slaughtered like an animal.

"Joseph!" I hear Arthor yell. "We have to go." He pulls me by the elbow and I shuffle unwillingly after him. What am I doing here? I don't belong here. It was a huge mistake to come here and now I'm suffering the consequences of my actions. There's no way I can survive these obstacles and I was stupid to think that I have a chance. In the end, my father was right: I'll bring shame to our family's name.

"Joseph, snap out of it. We have to go."

Suddenly, my cheek stings and I'm back at the start line with Arthor. I don't know how long I've been away, but every last contender has left.

"Get your act together, Joseph."

"You slapped me?"

"And I'll do it again if it makes your feet move," he says, shaking me.

I snap my arm away from his grasp and dash down the wide, rocky pathway—not so much to start the marathon, but more to get away from him—both because he slapped me and I don't want to run next to him. Soon he catches up to me, though we don't speak. I'm running so fast that we're panting.

My legs are strong from having biked up the steep mountains in Culmination all these years and my anger from Arthor's slap, combined with all that has happened over the past twenty-four hours, feeds my speed. My heart rate finds a steady rhythm, and as I continue to move ahead, inching closer to the last contender in front of me, I feel warmth spread through my body and beads of sweat gathering on my forehead.

Why am I doing this? When I planned this, it was to gain my freedom, yes, but it was mostly to help Gemma escape. At least that's what I've been telling myself all along. However, if I'm completely honest, she never asked me to get her out of there. I just assumed it was for her best interest. I knew best. But I didn't. I didn't know anything at all. So why am I doing this?

I pump my arms and move my legs faster, passing a few of the other participants. Nicholas' question pops into my mind. What is the first thing I want to do? If I survive, I will have to answer that question. And more. What are all of the other things I want to do? I realize Nicholas's question was exceptionally well placed. He must have known how down I was—how much I was struggling—and that I needed that question to move myself forward.

Arthor is the first one to break the silence. "Sorry I...slapped you. I didn't know...how else to get...your attention." He's sucking wind.

I know he did it to get me going, but I'm still upset. Besides, I really wish he would figure out that running alone is the best and safest option. Do I have to spell it out for him? Maybe if I try the opposite and run a little slower, letting all the others pass, Arthor will get tired of waiting for me and move ahead with the others. I slow my pace, but he keeps on me like a pesky mosquito. I speed up, but again, he's right there with me. Finally, I run as close as I can to the barbed wires lining the edges of the pathway, thinking, surely, he won't follow me there—or at least he'll say something. But no.

Doesn't he get that if one of us sets off a landmine, we'll both be blown to bits? Doesn't he see that absolutely no one else is running together? They all seem smarter than this.

I hold my tongue a while longer, and instead of continuing to mull over how upset I am at Arthor, I scrutinize the ground, searching for clues as to where the landmines are hidden. Then, I remember that there are shortcuts. But what shortcuts could there be in a marathon? Maybe there's a safe zone, a part of the path containing no landmines. I decide to look for the safe zone—maybe then I could keep running with Arthor.

I jog ahead, keeping at the tail end of the group with Arthor. Minutes pass, and I feel strong—like I could run forever. I thought for sure, by now, I would have heard or seen an explosion, but all I hear are the footsteps of the participants and an occasional shouted greeting between friends. After running for a good hour without seeing or hearing a single explosion, I relax a little. They never did mention how many landmines they had buried. Maybe there aren't as many as I had imagined.

"How far do you think we've run?" I ask, having almost forgotten that I was upset at Arthor in the first place.

"I'd say we're closing in on eight miles. You're doing really great, Heidi."

I give him a mean look. "Don't call me that here."

"Sorry. It just slipped out."

As we continue to run, Arthor's face becomes increasingly redder. It seems like I'm not really perspiring since the Savage Run uniform absorbs the moisture right away. But I know from the wetness in the nape of my neck, and the drops rolling down my forehead stinging my eyes, that I'm sweating like a pig. Once I become dehydrated, my performance will suffer—all of ours will—and the bad news is I don't think they will be providing any water or refreshments along the way.

We continue for a couple more miles in silence and my mouth slowly takes on the consistency of rawhide. The muscles in my lower body start to cramp; I'm used to biking, not running. It doesn't help that the clouds have evaporated and that the sun is scorching the skin on my face.

When I hear the first blast, my chest feels like it will implode on itself. The blast is far ahead, but I still see the smoke rise and hear the clamors. Now I can no longer fool myself into thinking that the road is safe and I can continue to run alongside Arthor.

Closing in on the place where the blast went off, I veer away as far as I can and keep my eyes glued forward. Still, my curiosity compels me to look, so I slow down, falling behind Arthor.

There's a crater in the road, about the size of my trailer back home—though nothing else. No body. No blood. No smell other than the scent of smoke. But the strange thing is that I didn't see or hear a hovercraft pass by. Was the landmine so powerful that it disintegrated the victim's entire body, blood and all, not leaving a single trace of the poor guy's existence? When the rogue Unifers usurped our land, it is said they used bombs that completely evaporated anything they came in touch with. Are these similar to the ones they used back then?

I continue onward, trying to think of other things, forcing my mind to move beyond the shock. I see Arthor running in the distance and intentionally run very slowly so I don't catch up with him. The blast makes me even more certain that I absolutely should not be running with him. It will get me killed. But then the guilt sets in. He stood up for me when I needed, vouching I was a friend of his from school, telling me he'd help me if I needed it during the Savage Run. Slapping me...plus, he's here running with me now when he could be solely worrying about himself. I think of how I betrayed Gemma and how much I regret not running to save her. But this is different—isn't it? Out here we're on our own. Back there, I was in charge of her.

When a deafening blast goes off much closer to me, I cower at first, but then reflexively look toward the sound. A body flies through the air and lands with a bounce. I avert my eyes, but not before I recognize the boy as one of the participants from Culmination. I don't know his name. His body lies lifeless—dismembered—on the rocks and dirt. Then there's the god-awful smell of roasting flesh. My stomach revolts, and I bend over when I feel the warm and acidic fluid rise up my throat.

"You okay?" Arthor rubs my back as I hurl.

132

I wipe the sides of my lips with the back of my hand, wishing I had some water to rinse the vomit from my mouth. "I'm fine."

"Just try not to look or think about it," he says.

"Yeah." I glance back at the boy, but there's no use in going over to him to see if he'll make it. His body is beyond repair—shredded—and the expression on his face is vacant—dead. A hovercraft zooms down from the sky and beams a ray on his leftovers, causing them to disintegrate. All the guys dying in the obstacles, is this the burial they'll receive? What will their families say when they find out?

Arthor runs ahead, but I intentionally wait until there's ample distance between us before I continue to run. He stops and waits for me. As I catch up to him, I speed up. But instead of losing him, he's right by my side. "What are you doing?"

"What do you mean?"

I have to say something. "It's way more dangerous if we run together. Seriously, if one of us sets off a landmine, the other one will die."

"Oh." He thinks for a moment. "But I'm looking out for you."

I huff. Why can't he just recognize it's a stupid thing to do?

"If you think it's..." he starts.

"Yes, I think so." I sprint ahead, leaving Arthor a good thirty feet behind me. Taking action is the best way to handle this situation—I mean, does he expect us to stand in the middle of the field and talk about emotions and how we should have each other's backs and all that stuff? Why do I have to be the rational one? Still, I can't help but glance back at Arthor and when I do, I see he's keeping his distance. I feel bad for him, especially since I'm only acting out of self-preservation. He's acting out of pure selflessness.

The next few miles are uneventful as far as blasts going off close to me. From time to time I hear one or two in the distance, but once I reach the site of the explosions, there's nothing but a gaping hole in the ground or some blood.

I run on for a while—maybe five miles—and when I hear another landmine go off, I don't initially react. However, when I hear a scream along with the blast, and continued wailing, I race toward the sound. I can't just let the guy lie there and die alone so I run to his side and kneel down next to him.

When I see him, I see that it's Clark from the capsule.

There's blood everywhere—on his clothes, in his hair and even between his teeth. He reaches a trembling hand up toward me, as if asking me to help him. But there is nothing I can do for him except watch him die.

"You did well," is all I'm able to say before he closes his eyes and slips away. I exhale with him and don't remember to take a breath until Arthor shakes my shoulder.

"Come," Arthor says. "You have to keep moving."

I hit his arm off my shoulder. "This isn't fair," I say. Arthor grabs me by the arm and stands me up. He nudges me forward, but my legs refuse to move on their own. Arthor shoves me again and somehow I'm able to move my legs one step at a time. He keeps on me, nudging me every time I slow down. But I can't keep going. I swivel around and lunge toward him. "Leave me alone, okay?" I take a swing at him, but he ducks.

Grabbing me by the waist and turning me around, he says, "Keep moving."

"I don't want to. Take your hands off me."

He wraps his arms around me and picks me up, leaving me helpless to do anything but kick my legs and scream. "You don't have a choice, Heidi."

"Stop calling me that."

"I'm going to set you down now, so please calm yourself. I promise I'll keep my distance as long as you continue to run. Will you agree to that?"

"Fine," I bark.

He sets me down and takes three big steps away from me, holding his hands up, his palms facing me. "I'm just trying to help you. I don't want to see you die out here, don't you see?"

"I don't want to continue."

"You might be saying that now, but...there's so much to live for. I mean...if we make it, our lives will never be the same again. Just hold that thought right there..." He lifts up his hand. "Right in front of you—like a beacon."

"I can't."

"Yes, you can. I've seen how you bike up those hills in Culmination. Don't tell me you're not strong enough. And if you can work that hard for someone else, I think then you can manage to do the same when your freedom is involved."

I can't face him because he's right. "You don't know what I've been through." Turning around, I sprint away from him. I don't want his help; I never asked for it. I just want to be left alone. But maybe I don't want his help since whenever I've received help in the past, so much more is expected in return. Yet, I can't deny that Arthor is different and doesn't seem to want anything in return.

As I continue onward, the muscles in my legs start to tremble. How much farther do I have to run? I still feel somewhat strong, but seeing these young men blown to bits is wreaking havoc with my mind. If I could just sit down and rest for five minutes to think, to process it all, I'd be fine. I just need a moment. To gather my thoughts. To make sense of it all. But I can't. If I stop, it's the same as saying I'm dropping out. So I continue—counting my steps. Just one more. Then another. And another.

True to his word, Arthor keeps his distance for the next few miles, only glancing back once in a while. Mile after mile, my mouth feels drier and drier. What I wouldn't give for a glass of water right now, and a shot of painkillers to dull the achiness in my feet. Biking is so much easier on the feet.

All of a sudden, I hear at least ten landmines go off back to back in the distance. I stop when I hear the cries of the wounded young men, and immediately I plug my ears. I can't listen to their screams because it's as if their voices bleed into my bones. From the corner of my eye, I see Arthor zooming past me. What is he doing? When he's about a hundred feet in front of me, he slows down to a jog and glances back at me. I keep moving. Reaching the place of the massive blast, I see that there's nothing left. Nothing but craters and blood. No injured participants. No bodies. I suppose if one is too injured to continue, then one is taken to the hospital. For the sake of their families, at least I hope this is the case.

My feet are dragging to the ground now. Surely, I must be coming to the end of the marathon soon. I have to be. My right foot has gone numb and I need to pee, but there's no way I'm going to stop in the open area to squat to relieve myself. That's one thing that's unfair about this; the guys can just whip it out and do their business. My head has been pounding for some time, and I know I'm in danger when I stumble over a small rock in my path. Catching myself with my palms, I let out a cry. They are still sore from my fall yesterday, and the wounds reopen and start to bleed. I roll onto my back and rest my arm across my eyes to shield them from the sun. It feels so good to rest. Every last muscle in my body screams for me to stay down. But it's not long before I hear footsteps, and when I uncover my eyes, I see Arthor standing above me.

"Don't you dare," I say, holding my arm out in front of me.

"Then get up!"

"No."

"Five...four..."

"Are you kidding me?"

"Three..."

I stagger to my feet and brush the sand and rocks off my palms. "There, happy?"

"Yes. Now run." He points.

"Since when are you my master?"

"I'm not your master. Just a friend."

I know his intentions aren't to boss me around or to hurt me; they're to help me. But the way he's doing it is driving me crazy. "Okay, okay, just run ahead. I'll follow." My voice is harsher than I intended, but I'm too tired to make amends.

We continue on like this for a while, him glancing back at me, me grumbling every time he does. From time to time, a landmine explodes—but instead of looking toward the explosion, I've learned to train my eyes on the back of Arthor's head. Maybe having him here isn't as bad as I thought.

The sun hangs high in the sky and every step has my legs screaming at me. What I wouldn't do to have my bike here. In the near distance, a whole bunch of landmines go off at once—fifty, sixty, maybe more—startling me enough to get the blood flowing to my brain. I stop and lean my hands on my thighs, giving myself just a moment to recover. Then, I hear whooping and screaming just beyond the gentle hill where Arthor is. He looks back at me, and his lips rise in triumph.

"We made it!" Arthor yells.

Chapter 13

My feet still ache, and I'm physically and mentally exhausted. I can hear the end of the marathon just beyond the hill, which gives my feet renewed strength. Go, don't stop. Go, Heidi. Cresting the hill, I see water. Blessed water. The sun reflects off the surface of the lake like a gold medal and a sudden surge of energy awakens my tired arms and legs. With every muscle in my lower body aching, I dash toward the lake and jump into it. I plunge my face into the cool water and drink deeply. I hadn't thought to ask if the water was safe, but everyone's drinking it, so it must be. Unless they want everyone to die at once, which would make the Savage Run a complete tragedy. It would do nothing for Volkov's popularity. I high-five Arthor, and his face is beaming.

"You made it," he says.

"Yeah, thanks for pushing me back there."

"You don't need to thank me."

I roll my eyes.

"Just keep going, okay?"

"Okay. And if you need it, I'll help you out."

We sit down and I pull off the Savage Run shoes. I dig my feet into the wet sand and feel the grains rubbing against my sore toes. I'm sure if we stick together, there will be an opportunity to pay him back.

A cameraman wearing a Savage Run outfit films me from a mere six inches away.

"Why are you filming?" Arthor asks.

"This is for President Volkov," the cameraman says.

I just ignore him. It's not like I have any extra energy to give him. A few of the cameramen are out on the water in motorboats. They'll probably be following us all the way, catching the gory details of the interaction between the e-condas and us. President Volkov wouldn't want to miss seeing how his precious creations interact with the inferior class. I try to look for any short cuts. Nicholas said not every obstacle course had one, but I had almost expected that at least one of the two first would.

Watching the other participants brave the lake, wading forward into the unknown deep, I can't help but dread what's to come. They've probably starved the predators for days so the slithering electrical monsters will eat anything offered to them.

Arthor and I relax for a few more minutes before delving into the second round, allowing our muscles to regain some strength before we put more demands on them. There's a flashing sign that reads if we wait longer than twenty minutes to continue, we'll be disqualified. This could mean a myriad of things including being shot like the young man who tried to get a head start in the marathon. The sign also reads to swim toward the setting sun, which would be westward. How long will it take me to swim ten miles when

I'm exhausted, hungry, and find it hard to stay focused? At least four hours, I'm sure. My arms grow heavy at the thought.

If I were still back at home, I'd be riding around on my bike, delivering medicine right now, trying to sneak a peek of the Savage Run coverage between runs. But I don't want to think about the life I chose to leave behind. Nor the people I betrayed.

I wiggle my legs a little—the achiness in my joints is impossible to ignore. Sitting down, my body has decided to revolt and feels even stiffer than while I was actually running. But I don't have the luxury of time to sit here and rest and I must keep going before I grow too sore, unable to get a move on.

I look over at Arthor. "Ready?"

"Yeah," Arthor says, his eyes void of their normal energy, his shoulders slumping. Instead of getting up, like I expect him to, he remains seated for a while longer. Eventually, he climbs to his feet and slowly tilts his head from side to side, loosening the muscles in his neck.

I wade out until the cool water reaches my waist, and stop to wait for Arthor. Unable to hold my bladder anymore, I relieve myself in the water. It's totally gross, I know, but they can hardly expect me to hold it until I have completed the entire first phase.

Of the three rounds in this phase, swimming is my least favorite, one of the factors being that I never really was a strong swimmer. Soon, the water reaches my chest, and I gasp at how cold it is. Once I get moving, I'm sure I'll build up body heat again. I grit my teeth, submerge my shoulders into the water, and start to swim. From the very first breaststroke, I think I felt something in the water—an e-conda?

"You good?" Arthor asks, swimming next to me.

"Yes. Just a little...nervous."

"And you're okay with me swimming with you?"

I can't tell if he's being difficult or playful. "That was only during the marathon."

"Good."

Unlike the marathon, the screams come right away. Ahead of us in the sunlight, I see a young man, his arms flailing, his voice screeching in pain. "Get away from me. Help! I withdraw! I quit! Help me!" He continues to scream for help, but no one comes to his aid. The Unifers in the boats just ignore him. Like me, everyone knows that if they swim over to help him, they're dead meat.

"This way," I say to Arthor, taking a long detour around the poor guy. If I think about it too much, I might panic. We swim on, stroke after stroke, and again, we hear screams. This time the screams come from a distance, so we don't see the person who's being attacked. It's a little easier to ignore these screams.

"Ah!" Arthor's eyes go wild with fear and he gasps. "I felt something."

For a moment, I'm unable to move. Arthor thrashes his arms into the water as his eyes search for an e-conda. All of a sudden, he lets out a shriek. "It shocked me!"

In an attempt to scare off the e-conda, I kick my legs as hard and as fast as I can. Then, as I feared, I feel a jolt, too, and a current rushes through my body, leaving my muscles immobilized. And everything throbs. Unable to move my arms or legs, I sink beneath the surface. Keeping my eyes open, I see dozens of thick, snake-like sea-creatures slithering below my feet, just waiting to make their next move. I tell my legs to kick, but they won't. I try to scream for help, but below the surface the water drowns out my voice—no one can hear me. Even if they could, they still wouldn't come. The water muffles the sounds of the e-condas' sharp shrieks, making them sound like a deeper octave of my bikes' squeaky breaks. I need to take a breath soon; the air is running out. Kick stupid legs, kick. This time, my right leg moves, and within seconds, I can move both my legs and my arms. Soon, I'm able to command all my limbs, enough for me to stop sinking and begin rising. I have to get up quicker—the surface is so far away. I see light up above, and with each stroke, my body feels stronger. Once I reach the surface, I gasp for air. Even though I wasn't under for very long, the exertion of kicking and punching the water to get rid of the e-condas has made me breathless.

Arthor is still above water. "We have to continue, or they'll eat us alive!" I yell. A motorboat approaches us with a Unifer holding a camera, coming to feed off our demise. They think they're so safe in their vessels, but I bet the e-condas could tip the motorboats over with one flick of their tails, and they would be fighting for their lives, too. I almost wish one of them would fall into the water. It's not fair how we have to fight so hard for our freedom while they were born with it.

Arthor and I swim as fast as we can, cutting through the water, kicking our legs. Adrenaline courses through me and I feel like I'm on the verge of death. This must be it. The hope that I'd make it through the first phase has vanished into oblivion. All I'm left with is envisioning my dead body at the bottom of the lake with a gigantic snake wrapped around me. Or maybe the e-conda will swallow me whole, and I'll slowly suffocate in its stomach.

A few feet in front of me, there's another young man who appears completely incapable of lifting his limbs, and his head is bopping in and out of the water. As I continue to watch him, I see the water is dyed with blood and he spews and coughs pink water from his mouth. A long, thick snake with a head twice as big as mine, spirals itself around the young man, causing him to scream louder. I hear a loud buzzing sound as the snake shocks the young man—a thousand volts of electricity streams through the poor boy's body. Before long, his screams melt into mellow whimpers, and he slides beneath the water's surface with the e-conda still wrapped around him, leaving nothing except bursting bubbles on the red water's surface. I become angry at once. How could President Volkov do such horrible things to young men?

Arthor lets out a cry, sounding like a cross between a scream and a sob. His arms and legs go motionless and his head starts to sink beneath the water's surface. With the drama dwindling around us, the Unifers turn on their engines, preparing to move onto the next location. A thought pops into my mind, and though it's a stupid one, I'm willing to try anything at this point. "Swim toward the boat," I say. Arthor doesn't respond so I grab him by the collar to keep him from sinking farther beneath the gentle waves. I haul him with me toward the motorboat's stern. When I reach it, I grab hold of the edge with my free hand, staying as far away from the moving propellers as possible, trying to stay as low in the water as I can so that the Unifers don't see me.

Almost before I'm ready, the motorboat takes off with a jolt. I feel my fingers slipping, but I refuse to let this be the end of my short existence, and cleave on as we're hauled away. The water gushes against my body and my fingers feel like they'll be ripped off if there's any more pressure. Water sprays in my face so I close my eyes. After some time, the boat slows down a notch, and I open my eyes to assess where we are. We've cleared the area where several attacks have occurred, so I let go. Sinking into the water, we stop moving. My hand and lower arm feels spent, like the muscles and tendons have been stretched beyond their limits.

I look at Arthor. "Can you move?"

"Yes, thank you. I would have drowned had you not..."

"We're not out of danger yet."

He leans his head back into the water. "Are you okay?" He swings his head quickly to the side, the drops from his hair showering the glassy surface. "Did they get you?"

"A little, but I'm fine." My legs sting horribly, but I don't dare to look at them, afraid the e-condas have burned my flesh to the bone, and if I see the blood, I'll lose my courage to keep going. If I bleed to death while swimming, so be it. "You?"

"I'm good. Let's keep moving," he says.

The next few miles are uneventful. Every time I think I feel movement beneath the water, I tuck my legs in beneath me, and silently pray it was just my imagination.

The clouds have returned, and as they turn to rose gold, a heavy fog rolls in. Now I won't be able to see Devil's Cliff in the distance—a hopeful beacon to swim toward. And with the fog there, it's also impossible to tell if I'm swimming westward.

"This is ridiculous. We don't even know where we're going," I say. "We could be going in circles."

"Just keep moving. The fog must mean we're close." Arthor flips over and starts swimming on his back. "They want to make it harder on us—not easier."

"Maybe," I give him. We swim on for another ten minutes before I say something. "How do they expect us to get through this fog?"

"They don't," Arthor says. "They only expect the elite to make it."

I shoot him an angry glare. "Whose side are you on anyway?"

He shakes his head at me. "Don't even ask me that."

I want to rip his hair out, but I think it has more to do with the fact that I'm exhausted and hungry than that I'm upset at him. As we keep swimming, I start to think about how I haven't even made it through the first of three phases, and how I'm already both physically and emotionally depleted. How easy it would be to give up and let myself sink into the watery abyss. I'm sure it wouldn't take long for me to go unconscious and slip into a quiet death. While contemplating this, I feel a warm current against my body. "Do you feel that?" I ask Arthor.

Arthor stops swimming forward for a moment and treads water instead. "We must be close to shore."

The new information makes me abandon the thought of my suicide operation. If we're almost there, it means I made it through round two. Eager to be done, I kick harder. But when my foot hits something hard, I immediately pull my legs close into my body and scream. It must be an e-conda, or worse, maybe there are a whole slew of them and that is why the water turned warmer. Unable to control my fear, I cry out and begin to thrash my arms and legs, sending the water in every which direction.

"It's okay. It's okay!" Arthor yells, taking my hands in his. "They're rocks. We've reached the shore. They're rocks."

I pause as his words start to sink in. "Really?"

"Really," he says with a broad smile on his face.

Chapter 14

Still not quite able to believe that we've reached the shore, I hesitantly stretch my legs downward. Soon the rocks at the bottom of the lake press against my feet—firm and unyielding. I exhale. Standing up, I gasp in relief; the water reaches just above my waist. We have reached the shore.

Ecstatic that I have managed to live through two of the three rounds in this phase, I jump into Arthor's arms, whooping and screaming. "We made it!"

He squeezes me back, and we stand wrapped in each other's arms for a long time. Not until I start thinking about how he's got his arms around me do I feel awkward. It's not that I'm attracted to him, and I don't think he likes me in that way either. But standing so close to him, sharing this, not only physical, but very emotional moment, it feels so good to have someone who understands what I've just been through.

I let go. "Sorry."

"No apology needed," he says.

When I turn toward the shore, I see bushes and trees—foliage—but I can't make out any more than that; the fog is still too thick. Eager to get out of the e-conda infested water,

I wade toward land, and the instant my feet touch the raggedy, stony shore, I lie down onto the rocks, my legs still in the water. I don't really care how they're stabbing into my back or how I'm cold and wet. I'm safe. And I'm alive. No more e-condas will come after me, and I don't have to worry that one of them might electrocute me or pull me down. How many young men lost their lives?

I press my palms to my eyes and release a laughing, crying sound, and with it, all the tension in my body releases. A moment later, it feels as if all my guts and muscles and bones have been scraped dry and pumped full of jelly. Though my survival has so much more to do with crazy luck than anything, the joy of having lived through the first two rounds is not any less.

When I finally resolve to open my eyes, I let my gaze wander up toward the sky, and there I see Devil's Cliff. It hangs over me like a bad omen. The mountainside is a jagged and vertical sloped monster of a rock, and it extends to the heavens like a pillar of fire—the height dizzying—the red surface looking like it could be something from Hell. Many participants are already climbing up the wall, their fingers and toes gripping onto the edges of the rocks. For the life of me, I can't see the top. The fog is still just as thick. Something tells me it could be much higher than what I dare to imagine. Or dread. How in the world I'm supposed to make it to the top of that mountain is beyond my comprehension. And with the sun soon to set, my muscles already way past spent, climbing Devil's Cliff at night will be impossible.

There isn't a single part of me that isn't achy or sopping wet, but I can't lie here all day. I scramble to my feet and look for Arthor. I find him standing at the base of the cliff reading a sign. Walking over to him, I notice that my legs sting, and when I look down, I see that they're riddled with minor burns. However, all my pain is temporarily forgotten when I see the back of Arthor's right leg. Part of his calf has a chunk removed. And we still have a cliff—the tallest cliff I've ever seen—to climb. But what's even more mind-boggling is that he hasn't complained about it a single time. I pause behind him. Will he be able to climb the cliff? My heart drops. If he can't climb the cliff by himself, I'll either have to abandon him while I continue to press forward or help him climb to the top.

Arthor turns around and points to the sign.

Fifteen-minute rest stop max.

Without warning, there's a scream from above, and then a loud thud behind us. Instinctively, I turn to look—but stop myself—I know what I'll find there, and I don't want to see it. I never in my wildest imagination would have thought that I'd grow so callous about a dead teenage boy that I'd refrain from walking over to him and showing my respects. But I don't. And I hate myself for it. Instead, I tell Arthor to sit down, and after he complies, I rip off a piece of my uniform to tie it around his injured leg. He moans a little when I cinch it, but stops when I stare him in the eyes.

Should I leave him behind? My chest squeezes.

I study the wrap, and it seems to help control the bleeding. He's going to slow me down significantly, and most likely, he won't be able to make the climb.

"Ready?" he says, gritting his teeth.

"Will you be...?"

He interrupts me, and says angrily, "Don't worry about me."

I force a smile, but suspect that it looks more like a pained frown. "Okay?" I walk over to the base of the mountain and press my palms against the red rock. When I look up, my stomach drops like I just swallowed a bag of concrete. Of course they had to put the hardest challenge last when we're thoroughly exhausted. A lump forms in my throat, but I force it down and put on a stern face. I lean my back against the cold, hard surface of my next challenge. I need strength, and I need it now. Glancing upward, I see a dozen or so participants ascending the wall, moving slowly, clinging to the mountainside like spiders. I study their movements—their strategies—to see if I can pick up on how to climb the cliff. When I try to survey the best route to climb, I happen to notice a strange pattern of rocks. I hear Nicholas' words in my mind. "All the things you need to succeed are within the obstacles..."

Every few feet there are protruding rocks—stepping stones up the mountainside. And all the guys climbing seem completely oblivious to them. I gasp.

"What?" Arthor asks.

I tell Arthor to come in closer and I show him what I see. The only problem is that the steps are just beyond reach of each other. Why would they go to such lengths to create those ledges if we can't even use them? Then, from the wall, I see movement; a ledge protrudes out from the mountainside as another vanishes just a few feet away. The steps appear and disappear at timed intervals. If I can just figure out the timing, we can climb all the way up.

Suddenly a ledge juts out right next to me. Arthor and I look at each other.

"Let's go," he says.

Without hesitation, I climb onto it and offer my hand to Arthor. He takes it willingly. The ledge is about two feet wide, and protrudes about twelve inches—just large enough for us to fit. Clinging to the cliff with Arthor right next to me, I see the next step jut out a few feet away and about a foot above where we are. I spring across the divide and onto the next ledge. Normally I'd be able to land without a problem, but since my legs are rubber from running the marathon and swimming for miles and miles, I wobble a bit. Once I have my balance, I offer my hand to Arthor. He takes it. We continue on like this for a while: me moving ahead, and then pulling him up. I notice that he's avoiding putting weight on his bad leg, which causes him to sway so much that I fear he's going to lose his balance and fall.

"You all right?" I ask after we've been going for some time.

"I'm feeling a little weak."

I look down at his leg and see the wrap I put on earlier soaked. "Just hang in there, okay?"

I turn to continue upward, but he grabs my arm. "Listen...if I don't make it...if I fall..."

"You'll make it. We both will," I say harshly. Unwilling to have this conversation now, I press onward. From time to time, I hear Arthor puff. I assume he must have put some pressure on his bad leg. But I don't stop. There's no time limit to complete this first phase, but we need to get back to civilization before Arthor loses too much blood.

We climb in silence, the shadows growing blacker by the minute. I wonder how dark it will get, remembering that in the northern countries, it supposedly stays light through the entire night. I see a drone hovering just by us—a camera—and then just as quickly as it appears, it vanishes. Nicholas said they'd be here, snapping illegal shots for the media. I just ignore them. As we hop from step to step, the space on each step seems to be diminishing. I don't mention this to Arthor, not wanting to cause him to worry, but as we continue to move upward, my fear is validated. The ledges are shrinking in size, and where it was fairly easy to stand together before, it has now become very challenging.

"They're smaller," Arthor says, studying the ledge we're standing on.

He doesn't ask the next obvious question out loud, but I know he's thinking the same thing as me: a little farther up will the ledges eventually vanish? "Yeah, I noticed that, too." With an injured, or partially removed calf muscle, Arthor won't be able to make it to the top.

"Let's just keep going," he says.

I nod, but for whatever reason, I look down at the ledge. The next thing I know is that my gaze focuses past it and all the way down to the bottom of the cliff. My head spins and I grab onto Arthor's arm.

"Careful," he says, steadying me.

I take a deep breath and go to the next step, but when my first foot touches the surface, it slips, and I fall. Somehow, I'm able to grab onto the ledge and hold on. With my heart in my throat, my fingers white-knuckling the edge, I scream.

"Hang on!" Arthor yells. He hesitates for a moment before leaping to the ledge I'm hanging from. Landing on both legs, he cries out in pain.

"Hurry, please," I say, feeling my fingers slipping on the smooth surface.

He turns so that he faces outward. Clenching his teeth, he bends down and grabs onto my wrist. "I can't pull you up alone, so you have to find a way to get one of your legs onto the ledge."

I kick my right leg up, however, it slips off the edge and I end up dangling in the air. I scream. Desperate to hang on, I press the bottoms of my feet against the mountainside to try to find a ridge to hold onto. The surface is smooth like glass.

"Kick your leg up and dig your heel in!" Arthor yells.

I swing my leg up again. This time I drive my heel into the step and it remains there. When I push off with my heel, it gives Arthor just the leverage he needs, and he pulls me up so I end up standing on the ledge, squeezing onto him for dear life. We stand like that for a few seconds, as I gather myself.

"We have to move on," Arthor says.

Somehow, I manage to push the weak part of me aside. Looking up, I see another participant a couple dozen feet above us. He is also using the ledges, but he doesn't have to share the small surface with anyone. From what I can gather, we're about halfway to the top—our method has worked. But now, we have to come up with a better solution than to climb together on the shrinking steps.

"We have to split up." I'm not quite sure how to bring up the obvious dilemma of who will get to go first, so I wait a moment, hoping he'll suggest something.

Arthor nods absentmindedly with his eyes half-shut. I think he's in so much pain and has lost so much blood that any suggestion is welcome. "One of us will continue on, while the other waits for the next wave of ledges to emerge."

I should be the one to stay behind; I'm not as wounded as he is. Yet, I can't speak the words.

"Just be careful," he says, his face taking on the color of snow, and then he reaches for and steps onto the next ledge.

At first, I can't believe it. What is he doing? We hadn't agreed on anything yet, and he just assumed he would be the one to go first. Not that I think I should be the one, but at least he should offer that to me. Shouldn't he? Without looking back, he continues onto the next ledge, and before I'm able to say anything, I feel the ledge beneath my feet move. Quicker than lightning, my heart instantly galloping, I find a couple of grooves in the mountainside, and hook my fingers into them. Unable to find any decent ridges for my feet, I just press them against the mountainside as best I can. I have no idea how long it will be until the ledge beneath my feet returns, but this I know: I will hold on and make it all the way to the top just so I can give Arthor a piece of my mind.

The groove between my eyes contracts as I watch him climb the next few steps. His movements are hasty and careless; he's not taking enough time to prepare for the next step before he leaps. It will indeed be a miracle if he doesn't tumble off the cliff. As for me, I'm stuck hanging until the next ledge appears.

After a few minutes, my forearms start to burn. It doesn't take long before my fingers go numb, which really worries me simply because numb fingers can't hold onto anything. I adjust my grip in the small crevice to try to relieve the pressure, but it only helps for a few seconds.

Arthor looks down at me and yells, "They're getting smaller. A lot smaller. I don't know about this, Heidi..."

"Arthor!" I yell, afraid we're being filmed or that some of the other participants climbing the wall heard him. He must really be losing it to call out my name so freely. Then a scary thought occurs to me: maybe he's out to get me and wants my secret to be discovered.

"Oh...sorry," he hollers.

"Just shut up, okay?" I want to vanish into the rock this instant, fully expecting the other participants climbing the wall to call me out, or for a hovercraft to appear out of nowhere, beaming me into oblivion. After waiting for a few minutes for something to happen, I start to think maybe no one heard Arthor say my name and maybe no one's coming for me after all.

A drop of sweat rolls into my eye and it stings. And then it starts to itch. When is the next step coming? I could be hanging here until the morning when I'll fry in the sun and slowly die of dehydration. The gnawing feeling in my stomach has been there a while—I've just ignored it—and I'm weak. A moment of weakness could cause me to lose my grip or balance, and I would tumble to the rocks below. My achy fingers have held on way longer than I thought they were capable of and my right hand is cramping something awful. I breathe through it—pant—but I have to face reality: I just can't hold on much longer. There's no use in crying for help, for what good will that do? I look up again and see Arthor is at the top now. I should have been the one to go first. If he were any bit of a friend, then he would have offered to stay behind.

Trying to ease the cramp in my right hand, I loosen the fingers just a tad. Unable to carry the majority of my weight, my left hand slips. I drop toward the earth.

I have heard that some people have their entire lives flash before their eyes right before they die, but this is not what happens to me. Oddly enough, when I squeeze my eyes shut, Mai's face appears, and she smiles softly as if telling me that everything will be okay. I believe her.

With a crash, my feet hit a hard surface. Knife-like pain radiates up my legs. When I open my eyes, I see that I've landed on a ledge. It wasn't the ledge I was waiting for—this one is farther down—but it's a ledge. I hunch down, and bring my clenched fists to my mouth, hyperventilating. I'm not going to die; I'm going to live. My mouth is dry, and my belly feels like it has been filled with gasoline and set on fire.

"Are you okay?" Arthor bellows from above.

"Yes," I say, my voice trembling as much as my hands. Focus, Heidi, focus. There's no time to sit here and cry. I need to continue on before this ledge vanishes, too. Locating the next one, I jump onto it. Still thoroughly shaken, I slowly make my way upward. Step by step, I continue on, and the farther up I get, the more confident I feel that I'll make it. As I ascend, the steps grow smaller, like Arthor said, and when I finally come to the last few ledges, they're so tiny that the balls of my feet barely fit. Fortunately, they're very close together so I can easily get from one to the next. Stepping onto the last ledge, Arthor reaches his arm out to me and helps me up to the top of the cliff—a flat, square surface void of any vegetation.

Unable to contain my emotions, tears spring out of my eyes and run down my cheeks. I collapse into Arthor's arms, and there's nothing I can do to stop my emotions from coming out in loud, ugly sobs.

Once I have calmed myself, I pull away and brush the wetness from my cheeks. Glowering at Arthor, I shove him in the chest so hard that he falls down.

"What was that for?" he asks.

"You took advantage of me down there."

"What do you mean?"

"Please—you went first and left me there to die."

"But you nodded toward me. I thought you meant for me to go first."

I think back to our exchange down there. "That's ridiculous. I didn't say anything. Besides, if you were a true friend, you'd at least offer to let me go first."

"So what you said when we were sitting in the lake...?"

I open my mouth to speak, but I have nothing to say. Remembering how I actually had said that I would help him if he needed it, I feel like a jerk. "Fine, whatever." Not wanting to remain on the subject, I step past him and walk to the other side of the cliff, stopping about ten feet away from the drop off. Behind me is the lake; in front of me is the ocean. I don't dare to look over the edge yet, but from where I'm standing, it looks to be way higher than two hundred feet.

Now that the fog has lifted, I see how the sun hangs low in the sky, hovering right above the surface of the ocean. The sky is a deep blue, the water below black, and the horizon golden. According to my father, the sun never sets during the summer in the northernmost countries. I never actually believed him until now. Looking to the right, I see a sign, and it says,

To complete Round 1 of the Savage Run program, jump off the cliff and into the water below.

I thought I'd feel like a champion completing all three rounds in the first phase, but now all I can think about is that I have two more grueling phases to complete.

"Will you take a moment with me?" Arthor sits down on the ground, reaches his hands behind his head, and looks up into the sky.

His suggestion takes me completely off guard and I wonder what he's really suggesting here. And besides, how can he be so casual about what happened? He didn't even apologize for leaving me behind or thank me for risking my life for him. I at least thanked him when he helped me. Doesn't he know that I nearly died and that he was partially to blame for it?

Too tired to argue with him, I lie down and glare up at the sky.

"I have something I've always wanted to tell you," he says. "I feel like I could tell you anything."

I hold my breath. Oh, no. I hope he's not going to tell me he loves me or something. But then I catch myself—what a ridiculous thought. If he cared about me in that way, or in any way really, he wouldn't have abandoned me the way he did—all too eagerly. Even if he did think I gave him the nod to go ahead.

"But if I tell you this one thing, will you share something with me, too?"

I hate confessions. Especially when they're forced out of me. I mean, I just completed three rounds of grueling obstacles—more like torture—and he wants to talk about secrets?

"Your deepest, darkest secret." He smiles at me.

Arthor must think he's going to die in this next leap and that is why he wants to get something off his chest. I look at him, his face pasty gray, his lips dry and colorless. My chest aches for him. I look around to make sure none of the drones are filming before I say, "Okay, I'll do it." To my surprise, it only takes me a second to know exactly what I need to share. Something that's been on my mind for years. Something I've never been able to speak out loud, not even to Gemma. And maybe, just maybe, it might help lighten the burden I've been carrying for so long.

"You want to go first?" he asks.

Of course he wants me to go first—now. "Sure." My heart's a nervous wreck, hopping all over the place. Why is this so hard to speak what's on the inside? "Can I sit up and do it?"

He chuckles a little. "Of course you can sit up. You don't have to ask." We sit up and look over the side of the platform we're supposed to jump from. The water sways and the sun reflects off the surface like an eternal flame.

"Ready?" I say.

"Yes."

I inhale until my lungs feel like they'll burst, and then I speak. "Sometimes I've wished I was a man."

Arthor is quiet for a minute before he whispers, "You mean...like...you're attracted to girls?"

160

"No, what are you crazy?" I punch him in the arm. It's illegal to be gay in Newland, usually punishable by death. "It's just..." My voice lowers, just in case someone is listening. "It's just so much easier for a man, you know. They have so much more power...and control. Sometimes it just sucks being a girl."

"I suppose you're right."

"Of course I'm right," I laugh a little.

"So that's the deepest, darkest secret you have?"

"It is. And the most powerful one, too. Maybe it's pathetic."

"No, not at all."

I hear footsteps behind us, and then panting.

"You guys ready to jump?" a deep voice says.

I turn around and recognize the boy with the white hair immediately. "Hey," I say. "Cory, is it?" I'm surprised he's here so late in the competition—I thought for sure he would be one of the first ones to finish.

Cory's eyes narrow into slivers as he scrutinizes me, and I can't help but notice that his tree-trunk sized neck is glistening with sweat. "Yeah. I remember you, too. I'm sure everyone's surprised you made it this far."

"Uh...yeah," I say. He must be referring to the poll from TV where I was voted the least likely to survive. Or how everyone's talking about me—I know they are.

"Seems you're smarter than most to pace yourself—especially when there's no real time limit on this phase."

"Sure." I shrug my shoulders. No harm in letting him think I was intentionally trying to be slow. Then something unexpected happens. A small bubble of excitement swells on the inside; I proved everyone wrong.

Cory continues. "But seriously, don't listen to them. They want to put you in a box and keep you there."

"I'm Arthor." He reaches out his hand toward Cory.

Cory takes it, smiles, and they shake. "Pretty bad gash you got there."

Arthor looks down at his leg. "I'll manage."

"Well, better be off so I can be done with this. Wanna join me?" Cory asks.

"We'll be jumping in a minute," Arthor says, eyeing me.

Cory salutes us, runs toward the edge, and hurls himself off the cliff.

I spring to my feet, rush over to the edge, and watch as he plummets toward the blue ocean. My chest feels like it contains a hundred bouncing crickets. When he hits the water, white blooms around him and he vanishes beneath the waves. Will he come back up? For every second that he remains gone, my breathing becomes a little shallower. I wait longer. No one can stay under water that long, can they? I scan the entire sea, but there are no bodies anywhere. And no hovercrafts to disintegrate the floating corpses. Most likely, Arthor and I are close to being the last ones to jump, so surely some of the participants must have died. But where did everyone go?

After waiting longer than I deem any human could survive without a breath, I take a step back. If he didn't make it, there's no way I'll survive the two-hundred foot fall.

I look at Arthor, who's not breathing either, rather gawking at the water as if he's expecting Cory to suddenly appear. Trying to get my mind off Cory's death—and what his death means when it comes to my fate—I ask, "So, what's your secret?"

Arthor's lips draw to a line and he sits back down. "Will you promise me you'll still be my friend after I tell you?"

I sigh. If this is one of my last moments, I'm not going to waste it holding onto a grudge. "If you want me to."

He nods. "Ready?"

I nod.

He leans in and whispers, his hand cupped to my ear. "I'm gay."

I do everything I can to not react in any which way—not shocked, or confused, or disturbed, the very emotions I'm feeling at the moment. Shocked. I never suspected anything; he seems as straight as any other guy I've met. Disturbed. I always thought gays were so different— strange. He must think I hate him, especially after how I reacted when he thought I might be gay. I have to admit, I don't really know a lot about the subject. Sometimes gay citizens are given the chance to join a rehabilitation program, which supposedly cures them. I've even heard President Volkov say there's no such thing as a homosexual person, but that homosexuality is a disease that can be developed from watching indecent programs. It doesn't sound quite right to me.

"No response?" he says, chuckling lightly, grabbing behind his neck.

"Well, I just never thought...er...I'm surprised," I say with all honesty. "But thank you for telling me." My father hates gay people, says they're the scum of the earth and that it states in the Bible that they're an abhorrence in the sight of God. I believe in a God, too, but somehow I can't imagine that a loving God hates any of his children.

Arthor sighs. "It feels good to get that off my chest."

"Have you told anyone before?" I ask.

He shakes his head somewhat sheepishly.

"Not even your parents?"

"No. Well, Tristan was the only one who knew. And my...boyfriend." He glances at me from underneath his eyelashes.

His boyfriend? Who could that be? I never once saw him with anyone I'd suspect of being his boyfriend. All these years, and I never knew.

"My parents suspect, I think, if they don't know already. My father seems to avoid me whenever he can."

"I'm sorry."

He claps his hands together and rubs them briskly. "Well, let's do this thing." Struggling to his feet, limping on his one good leg, he toes the edge of the cliff and peers down.

I stop him. "Wait...can I...hold your hand?" I don't know where that came from, but something inside me needs someone right now. And somehow, revealing to him my deepest secret, and him revealing his to me, it feels natural to share this defining moment with him.

He smiles. "Sure. On three?"

I stand up and walk over to the side of the edge, looking down on the same bottomless sea that just swallowed up Cory's body. My head starts to spin and my legs turn into two wobbly stilts. It's way farther than I've ever dreamed of jumping, and way farther than I can see myself surviving. Should I quit? If I pull out of the obstacles, I'll be sent back home—nothing would be worse than that. I just need to do this before I think about it any more or before I lose the little ignorance I still have left and change my mind.

Trying to get a hold of my erratic breathing, I think about what Nicholas said to me before I left the Conference

Center: "And for the last jump, make sure you jump feet first, no interlocking of the fingers, close your eyes and plug your nose."

Instead of reaching for my locket, I take Arthor's hand in mine and clasp my other hand underneath my armpit. Don't think. Just count. "One...two..." I can't. I'll die. Tristan. No—don't think, just do it.

"Three!"

Chapter 15

There's a time in all our lives when we come to the realization that no matter what we do or how we choose to spend the hours and days that are ours, death is the only outcome. It's crazy really how we walk around as if that momentous day will never arrive—like it's a myth or an illusion—avoiding thinking about that instant when we will no longer exist. Maybe it's a survival instinct. If we truly understood that death could snatch us before we're even aware of it, we would be freaking out, desperate to avoid the inevitable, searching for a remedy that would immortalize our bodies.

But it's too late for me.

Arthor and I jump over the edge, and the sudden drop makes me breathless. The wind whips against me and howls in my ears, but I keep my eyes shut and continue to squeeze Arthor's hand, telling myself that by doing so, the impact will be less painful.

As if by chance, I remember to plug my nose and not a second later, a force as hard as concrete smashes against my feet. Cold liquid rushes around my body, and I sink into the seemingly bottomless ocean. At first, I'm glad there are no hidden rocks I collide with, but when I continue to drop at a fast pace, it occurs to me if I don't stop sinking, I might never make it back up. Just like Cory.

I kick my feet and move my arms, but I continue to sink. I kick more vigorously, but the faster I move my limbs, the more my lungs burn and the farther I'm drawn under. I exhale halfway. When I open my eyes, thousands of bubbles surround me, obscuring my view in the dark ocean. At first I become desperate because I can't see anything, but then it occurs to me: these bubbles must be coming from somewhere and sinking deeper and deeper is all part of the plan. This is why Cory and all the other participants vanished. I'm desperate to take a breath, but am able to hold off a little longer, believing that I'll soon be safe. Then I exhale completely.

My thoughts are confirmed when I get to the ocean floor, and I see light shining from an open hatch. Arthor and I are sucked toward it and into some sort of a capsule. The pull is so strong that I become stuck to a wall right next to him. But things are not happening fast enough. As I inhale, the salty fluid burns my throat and chest, and I start to heave. Unwilling to die alone, I take Arthor's limp hand in mine.

The door to the container closes with a bang, and not a second later, the water drains out of the capsule and is replaced with air. Collapsing onto my hands and knees, I vomit the water out and gasp for air.

"Please take your seats and secure your harnesses," a woman's voice says.

I continue to cough until all the fluid has come up. When I come to myself, I see Arthor still lying lifeless on the floor.

I crawl over so I'm kneeling next to him, stoop down beside him and bring my ear to his mouth to check for breathing. My heart nearly stops when I realize there's no sound or movement.

"Arthor!" I scream, taking him by the shoulders and shaking him.

The female voice says, "Prepare for departure."

I try to lift Arthor up, but he's too heavy. Instead, I lie on top of him and hold onto the bottom of a seat in hopes we won't go flying when the capsule takes off.

"Three, two, one..."

The capsule ejects to a start, and unable to keep my grip, we are thrown into the back wall. My skull hits against the glass, and I fall to the floor with a thud. The impact is so hard my head spins. I get the wind knocked out of me, causing me to gasp for air once more. As I catch my breath, I kneel beside Arthor, place the base of my palms on his chest, and start to compress. His face is limp and gray.

"Arthor, wake up!" I compress his chest again—harder this time—and grant him a few more breaths. "Come back." I grab his shoulders and shake them. "Just don't die..." I push on his chest again, putting all my weight into it.

Finally, he starts to cough and water spurts from his throat. My heart leaps in my chest, feeling like it's going to burst. I can't tell whether I'm laughing or crying.

"Arthor, can you hear me?" He doesn't answer. I lift his head and place it in my lap to get it off the hard, cold floor. I run my fingers through his wet hair and as he continues to breath, the color slowly returns to his face.

"Arthor," I whisper, but he still doesn't open his eyes. The capsule continues forward and every few seconds I glance at his chest to make sure he hasn't stopped breathing.

* * *

The five minutes it takes us to get back to Trollheim seems like days. When we arrive, hordes of people wait outside on the UVC station brick platform, and several of them are waving Culmination's flag. What are they doing here, and how do they know about us? They cheer loudly when they spot us and try to break through the wall of Normark security guards who are struggling to keep the onlookers contained. Once the capsule has reached a complete stop, the doors open and a cool breeze gusts in, causing me to shiver. Just then, Arthor mumbles something. I gently press my palm to his face and when he opens his eyes, I take his hand in my other hand.

"You're going to be okay."

Nicholas enters the capsule first, and the moment he sees me, he exhales so loudly I can hear it.

"Welcome back," he says and throws a blanket around my shoulders.

I didn't think seeing him again would have any effect on me, but when our eyes connect, I feel safe again.

Mai enters and spreads a blanket across Arthor's body. Taking one look at Arthor's leg, she scowls. "Oh, dear. It's worse than I thought. Much worse. Nick..."

Nicholas examines Arthor's leg carefully. "He'll bleed to death if we can't stop it."

"Well, what are you waiting for?" I ask.

Nicholas' face grows weary. "If he is to receive medical treatment, his parents have to pay for it."

"What?" I shout. "They don't have money like that."

"Joseph," Nicholas says in a low voice. He stands up and shouts at the reporters who have slithered their way into the capsule. They retreat back outside.

"I don't remember that being in the contract," I say.

"It's there." Mai glances at Nicholas. I'm about to object, but before I get a single word out, Mai says, "Let's bring him back to the hotel. To my room."

"Yes, let's," Nicholas says. We don't even get a stretcher so Nicholas and one of the security guards lift Arthor to the transporter that's waiting for us outside.

"We love you, Joseph," I hear some girls beckon from the crowd, and when I look over at them, they giggle. My cheeks flush with blood. I get into the transporter and sit between Arthor and Nicholas. Arthor's eyes are rolling to the back of his head. It makes me furious how President Volkov can spend so much money on the obstacle courses, but not find it in his heart to provide medical care for those who suffer injuries.

"You and Arthor are the last ones from the Culmination participants who made it back. We're pleased you made it," Mai says with a soft smile, sitting in the front seat with the driver. "I have to be honest; no one thought you would survive."

"Except for me." Nicholas takes my hand, squeezing it ever so softly, and even though I feel halfway dead, his warm skin sends tingles through me.

"How many survived?" I ask.

170

"The numbers are still rolling in, but when I checked a few minutes ago, it said that roughly half the participants either died, or withdrew," Nicholas says.

"Half? Now I feel guilty for having..." I close my mouth, not wanting Arthor to know about my advantage during the marathon. But half of two thousand and thirty-nine is shocking, especially after the first phase.

Mai glances back at Nicholas and clears her throat.

"What?" I ask.

"We'll talk about it later," Nicholas says. "Let's make sure Arthor is stable first."

I'm curious to know what Nicholas has to say but I drop the subject.

Mai catches me up on how some of the other registrars thought Arthor was an idiot for helping me through the marathon, but when I helped him climb Devil's Cliff, they recanted, saying Arthor was perceptive for having teamed up with the smart contestant. Nicholas shares how his father was very surprised that I survived the first phase, and how it shows that intelligence trumps physical superiority. I don't like hearing that President Volkov is paying attention to me.

"How come there are so many reporters here?" I ask.

"A few reporter drones made it into the obstacle courses, and now it's all over the news."

I remember seeing one on top of Devil's Cliff. "Oh..." What if they recorded what Arthor and I said? Or when Arthor shouted my real name? My shoulders become tense. I do remember looking around before Arthor and I spoke about our secrets, but I can't be certain.

A short time later, we arrive at a skyscraper hotel with a golden Viking longship in the front courtyard. Mai explains that we were supposed to stay in Volkov Village again, but that it was delayed due to Hurricane Chloe. When Prime Minister Halvor of Normark, a huge fan of obstacle courses in general, and a supporter of equal rights, found out about the dilemma, he immediately offered to house us in the Valhalla Hotel.

I don't mind one bit.

A bellboy with white gloves and silver buttons on his suit opens our doors and greets us with a warm smile. But when he sees Arthor's leg, his grin drops several notches.

"To the hospital, perhaps?" he asks and looks at me.

"No." Mai gets out of the transporter and walks around it to where the bellboy is standing. "Help us get him inside. We've already checked in. Room 10545."

"Uh...most certainly, ma'am," he says. Nicholas and the bellboy lift Arthor's arms above their shoulders, and help him out of the transporter. Arthor groans, but they continue to drag him toward the hotel.

I follow after, walking with Mai. The interior has vaulted ceilings with serpent-like woodcarvings and metal sculptures that resemble birds. We cross the marble-floor foyer and Mai presses the button with the number two hundred and thirteen. If I weren't as exhausted as I am, I probably would love this place, but right now nothing seems important other than Arthor getting the help he needs and that I get some rest.

The elevator doors open and we go down a long, narrow, carpeted hallway. I hardly remember walking from the elevator to the door, but somehow I manage to get there. Nearly unconscious, I glance at the clock and it reads 5:07 a.m. Mai's room is a two-bedroom suite with a full kitchen, a living area, and an office. Mai finds a first aid kit in the

172

bathroom while the bellboy and Nicholas take Arthor into one of the rooms to lay him on the bed. Arthor's eyes are open slits and drops of sweat roll down his face.

Mai comes back with a white box, flings it on the bed, and opens it. Wasting no time, she undoes the makeshift bandage I put on and douses a cloth with alcohol. "I'm sorry. This is going to hurt."

Nicholas stays her hand. "Maybe we can give him something for the pain."

Mai nods and Nicholas leaves for a moment, returning with a glass filled with dark yellow liquid. "It will knock him out."

Arthor downs the entire glass and rests his sweaty head back onto the pillow. "We made it, Heidi," he whispers.

I take his hand in mine. "We did."

"We'll wait to tend to the wound until it takes effect," Mai says. "Care for some food, Heidi?"

"No," I say, staying by Arthor's side. I won't be able to stomach anything right now.

"Go eat. I'll watch him," Nicholas says sternly.

I don't feel like eating anything, but I'm too tired to object, so I follow Mai out to the kitchen and have a seat by the table. Every inch of me is still uncomfortably sore, and I desperately need to get cleaned up—I can even smell myself.

Mai sets a huge bowl of pasta and two tall glasses of water in front of me, the beads of condensation trickling down the outsides of the glasses. I gulp the entire first glass down and start on the pasta, eating it quicker than I should after having not eaten for twenty-four hours.

"Your room is right across the hallway from mine, but you can stay here until Arthor is stabilized."

"Thank you." I pick at the pasta. "So what was that all about back there?" I ask.

Mai squint her eyes at me. "Oh." She nods her head. "The landmines were rigged to go off at fifty pounds."

I stop eating. "They changed it?" I ask as calmly as I can, giving Nicholas the benefit of the doubt. He told me they were rigged to go off at one hundred and fifty pounds, and he wouldn't lie to me. Would he?

Mai continues. "We found out about the change right before the Opening Ceremony, but it wasn't something we were allowed to share with you."

"I went out there thinking I was safe."

"Yes, but thankfully..."

I don't listen to the rest of her sentence, only stand up and charge back into Arthor's room where Nicholas still is. "You lied to me?" I ask Nicholas.

He takes me by the arm and leads me out of the room, closing the door behind him. "I didn't think it would be good for you to know. You would just have worried about it and I needed to keep you emotionally stable." He stares at me unapologetically.

"You needed to keep me stable? Like I can't do that myself? Like you can...control me?"

"Not like that." He huffs. "If I would have told you beforehand that you would probably be blown up, wouldn't it have made you terrified?"

"It would have," I admit. "But I have a right to know the truth."

"We weren't allowed to say anything, Heidi."

"Not being allowed to say or do something hasn't stopped you before."

His intense eyes bore into mine. "I get to decide what I share. Will you just trust me that I'm trying to do what's best for you?"

"Which is what, exactly?" I pinch my lips together.

"To keep you alive."

I point my finger at him. "I've lived as a Laborer my entire life—"

He rolls his eyes. "Heidi..."

"—where I've been told what to do, what to think and what to believe. I can't live like that anymore." No, it's more than that. I shake my head. "I refuse to live like that anymore. Knowing the truth is the only freedom I have."

His eyes grow worrisome and he breaks our eye contact by looking down.

"What?" I ask.

He shakes his head. "Did you finish eating?"

"No."

"Why don't you go and finish eating, take a nice hot shower, and get some rest. Tomorrow we're attending the fundraiser at 8:00 p.m." He pauses and the right side of his lip curls into half a smile. "Only if you want to, of course. It's all optional."

I don't know what makes me think that I can punch him in the arm, but I do. Immediately, I regret it. "I'm sorry...I'm really tired, and..." When he starts to laugh, I can't help but smile a little.

"Remember, you're not a Laborer anymore."

Right as I open my mouth to say that I am a Laborer, I think I get what he's trying to do: get me to change my perception of myself.

He takes my arm and leads me back into the kitchen. "Please eat."

I sit down at the table and take a bite. After I finish my food, Mai escorts me to my room just across the hallway. It's identical to the room in Mai's suite where Arthor is staying. She leaves me a key card and says to come back once I've finished cleaning up.

I hop into the shower and turn the setting on hot. The water scalds my skin, but it feels so good, like I'm washing away all the grueling events in phase one. Someone has laid out fresh clothes for me on my bed and I slip on the silky blue pants and a loose white t-shirt with the Savage Run logo.

I return to Arthor's room and see his leg is bandaged; they must have wrapped it while I was in the shower. I sit down on the bed and hold his hand, watching him sleep peacefully. His skin is colorless, his cheeks sunken, and it's only a matter of days before he'll die unless he receives professional medical treatment.

"You really should get some rest, too," Nicholas says, entering the room.

My eyes feel like they have gravel in them, but I say, "I'm fine." I turn back to Arthor.

Nicholas sighs a little. "I know you think you are, but tomorrow is a long day and you still haven't seen the worst of the obstacles yet. Do you need anything to help you sleep?"

I cringe at his words. 'Still haven't seen the worst.' I can't imagine that I'll be able to survive anything crueler than I just went through. I look into his blue eyes as he sits down next to me on the bed, his knee resting against my sore thigh.

"You did a great job out there, but this next round will be even more difficult than the first one."

"I can manage," I say.

He sighs in frustration. "Would it be so hard to accept my help?"

I've always relied on myself, never having found anyone I felt I could trust completely. Except for Gemma. And she's dead. "I just don't...when I have in the past, they've always let me down."

"I won't let you down." He touches my elbow briefly.

I feel a flutter in my abdomen. "You don't have to help me."

His eyebrows rise.

"I know what's best for me." I look down at the red carpet and pretend to kick something.

"I won't let you down, Heidi."

I don't believe him because everyone always does eventually. "It won't matter if I'm careful or risky out there; it seems like surviving has more to do with luck than anything."

"Listen, you may be physically weaker than any of the other participants, but you're a whole lot smarter than most of them, too. You pick up on things others don't, so just use it to your full advantage." He nudges me with his elbow.

Heat rushes to my cheeks, and a lot of the exhaustion I was feeling earlier has melted away. "Is that the secret to survival? Picking up on things?"

"There's no secret. Everyone knows the shortcuts are out there, but many can't seem to find them." He places his hand on the mattress and leans in. "At one point I wanted to join the Savage Run myself, to prove to my father that I could do something worthwhile. I'm not as strong as some of these guys, but I'm reasonably fast. And it's easy for me to determine where the shortcuts are—my mind has always been going at a hundred miles a minute trying to decipher everything. I planned to find the shortcuts in every single obstacle, just like the one you found in Devil's Cliff."

"What happened?"

"My father forbade me to register. Said he'd change my status to a Laborer if I tried. Like I said before, he wanted me to be the venture manager, but as a compromise, he let me become a registrar."

"Do you enjoy what you're doing?" I whisper.

His eyes scan my face, starting with my eyes, until they reach my mouth where they linger for a long time, and he says, "I do."

The room has become unbearably warm, and I stand up and start to pace. "What about the next phase?" I ask. "There doesn't seem to be a way around those obstacles."

"That's a tricky one, but try to find a pattern on the disks or on the beams. The most obvious route isn't always the smartest or the easiest."

"What's the hardest obstacle you've ever seen?"

He thinks for a moment. "It depends on what you're afraid of, but I'd have to say the underwater swims. In one competition, participants had to swim for longer and longer periods of time beneath murky water before they came up for air. The last stretch took some of them three minutes to complete and many drown." A wrinkle appears between his eyebrows and he looks down. "That would be the hardest one for me."

Why would he be afraid of water? "I'm not really great at swimming either, but my main weakness is small spaces." My shoulders feel tense just thinking about it, having to crawl through the Caves of Choice in phase three. He stands up and walks over to me, never breaking eye contact. His blue eyes draw me in—away from where I've been, away from the pain. What is it about him that puts me at ease?

"You've already proven that you don't give into your fears," he says.

"That's because..." It's difficult to speak my mind when he's so close to me, breathing the same air. "...I never felt like I had a choice; it was just something I had to do." Mai comes into the room, and with her entrance, the air returns.

"So, there's a problem," she says.

I immediately think that President Volkov knows, and it's as if I've been whacked in the solar plexus.

"What?" Nicholas asks.

"We don't have a tuxedo for Heidi for the benefit," she answers.

"That's a relief." Nicholas puffs.

"This is serious," Mai says. "It's not like we can just go out into the store and get her one in her size."

"I thought you were going to say something along the lines of that my father had found out Heidi is a girl," Nicholas says.

"No, of course he doesn't suspect at all. I just spoke to him and he's giddy that Joseph the underdog actually made it," Mai says.

"Giddy?" Nicholas' eyebrows crinkle. "I've heard my father described as many, many things, and giddy isn't one of them."

"We absolutely have to solve Heidi's apparel problem," Mai says.

Nicholas brings his hand in front of his eyes and shakes his head. "I'll order one and it will be here within the hour."

I nap on the couch while we wait for the tuxedo to arrive. When it comes, Mai wakes me and helps me get into it. It's way too big.

"My tailor's in town. I'll call him," Nicholas says.

"Well, we can't let your tailor get too close to her, if you know what I mean," Mai says.

"Don't worry. He's a master at what he does, and I guarantee he'll keep quiet."

The silver-haired tailor arrives within the half hour, carrying a container and a full-length mirror. After he sets up, he has me stand in the middle of the room in front of the mirror. He takes out these paper pieces and starts pinning them to my Savage Run outfit, using his tape measure. His gray eyebrows crinkle a bit as he writes the measurements of my chest and shoulders down. He measures my hips, and then grunts a little as he writes those measurement down. He glances at Nicholas over his glasses. Nicholas remains silent.

"I need to measure the inseam. Do you dress to the left or the right?" the tailor asks.

"What...?" I look at Nicholas.

"Right or left," Nicholas says.

"Uh..."

"I'm sorry, let me rephrase. On which side do you hang?" the tailor asks.

"Hang?" I'm thoroughly confused.

"Just pick one," Nicholas says through his teeth.

The tailor looks at Nicholas with questioning eyes, with dozens of pins sticking out of his mouth. "You can't just pick one...either you hang to the..."

"Uh...right." I blurt out, my cheeks flushed now that I understand what they're talking about.

The tailor's eyebrows rise again. "Hmm...that's rare."

Great. I had to pick the rare side.

He measures me from the crotch to the floor and then finishes up with my neck and arm measurements. "You're a girl," he says, studying me carefully. He glances at Nicholas with his old, tired eyes.

"For your confidentiality," Nicholas says, pressing money into the tailor's hand when he leaves.

"Are you sure he'll keep it a secret?" I have to ask since Mai doesn't question him on it.

"I would trust this man with my life," Nicholas replies.

I hope his trust isn't misdirected.

Chapter 16

After being measured, I can no longer keep my eyes open so I go to my room to get some sleep. The sun has risen higher up in the sky so it's light outside. I pull the navy-colored, velour curtains in my room to block out all brightness. Dreaming, I relive the horror of the e-conda lake and of the screams of the boys who were blown up by the landmines. When I wake up with a jolt, it's pitch black and the clock reads 10:03 p.m. I slept all day? I try to fall back asleep, but images from the obstacle courses keep attacking my mind. I decide that I should check on Arthor.

When I go to sit up, there isn't a single muscle in my body that doesn't feel like it's being ripped apart. I'm so sore. I set my feet on the floor and will myself up to a standing position. Barely able to carry my weight, my legs scream at me. The smallest movement causes severe pain, and even a simple effort like moving my head from side to side is extremely difficult.

I still have the key card Mai gave me, so I slowly drag my feet to my door to go to Mai's room. But when I open it, there stands a Unifer. In fact, the entire hallway is lined with Unifers, except for a few doors at the very end. They must be empty.

"I'm not authorized to let you leave," he says.

"I'm allowed to go into that room over there. I have the key card." I lift it up to show him.

He glances over at the Unifer in front of Mai's door.

"Here, I'll show you. Do you think they would have given me a key if I wasn't allowed in there?" I ask.

"Go ahead, but I can't let you go anywhere else."

"That's okay." I slip out of my room and enter Mai's room.

However, when I get there, I find the place completely dark and empty. The thought that he died hovers in the back of my mind, and a lump forms in my throat. Not willing to concede to the thought, I search the room thoroughly, but to my great distress, I can't find him there. And Nicholas and Mai are gone, too. Couldn't they have left a note or something? My first instinct is to go looking for them, though I hardly think I'm allowed to—having the Unifer guarding my door and all. If I were on Volkov Village, I'd be locked in my room with nowhere to go. But here they didn't really tell me I couldn't go anywhere. I could feign ignorance. The only problem is getting past the Unifer.

A slight breeze catches my attention and I see the sheer curtains moving a little. A window. I walk over to it and peek outside. It's rather far to the ground below, so climbing down won't be an option. Plus I'm too sore. Then I see another curtain waving in the wind all the way down at the end where there weren't any Unifers in front of the doors. There's a wide ledge right below, so I could technically...but

I should change into regular clothes first so no one recognizes me. I slip into one of Mai's jeans and a plain black t-shirt so I still look like a boy. They're a little big, but it's not like they're going to fall off me.

I go back to the window and slide it open all the way. Then I quietly remove the screen, and climb out. I press up against the wall and inch my way sideways toward the end of the building. The wind is strong and gusts against my body, rocking it gently from side to side. Though my breathing has become staggered, this is nothing compared to what I've been through. I make it to the end in no time and climb in the window. The room is empty, and the bed has no sheets on it. Opening the door, I peek down the hallway. The Unifiers stand at attention, but they don't turn their heads to the creaking door. I step out of the room, turn my back to the Unifers, and head straight for the elevator. Once the doors close, I'm able to breathe a little easier. I take the elevator downstairs to the foyer and approach the middle-aged woman behind the counter.

"They took the sick boy to the hospital," the woman answers. "They said they'd be back in a couple of hours and that was about an hour and a half ago."

Relieved Arthor is receiving medical treatment, but curious as to where the funds might be coming from, I thank her. Having now regained some of my energy from the mounds of pasta I ate, the gallons of water I drank, and the long nap I took—and with thirty minutes to kill before they return—I go back into the elevator and take it to the two hundred and fourteenth floor—the rooftop. When I exit, I walk into a garden of flowers, plants, and benches. Rarely have I ever seen this many flowers in one place, and the beauty takes my breath away. I walk over to the side of the building but stop before I reach the railing; the two hundred foot jump is still too fresh in my bones, and I can't get myself to look down. Instead, I sit down on the bench and gaze up at the heaven above, the sky barely dark enough for a couple of stars to appear.

"What are you doing up, Imp?"

I turn around to see Johnny standing before me. What is he doing here? "I was just leaving." I stand up and start to walk back toward the elevator, acutely aware that Johnny could very well pick me up over his head and hurl me over the edge, which is probably what he's thinking about doing.

Johnny moves in my way. "No one's here to defend you now, are they?"

I think about bringing up the fact that he's supposed to be in his room, but it would only highlight the fact that I'm not in my room either, so instead, I say, "I'm really surprised you made it."

He chuckles for a moment. "Yeah, ditto. How did you ever manage?" He gets a sly smile on his face.

The hair on the back of my neck rises when Johnny takes a step closer to me. I attempt to swerve around him, but he grabs my arm and shoves me backwards toward the railing so I'm pressed up against it. He's going to kill me.

"You know, there's something not quite right about you, but I just can't put my finger on it." He squeezes my sore arms so hard it constricts the blood flow.

"Let go of me!" I yell, but he squeezes my arm even harder.

"Say, what kind of a Laborer are you back home? Maybe then I could remember where I'd seen you before."

"None of your business."

"Is there a problem here?"

Johnny and I turn around to see Nicholas standing there.

"No, Joseph was just explaining to me how the first phase was," Johnny spews, releasing my arm.

"Yeah, because your memory is so bad that you don't remember," I retort.

"I think you should leave now, Johnny," Nicholas says. "Before I report you out of your room."

"Well, Joseph's..." Johnny starts.

"Now."

"We'll have to catch up later." Johnny points his finger in my face before he walks off.

I'm relieved that Nicholas showed up at a very convenient time, but I cringe thinking about the lecture he's going to give me. Technically he could send me home, but I figure that he won't since he didn't send Johnny packing. Which brings up the question: why didn't he?

"You really shouldn't..." Nicholas starts to say, but he stops himself. "Are you okay?"

"I couldn't sleep." I look across the view on the thousands of lights below, now brave enough to slump against the fence next to the drop off. "I needed some fresh air. To clear my mind from...you know?"

He doesn't say a word—just looks at me.

"How's Arthor?" I ask.

"We took him to the hospital."

"But I thought..."

"A benefactor paid for his medical treatment. He's in reconstructive surgery right now and will be ready to go when the second phase of Savage Run begins."

"I'm glad to hear." My body feels lighter. "Wish I could take a day off. That slacker." I laugh nervously, my heart still pounding hard from being approached by Johnny. Or maybe it's because Nicholas is so near. "His family could never pay for something like that."

"An anonymous donor paid for it."

"Of course." I don't quite know what to say, but the silence isn't awkward as it is with so many people. It's more like the silence between us validates that no words are needed to relate.

"Dare I ask you to walk me back to my room?" I smirk.

"How did you get out?" he asks.

"I climbed out the window. Are you going to send me home?" I ask—just in case.

"No."

"Why didn't you send Johnny home?"

"It's complicated."

"Another one of those things that you're unwilling to share?" I tease.

He smiles. "Fine, I'll tell you. He's the illegitimate son of President Volkov."

My eyes pop open. "What? Are you joking?"

"I wish I were." He huffs and leans on the railing, his eyes gazing out into the distance. "Johnny doesn't know."

"Didn't Johnny's mother say anything to him?"

"His mother is dead. He was raised by his grandmother," he says.

This is why he wants to provide her with a better life. "So, he's your half brother."

"Yes."

"Wow...that's...unexpected. When did you find out?"

"My father just told me today."

I see the pieces coming together. "That's why your father let you become a registrar."

He gazes at me for a moment. "You pick up fast. My father wanted me to personally invite Johnny to join the Savage Run, to test him. I suppose to see what Johnny was made of. My father always has some agenda—his agenda. I thought that this one time...but it's never-ending."

"But when you become president..."

"Now that's even questionable. If he doesn't like the way I plan to run the country..."

"Oh...you're so done for."

He barks a laugh. "Thanks," he says sarcastically.

"Sorry."

"Don't apologize. You're exactly right."

"Well, as I see it, the only way to win is to play the game and beat everyone at it. And I mean, who's to say you can't make your own rules?"

"Spoken like a true outlaw."

I smirk, a little guiltily. "I suppose. Thank goodness you went along with it. Anyone else would have refused to register me or left me to Master Douglas." Shivers go up my spine.

"Partners in crime."

I laugh at first, but then think about it. "That's kind of sad."

"Or exciting." He stares at me for a moment. "Well, speaking as your registrar, you need to get some rest."

"Are you ever going to let me have any fun?" I ask.

"Not until the sun stops shining."

"Well, technically it goes down every night..." I say.

"Not in this country."

Chapter 17

Before bed, Nicholas gives me a pill—says it will take away the bad dreams and help me recover from the soreness more quickly. I take it willingly and like he said, I sleep like a baby and wake up much less sore.

All morning, Mai works on making me look presentable. She manages to remove all my sores and burns with a nifty little device called the Heal-R, so in that respect, I look okay, but the tuxedo does nothing to make me look more muscular. Sissy boy—was that the word Sergio used? Of course it's hopeless, Mai keeps repeating. Somehow, men with at least some substance to fill out the black and white suit look way better than a twiggy girl like me. Go figure.

Around noon, when Mai has just given up on me, a couple of paramedics bring Arthor to her room. The color in his cheeks and lips has returned and though they're rolling him in on a wheelchair, he asserts with rather colorful language that he can walk just fine. The second I see him I throw my arms around him.

"You scared me," I say.

He hugs me back. "Well, I couldn't just let you continue the obstacle courses without me. And look at you, all handsome." He winks at me.

I think about the last conversation I had with him and how we had shared our deepest, darkest secrets. My heart swells in my chest for him and I feel like I need to protect him—from what, I'm not so sure. His leg looks like new and he looks exactly the way he did before the obstacles started: red, curly hair, light eyebrows, and a wide grin on his face.

"Back to bed with you," Mai says to Arthor. "You need to rest up before the second phase starts tomorrow." She takes the wheelchair from the paramedics and wheels him into the bedroom.

"This isn't necessary," Arthor says begrudgingly on the way to the room.

I follow after.

"We had a deal," Mai says. "You promised to rest if we'd allow you to compete."

Arthor hops into bed and huffs.

"Are you sure he can't come?" I ask Mai, seeing he's back to his old self.

"No. The medication needs to run through his system, and while he appears and feels completely recuperated, he still needs his rest. I'll be staying with him to make sure he gets it."

Mai lets me stay in her room while we wait for the fundraiser to start. I change out of my tuxedo and slip on my light blue Savage Run outfit. Glued to Arthor's side, I watch him drift back to sleep. Soon I, too, find my eyelids feeling unusually heavy and lie down next to him. Within moments,

I'm out. When Mai wakes me up, she says it's an hour until the fundraiser starts. I've slept for at least seven hours.

Once I've changed back into my tuxedo, I go out into Mai's living area. Nicholas is tying on his shoes and is wearing a black tuxedo nearly identical to mine. But unlike me, he looks really handsome in his—like he was born to wear such a fine suit. His hair, combed slick to the side, appears darker than usual, making him seem years older, and there's something about him being dressed so formally that has me weak-kneed.

"Ready?" he says, standing up and pulling his jacket down.

I really wish I were wearing a dress right now, not this man-suit. I roll my eyes. "Sure."

"You look great," he says.

I can't tell if he's being serious or if he's just trying to make me feel better—either of which I don't want. For some reason I find myself wanting to look nice for him. I shake the thought out of my head.

We take the elevator down to the foyer where many of the participants have gathered. Tuxedos range in color from white to red to green, to pink, and black. The moment I see Johnny in the hotel lobby, I remember our little incident on the roof. And he's Nicholas' half brother. How did he end up being such a jerk? He wears a smug grin, and glares me down from across the room as if he owns me. I want to claw his eyes out, but it would be stupid to infuriate him more; there will be no one to protect me once I'm out in the obstacle courses again.

The participants from Culmination fly together in a hovercraft to the Dovre Manor—the castle where the fundraiser will be held. There are only seven of us left, including Arthor, and I see that Danny and Timothy made it. The others I don't know the names of, but I'm sure I'll get to know them tonight. I should be jumping up and down, having survived over all the others, but instead, I think about all the families who lost their sons and how most likely, I won't be participating in the next fundraiser. Next time my seat will be empty.

"The Savage Run event coordinator has flown in female students from the University Trollheim. You may dance with, speak with, and take walks with these young women, but nothing more. Men, be on your best behavior." Nicholas glances over at me, probably knowing how awkward the evening will be, and already is, for me.

We approach the Dovre Manor—a gray stone castle with two circular towers, and a drawbridge allowing crossing over the murky moat. There is a hedge maze behind the building, and the shape of the Savage Run wreath is mowed into the front lawn. The hovercraft lands on a helipad, and not wanting to attract attention to myself, I wait until everyone else has gotten out. When I step out, fireworks light up the still light sky and the hundreds of formally dressed people standing on the lawn cheer for us.

I hope no one will notice me.

I follow Nicholas toward the castle, but don't get far.

"You're Joseph, right?" a platinum blonde, middle-aged woman asks as she grabs my elbow.

I stop and nod, anxiously watching the others continue on.

"Excuse my intrusion, but we came all the way from Normark just so we could be here tonight, and you were one of the participants we wanted to meet. My husband, Dr. Konders..." She gestures to the dark, lanky man with a mustache standing next to her. "...and all our friends were so impressed by your bravery that we decided to donate a good little chunk of change to the Savage Run on your behalf."

"Though it's a shame you won't see much of that money," Dr. Konders says. "It goes to pay for other administrative fees and such. Nicholas has been heavily involved in getting us to commit. I was skeptical that the program could do what he claimed: be a catalyst in bringing equality to Newland. Until the moment I saw you. After you—an emaciated little slave boy—showed up all those muscle heads out there I believe I witnessed the beginning of the end of your hierarchical society." He raises his glass to me.

"Thank you, Sir," I say.

Mrs. Konders continues. "You are such an example to everyone who has dreamt of becoming something more. Finally, a man who doesn't shrink in the face of the impossible."

I want to sink into the earth; I doubt they would tell me that if they knew who I really am.

"Besides, our daughter just loves competing in obstacle courses," Dr. Konders says. "Now personally, I don't think it's quite the womanly thing to do—"

"Edgar." Mrs. Konders smiles and pats his arm.

"—but if it makes her happy, then let her compete."

"That's amazing." My eyes widen.

"That's right—equal rights," Mrs. Konders says. "We believe in freedom, and it is so great that President Volkov has started to make changes in that direction. We were wondering when he'd finally catch up." She laughs a little.

"And to have such a liberal thinker as Nicholas soon to take over the presidency, that's a true blessing."

"Indeed. We brought a couple of friends tonight, and they, too are donating on your behalf." Dr. Konders pulls out a gold-plated watch from his pocket, checking the time.

"It was a true honor meeting you. Sorry we kept you. You should probably catch up with your group," Mrs. Konders says. "Good luck out there, Joseph. We believe in you. And if you ever need anything, please don't hesitate to contact us."

Dr. Konders hands me a card with his contact information.

"Thank you." It's becoming apparent that Nicholas has supporters, too, and though he is still at the mercy of his father, bound to obey his every rule, Nicholas is building an empire for himself, in his own way.

With my eyes lowered so I don't have to talk to anyone else, I walk across the wooden bridge and enter the castle's foyer. I walk toward the sign that reads "Great Hall," and enter a large room with a sea of roundtables and golden chairs. Each table is decorated with yellow and purple flowers that sparkle and millions of twinkling lights hang from the dark wooden beams in the ceiling. Beautiful music streams through the room. I see President Volkov sitting at one of the tables, and I remember that Mai said he was so impressed I made it. I desperately hope he doesn't make me get up on stage again. Dr. and Mrs. Konders pass me and join President Volkov at his table. I feel sick to my stomach.

Nicholas steps up next to me. "Chopin."

"What?"

"That's who they're playing." He nods his head in the direction of the string quartet in the corner.

I listen for a moment over the hushed chatter, and the tune helps me relax. "It's lovely."

"Let me show you to our table," he says.

"Okay."

Our table has a golden plaque on it that is inscribed with 'Culmination.' Each setting has three forks, a spoon, two knives, three different-sized glasses, a cloth napkin, and a place card. Taking my seat, I notice I sit between Nicholas and Timothy, and not next to Johnny—he sits across from me. Thank goodness.

"I swear I know you from somewhere," Timothy says, running a hand through his curly blond locks. "But I just can't put my finger on it."

"Really?" I say. "Because I remember everyone I meet, and I can guarantee you that I've never met you before." I sip my water, making sure I hold my glass like a guy. And sit like a guy. Gosh, I feel so out of place. I even think I see Johnny laughing at me, and sure enough, when I turn to look at him, he's sneering and staring me down. I quickly look away.

"I thought we could each take a moment to introduce ourselves to each other," Nicholas says. "As I understand, some of you haven't been introduced. Tell us your name, your class, and the reason you registered for Savage Run. Let's start with Johnny."

Johnny keeps his eyes on me. "I'm Johnny—Advisor. Soon to be Master. I believe you all know why I'm here, but I can say it again. I'm here to help my sickly grandmother."

When he says the word "grandmother," his voice softens just a tad.

"I'm Abraham, but you can call me Abe. Advisor." He has huge lips, small, black, beady eyes, and his skin is a deep espresso. "I'm here 'cause my mamma kicked me outta the house. Said I needed to make my own livin'."

We laugh a little, but I notice how when he laughs, his eyes still look sad.

We skip Nicholas because we all know who he is. "I'm Joseph—Laborer."

"Aka, the Imp," Johnny inserts.

I narrow my eyes at him. "Very funny. I'm here because I don't want to work with my father anymore." It's a safe answer, and it's true; no one should be able to figure out who my father is or who I am from that comment.

"Just out of curiosity, what does your father do?" Timothy asks.

"He works at the hospital." Many Laborers work there cleaning and cooking. It should be a safe enough answer, but it worries me how Johnny's dissecting me with his eyes.

"Next," Nicholas says.

"I'm Timothy and I'm an Advisor." His transparent green eyes remind me of a fish's. "I'm here...I don't know why. I was just bored with my life, I guess."

We laugh.

"I'm Danny, an Advisor. Here to make the family proud. Here so my kids can grow up without the restrictions I've fought all my life."

"Dude, you're already planning to have kids?" Timothy asks.

"Well, one day."

"Let's keep going," Nicholas says.

"And I'm Fletcher." He grins and reveals crooked teeth. He is almost as small as Arthor, making me think that maybe he is a Laborer, too. "I'm an Advisor and I'm here because I want to become a doctor."

Just as we finish, the lights dim, signaling that the program is starting. A female announcer takes the stage, welcomes us to Dovre Hall, and explains that this very castle is thought to have been built on the graveyard of trolls. She specifically welcomes the benefactors of the Savage Run, and hopes they all brought their checkbooks tonight. The gathering laughs. Referring to the programs on our plates, she says first we are to eat, after which we'll head to the ballroom where there will be dancing and socializing.

While she's speaking, my eyes wander from Nicholas to Johnny, back to Nicholas again. They don't look alike at all. Johnny's face looks like it's permanently locked in this sour expression, while Nicholas seems to have a smile waiting to appear at any time. Other than the dark hair, there are no similarities. I think I remember that President Volkov had dark hair when he had some. Now he's just bald.

The woman up on stage wishes us a wonderful evening and leaves the stage. The first thing I'm going to do after we eat is to find myself a secluded room so I don't have to face Johnny anymore or dance with a girl. That would just be too weird.

"So where's Arthor?" Timothy asks Nicholas. A waiter brings us each a plate with steak, au gratin potatoes, and creamed carrots.

"He's recovering. He'll be back participating tomorrow," Nicholas answers, taking his first bite.

"You know," Johnny says loudly, sawing at his meat. "It's funny how we all chose to climb Devil's Cliff the legit way, and how Joseph cheated his way up the mountainside."

I groan inwardly. Great—here we go again. "What I did was perfectly legit. We were all informed about the shortcuts before we started."

"It's just a trap to see who will take the easy way out. Didn't you figure that out?" Johnny counters.

"Or it could be a way to see who's smart enough to use the resources provided," I retort.

A vein in Johnny's forehead bulges and his eyes bore a hole into me. "Are you saying that you, a Laborer, are smarter than all the Advisors in the program?"

"Did anyone else use the ledges?" I ask the others.

"I did," Timothy says.

"Me, too," Danny says. "They said we should look for them, Johnny."

"I was one of the first ones there with Johnny. I couldn't find it," Abraham says.

It goes completely silent and I'm sure we're all thinking the same thing: Johnny will never admit it, but he wasn't able to find the short cut.

Johnny leans forward and is about to say something to me.

"The important thing..." Nicholas asserts, "...is that we're all here—alive."

"You're always defending Joseph—what, do you have a thing for him or something?" Johnny looks at the other guys for validation.

"Dude, that's not even funny," Timothy says, chewing on some meat.

199

"This is so not fair. You guys are naïve if you think there isn't something shady going on." Johnny stands up and throws his napkin on the table. "Here I am risking my life so that my grandmother can have a better life, and no one but me cares that Joseph is getting ahead by cheating." He walks off.

"Well, that was uncomfortable," I say, but the others don't laugh or acknowledge me at all. "How is it cheating when we were encouraged to take the shortcuts?"

Nicholas shakes his head at me and I take it as him telling me to drop it, which I gladly do. I eat my food without saying another word, eager for the meal to be over. After I finish, I excuse myself and head for the men's room. Never mind. I don't want to sit in there locked up in one of the stalls all evening, listening to all types of sounds. Returning to the great hall, the guests are already on their way to the ballroom. When I turn around, I see Nicholas walking a few feet behind me. I greet him with a nod and continue to the other side of the ballroom where it's less crowded. Nicholas remains a few feet behind me the entire time. Does his following me around have anything to do with the fact that Johnny is here?

The string quartet starts to play a slow waltz, and a young lady appears out of nowhere asking me to dance. I balk for a moment, cursing myself quietly for not having just sucked it up and locked myself up in the men's room. "I don't really know how to dance."

"It's okay. You can follow my lead." She smiles warmly and latches her arm around my elbow, leading me to the center of the dance floor.

This is humiliating on so many levels.

Taking my hand and wrapping it around her waist, she says, "My name is Eva Dahl, and you're Joseph, right?"

"Yes."

"You're all the rave amongst the tween girls around here. You're a little young for me, but my younger sister made me promise that I'd dance with you."

I suppress a smile. Trying to move with her, I trip and manage to step on her foot.

"A waltz has three beats to it, like so." She shows me and I'm able to pick up the rhythm pretty quickly.

Once we're moving again, she says, "It was such a wonderful thing you did for Arthor. I thought he was going to die for sure."

"Thanks." I try to make my voice sound a little deeper.

"You look much younger up close."

"How old are you?" I ask.

"Seventeen." Picking up on how I won't be doing the talking, she starts to tell me at length about herself. Her parents are making her study science at the University of Trollheim, but she'd much rather be a singer. And, oh, what she wouldn't give to have a man take her away from her wretched life so she can finally be free from her father's control.

"I completely get that," I say.

Her big brown eyes pop open. "You do?" She must assume that since I'm a boy, I have more freedom than her— and if I was a boy maybe I would have had some freedom— but as it is, our situations are extremely similar, the only difference being she's a free person as far as her status goes, and I'm a slave to every Master.

"Sure, just maybe in a different way," I say.

"So tell me about that Johnny guy. He's pretty hot."

"Er..." I answer.

"I mean, what's he like? He seems like one of the strongest, bravest guys out there."

I nod and am amazed at how quickly she can change the subject. "He...uh...he's pretty strong. Not really a nice guy, though."

"Hm. So what's it like to be a Laborer? I mean, here in Normark we're all considered equals. There are no slaves and no Masters. We're all Masters, I suppose."

"It's horrible," I confess. "I'd do anything to live the way I want to."

"Even risk dying..." she says dreamily. "That's so brave. Maybe if you survive, you could come visit my sister and me in Normark?"

I hardly think I'll ever be visiting her, but since the odds of me surviving the Savage Run are slim to nothing, I say, "I would enjoy that."

"Now...where did Johnny run off to?" She scans the crowd. "Oh, I see him." She hands me a pen and a postcard with my picture on it.

"Where did you get this?" I ask.

"My dad has connections, and my sister gets pretty much anything she wants...so...will you sign it?"

I start to write my name. "H..." But I quickly turn it into a J and sign my last name. "There."

"Thanks for dancing, Joseph. And for the signature. My sister will love it."

She leaves me standing alone on the dance floor and heads toward Johnny.

"Thank you for the dance," I say to myself. Zooming as fast as I can, I migrate toward a dim hallway and look for a place where I can be alone. Eventually, I find a dark room with built-in bookshelves, with a brown leather sectional, and a huge wooden desk. Just as I'm about to shut the door, Nicholas slips in behind me.

"Having fun?" He laughs heartily.

"Wipe that clever smile off your face."

"It was quite amusing to watch." He chuckles a few more times.

"I didn't think it was funny." Despite myself, when I think about it, I can't help but smile. "Okay, it was a little funny. But she just wanted to dance with me to get a signature for her sister and to ask about Johnny."

"She'd be smart to stay away from him."

"For sure." I walk over to the sectional and sit down. "This whole evening feels so...awkward."

Remaining by the door, he says, "You can stay in here the rest of the night if you want. I'll tell everyone you needed to get some rest."

"Thanks." There's a pause in our conversation where we look into each other's eyes. Realizing that I have stopped breathing, I look away.

"I'm sad she beat me to it though." He moves closer to me.

My eyes have a mind of their own and find their way back to his. "Beat you to what?"

"I promised I'd take you dancing if you made it past the first phase."

"Oh...that. Well...I won't hold you to it. I know what you meant."

He takes a step closer to me and reaches out his hand. "I meant what I said. Besides, now that we're partners in crime, I can't go back on my word, can I?"

I smile a little, but my breaths have become quick and shallow. "What, here?"

His right eyebrow rises.

"But there's no music." I don't know why I'm trying to make it difficult for him because if I'm honest with myself, I know I'll enjoy dancing with him.

"Come here."

After a moment's hesitation, I reach my hand out. When his warm skin meets mine, it's as if electricity surges through me. He pulls me to a standing position and draws me in so close that his chest touches mine. He begins to hum and his voice vibrates through my core.

"Doesn't it make you feel weird dancing with me since I'm in a tuxedo?" What a ridiculous question.

His eyes lock with mine. "Not really."

His palm presses against the small of my back so heat collects there, and when he rests his newly-shaven cheek against mine; I can feel my pulse in my ear. For how long we stand and sway like that, I don't know.

"Can I ask you something?" I finally say.

"Anything."

"What is your opinion of a...gay person?"

"What do you mean?" He thinks for a moment and then chuckles. "I guess someone would think we were gay if they walked in on us."

"Well—that—and I'm interested to know what you think about it."

"Why?"

"My father hates any gay person, but I think they're just like everyone else."

"I wouldn't condemn them."

"But it's against the law," I say.

"Unfortunately, yes." He lifts his hand from the small of my back, reaching farther across, pulling me closer.

It's become difficult for me to think straight. "So do you think it's wrong?"

He ponders for a moment. "My father would say it defies natural laws, that it isn't conducive to the propagation of life, that it devalues traditional marriage, and that it turns moral wrongs into civil rights."

"Do you agree?"

"It isn't conducive to the traditional family."

"But do you think it's wrong?" I press, a little irritated that he's avoiding answering my question.

"I don't believe in right or wrong anymore. I only believe in what works for society and the individual alike."

"And when those two clash?"

He looks me in the eyes and for a moment, I think I can see his soul. "Then we must be brave enough to stand for what we believe. As long as we don't hurt anyone, we should have rights to our opinions and to be able to live the way we see fit."

"Well, you have that right," I say, thinking about my own Laborer status, which gives me the right to basically nothing. Especially not living the way I see fit. "It's all so easy for you. Do you ever try to imagine what life might be like without your freedom?"

"I must admit I haven't. Not until..."

I interrupt him. "So how can you say that we must be brave enough? Do you think that just by being brave and standing for what we believe, things will suddenly become fair? If a Laborer stands for what he or she believes, they're punished for it."

"Listen, you don't have to be so upset with me. I agree with you. And I want to change it."

I just stare at him blankly for a while with nothing to say.

He cocks his head to the side, his eyes narrowing. "What?"

When I realize I've been gawking at him for the last minute, my cheeks become hot. I look away.

Leaning his cheek against mine, he says. "You don't have to fight against me."

The knot in my gut melts away.

Suddenly, the door flings open and I hear loud laughter. Johnny enters, pulling Eva inside with him. Nicholas and I step away from each other immediately, but it's too late; I know they saw us.

"Oh, sorry," Eva says, but when she recognizes me, she says, "Oh, my."

Johnny's face lights up and a devious grin sprouts from his lips. "Wait a minute, I knew I'd figure it out." He wags his finger at me. "Your father's that crazy, holier-than-thou pastor at the hospital, and you're that girl who rides around delivering medicine. What's your name...? Heidi!"

Chapter 18

Nicholas dashes across the room and pulls Eva and Johnny inside, slamming the door shut behind them.

"Wait. What? Joseph's a...girl?" Eva's eyes widen.

"No I'm not."

"I know who you are. You delivered medicine to my grandmother like a hundred times, and I bet if I told President Volkov, he'd have no problem believing it," Johnny asserts.

I wonder how Johnny saw me because I don't ever remember meeting him.

"Listen to me very carefully," Nicholas says. "Heidi had extreme circumstances and if I didn't register her, she'd be dead by now."

I can't believe he's telling Johnny about this.

"You knew about it and registered her anyway," Johnny says.

"I did it because she deserved a chance to live. Like you do," Nicholas replies.

Johnny sneers. "I can't wait to tell Pres. about this."

"Why would you do something so cruel?" Eva props her hands on her hips.

Johnny hesitates for a second. "Obviously because it's illegal."

"Just let her go, Johnny," Eva says. "It would be so amazing if a girl could complete the Savage Run." She turns and smiles at me, and it feels good to have someone defend me.

"Pres. needs to know about this," Johnny says and reaches for the doorknob, but Nicholas presses the palm of his hand against the door, keeping it shut.

"What makes you think my father will trust you over me? I have Joseph's government issued ID," Nicholas says.

"She's a girl." Johnny points at me.

"This isn't your battle. Turn a blind eye," Nicholas says.

"Whatever," Johnny says. "She'll probably die in the next phase anyway."

Eva puffs. "Wow, Johnny. That's really cruel." She faces me. "I'll keep your secret, Heidi. It was really an honor to meet you, and know that I'll be rooting for you. Oh, and do you mind signing your real name?" She hands me the card and pen again.

"Seriously?" Johnny says.

Begrudgingly, I sign it. After hugging me, she opens the door and walks out.

"I make deals, Nicholas. What are you going to offer me?" Johnny says.

"I have plenty of dirt on you, Johnny. If I leaked any of it to my father, he'd disqualify you from Savage Run."

Johnny's face turns pale. I wonder what kind of dirt Nicholas is talking about.

"So if you keep your mouth shut, I'll do the same," Nicholas says.

"Fine, but don't think this is over." Johnny opens the door and slams it shut behind him.

"What do you know about him?" I ask.

"Plenty of stuff. I don't want to overload you with it, though. Just keep your focus on getting through the obstacles."

He's keeping information from me again, but I don't really care to know about all that Johnny has done, so I let it go. "Do you think he'll tell?" I lean my back against the door.

"If he does, he's a bigger jerk than I thought." Nicholas places his hand on my shoulder and slowly lets it glide down my arm all the way to my fingertips before letting go. I'm tempted to take his hand and just feel the strength that's there, borrow a little of what I'm lacking at the moment. But I shouldn't. I need to rely on my own strength.

"Why did he have to remember me?" I ask.

For a moment, he looks conflicted, but then he brushes the back of his hand against my cheek.

No man has ever touched me with such tenderness—I didn't think it was possible.

He says, "I should get back to the others."

I want him to stay. It must be because I'm scared to be left alone with all my demons—no other reason makes sense. But I need to learn how to fight the demons myself. I reach behind my back and push the handle so the door opens. "I'll hang out here until the benefit is over."

"I think that's a wise decision."

Stepping out of his way, I let him out. The knot in my stomach returns as soon as the door closes behind him.

Johnny knows. And I'm ninety-nine percent sure he's going to tell.

* * *

At the end of the night, Nicholas escorts us to the hovercraft and we're flown back to our hotel. The first thing I do when I get to my room is to check up on Arthor. He's sound asleep. Mai tells me he's been in and out for a couple of hours and that everything looks promising for him to continue the obstacle courses tomorrow. I'm not sure whether I'm the one protecting him or if he's the one protecting me, but either way, what's probably true is that we need each other.

When I go back into the living room, Nicholas has vanished. I know he'd tell me to go straight to bed, and I do think it's the best thing for me considering I have to be up at six a.m. tomorrow. I go back to my room, but the thoughts start the second my head hits the pillow. What if Johnny already told President Volkov about me? What if they arrest me? Tonight? I open my eyes and sit up in bed. Inhaling slowly, I attempt to calm myself. Walking usually helps calm my mind, but technically I'm not allowed to wander around alone. If I dressed up as a girl and went to a more public place, no one would notice me. It's not like anyone else is wandering around, except for maybe Johnny, but he already knows about me and if I'm in a public place and wear Mai's clothes, any man would stand up for me if he started to attack me.

I go back into Mai's room—the Unifer lets me pass without a word—and when I see there's no one, I find a hot pink tank top, a pair of tight-fitting jeans, and a floral scarf to wrap around my head. I also apply a generous layer of Mai's lipstick and stick her sunglasses in my back pocket.

I climb in and out of the windows again, take the elevator to the main floor, and head toward the upbeat techno music. Entering the restaurant, I see colored strobe lights bouncing off the floor and walls. After I see there aren't any other Savage Run participants here, I put on Mai's sunglasses and sit down at the bar. The people on the dance floor move their bodies freely, and it makes me want to join them. I don't feel confident enough to let myself go so thoroughly.

Shortly after, the bartender brings me a drink.

"Excuse me, Sir. I didn't order this," I say.

He points to someone sitting at the end of the bar, and I recognize the guy as the registrar from Asolo—Cory's registrar. I half-expect him to come over and sit by me, but when he doesn't, I nod a thank you.

The beverage has a strong taste to it—like I imagine liquor would taste—but this is very sweet, and besides, the registrar wouldn't order me, a young lady, an alcoholic beverage, would he? In any case, maybe if it does contain alcohol, it will help me relax a little. I drink the whole thing down and ask for another. The registrar happily pays for the next one. After drinking the second one, I don't feel any more relaxed. It must just be an exotic juice or something so I tell the bartender to keep them coming. After I start on the fourth one, the registrar stands up and starts to make his way toward me. But as I'm trying to figure out how to escape this situation, I hear a voice behind me. The other registrar leaves the restaurant.

"Out roaming again?"

I turn around and see Nicholas, and immediately try to come up with a good excuse for being out. Dressed like a girl. "I..."

The bartender hands me another drink.

Nicholas' face becomes stern. "What are you drinking?"

"It's just...juice...soda juice...soda?" I'm starting to feel a little warm so I grab the menu off the counter and fan myself with it.

He picks up my drink and smells it. "It's spiked, Heidi."

"Spiked?" I ask, looking for the bartender, but he doesn't seem to be around at the moment.

"As in an alcoholic beverage."

"No..." I laugh.

Nicholas scoots the barstool closer to me and sits down. "You need to go back to your room right this minute and get to sleep."

"Tried already." I rest my chin in one hand and drum my fingers on the counter with the other. "Didn't work."

"Maybe I can help you with that."

I give him a mean look. "I'm okay. Besides, I want to live every moment I have left to the fullest. You know, I might die tomorrow." The music is so entrancing that I want to move my body to the beat. For some reason, I feel much less inhibited than I did a few minutes ago and I shoot to my feet. "Wanna dance?"

He stands up with me, but continues to wear a frown. I walk toward the dance floor and Nicholas grabs my elbow, stopping me. "There are other registrars here."

"They don't recognize me. I want to dance. None of this prim and proper dancing stuff." Right when I say it, I wish I could take it back. Because the way Nicholas held me when we danced earlier, has forever been placed with the group of memories I cherish. His expression remains unchanged—cold. Maybe dancing with me didn't mean anything to him; he was just set on keeping his promise. I pull my arm away from his grasp and step onto the packed dance floor.

A young man comes up behind me and places his hands around my waist. I giggle and lean my head back onto his firm chest.

Nicholas steps onto the dance floor. "Get lost."

"Sorry." The young man leaves.

Acting on impulse only, I lock eyes with Nicholas and wrap my arms around his neck.

He immediately removes my arms, and looks around the room to see if anyone is watching.

"Come on, Nick. They can't see us in the crowd. Have some fun." I throw my head back and feel like a laugh just waits in the back of my throat. "You have to live in the present." Words are coming out of nowhere and I'm sure once I return back to my normal self, I'll be embarrassed.

"I do," Nicholas says flatly.

"Then what are you afraid of?"

He sighs. "Nothing."

Yeah, right. "It's dark in here; don't worry; no one will see us."

He shakes his head and looks away.

"You need to move more," I say, placing my hands on his hips.

"If you don't go to bed..."

I interrupt him. "You know, you're not very fun to be around sometimes. Most of the time."

"Sorry to disappoint," he says.

"Well, you could always lighten up." I laugh and then I feel the sudden urge to kiss him on the cheek and before I know it, my lips meet the skin right next to his dimple.

"Careful," he says, the muscles in his jaw tightening, but he doesn't stop me.

"Or what?" I challenge him, running my hands through his hair. Would it be too crazy if I kissed him on the lips? The thought brings a smile to my lips and I giggle a little.

"What?" he asks, seeming slightly amused.

Then a cage catches my attention and I want to see if I can dance inside it. I run over and climb into it, grabbing onto the bars. Closing my eyes, I let my body rock to the music.

"You're not yourself," Nicholas says, glaring up at me.

Does he like what he sees? "It's okay. I'm just having fun."

Taking my hand, he pulls me down from the cage, and drags me off the dance floor.

"I'm not done yet," I object.

"Yes, you are." He pulls me into a corner and behind a curtain, his hands pressing up against the wall behind me—confining me. His shirt is fitted enough so I can see his chest and shoulder muscles and I notice how he smells like cologne.

"You smell good."

"You're drunk."

I scoff. "I'm not drunk," I say, feeling my head swimming. I wish he'd see me as something more than just a participant he needed to take care of. "I don't need a babysitter."

He shakes his head. "I know you don't. And I'm not here to...I just want you to be safe."

He leans his forehead against mine and it seems like all the air in the room has been sucked out. His mouth is open—an inch away—and I want to touch my lips to his. But he pulls away before I'm able to try.

"Can I take you back to your room now?"

"Fine." I roll my eyes. "Just no sleeping powder."

Before we get on the elevator, he stops and squeezes the bridge of his nose.

"What?"

"I can't take you back up there dressed like this. The Unifers..." He looks around the foyer. "Can you wait in the Ladies room and I'll get you a Savage Run outfit?"

"Okay."

"Just don't go anywhere, you hear?"

"Yes, Sir."

I head to the Ladies room and he takes the elevator upstairs. A few minutes pass and I hear knocks on the door. When I open it, he hands me a plastic bag.

"Don't forget the lipstick."

After I change, he escorts me back to my room, closing the door behind us. I hand him the bag of Mai's clothes. The Unifers don't say anything, though I'm sure they're wondering how I got out. But who questions President Volkov's son?

"Will you be okay?" He leans against the door with his hands behind his back, holding onto the door handle.

Somehow I know when tomorrow comes I'll feel horrible about the way I acted, and I look away. "Sorry I...I don't know what I was thinking."

"Consider it forgotten. But this has to stop."

His words are like a Master's, pounding me into submission. Who am I fooling? He wouldn't want me. He's the next president of Newland, a free man, a god in some people's eyes. I look down. He takes a step closer and lifts my chin until our eyes meet. Electricity spreads through me, making me even more confused. "You be careful out there tomorrow, you hear?"

I nod. Is his touch just that of a friend? A concerned representative?

"I'll see you in the morning."

Or is there more behind the tender way he handles me? "Good night." I watch him shut the door. My head falls back, and a strenuous sigh escapes my lips. Gosh, I'm such an idiot. I bury my face in my hands and fret. "Stupid, stupid, stupid." I undress, take a hot shower, pull on the Savage Run outfit I wore before, and then go to bed.

Chapter 19

The next morning, I wake up to Mai flinging open my curtains. Immediately, I remember what happened last night and I grunt.

"Rise and shine." She's in her white leather pants, white Savage Run shirt, and black stiletto heels. Her black hair is straight and reaches her waist.

What did I do? I haven't even seen him and already I feel mortified. He must think I'm such an idiot. Which of course, I am. I don't have time to think about some guy or make moves on him. Or get drunk. I want to sink into bed and disappear.

"When did you get up?" I sit up and my head spins. This is not good. The first obstacle—the floating disks—requires me to have impeccable balance.

"I never went to bed. Too many things to take care of."

Half conscious, I throw the sheets off, and make my way across the hallway to check on Arthor. Passing through Mai's living room, I notice Nicholas isn't here yet. Did he come back at all last night?

When I get to Arthor's room, he's sitting on his bed, already wearing a yellow and red Savage Run outfit, pulling on his shoes.

"Ready for phase two?" I ask.

"Yes, my leg feels just like new again. How about some breakfast?"

I hadn't noticed how tense my neck was until it relaxes with his answer. "Let me just get ready first." Just as I get to the living room, Nicholas enters with a glass in his hand. The instant our eyes connect, my stomach twists like I just ate a jar of worms. Was last night as bad as I remember? Did I actually try to...kiss him? Wait, I did kiss him—on the cheek. And anyone could have seen us. Mortified, I look away. The drink must really have been strong for me to do something so irresponsible. I take a deep breath and try to clear my thoughts. This is beyond ridiculous. I don't need this kind of complication right now; what was I thinking?

"Hi." Nicholas hands me the glass and tells me to drink the green liquid. His expression is perfectly normal and it makes me think that maybe I'm exaggerating what happened. "Sleep well?" he asks.

"Yes." I gulp the drink down as fast as I can, trying to ignore the beverage's sour, grassy aftertaste. "Can I have a word?" I whisper.

He shoots me a glance, as if saying no.

"I just want to...I just wanted to say..." It's hard to get the words out. "Thanks for bringing me back to my room last night."

His face is unforgiving. "It's hard to be partners with someone who keeps breaking the rules, Heidi."

Like he keeps the rules all the time. Well, obviously he wants to ignore what I did last night, so I should, too.

Mai parades into the room and sits down at the kitchen table. "We have an hour until we need to be at the UVC station. Do you have any questions before we leave?"

"Just survive, right?"

"Right," Mai says with a stern smile.

I place my empty glass in the sink. Though it tasted horrid, my head feels clear again and it took away the nausea. With no time to spare, I head back to my room and take a quick shower, after which I slip into my new Savage Run outfit.

Just as I finish dressing, there's a knock on my door and Nicholas enters. We're alone again, and I have no idea what to say. I really hope he doesn't bring it up.

"About last night...if you do something like that again, I'll have to disqualify you."

Something like what? Try to kiss him? Leave my room? Get drunk? Dress as a girl? I didn't think he would revert to threats. "You know, you're so two-faced."

"We don't have time to hash this out." His eyes darken.

"That's the problem with all you Masters. You have to control everything—even conversations."

He rolls his eyes. "I'm your registrar. It's my place to tell you what to do."

"Sounds just like something your father would say."

His lips squeeze to a line and his nostrils flare. "I'm here as your registrar. Will you let me deliver the message?"

Still boiling on the inside, I consider it for a moment, but I finally nod.

He takes a deep breath. "In the balancing phase, look for other paths—plateaus even. Remember, it's just a game, and there are many ways to finish, not just the most obvious."

I nod, forcing myself to calm down and think about the obstacles, not at how angry I am with him. "Are there shortcuts to every course?"

"I don't know." He reaches behind his head and cups the back of his neck. "They track your time from the moment of your first step to when you get back on the capsule, understand?

"Yes."

"It's not about who's first. It's about finishing in the top fifty percent, so pace yourself."

My nerves creep up my spine toward my neck.

"Usually women have better balance than men, so this next phase should go in your favor," he says. "And the drink I gave you should help remove any toxins in your body from last night."

I stifle a groan. Not thinking about it.

"You have little to worry about." His eyes soften a tad. "You have a gift. Use it. I've seen the videos from the obstacle courses. When you're in the worst of it, you have no fear, only instinct, and that's what's needed out there."

I want to scream at him. One minute he's threatening me, the next, he's building me up. But instead, I turn toward the window and look across the city.

"You have the edge over everyone. You're unique. You're strong."

I don't feel strong.

"What do you want, Heidi?" He's right behind me now and places his hands on my shoulders.

"I want..." I can't think straight when he's so close to me. I try to refocus my thoughts. "I want to be free." I turn around to find his burning eyes, and I notice how his breathing has become as shallow as mine.

"In another life...maybe..." He pulls me in close to him, his arms wrapping around my thin frame. I press my hands against his broad back, the side of my face resting against his chest and we stand for a while without words. What was he going to say? In another life I'd be free? In another life I'd live?

He releases his arms from around me and his eyebrows are drawn low over his eyes. "You will get through this next phase, you hear?" His voice has become demanding. "Just stay close to Arthor."

"But..."

"Promise me," he repeats.

"You're forcing me to make a promise I can't keep," I say.

"I'm not forcing you. I'm just getting you to commit."

"What's the difference?"

"Think about it. You'll figure it out." He briefly presses his lips to my forehead and then without another word, leaves my room.

* * *

Nicholas and Mai take the remaining seven of us to the UVC station—the official starting point of phase two. No one speaks the entire way, each of us engrossed in our own thoughts about what's to come or perhaps what has transpired. How many of us will die today? I glance at

Nicholas only once, and catch him looking at me. He doesn't smile, but his eyes turn soft.

After we exit the transporter, we look for the number sixty-seven—the capsule the Culmination participants are to leave in. Bumping shoulders with other participants, following after the others, I push my way through the crowd. I pass a participant who's sobbing. He has a huge red birthmark on the right side of his face, reaching all the way from his ear to his nose and from his hairline to his jaw. His arms are flailing and his representative is shouting at him to get a grip. The young man braces his chest, his shoulders jarring with silent cries, his ribcage rising and falling quickly with every strained breath. I think we all feel the way he does, but the rest of us are controlling our fears. Why can't he?

Noticing that I've fallen behind the others in my group, I run to catch up. When I find them standing by our capsule, Mai stands a little removed from Nicholas and the participants, and she's yelling at someone on the phone. President Volkov?

Nicholas extends his hand to me like a proper representative should, nodding confidently toward me, scrutinizing me. Is he still waiting for me to say I'll commit to getting through this next phase?

"Fine. I'll commit." I say.

He inhales, and his shoulders drop a half an inch. "Good."

"Commit to what?" Johnny asks.

"It's just something for the Imp and me," Nicholas says, not taking his eyes off me.

222

The UVC emerges from the tunnel with a swooshing sound, and I file onto it with the other Culmination participants. I take my seat and buckle my harness, and as the doors slide shut, my chest tightens. When I look out the window, Nicholas is watching me, his expression unyielding, yet melancholy. He nods and mouths something, and even though I can't hear his voice, I know what he's saying: "Partner."

I nod back, an aching weakness taking hold in my chest. Before I'm ready, the capsule whisks me away, but I continue to hold his eyes until I can no longer see him—and in my mind, even longer.

"Who's going to protect you now, Imp?" Johnny says.

To my, and from the look on his face, Johnny's surprise, Arthor declares, "I am."

Johnny huffs. "You think you're strong enough? You'll see, once we get out there. There's going to be so much going on that you can't possibly be there all the time."

"He's not the only one who needs to watch his rear," Arthor says. "So back off or you won't know what hit you."

"Hardly." Johnny looks at me with a devilish smile, the wheels in his head turning, probably thinking about how he'll finish me off. I need to stay as far away from him as I can. "Besides, I know your secret, and I know the best way to hurt you."

That could be interpreted in many painful ways. I feel the blood leave my face.

"Dude," Timothy says to Johnny. "Quit being such a jerk. We should hang together, us guys from Culmination."

"Yeah, the more of us that make it, the more connections we'll have once we become Masters," Abe says.

"You only say that 'cause you need somewhere to stay since your mamma kicked you out," Johnny says. "Besides, I caught Joseph dancing with Nicholas last night. And smooching. Betcha didn't know he's gay."

"What?" I exclaim. "You're absolutely crazy!" I know exactly what he's doing—turning everyone against me. After this, they won't know how to act toward me, just like people don't know how to act toward someone who's different than them. And instead of seeing a person, they see only a problem, in which the only two solutions are hostility or avoidance. I suspect they'll be avoiding me, afraid I'll be hitting on them. The imp. The gay imp. However, I doubt he knows that Arthor is gay, and this confrontation has a secondary effect: the more I deny being gay—saying it's crazy—the more I'll hurt Arthor. And of course it's already working because everyone in the capsule is either staring at me or avoiding eye-contact at all costs. "It's not true..." I look at Arthor and I see the subtle disappointment in his eyes. "I'm not gay."

"I saw the way you were looking at Nicholas."

"So what if he is gay?" Arthor's voice is bold. "I know several people who are, and they're actually some of the nicest people I've met."

"I don't care if they're nice. It's illegal," Johnny says.

I smile a little. "Well, I'm not gay, but I can definitely vouch for what Arthor is saying."

"I know someone who is gay, too," Fletcher says. "He's really nice."

"Dude, gays are just disgusting," Timothy says. "I was hit on by one once and...it was just gross."

"Seriously, are we really going to talk about this all the way to the obstacles?" I say.

"Yeah, Johnny." Arthor says. "We have more important things to focus on right now besides determining if we side with the gays or not."

With that, the topic dies down, though I notice that the guys look at me with guarded eyes. We settle into a conversation about Culmination and how unfair the hierarchy is in our country. I learn that the Advisors are just as upset about their inferiority to Masters as Laborers are—maybe even more so—because they live between both classes, never being good enough to be a Master, yet not feeling they have the right to complain since they aren't as destitute as Laborers.

When the conversation ends, my mind wanders back to Nicholas. He's been paying a lot more attention to me than I thought. I've been such an idiot around him. Gosh—drunk? I exhale. But one thing I don't understand is why he kissed me on the forehead. It was so quick, like he wanted to do it before I could pull back and get it over with before I had a chance to respond. Maybe now I'll never know.

We emerge from the underground tunnel, and the capsule stops at the top of a mountain, overlooking a black desert valley. Even before I get out, I see multiple rows of white disks floating high in the air above something that looks like long, crystallized metal blades. Participants are already hopping from wobbly disk to wobbly disk above the jagged chasm below, white knuckling the edges when they land, and helicopters with reporters are flying above them.

Hot, sticky air enters the capsule when the doors slide open. I step outside onto the wooden platform and read the sign.

Phase 2, Round 1 must be completed in 10 hours. Afterwards, the disks vanish. Each participant's timer starts when his feet touch the first disk and only the fastest fifty percent will be allowed to continue.

Clearly, I'm not as fast as the majority of these guys—the thousand or so left—and the thought of having to compete against them makes me nervous. I step to the very edge of the platform to see if I can find any clues as to what the shortcut might be. However, nothing indicates that there is a shortcut, so instead, I assess how much force I will need to hop onto the first disk. It's not too far away, but far enough that I have to jump to get to it. I look down into the gorge and see a body, his limbs bent in unnatural directions. Grimacing, I look at Arthor.

"Is your balance good?" he asks.

"I've been known to walk on fences, but nothing like this. You?"

"Not even close."

Johnny speeds past me, shoving me off balance, and hops onto the first disk, crouching as he lands. "See you guys later...maybe."

"You mean you don't think you're going to make it?" I yell at him.

Johnny stands up and turns around, his feet firmly planted on the disk. "Oh, I'll make it all right, but I doubt that you two will."

Arthor looks at me and says loudly, "You're going to make it, right?"

I nod. "You?"

Arthor nods and looks at Johnny. "There you have it. See you across the gorge. Or maybe we'll be looking down on you as we pass."

Johnny gives us a dagger glare and keeps going, hopping from one disk to the next. I don't want to admit it, but by the way he moves, I can tell he's an exceptional athlete. Danny, Abe, and Fletcher follow Johnny.

"Good luck, you two," Abe yells.

"You too," I say.

Another capsule zooms in behind us, and the young man with the huge red birthmark on the side of his face gets out with four others. They fly by us, and start leaping from disk to disk, landing effortlessly, like dancers. I wonder how the boy with the birthmark managed to control his fear, remembering how he was freaking out back at the UVC station. It doesn't seem like balance is an issue for him at all, so why was he so nervous? On the tenth leap, however, the disk wobbles a little more than the other, and that causes him to lose his footing and slide off the disk.

I bring my hand to my forehead and gasp. I don't want to watch this, but I'm unable to tear my eyes away. At the last second, his fingers clamp onto the edge and his legs dangle beneath him. Then the inescapable happens: his hands slip and he plummets toward the ground, shrieking.

"No!" My voice echoes across the chasm. His body shrinks the farther he falls, far beyond what I thought he would, still not hitting the ground. Still screaming. Still dropping. When his body crashes into the rocks, the gorge is instantly quiet, like a prayer. I look up to see that many participants have frozen where they stand and are peering down at the fresh corpse. My eyes connect with a young man a few disks ahead of the tenth. For a moment, his face twists in pain, and then he pulls at his neckline and screams.

A friend? A brother?

This is not how I wanted to start this phase—my heart pounding so hard I think it might burst. I need to calm myself before I continue. Trying to balance with shaky hands and knees will get me killed quicker than the boy with the birthmark on his face.

Arthor takes my hand. It's cold and clammy, yet comforting beyond words. "We'll be more careful."

"Any clue as to what the shortcut might be?"

He shakes his head.

"Did you see how that disk seemed looser than the others?" I say.

He nods. "I think they're all coiled differently. Just in case we needed a little more challenge." He produces a noise that I think is supposed to be an attempted laugh.

I have to get the falling boy's screams out of my head before I can start. I close my eyes and try to think of something that might calm me and Gemma's face appears. I hear her laughter and before I know it, I'm back in Culmination, considering my choice. I shouldn't have left her. And where is she now? Did Master Douglas throw her remains into the lake? Or maybe the mass grave right outside of Culmination made for Laborers? I hear her yelling for me to win this for her. Somehow her words give me the strength I need. I open my eyes. I will win this for her.

"Ready?" Arthor asks.

"Yes. Let me go first." I force myself to focus on the disk in front of me instead of on the plunging ravine below. The disk's diameter is about the length of my height—small, but not impossibly so. "I can do this." Squeezing my hands into fists, I bend my knees, push off the platform, and thrust my legs forward. When I land, the disk wobbles, and knots tie in my stomach. I crouch down quickly, pressing my hands onto the glassy surface, so the swaying ceases. One down—how many to go? Looking ahead, I can't even see the end of the disks. Slow and steady, I tell myself.

I bend my knees again and leap to the next disk; it barely moves. I keep pressing forward, and by the eighth disk, I feel like I have the hang of it. But before I hop onto the tenth disk, I remember how it wobbled much more than the others. I jump as lightly as I can and when I land, the disk plunges a few feet down and rebounds so quickly that I become airborne. Coming back down, I crouch close to the disk. My palms are sweaty. Not good. The disks are slippery enough as it is. I peer back and see Arthor jumping from one to the next.

"This one's temperamental," I say.

He nods and gives me thumbs up.

I wish there was someone directly in front of me so I could watch him, but the others are so far ahead I can't remember which ones drop and which ones don't. I'm growing concerned that I won't be in the top fifty, but I'm afraid that if I speed up, I'll get sloppy and lose my balance.

I press forward, and every once in a while there are a few more touchy disks like the tenth, but soon I pick up on the best way to land whether the disk is firm or wobbly. As the day progresses, it becomes increasingly hotter, and my thighs and the bottoms of my feet start to burn. Yet the end is still nowhere in sight.

"Do the disks seem to be farther apart?" Arthor yells to me.

"Maybe a little." I pause to wipe the sweat off my brow, and automatically my gaze wanders toward the bodies at the bottom. It's too far to make out their faces, but I hope it's no one from Culmination. Suddenly, I hear a clap of thunder. I look up, and in the distance I see dark clouds that are headed in our direction.

"We have to move faster," Arthor says.

"We're not going to make it before the rain comes."

I pick up my pace, even though I would still rather go slow and steady. My legs are trembling now. Not from being afraid, but because they're tired from all the squatting and stabilizing, and my mouth is dry. On the next disk I slip a little and I let out a yelp.

"You okay?" Arthor asks.

"Yes." I know I can't afford to make these kinds of mistakes.

After moving slowly again for some time, the first raindrop taps my forehead. And then, another. And then, as if by the push of a button, the heavens open. The rain soaks me in just a few seconds. I slide my shoe across the surface of the disk. It's slippery—dangerously so. What do I do? Try one more disk and see if I can manage to land without falling? If I wait too long, I'll never be in the top fifty percent, and though I don't know exactly how long we've been going, I would estimate that we have about half our time left.

I have to chance it.

"I'm going to try," I tell Arthor who is one disk behind me.

"No."

"If we wait, we'll never make it!" I yell.

"Hold on." His hands hit his temples and rain drips off his short, red hair. "Let me jump to you and if I slip, you can catch me."

If he jumps to my disk and he slips, either we will both fall together, or we can hold onto each other, preventing us from falling. If I jump to the next disk and slip, I'll have no one to catch me. Arthor's suggestion is better. "Okay."

"Catch me if I fall?"

"If you fall, I fall," I say, reaching my fatigued arms out, ready to catch him.

"On three," he says.

"One...two..." He bends his knees. "Three!" He flings his arms and legs in front of him, but just as he lands right next to me, not only does he slip, the disk plummets toward the ground. My heart leaps into my throat. I grab Arthor's arms and open my mouth to scream, but not a single sound comes out. Just when I think I'm going to pass out, the disk stops mid-air, and Arthor goes skidding down the side of it. Still cleaving onto him, I fall flat on my abdomen across the rounded surface, and we end up hanging on either side of the disk—my nails digging into his wet skin and his in mine.

"I'm okay, you okay?" He's panting.

I manage to belt out a yes, but I'm losing my grasp fast—the rain making his skin smooth and slick.

"We have to climb up symmetrically. Together. Balance it out." His face contorts into a pained expression. "I'll swing my right leg up onto the top. You do the same. On the count of three."

On three, I kick my leg up—digging my heel into it like I did on Devil's Cliff. The disk wobbles a little. "Pull my arms," I say, and we come closer. From there we're able to drag ourselves up to a standing position. We cling onto each other for a moment, afraid if we move, we'll slip back off the disk. The raindrops fall heavily on the top of my head.

"We're going to be okay."

I look at my hands and notice that my fingers are still digging into his flesh, his blood beneath my nails.

"Sorry." I slowly unclamp my cold, cramped fingers, and any resolve I had to survive this course feels like it's being crushed in my chest.

"Heidi, we're fine." He touches my hair, but I slap it away.

I almost wish we had fallen so there would be an end to this. "How can you say that? It's still raining and we don't know how much further the disks go on." I pause to sob, knowing I'm not angry at him, only at my own fear. "And we'll never get back up to the disks now. We'll stay here and then..."

He grabs my shoulders and shakes me gently. "Heidi, Heidi, just turn around."

"What?"

"Turn around." I look up at him for a moment, his pale green eyes beaming, and glance in the direction he's pointing. There, right in front of us is a path. The four-foot wide alleyway looks like it's made of glass or plastic—some type of transparent material. But with the rain pummeling down over us, I can see the water pool around the edges. If we hadn't both gotten on the disk, we never would have seen it. Had we not thought to work as a team, we would have struggled our way forward until nightfall. And never made it. I remember Nicholas talking about plateaus, and I'm curious if he actually knew about this or if it was just a lucky guess.

"The only problem is, that the path is about five feet away," I say.

"And it could be a trap." Arthor rubs his palms to his face, removing the raindrops.

It could be. "But how would it hold water if it couldn't hold us?"

"True."

"We can jump together," I suggest.

His eyes grow determined. "Let's do it."

I instinctively take his hand and he squeezes mine. I notice how remarkably safe I feel with him; he doesn't expect anything from me other than friendship. "On three again?"

"Yes. One..." Will there be a firm foundation to land on? "...two." My knees shake and I'm sucking wind. "...three."

With all my might, I push off from the disk. Mid-air, and about halfway to the path, I don't know if I'll make it. I let go of Arthor's hand and thrust my legs forward. Landing with my toes on the edge, I contract my abdomen and throw my arms out in front of me, hoping that will make me fall forward. And it does.

Once I find my balance, I squeal in delight and give Arthor a high five. We embrace briefly, but know we don't have any time to waste. We jog down the road, passing participants who have gotten stuck in the rain. Some of them point and yell at us. Should I share my secret with them? It would only be fair. But the instant I see Johnny hovering above, I decide not to tell anyone how to get down here.

Chapter 20

After we have jogged for about two more hours—passing all the contestants—the pathway takes us down to a vast, concrete-paved area. Four long rows of small, white spacecrafts are situated in front of us, and each ship has a number on it and Newland's flag.

"President Volkov literally meant out of this world." Arthor's mouth drops open.

"You mean..." For some reason, it hadn't yet dawned on me that I would actually be going into space. I don't like it one bit.

There's a sign in front of the spacecrafts and I read it.

Memorize this password:

@w3v+04$*13nzZjiJ=?..:<6c4eigh802>1

Then get on a spacecraft.

"This is awesome," Arthor says, smiling. "My own spaceship."

235

"Yeah, but did you read this?" I point to the sign.

The grin on his face melts away as he reads. Tracing the edges of the sign with his fingers, he says, "I wonder what this password is for."

"I don't even want to think what we'll need it for up there." I look up into the sky. "Everything's life and death in these obstacles, so I hardly think space will be any different."

He nods.

I study the password for the next ten minutes, wracking my brain—cramming—trying to remember the order of the ridiculous amount of symbols. Being a prescription delivery driver back home, I had to memorize quite a few codes with both numbers, letters, and symbols, but nothing as long as this.

"I think I have it," Arthor says after an inordinately short amount of time.

"Seriously?" In school, he used to be a whiz at memorizing preposterously long words, words that I still don't know what they mean.

Arthor climbs into the first one, his hands running across the panel of buttons—a smile on his face. "I've always wanted to go into space."

"Yeah, I kind of figured that from your overenthusiastic reaction earlier."

"If I were a Master, that's what I would want to be—an astronaut. What better place to be?"

I can think of a few. "Good luck up there." I reach my hand out to shake his and he takes it, pulling me in for a long hug, his damp suit pressing against mine.

"Meet you back down here," he says sincerely.

He releases me, and I watch him press his index finger onto a small, red reader, causing the hatch to open. He gets inside and the next thing I know, the hatch closes and white smoke billows out from beneath the spacecraft. I step back and watch him being catapulted into space, vanishing into the clouds. I really hope I see him again.

I study the sequence some more, and when I finally think I have it, I get into the spacecraft right next to where Arthor's used to stand. The door closes, and at the same time, blue and white lights appear on the dashboard. The spacecraft hums for a moment before a cloud of white smoke swells around it, and two seconds later, my head feels like it's spinning out of control, my stomach like it's being wrung inside out. The ship shakes violently, and I close my eyes afraid they'll come out of their sockets. I repeat the long sequence in my head to keep myself from becoming too nervous.

Slowly, and the higher I climb, the shaking decreases. Once I reach a certain height, the ride is so smooth, it feels like I've stopped moving. I open my eyes and see a black sky dotted with thousands of stars. Below me is the Earth—blue, white and green—and for a moment, I forget that I'm afraid. I pass an orbiting satellite, the light gleaming off it. My spacecraft heads toward a large, gray space station—two identical diamond-shaped vessels held together by three rods—and enters via an oval opening. Was this space station built specifically for the Savage Run?

Gliding inside a circular atrium, I am sucked into one of the many small cells in the wall, and the narrow passageway seems to be lit the same way the inside of the UVC station was: with illuminate walls. I have no idea what this obstacle will be, which makes it difficult to mentally prepare for it, and even harder to stay calm. My spacecraft stops, and when the door opens, I get out in an excited hurry. To my surprise, Arthor is waiting there with a Unifer.

"Follow me," the Unifer says, and marches down the silver corridor.

"What's the obstacle?" I ask.

He doesn't reply.

"Do they control you so much that you can't even talk?" I ask.

The Unifer remains speechless. After taking a right and going up some stairs, he stops in front of an invisishield door. I've only heard of these types of shield doors that no one or nothing can get through—not even bullets or fire.

"Stay here," he says to me, waving his hand in front of the door so the clear shield vanishes. The Unifer instructs Arthor to go into the room next to me, and Arthor does as he's told.

I step into the empty room and peer out the apple-sized window. The other diamond-shaped section of the ship is on the opposite side of the gulf. Looking over at Arthor, through the transparent walls, I note how tense his body is.

The Unifer steps out of the room and with the swoosh of the door, the invisishield is back up. He presses a button on the outside and says, "Listen very carefully. Exhale all the air in your lungs and then do not inhale again, understand?"

I nod my head, as does Arthor.

He continues. "And you must each punch in the code to continue on."

Before I'm able to recognize that this is the commencement of our next obstacle, the wall separating space and me vanishes, and I'm sucked out into the black gulf. Everything happens so fast; I hold my breath, the freezing air assaults my skin, and momentarily, my legs and arms flail, not finding anything to grab onto. I open my mouth to gasp, but instead, the air is extracted out of my lungs. Remembering what the Unifer said, I close my mouth so I won't inhale.

Arthor is a few feet away from me—too far removed to grab hold of. My eyeballs feel very dry even though I feel like I'm crying. Fortunately I'm not being pulled into the big void of space, but I am moving quickly toward the unit on the other side. Right before I collide with the exterior wall, I reach my hands and feet out, and then crash against a freezing metal door.

Fumbling, I grab hold of the handle so I don't float off into the void again. It's only been about ten seconds, but I have to take a breath soon or I feel like I'll pass out. A keyboard with numbers, letters and symbols are to the right of the door.

That's what the code is for—to get back inside. My first instinct is to start entering the symbols right away—before I can even think—but I don't know whether I only have one shot at getting this right or whether I will have more chances.

Looking over at Arthor, who's at another door, I see him punching numbers and symbols. The keyboard flashes green and his door opens, taking him back inside. I stare at my own keyboard again and start to enter in the code, but when I get about halfway through, I freeze. I can't remember it. Within seconds, the keyboard flashes red.

Should I start over? Continue where I left off? I need to take a breath. In a desperate attempt to get some oxygen, I inhale, but instead of getting air, the saliva on my tongue starts to boil. I enter the code from the beginning again—this time able to recall the entire sequence—and the door opens and sucks me inside. The instant the door closes, I fall to the slick floor, gasping for air. The room almost turns black, but the more I breathe, the lighter the room becomes.

"Are you all right?" Arthor asks through the clear wall. His voice sounds hollow.

Feeling my arms tremble, I look over at him. "That was just a nightmare. I can't believe I remembered the code."

He touches his fingertips against the wall. Standing up, I meet him there.

"I wish I had your memory," I say.

"You passed the test. You had what you needed at the time you needed it."

"I'd rather run a hundred marathons than have to go through that kind of thing again." I look out the window and see other participants floating through space toward other doors. None of them should have to die this way. Not even Johnny.

We wait a few minutes for the door to open, but the door remains closed.

"Maybe they're waiting for us all to return together," Arthor says.

I stare aimlessly out into the blackness beyond the see-through wall. "Or do you think they'll make us go through that again?"

"Why would you think that?"

"Because our spacecrafts are on the other side," I say.

Like an answer to my question, the wall in front of me vanishes again, and I go sailing out into the emptiness. I know better what I'm doing now, so I'm not as terrified as I was the first time, but can one ever really stop fearing for one's life?

This time, Arthor and I float farther apart than before. Just like before, shortly after I hit the side of the space station and latch onto a handle. Right as I'm about to punch in the code, I read the plaque next to it.

Enter the code backwards

What? Backwards? Having no time to think about it, I begin to key in the code, and for some reason, I am able to enter it without really struggling. The door opens. I'm back inside a room full of oxygen. How did I manage that so easily? I look for Arthor. He was just at the door three doors down from me. To my surprise, the backdoor to my room opens, and I rush into the corridor to search for Arthor. But he isn't there. I run to the door that I think is his, gazing through it, and there he is still outside punching in the code. He sees me and bangs on the shield with a fist. He can't do it. I slam my hand against the invisishield.

"Arthor!"

He shakes his head, as if to clear it, and his brows grow dark over his eyes. Punching in the code again, his face turns redder. And redder. Purple. I stop breathing. "Arthor."

Finally the shield opens and he is pulled into the room again. My hands rest against the transparent sliding door, my eyes intently on him.

Coughing, he looks up, saliva dripping from his mouth onto the floor, and when our eyes meet, I smile.

The Unifer leads us back to our spacecrafts, and soon I'm reentering the atmosphere. The spacecraft starts to vibrate. Then it shakes. I grab onto the straps of my harness and close my eyes, surrendering to the jagged movements. Approaching the ground, the shaking decreases, and I reopen my eyes. My spaceship has slowed down considerably, as if it's floating down from the sky.

Below me, I see two participants hopping onto bikes. I smile. Our next challenge should be a breeze for me. I see someone sprinting toward the bikes; I think it's Arthor. There are three spacecrafts that lie in a green field next to where the hundred or so other spacecrafts wait. The rest must still not have made it here yet, so I'm feeling pretty confident that I'll be able to finish in the top fifty percent. Then I notice that to the side of the three spacecrafts, stands a guy dressed in black. He almost looks like Johnny, but it's difficult to see him from here. I notice that he is carrying a long, cylinder-shaped object on his shoulder and he's aiming the device directly toward me.

Every single muscle in my body freezes. What's happening?

Just as I finish thinking the thought, a sudden burst of light flares from the guy's shoulder, launching a missile.

Three seconds. That's exactly how long it takes the missile to collide with my spacecraft. And my last waking thought is I don't have to pretend to be someone I'm not anymore. Finally, I'm free.

Chapter 21

When I wake up, all I can feel is an intense burning sensation across my abdomen, hands, and face. The burns feel like a thousand needles stabbing my skin at once and my muscles keep tensing, unable to relax through the pain. The air around me vibrates, creating a buzzing sound, and the surface beneath my back is cold and unyielding.

Where am I?

When I try to open my eyes, my eyelids stick together. I eventually manage to lift my right eyelid and see that I'm inside a white cell without doors or windows. There's a symbol on one of the walls that looks like a rod of lightening. The cell must be electrified.

After the missile hit my spacecraft, there was a bright light, a plume of flames, and black, thick smoke. That's all I remember before everything went black. President Volkov must have found out my secret after Johnny tipped him off. I can't think of anyone I hate more right now than Johnny. And was that Johnny down there? It was too hard to tell.

But somehow, having President Volkov find out comes as a relief. Now I don't have to hide anymore, pretend to be someone I'm not, put on a façade just so I can race to be free; there's freedom in the truth, however small that freedom might be. My chest slumps. I was so stupid to enter the Savage Run; I should have stayed home, but then again, I couldn't have because then Master Douglas would have killed Gemma and me.

Wait, no—the memory of Gemma being shot comes as a sudden stab to my chest. She's already dead. Gemma. How could I forget? I sob only once, for the contraction of my abdomen feels like my skin is being ripped off my flesh. I try to sit up, but even with the tiniest of movements, I wince in agony. Every inch of my body hurts, and I'm certain I have more than one broken bone. How could I not? Having fallen from the sky.

Studying my hands, I see that the skin is red and blistered. I'm afraid to look, but the rest of my body must be equally as burned—if not more. For the next few minutes, I lie as motionless as I can, but there's no relief from the pain whether I'm moving or lying still.

Finally, pushing through the pain, I gather the little strength I have and sit up. Screaming, spitting and groaning as I pant, I rise to my feet. My right foot feels like there's something loose inside, and it hurts so much that I can't put any pressure on it. I go to lean on one of the walls, but then I remember that they're electrified.

"Help!" I yell. "Help!"

I wait in the obscure chamber. Wait to be killed, or wait for someone to rescue me. President Volkov knows; it's the only explanation. But if he found out I am a girl and he wanted me out of Savage Run, couldn't he just have shot me dead? Maybe he'll think I will go away if he sends me back home. Or maybe he's not certain that I'm a girl and he wants to verify it before he kills me. On the other hand, the thought is a little ridiculous—I hardly think President Volkov has time to deal with a young girl like me—but why else did all this happen?

But the worst part isn't that he found out. The worst part is that I have to sit here defenseless and try to anticipate what my punishment will be. Smaller transgressions than mine frequently result in the death penalty.

There's a clicking sound, followed by one of the walls fading, revealing a Unifer holding a cup. "Drink up." He hands me the cup and waits.

I peer down at the neon green liquid. "What is it?"

"You can either drink it or I can pour it down your throat."

Not wanting him to touch any part of me, I press the cup to my lips and swallow the cold beverage. With no consideration for my burns or possible broken bones, the Unifer grabs my arm, and pulls me into the hallway.

When I put pressure on my right foot, I let out a cry and can barely keep my feet from giving out under me. He hauls me down the short, gray hallway, and I'm certain he's either taking me to President Volkov or to be executed. Unifers run down the hallway, passing us on the right.

The Unifer pushes open a door that leads to a set of stairs. He's moving so fast that I can barely keep up, and now I'm sucking wind and my lungs burn. I start to cough. At the bottom of the staircase, he opens another door that leads us into a large foyer. The place is crawling with Unifers in their blue and green uniforms, but there's one person that catches my eye. He's dressed in black and gray, and he's looking right at me, like we're the only two people in the room, like the distance across the divide is nothing. Nicholas runs toward me, and with the last morsel of willpower I have, I wrench my arm out of the Unifer's clasp, stumble toward Nicholas, and sink into his arms. The room spins around me again, and I vanish into the blackness.

* * *

When I wake up, I'm completely naked and my body is submerged in blue liquid in a metal tub. The liquid tingles on my skin and the only thing that still burns a little is my face. I look at my hands, noting that the blisters are gone. Nicholas must have brought me here. Well—there's no hiding the fact that I'm a girl anymore, and most likely, the entire world knows now. The thought scares me half to death so why do I feel like the greatest burden has been removed from my chest?

A short, curvy nurse enters and gives me a smile. "Hello, Heidi. Can you hear me?"

"Yes." I move my hands in front of my chest to cover up, and to my amazement, it doesn't hurt.

The nurse checks the monitor I'm hooked up to. "My name is Paula and I'm your nurse. Now don't mind me, sweet thing. I've seen it all a million times. Everything looks great." She dips a washcloth in the bath, and wrings it over my face, immediately removing the stinging. "You have one more hour in there and that should be enough to take care of the burns and broken bones. In the meantime, can I get you something to drink?"

"Water." I hear footsteps, followed by a door closing, then silence. The door opens again, and the nurse hands me a white cup with a straw in it. When I suck on the straw, cold water enters my mouth and runs down the inside of my throat, quenching my thirst. I take a deep breath, and to my relief, again, the motion doesn't hurt.

"I'll be back in an hour. If you need help, sweetie, press this." She points to a red button by the tub before strolling out the door. She dips the washcloth in the blue liquid again and twists it over my face so the fluid cascades over my skin. Then she leaves.

After an hour has passed, the nurse helps me out of the bath. My foot is a little sore, but I have no problem putting all my weight on it. Glancing into the mirror across the room, I see that red marks cover my abdomen, arms, and face, where the burns used to be. But they don't sting at all. She helps me slip on a white gown and tells me to sit in the wheelchair. She wheels me down a long, white corridor with lots of doors, and takes me into another room where two Unifers stand guard. I think I recognize one of them as Nicholas' bodyguard.

Inside the room, Nicholas lies on a hospital chair curled up into a ball—his eyes shut and his mouth slightly open. He looks like he could be just any other guy—so young and full of hope—not someone who constantly struggles to play by a tyrant's rules, not like the next president of Newland. The nurse helps me into the bed and hooks me up to new monitors.

"How are you feeling, sweetheart?" she asks.

"Much better, thank you."

"I'll be right around the corner if you need me." She exits the room, closing the door behind her.

As if on cue, Nicholas opens his eyes, stretches his legs out, and plants them on the floor. When he sees me, it takes him no time at all to stride across the room to my bed. He sits down next to me and briefly strokes my arm while looking into my eyes. There's so much care as he caresses me, so much tenderness.

I don't know exactly why, but I can't stop myself from leaning forward and wrapping one of my arms around his neck. Very gently, he scoots closer to me and he eases his arms around my back, his palms resting against the skin where my hospital gown doesn't cover. I wrap my other arm around his neck, too, and bury my face in his chest. Tears fill my eyes, and I start to breathe erratically. He pulls back and strokes my hair, kissing the wetness from my cheeks and the edge of my mouth, his breath playing like butterflies on my face. We embrace again, and he holds me until I'm able to stop the sobs. This must be one of those moments I've heard about, when after having gone through a traumatic experience, you need someone to connect with. And since Nicholas is close right now, he's it. Or is it more? He's been there for me, and showed me kindness, confidence, and encouragement. He waited for me in a hospital, for how many hours, I don't know.

"How are you feeling?" He strokes the last tear on my cheek away with his thumb.

His touch sends a dull, achy current through me and I want the space between us to be nothing like it was just a second ago. "How...did I get here?"

"I brought you here in an ambulance."

"Before that. Does your father know? Why did they release me?"

"Are you up to hearing the whole story?"

"Yes."

He clears his throat. "Right before you returned to earth, my father announced to the benefactors that a girl had registered illegally, and that the penalty in our country is execution."

"Johnny told him."

"Yes. Within minutes of your spacecraft being shot down, Dr. and Mrs. Konders had contacted the benefactor in Normark, and every last one of them threatened to withdraw their funding if my father didn't let you continue."

"Why would they do such a thing?" Then I remember. "Oh, they have a daughter who competes. And they're your friends."

"More like...family. In Normark, like in most countries around the world, slavery has been abolished for decades. There are no classes—everyone is equal. Women are equal. It's a beautiful thing. Dr. Konders knew the rules going in; only males were allowed to register. But when he learned that you were going to be killed...he wouldn't have it."

"I know the countries agreed to host Savage Run because of the oil they'll receive, but why did your father get the other countries involved? What's in it for him?" I ask.

"I'm not sure, but whatever it is, he's doing it to gain more power. And it's a way in which he can demonstrate that he's a charitable person. Giving to those who cannot give to themselves." He scoffs.

"So will he let me continue?" I ask.

"Yes." His voice almost sounds disappointed.

"Why didn't he just kill me?"

"I think he tried to...but somehow you survived, and by then, Dr. Konders had contacted him." He takes my hand and squeezes it.

"I saw someone aiming the missile toward me."

"Who?"

"I'm not sure, but for a moment I thought it looked like Johnny."

His eyes widen just a tad. "Oh."

I lean my head back into the pillow. "Who's paying for me to be here?"

"The Konders."

"Did you have anything to do with that?"

"No, they just volunteered."

"So does everyone know that I'm a girl now?" I ask.

He shakes his head. "Except for the benefactors. It was part of the deal: keep your gender a secret."

I pause for a moment, thinking about how liberating it felt not to have to hide the truth anymore, trying to wrap my mind around going back to being Joseph again. "What if I want to continue as myself?"

He shakes his head. "That's not an option."

I punch my fist into the mattress. "I'm doing it." I can't live a lie anymore; pretend to be something I'm not.

"Just wait until the end, Heidi. Revealing it now won't do you any good. It will only give my father more of a reason to try and have you killed off."

"No. I have to do this. This way—I don't know—I guess I can prove that I'm just as good as anyone else."

His eyes turn soft. "You already are just as good—better even."

Should I continue on as Joseph? Maybe Nicholas knows something I don't—like what President Volkov might do if I defy him—and I should do as he says. Plus, there is danger in my real identity; I'm the only female participant out there and could easily be taken advantage of. I will be looked upon as weak. But deep down, I know I can't go on pretending. Not for a single second. Not wanting to talk about it anymore, I change the subject. "How long have I been out for?" I ask.

"Since yesterday."

"So it starts again tomorrow?"

"Yes—my father excused you from the last round in phase two due to the accident. And don't worry, you'll be back to your normal self by then."

"What about Arthor, is he all right?"

"There are about four hundred participants left. But of course, Arthor made it. He made the top ten percent, actually."

I want to ask about the others, but I am too tired right now.

The right side of his lips rises and he glides his warm hand between mine so our fingers interlace.

I look down at our joined hands, completely confused by the fact that with a single touch from him, I feel like I could entrust him with everything that I am and hope to become.

"Are you able to watch the obstacle courses?"

"Yes—there are cameras throughout so we can see most of it. But I don't like watching you out there. It scares me."

Being strong, I know how to do that—it's familiar. Being vulnerable—that's dangerous. But with Nicholas, I want to go there. He makes me feel safe.

"I need to visit the other participants." He stands up and heads toward the door before I'm able to stop him.

I want to say that I need him to stay, but words are too far lost to speak. Finally I'm able to blurt out, "Wait."

He turns around.

"Can I talk to Mai?"

"I'll send her in. See you at the benefit." He cracks the door open, and looks straight at me, his blue eyes lingering on my face for a long while. He turns to leave, but before he does, he glances over his shoulder. "Oh, and you'll be staying back in Volkov Village tonight in the room you were in before. It will be taking you to the O-Region."

Volkov Village? The hole in the floor toilet. Great. No mattress. I guess I can handle anything for one night.

Chapter 22

Just when I throw my legs over the side of the bed to see if it hurts to stand up, the door opens. Mai enters with a garment bag draped over her shoulder and a bag in her hand. She's wearing a hunter green, spaghetti-strap, floor-length gown and her black, loose hair has green glitter on the edges. She stares at me for a moment as if she's seen a ghost. "How are you?"

"Much better than before, thank you."

She sets the bag onto the floor and hangs the garment bag from the top of the curtain partition. She unzips it, revealing a tuxedo.

Oh, that again. "I wanted to talk to you about something..."

"Okay." She pulls the tuxedo out of the bag and lays it on the bed next to me.

"I want to continue on as...myself."

She pauses and slowly looks up to me. "Are you sure?"

I nod.

"Have you spoken to Nicholas about this?"

I roll my eyes. "Yes, and he didn't think I should."

Mai marches over to the door and closes it. Returning to my bedside, she says, "I think you should do it."

"You do?"

"Absolutely. If President Volkov tries anything, the benefactors will know, and they will withdraw their support. That's the last thing he wants, so coincidentally, it's the safest move for you." Her black, round eyebrows rise. "Luckily, I have something for you."

"What?"

She reaches for the garment bag again, and this time pulls out a halter-top, floor-length mint green dress that has crystals on the bodice and the hem. "A donation from a..." she reads a small yellow card attached to the dress, "...Mrs. Konders."

I wonder if Mrs. Konders' gift is her way of telling me that I should continue on as myself. Her words come back to me: equal rights. "It's lovely."

"What about Nicholas? He'll kill me."

"He most certainly will."

I chuckle a little at her response.

"But it's time to start thinking like a Master. You are now free to make your own rules. And if Nicholas tries to stop you, he isn't doing his job properly."

Coming from Mai, her comment shouldn't surprise me, but it does. "Have you known each other for a long time?"

"Oh, for years. I used to be his martial arts instructor. It's a long story how I got involved in that, but in short, after having been assaulted for the fifth time, and almost losing my life in the process, I decided to learn something about self defense."

"Is that how you came to be a Savage Run registrar?" I ask.

"I'm the top Jeet Kun Do artist in the world, and since I knew President Volkov from training his son, he offered."

"Jeet Kun...?" I ask.

"The art of expressing the human body in combat," she explains. "The goal is to empty your mind, to be formless—shapeless—like water, and to have the ability to adapt to any combat situation."

"Was Nicholas good?" I ask.

"The best student I ever had. He mastered the discipline in three years and became the national champion."

"You were a Laborer before...?"

"He's the reason I've been able to reach so far. The pain he gave me drove me. When my husband and I married, we were both Masters. He lost his freedom to gambling. As a good wife, I followed him and took upon myself the status of a Laborer, but he soon became cruel and bitter. I was too much of a coward to stay." Mai's eyes glaze with wetness. "But it was so long ago, and I have almost been able to forget."

"I don't know if I'll be able to forgive my father."

For just a split second, her face expresses unimaginable pain and she looks away. "Remember, a strong person holds on and hangs in there until the bitter end, but a wise person knows the exact moment to let go. Let it go, Heidi. Set yourself free." She faces me and her eyes are set with tears. "Though I know, some things one can never forgive oneself for."

I want to ask her what she hasn't been able to forgive herself for.

"Let's see what's happening in the world. TV on."

A news reporter is talking. "So is it a wise move of President Volkov to allow the young man to continue to participate in the Savage Run, only days after he was shot down? And despite the numerous rumors alleging that Joseph Wood is a girl?"

"How did that leak out?" Mai says.

Johnny. Master Douglas. My father. The apothecaries I work with. The list is endless.

The reporter continues. "Or does his decision have to do with the fact that the benefactors suspected that it was foul play and threatened to withdraw their funds if President Volkov didn't let Joseph Wood continue? But in another story intimately related to this, Master Douglas..." Mai commands the TV off.

"No, wait!" I yell.

She looks at me, baffled, but commands the TV back on.

"Tragically, his seven-year-old daughter died in a drowning accident the day of the Savage Run Registration...."

I remember the happy little girl who planted a kiss so freely on Master Douglas' cheek. That innocent girl is gone, and for the first time, I feel something close to empathy for Master Douglas for having lost someone who brought such joy to his otherwise angry eyes. I wonder if Master Douglas knew that his daughter had died before he shot Gemma.

"...Master Douglas alleges that Joseph Wood is Heidi Cruise, and that she is an outlaw. He claims that Heidi kidnapped his housekeeper, Gemma Brooks, when Gemma was supposed to be caring for his daughter. Master Douglas has also stated that Heidi tried to have his housekeeper register for the Savage Run with her. When asked what happened to Gemma Brooks, he said that she's been put under strict house arrest."

My monitor beeps more rapidly. "Gemma—alive?" No, it can't be. He must be lying. To cover up that he killed her. But why would he do that when it's his right to kill any of his Laborers for whatever reason he wants? However, if he is telling the truth, Master Douglas is probably treating Gemma even worse than before. Way worse.

Nausea wells up in my stomach. If what he's saying is true, Master Douglas wouldn't have killed us. But now Gemma might be suffering even more because of what I did—because I abandoned her.

I hate myself and Gemma probably hates me too—or she should. I have to find out if she's alive, and I have to make it up to her—for all the times she's been there for me. That she yelled for me to run. I have to place first, second or third in Savage Run so I can hire an advocate and buy her freedom. And I don't care how much grief Master Douglas will give me; I'm going to make him sell her to me. I press my hands to my face and moan.

"Heidi, there's nothing you can do for her right now. Focus on what you're doing and things will take care of themselves." She commands the TV off.

"No, you don't understand. He's a monster, Mai."

"I believe it. Trust me, more than most. But there's nothing you can do right now. Now is the time we have to get you ready for the benefit." Reaching into the bag on the floor, she lifts out a matching ivory silk bra and underwear and hands them to me along with the dress. "Go change."

My mind still on Gemma, I take the undergarments and dress and lock myself in the bathroom. Alone, I let the clothes slip out of my hands and fall to the floor. I sink down, clasping my head, breathing irregularly. Gemma. I don't know for sure that she's still alive, but why would Master Douglas say she is? Is he trying to send me a message? Use her against me? Maybe he blames me for his daughter's death and wants me dead to avenge her. I shake my head, trying to center myself. I wish Nicholas were here; he'd help me get through this.

Somehow I find the strength to stand up and start to undress. Slipping out of the hospital gown, I catch a glimpse of myself in the mirror. My hair is greasy and messy, my lips chapped, my eyes red, and my skin blends well with the white walls. The ugliest girl in the world. Not that I was so beautiful before, but I used to be somewhat decent-looking when I had my long hair and rosy cheeks. Now, I'm just emaciated, pale, and plain old homely.

Mai knocks on the door. "You doing okay in there?"

"Yeah, just...just a minute." I slip on the silky bra. Doing something helps me get my mind off Gemma. Not much, but just enough to where I can function. The padding makes it look like I have a full chest. The boys will make fun of me—especially Arthor.

I step into the thin, silky panties, the fabric tickling my skin as I slide them up over my knees and thighs. Is this what Masters wear? The barely-there material seems flimsy compared to my coarse cotton underwear, and it's almost as if I'm not wearing anything at all. I slide the dress on, the fabric heavy and smooth against my body. Opening the door, I ask Mai to help me zip up the back of my dress.

"It's a little big around the shoulders," she says. "No worries. Nicholas' tailor is here."

But something doesn't feel right. "This is all wrong. I can't wear this. This isn't me."

"What were you thinking?" Mai asks, a curious grin on her face.

"Will you get the tailor for me?"

She nods and slips out the door. When Mai returns with the tailor, he wags his finger at me and smirks.

"I knew you were a girl."

I laugh, remembering the embarrassing moment. The tailor's eyes light up when I tell him what I'm looking for, and while he works to alter the dress to my specifications, Mai starts on my hair and make-up.

Mai works on me for about an hour and a half, applying make-up, curling my short hair, shaving my legs and armpits, and plucking away at my eyebrows. When she's finished, she shows me to the mirror, and to my astonishment, the girl looking back at me has rosy cheeks, red lips, and bright eyes. In short, I resemble a high-society Master. My hair is short and smooth, and curls playfully at the ends. My skin carries no blemishes and glows slightly.

"Now for the dress," the tailor says, handing it to me, and once I've changed into it, Mai takes me to the transporter.

On the ride to Casa Libre, I run my fingers over my palms, amazed at how I feel no pain; they're just sensitive to the touch. Thinking about Gemma has made me determined to give it all I've got both here tonight, and tomorrow, when I begin the third phase of the obstacle course. I have to survive, finish what I started, and free her myself. Nothing will stop me this time.

The sharply sloping, triangular building reaches the clouds, and it glows orange in the night. When our transporter stops, reporters storm around us, lights flashing like a lightning storm. I see Nicholas through the window and he's wearing a black tuxedo with a gray vest and tie. My heart hammers in my chest. What will he say? He's going to be so angry with me; that's for sure.

Before opening my door, he sees me through the glass and pauses, his mouth opening ever so slightly. I hear a deep man's voice announce: "Next is Joseph Wood."

Nicholas opens the door and offers me his hand. Still no hint of anger. The reporters storm around us and push their cameras and microphones in my face. Can they tell who I am? Do they understand that it's me?

"Hey look, it's old Lady Liberty," a reporter says.

"Where's Joseph?" I hear one of them call.

Nicholas pushes past them, hurrying me inside. We get inside the foyer and it's like entering a cave in a lightning storm. Nicholas stops and his eyes scan the room, his hand pressing against the bare skin on my back.

He takes my hand, pulls me with him up the curving stairwell, and guides me gently into the walk-in closet, closing the door behind us. Being this close to him where I can smell his musky cologne and feel the heat of his body against mine, my heart starts to race. I step back so I'm pressed up against the itchy coats, the smell of wool and linen filling my nostrils. "Are you mad at me?"

"Is that supposed to be...?"

"It's inspired by the Statue of Liberty. Your tailor helped me."

260

"Of course he did." His nostrils flare as he exhales sharply. "I am extremely disappointed, but that's beside the point right now. If someone offered you a way that you wouldn't have to go back out into the obstacles, would you take it?" His bright blue eyes cut into mine and for a moment, I'm speechless.

"Is that a hypothetical question?" I ask.

"No." His stare is intimidating.

"I...I have to have my freedom."

He exhales through his nose. "That could be arranged—later."

"How?"

He sighs, his breath tickling my face. "The Konders."

"I...I don't know. I mean, I want to live, but part of me wants to see through what I started. And Gemma...I need to..." He said I could have my freedom 'later.' "How much later?"

"I don't know. Months, but no longer than a few years." He takes a step closer to me and presses his fingers to my lips, trailing them down to my chin and neck.

I don't understand what he's doing, so I look away, afraid he can tell how beside myself his touch makes me feel. "It's too long. Gemma will be dead by then or wish she were."

He takes a deep breath and exhales slowly. "There's so much fight in you, Heidi. Sometimes it's better to just let it go."

I feel like all the air in my lungs deflates. "Let it go? Gemma might be alive. I can't let go."

His eyes darken. "I just don't want to see you die out there. It was frightening how close you got last time."

"It won't happen again," I say harshly.

"No—Heidi—it's just what happens out there. If my father doesn't get to you, the obstacles are made to push you to the limit and eliminate anyone who has a moment of weakness. One small millisecond of being unfocused will cost you your life."

"I know that, Nicholas." What's his point?

"I don't mean to—it's just..." His voice trails off.

"What?" I snap.

He shakes his head. "Will you just answer the question?"

"No, I wouldn't take the offer." I try to read his reaction as his eyebrows gather in the center.

"Why not?" he asks.

"I have to place in the top three so I can buy Gemma's freedom. And because for once in my life, I have control over what happens to me. For once, I can fight back without being beaten into submission. And I don't even know what the Konders want with me. Do they want to own me? Control me? How can I accept help from someone I don't know if I can trust?" I retort.

"Well you accepted the help from the Konders' at the hospital." His eyebrows rise.

"But that was different."

"I beg to differ."

Of course he does.

"Sometimes one just has to learn to trust."

"There's no one I can trust. Not even myself."

He gets this icy glare and for a moment I think he's going to blow, but instead, he says very slowly, "I just want you to be safe—that's all."

"There's no safety for me anywhere, don't you see that? Where I come from and where I'm headed is the most dangerous place of all."

He leans his temple against mine. "I...could be there for you. Help you."

My throat is suddenly hot and dry, and I feel my heart rate all the way down in my lower abdomen.

He chuckles—nervously, I think—and he runs his fingers across my collarbone.

I stiffen, unsure what he's doing, but not wanting him to stop. "I hardly know you, Nicholas." I bite my lip.

He knits his fingers through my hair, gently tugging at my neck, and his gaze lowers to my mouth. His breath trembles and then he presses his mouth gently to mine. The scratchy coats rub against the bare skin on my back and his kiss is silky and wet and soft. Pulling back, our noses still touching, he pauses as if waiting for my reaction. Wanting him to kiss me again, I nod my head, encouraging him, my knees feeling as weak as they did back before I jumped off Devil's Cliff. My hands find their way around his waist, beneath his coat and I pull him closer so our bodies press against each other. I don't know what I'm doing, but it feels so good to have him this close—to taste his minty lips. When he swivels me around and pins me against the wall, I think I could stay with him forever. I could accept.

He kisses my neck and my chin and our lips find each other again. This time, I feel it all the way down in my toes, and it's a little scary how my body screams to be even nearer to him. His fingers trail down my spine and I arch my back and lean my head onto the wall behind me. I don't understand this force that is so strong, making me want to give up everything to be with him, making me forget all the cruelness I have suffered at the hands of other men.

But I can't.

"Nicholas," I say, turning away from his lips, my body cursing me—me needing him.

He breathes deeply and leans his head against my bare shoulder. "Heidi."

I press my lips together, wanting to say that I need him, but I'm too afraid to be this vulnerable, to need someone. And to admit it.

"Just think about the offer," he whispers. "I know you've been hurt, but I promise I will never hurt you."

How can he promise this, the son of the man who wants me dead? "I can't do it, Nicholas. I can't betray Gemma again."

He lifts his chin and gazes into my eyes. "Then how can I help?"

"Don't ask me to abandon Gemma."

He squints his eyes. "Fine."

"We should probably go."

He nods and stands aside so I can pass. It takes everything in my power not to pull him in again and keep kissing him, to explore him in ways I have never explored a man, but Gemma is the one who truly needs me. I walk past him, his fists clenched, his jaw tense. I open the door.

Mai gives me a baffled look when I step out of the closet, but quickly reverts back to her stern self. "Ready?"

"Ready," I say, trying to cover up my flushed cheeks and pounding heart.

Chapter 23

I walk with Mai down the stairwell and pause about three-quarters of the way down. One of the reporters notices us, and within moments, they're snapping pictures and elbowing past others for a better spot.

"Is it true that you are Heidi Cruise?"

"It is."

A gasp goes through the room, followed shortly after by sudden bursts of clamor.

"There will be no interviews," Mai says. "Now, if you would be so gracious, please let us pass so we may get to our dinner."

The reporters don't budge so instead, Mai takes my hand and leads me upstairs. "There's another way to get into the ballroom." We climb the stairs and take the long, red and gold hallway to the other side of the building. Riding the elevator down, it brings us back to the main floor and into the foyer just outside of the ballroom. A large sign reads:

No reporters allowed beyond this point.

I sigh in relief.

To my great dismay, the first person I see when I enter the ballroom is Johnny. He's sitting at a round table with four benefactors, looking pissed off at the world. I'm not sure whether his sour expression is because he's upset at something in particular or just because, well, that's pretty much his usual expression. The tall windows on either side of the long, rectangular room have bright red curtains, and the walls and ceiling are adorned with gold wooden carvings.

When Johnny sees me, his eyes grow even more contemptuous; he probably thought I was a goner and that he didn't have to deal with this crap. The people sitting next to him aren't even engaging him in conversation, which tells me he's not very popular among the benefactors anymore. Not that I think they know that he was the one who shot me down, but I'm sure he's been revealing his true colors, turning benefactors off. I have to suppress a victorious smile. But then I change my mind and walk over to him and smile.

"Long time no see," I say. The room goes silent and I feel hundreds of eyes and ears on me. Has word reached here about who I am?

Johnny rises to his feet. "No hard feelings?"

"None at all." I coil my hand into a fist and sock him as hard as I can across the face. Being the gorilla he is, he doesn't move much, but it feels good to hit him. Never mind that my hand hurts like crazy.

He steps into my face. "I'm not going to hit you here, but don't think that I'll ever forget what you just did to me. Just wait until phase three. I've got something special planned for you."

I swallow hard, but before I can formulate a retort, Nicholas comes up next to me and grabs my arm. "Let's find our seats, shall we?"

"I know you two are an item. Don't expect me to go easy on her out there just because she's a girl," Johnny says.

"You touch her, and I'll make sure you never receive your status as a Master," Nicholas says.

The right side of Johnny's lip rises and he smiles at me like he knows something. I go with Nicholas and as we're walking over to our table, he says, "I don't like his smile. Just stay away from him."

"I'll manage him, don't worry."

Nicholas glances at me like he wants to kill me, but he doesn't respond. Walking through the room, I notice how few contestants are left. I search for the participants from Culmination, but can only locate Danny—he's easy to spot with the eagle tattoo at the back of his head. Then I see Timothy.

We arrive at a table where Mai and Arthor sit with six other benefactors.

"I'm sitting somewhere else," Nicholas whispers into my ear before he takes off.

The moment I sit down, the benefactors swarm me with questions. I answer as best I can and as truthfully as I can. "Of course I hope I will make it, and I feel much better than I did the same time yesterday." They laugh and coo at my replies.

After eating filet mignon, mashed potatoes, and squash medley, President Volkov takes the stage. I wonder if he smears his head with Vaseline, it's so shiny.

"Dearly beloved friends," he says. "We have all seen the way the Savage Run has changed in the past few days. Acts of bravery have abounded, acts of selfishness and ill will have emerged, and illegal acts have been exposed." The gathering laughs. "But more than anything, we have all grown to love the most popular participant we have. The only one who dared risk his life for another. Namely, Cory Cunningham."

Mai and Arthor glance at me simultaneously. Not that I think Cory doesn't deserve to be highlighted, but I suspect Cory's honorable mention has more to do with President Volkov's desire to diminish any attention I might garner than with celebrating brave participants. I don't care. I look for Nicholas and find him sitting just two tables away from me with Timothy. I haven't been able to locate Abe or Fletcher, making me think that they died or dropped out of the program. Or maybe they didn't make it in the top fifty percent. Whatever happened to them, it only leaves us five remaining.

President Volkov continues, "Cory's bravery and valor in the Savage Run has caught our eyes. A friend to all, a saint to some, his heroism is something that cannot be bottled and sold anywhere. And that such a young man would so willingly risk his life for others who are participating in this program, is beyond me."

I glance over at Arthor, who is the real hero in my eyes. I don't know what heroic feats Cory has done, if any, but Arthor's been a true friend indeed and without him, I wouldn't be sitting here today. Arthor gazes at me with no look of disappointment in his eyes, no look saying he should be the one highlighted today for his valiant deeds.

"You're my hero," I whisper, reaching across the table and squeezing his hand.

Arthor gets teary-eyed.

When I look at Nicholas, he quickly looks down, his face sunken. I don't know what to do with my growing feelings for him. I want to stuff them away because I'm afraid I might get hurt if I open up to him.

President Volkov continues talking about the highlights of phase two and even has Cory stand up in his seat when he reviews the events of the bike ride across burning beams. Even though biking would probably have been my best obstacle, I'm glad I didn't have to bike across burning beams.

"That kind of bravery, Cory, is what this program is all about," President Volkov says. "Now, please come here, Cory, to receive a medal for your bravery and valor."

"President Volkov showed me the whole damn thing," the old man with yellow teeth says. "He just helped someone patch up his tire. The greatest act of bravery I saw was between you two in phase one. No one was supposed to see that; but it was filmed by a drone and circulated in a secret email." His disheveled, gray hair, makes me think that he is or used to be a Laborer, but there's no way he could be a Class-3 citizen and attend this event.

"Thank you," I say. President Volkov must be showing different clips to selected benefactors.

After dinner, everyone scatters to different places, and I'm left alone with the old guy at the table. Out of nowhere, Johnny appears. "May I have this dance?"

"Uh..." I look around the room for Nicholas, but don't see him. But being here in a crowded room, I must be safe—the safest I'll ever be around Johnny. And I'm curious to find out why he asked me to dance. Besides, keep your friends close, your enemies...I stretch out my hand. "Sure."

Once we're on the dance floor, he takes my right hand in his left and reaches around my waist. I force my lips to remain pleasant.

"Trying to get Pres. to end your life early?"

"What?"

"The dress."

"Oh. I thought it would be fitting."

"Well, it sure had him squirming when I brought it up to him."

"How thoughtful of you to mention me."

"Of course. Hey, listen. I'm sorry about ratting you out."

"And shooting me down?"

Air hisses between his big teeth. "You saw me, huh?"

"Yes."

"It was an order."

"So you're President Volkov's mole?" I want to ask in a roundabout way if he knows or will reveal to me that he's President Volkov's son.

"Oh, I'm more than that. I run the show on the ground. Here's a piece of trivia for you: do you ever wonder why I joined Savage Run?"

"No."

"The real reason isn't because of my sickly grandmother. The real reason is because Pres. didn't want to see Arthor's kind secretly get into the Savage Run and smear the honor of his masterpiece."

"Arthor?" He leans his cheek against mine, and I angle my head away.

"He's a disgusting breed, don't you think?"

So he did know what he was doing on the UVC. "I don't understand what you mean," I feign.

"Stop lying. His unnatural inclinations make me sick. Those kind of people deserve nothing else than to be put to death."

"How can you say that?" I see crimson. "Just because he's not like you?"

"So you condone his ways? Interesting. I live to serve the laws of the land. I live to see justice done. And I will fulfill my duty in putting Arthor in his rightful place."

"You're planning to kill him?"

He nods slowly. "Before the first round started, Pres. cut me a deal. We can't have gays in the Savage Run, and we especially can't have a gay guy winning his freedom." He scoffs. "Pres. told me to get rid of Arthor and make it look like a natural occurrence. Problem was, you two started hanging around like turtledoves and I couldn't get to him. The kill needed to be clean and not cause suspicion. But then I found out you were a girl...and, that Pres. wants you dead, too. It will be a very interesting third phase."

Suddenly Nicholas' plan doesn't sound so bad. I'll trust the Konders' any day over Johnny. If President Volkov still wants me dead...I'll never have my freedom even if I do make it to the end. Even if I place first. So what's the use in continuing? Gemma. Arthor. I have to continue. Maybe...we can put enough pressure on President Volkov and get all his benefactors to withdraw completely in the event I'm killed.

"Heidi," I hear Nicholas' voice behind me.

"She wanted to dance with me," Johnny says, letting go of me.

"I'm fine, but I'm done." Johnny and I stare at each other for a moment and then Nicholas and I leave the dance floor. "We need to talk."

* * *

After I tell Nicholas what Johnny shared with me, he recruits Mai to round up Timothy, Arthor, and Danny, and then he has the chauffeur drive us back to Volkov Village. Johnny included.

We pretend to go into our rooms, but once Johnny is locked up, and we're dressed back in our Savage Run outfits, Mai brings Timothy, Arthor, Danny, and me back to Nicholas' townhome.

Nicholas crams us around his small, round kitchen table. He remains standing and asks me to share with them what Johnny told me, down to the last details.

"Now don't think Johnny will stop at just these two," Nicholas points to Arthor and me. "He'll do whatever it takes to take first place. All of your lives are in danger—more so than just from the obstacles. I know it's a lot to ask, but we need to protect you from Johnny. On my end, I'm going to talk with the Konders' and the other benefactors, to put pressure on President Volkov so he won't meddle with the obstacles."

"What makes you think he'll do that?" Timothy asks.

"I know my father, and he has his reasons, believe me." He glances at me briefly.

Of course, wouldn't President Volkov be excited to announce to the world that his "lost" son has finally returned, and not only that, that he won the entire race on his own merits. Nicholas has far more to fear than anyone can fathom.

Timothy's the first one to speak. "Dude, I...I don't have time to mess with this kind of stuff. I just came so I could be free. And no offense, man..." He looks at Arthor. "But I just can't handle being around gays. You creep me out."

"How can you say that?" I blurt out.

Nicholas places his hand on my shoulder. "Timothy. Just know that Johnny will be hunting you, too."

"I know how to avoid him."

"Danny?" Nicholas says.

"Timothy, you're an idiot," Danny says. "I'm in."

"Dude, don't hate me. I'm just being honest."

"An honest jerk—what a relief," Mai says.

"Can you just take me to my room so I can go to bed?" No one answers. "Please."

"Just one more minute," Nicholas says. "I can't provide you with any weapons—the Unifers would find out and you'd be disqualified—but just being aware of the fact that Johnny is after you will help you tremendously. I will also speak to a few other young men in the Savage Run—guys I trust—and they'll be looking out for you as well. If you can just survive the next phase, you'll be out of the thickest. Though I'm warning you, especially Arthor and Heidi, President Volkov may have other things up his sleeves."

"Like what?" Arthor asks.

"He knows about you. Most likely, he won't grant you your freedom."

I take Arthor's hand. "Do you still want to continue?"

He thinks for a moment. "If I go back home, it won't be any better. At least here I have a chance to..." He pulls his hand away from mine and crosses his arms in front of his chest.

"To what?" I ask softly.

"I don't know."

I don't want to say it, and he doesn't seem to either, but no matter what he chooses to do, he's going to be seen as a freak of nature, a misfit, and a diseased human being. It's the way I first reacted. It's the way our society has conditioned us to think. And what's so sad is that there's no way he can win here or at home.

"I just really want to win this so I can prove to everyone..." Arthor says.

Mai slams her fist in the table. Everyone jumps—Nicholas included. "This kind of 'poor me' attitude will get you all killed. 'I just really want to win.' Arthor." She shoots him a glance, her voice mocking. "Every single contestant who registered for this program wanted to win. But that doesn't mean they will." She stands up and starts to pace. "You have two choices, guys. One: Feel sorry for yourselves and go in tomorrow with a demeanor that reeks of weakness. Two: Stop your whining and claim your freedom."

For a moment, the room goes silent.

Mai says, "You're making this about gender, about sexual orientation? Forget about all that crap; your lives are on the line here!"

"She's right, guys—Heidi," Nicholas says. "If you want to win, you need to give up all the reasons why you think you'll lose. If you stay together, you should make it."

"Now, it's late and you need your rest," Mai concludes.

Mai and Nicholas escort us back to our rooms. I lie down on the wooden bed and stare into the ceiling as I try to go to sleep. Should I have taken Nicholas up on his offer? It would be nice to have someone take care of me for a change. But I don't know him well enough to trust him, do I? It's not as if I have a good example to compare him to. Take my father, for example. I'm sure he treated my mother the same way he treated me, and that's why she left. The woman who carried me for nine months and left me to be raised by a man who cares for no one but himself. The woman I've learned to both yearn for and despise in my quiet moments. She gifted me the most important thing I own—my life—but left without giving me a clue as to who she was or of how to navigate my existence.

And Master Douglas. Ugh. Another cruel man. Are all men like that? Arthor seems different, but he could just be acting selfless to gain recognition. Somehow I know that he's not that type; he seems genuine. Nicholas seems genuine, too. A warm feeling spreads across my chest when I think about him and how he kissed me in the closet. I touch my lips. There's something so fragile about us; I'm almost afraid to think about it, worried it will slip away. Does he sense that fear in me? Or maybe he recognizes it, and carries that same fear inside.

There's a knock, and when the door unlocks from the outside, I stand up and crack it open.

Nicholas stands outside in the hallway.

"Hi." Even at the eve of the final phase of Savage Run, my body responds involuntarily by turning into a thousand electrified butterflies.

"I wanted to see if you were all right." His eyes grow dark and there's a storm of passion beyond the deep calm.

"I'm fine."

"And I also wanted to inform you that just short of five million Newkos have been donated in your name."

"Uh...Wow! I hadn't expected that." More leverage on President Volkov.

He smiles a little. "Well then." For several seconds his blue eyes are on mine, and he just stands there without saying a word.

It has become awkwardly silent so I just blurt out the first thing I think of. "Why did you kiss me?" What a stupid question.

He gets a puzzled look on his face, but says nothing.

I open the door a little more, turn around, and walk into the room, hoping he'll follow. I hear the click of the lock and my heart leaps into my throat. "I mean..." I swivel round and our eyes meet across the divide.

He presses his perfectly arched lips together for a moment before saying, "Don't go tomorrow." In his voice, I hear a man who is as afraid as I am of losing what little we have together—that little something that is so much more than anything else I've ever had before with anyone.

"Why are you asking me to stay when we already decided that I'm going?"

"I'm worried about you—out there. And I do what I can to protect those I care about." He steps forward and takes my hand, pulling me in so my chest touches his.

I look down, but he puts his hand underneath my chin, raising my eyes to his. I have stopped breathing completely and nothing and everything makes sense at the same time. I can't think at all when he is so near and for whatever reason, right now, I'd give him whatever he asked for. My mouth parts as we stand in this moment that has stopped the world.

"You don't have to go," he says. "I can take you to the Konders'."

I step away so I can think clearly, bracing my chest. "Haven't you been listening to me? I have to get Gemma. I can't leave Arthor."

"You don't owe either of them anything."

I swivel around, and suddenly my pulse rises. "I owe them everything! Never mind. You wouldn't understand." I move into the shadows of a wall, deeper and farther away. "Why are you trying to talk me out of this?"

"Because I'm afraid, okay?" His hand hits his temple and his voice cracks.

For an instant I'm stunned into silence. "President Volkov's son—afraid?"

"I can't stop worrying about you, that you'll...before I can get to know you and before I've had the chance to tell you..."

I stare at him in silence.

"Heidi, I can't explain it, but when I'm around you, everything makes sense." He strokes my arm.

I feel it too. It's like I'm able to do things I couldn't before, be braver, stronger, more. But something holds me back from saying it and instead, I say, "I...I don't know what you mean." My words taste like ashes in my mouth.

The muscles in his shoulders and arms tense beneath his Savage Run shirt. He groans.

"What?" I say as ignorantly as I can. I'm a horrible person, but in the short time we have left I can hardly get him to understand that I just can't trust any man. I can't allow myself to be vulnerable.

"If you can't even be honest about how you feel, what's left of life to live?"

"It would never work and if you were smart, you'd see that, too." Not only have I told him he's stupid, I've managed to tell him we're no good for each other. Both of which are lies and I hate myself right now.

"Is that the kind of crap you tell yourself?" His eyes gleam with anger.

"It's not crap, it's..." I pull further back, farther into the shadows until a cold wall presses against my back.

The muscles in his jaw tense. "Do you want me to leave?"

"No." The word just tumbles out.

"Then what do you want?" He pinches the bridge of his nose.

"I just...I don't know," I want to get away, want to be out of this uncomfortable situation, but my body won't budge like I'm commanding it to. Instead, I find myself approaching him, taking his hand to draw him close, and pressing my lips to his. I just want to be safe. And being with him makes me feel safe. Nicholas cradles my head in his hands, his mouth moving across mine and when I feel their wetness, I open my lips and a moan escapes. "I'm no good for you."

"Let me be the judge of that." His mouth meets mine again and he kisses me with so much tenderness, my fear seems to melt away. His kiss grows passionate and when his tongue briefly meets mine, I gasp and my senses become lost in the moment. His hands find their way to my back, underneath my shirt, and his palms are hungry and warm and strong. Strong arms that are gentle and kind, not harsh and cruel.

He kisses me deeply one more time and then he reaches around my shoulders, cocooning me in his arms.

"I'm so tired of trying to be strong all the time. And I'm scared. But I can't give up until Gemma's safe." A weight drops from off my shoulders.

"You already are strong. And I'm scared, too. I'll do everything I can to help you get Gemma." He kisses me on top of my head. "There are many things I don't know, but the one thing I do know, is that when I'm around you, I feel like I've finally come home."

I look up into his eyes and kiss him briefly.

He smiles. "I should go. I just didn't want you to go out there tomorrow not knowing that I care."

I watch him leave my room, and this time, I slip into a deep sleep almost right away.

Part 3

The Choice

Chapter 24

Early the next morning, I dress in my last Savage Run Uniform: a red tight-fitted suit with black stitching, a yellow saber-toothed tiger's head on the front, and my name written on the back. Now that the news is out, at least I don't have to squeeze my breasts flat.

When I get outside the Nissen hut, Timothy, Arthor, and Danny stand in a triangle. Johnny stands by himself with his legs wide apart and his arms crossed in front of his chest as if he thinks he owns the place. Nicholas and Mai stand to the side and are talking quietly. I inch close to them to see if I can hear some of their conversation since they don't seem to notice that I have come out.

Mai whispers, "Why did she have to leave? When she was there, I knew where I had her; she was safe."

When she was there? Who is 'she' and where is 'where?' I knew where I had her? Who are they talking about? Me?

"You of all people," Nicholas says, "should know that freedom is more important than being safe."

I move my head discreetly in their direction, but then Nicholas notices me. "Heidi. Good morning."

Mai turns away from me and walks directly over to Arthor. I'm not quite sure what to say. Does Mai know me from somewhere? No, she couldn't be talking about me. She wouldn't keep that from me, would she? I look at Mai, but she has her back to me so I can't see her expression.

"Listen up, everyone," Nicholas says, and the others gather around. Mai's gaze is down. I focus on what Nicholas says instead. "In this phase, you'll be in the volcano lands, you'll crawl through the Caves of Choice, and you'll brave Savage Jungle—all in the O-Region."

The thought of creeping through the caves makes it difficult to breathe. When I was five, my father locked me in the chest that he keeps next to the couch. I overslept and he wanted to teach me a lesson so he kept me in there for an entire day without food and water. Since then, whenever I'm in an unusually tight space, I start to hyperventilate.

No one speaks as we make our way down the hill toward the entrance where our transporter waits. The guys are probably thinking about Johnny—I know I am. How will we manage to stay away from him and not get killed? We get in the transporter and head toward Volkov Airport. On our way, I see a half dozen drones following us. I wish I could get rid of them somehow. I try not to look at Johnny, but it's difficult to avoid his prying eyes. I look at Mai, but her eyes are down.

Five gray cargo aircrafts wait on the runway. The remaining participants are at the airport, as are their representatives. A drone is hovering around 'Cory the Great,' as he's been dubbed by the news. The transporter stops about a dozen feet away from the aircraft I'm assigned to, and just as I'm about to get out, Mai takes my hand. I sit back down.

"Before you go, Heidi, I wanted to let you know how proud I am of you. You're an inspiration to young women everywhere and I am honored to have been your representative. You'll make it, okay? Just never give up."

"I won't."

"Everything is and always has been as it should be." She wraps her arms around me and we hold each other for a long time. Even when I try to let go, she continues to hold on. Her embrace feels like Ruth's, filling me up with whatever it is that I've been missing. I want to ask her about what she said to Nicholas, but I can't get the words out. And besides, if she says she knows me from somewhere, we don't have time to talk about it now. Maybe I'll bring it up after I finish the last phase.

"I'll see you on the other side," I say.

Her dark brown eyes look at me with gentleness. "Be braver and stronger than ever."

It sounds like what Ruth said. I hope I can be.

I step inside the aircraft—it's a cargo plane with seats on the sides—and immediately a Unifer tells me to go all the way to the end and take the very last seat. Passing the other participants, I see Johnny sitting in the first seat. The right side of his lip is bruised and I can't help but feel pleased that I was able to cause him some pain. But when he smiles at me like he's planning my demise, the pleasant feeling vanishes.

I push past Johnny like I don't have a care in the world and make my way to the back, looking for Arthor. But he isn't here. I see Cory's white hair in the second to last seat. I gulp. He's intimidating. And President Volkov's pet. But it's not like I can pick and choose where to sit. Besides, perhaps I can get some tips from him.

"Trying to steal my fame?" Cory says as I sit down. But then he laughs and leans over. "I hope you do well, Heidi," he whispers. "It would show that pompous President Volkov that he's wrong about women. And wrong about you."

His comments surprise me. "Thanks." I buckle my seatbelt, and note how his thighs are about the width of my waist.

"What you and Arthor have done for each other throughout these past few days is amazing. I wish I could have been so lucky to have the kind of friendship you have."

"Yeah, he's pretty amazing," I say.

"As are you."

I wait for him to say 'for a girl,' but he doesn't. "Congrats on your recognition. President Volkov seems to really...look up to you." I try not to sound disgusted.

He leans over again and whispers, "It's nothing more than an illusion to promote President Volkov's cause. I know he's using me, but what he doesn't know is that I'm using him."

"Oh?" I look around to make sure no one is listening in on our conversation.

"He thinks he's so generous to offer us lowly Laborers and Advisors our freedom, but what he doesn't know is that one day, when we're strong enough, numerous enough, we'll rise up against him and bring equality back to Newland."

I'm shocked by his words. Maybe I have misjudged him completely. "Well, when you're ready to begin that fight—"

He laughs, his ice blue eyes dancing. "Let's get through this next phase and then we'll talk."

The trip to the O-Region takes a little over an hour. Cory tells me that when he completes the Savage Run, he plans to marry his fiancé, June—a Master. June's family won't let them marry unless Cory becomes a Master, so he had to sign up.

Approaching the O-Region, I wish I could look out a window, but there are none.

"Everyone up," the Unifer says. "Reach underneath your seats and get your parachutes. You have one minute to put it on."

"Looks like we're skydiving," Cory says.

I unbuckle my belt, jump out of my seat and lift it up. Underneath, crammed into the seat, is a parachute. My hands are already shaking so violently that I struggle to pull it out. I watch as Cory puts his parachute on and then I strap my parachute around my hips and shoulders and lock the belt, securing it properly just like he did.

"Goggles," the Unifer says, handing them out as he passes us.

"Have you done this before?" I ask Cory.

"Oh, yeah, about twenty times. It's a rush." He smiles and the goggles make him look goofy. "You?"

"No, but I'm sure it will be a blast," I say sarcastically. My fingers are cold and sweaty, and it makes it difficult to adjust the goggles in place. A few seconds later, the back of the aircraft opens, and a hurricane of a wind whirls through the fuselage. A god-awful smell that reminds me of rotten eggs streams through the cabin.

Cory inhales deeply. "Ah, the smell of volcano."

I wrinkle my nose and grab hold of my seat to steady myself as the plane bumps forward.

"Now would be a good time to locate the ripcord on the parachute," the Unifer says. "After you've jumped, count to ten, and then pull it forcefully to release the chute. At the end of round three, there are eight cages. Only the eight fastest contenders get a cage and will be racing for the top three spots. So get your butts down there—ASAP!"

I grit my teeth. One of those spots is mine.

"The first one across the finish line is the ultimate savage. Good luck." He lines us up and when he passes me, he gives me a strange look. Is it because I'm a girl? Or is it something else? I stand behind Cory and he's clenching his fists, exhaling sharply, and pumping his fists, like he's revving himself up to go.

Another Unifer at the rear end of the plane starts yelling for us to jump, shoving one participant out every ten seconds. The line is moving fast, and I'm not ready to jump.

Three participants stand ahead of me. A few seconds later, two. Cory jumps. I stand at the edge, seeing the yellow and red parachutes open beneath me, the lava-filled island moving by slowly. The wind tosses my hair and fills my ears with a loud hissing sound. I sway forward, the turbulence and wind pushing me back, making it difficult to advance.

"This is the end of the line for you," the Unifer says.

Before I'm able to make sense of what he says, he shoves me out of the plane, and I plummet toward the ocean below.

Chapter 25

My first instinct is to knot together in an infant pose, my arms and legs drawn close to my torso. But this only causes me to roll. Instead, I slowly reach my arms and legs out, and as the wind pushes against my limbs, the spinning decreases until I'm being steadily drawn toward the earth's crust. As my hands reach for the ripcord, it feels like they're moving in an ocean of molasses, the wind is so strong. Searching frantically, I finally locate the drawstring and grab hold. I slowly count to five—I gather I've already lost five seconds—and then pull the cord.

Nothing happens.

I pull it again, thinking I might not have yanked it hard enough. Still, nothing happens. Jerking it over and over, the Unifer's last words replay in my mind. "This is the end of the line for you." They must have done something to my parachute so it won't open!

"Pull the ripcord, Heidi!" Cory yells.

Passing him with frightening speed, I see him sailing downward with his open parachute. "It won't open!"

"Pull harder!"

Looking down, I estimate that at this speed it will only be a matter of seconds before I collide with the black lava rocks below. They rigged it, is all I can think. President Volkov won. I lost. I failed Gemma. I failed Nicholas. I failed myself.

All of a sudden, someone rams into me from behind and hooks his arms and legs around my body. I look back and see Cory. "You're crazy!" I scream as we spin out of control.

"I know!" He smiles like he really is, but he feeds off of this kind of insanity. "Hold on."

The ground is so close and I can see the green grass and smell the scent of it mixed with the sulfur. He helps me turn around and I lock my arms around his thick shoulders, my legs around his firm hips. We'll die together, and he doesn't seem to care one bit. He really is insane.

Cory pulls his ripcord, causing the second chute to open, slowing our plunge. "Brace for the fall."

Just before we hit the earth, I extend my legs and let go of Cory's neck. We crash into the ground—not so fast that I think anything's broken, but hard enough that my knees and ankles throb from the impact. Before we've recovered, the parachute catches a breeze, dragging us with it a few yards. Cory pulls a handle and the parachute detaches, setting us free.

"That was freaking amazing!" Cory laughs, lying on the rocks next to me.

"You're crazy." The adrenaline is slowly wearing off, but my entire body is shaking like a leaf.

"What happened to your chute?" He sits up and undoes his straps.

I remain lying down. "President Volkov made sure I got a malfunctioning parachute..."

"Are you serious?"

I nod.

"Nicholas warned me last night, but in all honesty, I didn't believe him. If this hadn't just happened, I still wouldn't have believed him. But he's right. And I'm here to help." He stands up and offers me his hand. I take it and he hauls me up.

While tearing out of my harness, I look for a sign or some type of instructions of what we're supposed to do, but there is none. However, it's hard to miss a few participants running toward the erupting mountain.

Cory's eyes are already staring the volcano down. "Let's do this thing."

Eight cages. One of them is mine.

We start to run right away. The ground is black with a few splotches of grass and white flowers. The island is a mountain shaped like a cone with a small jungle area and a white ash cloud billowing from the peak, lava running down the side of it.

"So are you two...you know..." Cory starts.

"Don't go there," I snap, running alongside him, trying to keep up.

"Just wondering."

We sprint up the rocky, black hill toward the base of the volcano, and I'm breathing heavily.

"I saw what happened," Arthor says, coming up beside me, panting.

"Yeah, that...prick," I reply between breaths. "I got a defective parachute."

"Volkov sure wants you dead," Arthor says.

I'm glad Arthor is here. I know I can trust him. We run all the way until we get to the base of the mountain. There are hundreds of buckets, a scale, and a sign that says:

Fill two buckets with twenty-five pounds of rocks in each. Carry buckets to the opening of the volcano.

Fifty pounds—roughly half my weight. Like the others, I grab two buckets and start to load them with black rocks. Once they're filled, I prop one of the buckets on top of the scale and weigh it. Twenty-three pounds. I add another two rocks and the scale tips to twenty-five pounds. As quickly as I can, I repeat the process with the other bucket. Some of the participants have found thick sticks and are laying them across their upper backs, hooking one bucket on either end. I head into the wooded area and search for a stick. After searching for a few seconds, it becomes clear to me that all the good ones are already taken.

Defeated, I return to my buckets. Wrapping my fingers around the handles, tightening my core, I lift them up. Fifty pounds is much heavier than I thought it would be. Some of these guys probably weigh two hundred and fifty pounds, and picking this up is like picking up a pair of shoes or a washcloth. But even though this isn't fair at all, I'm not going to let President Volkov win. Instead, I'm going to make my anger fuel my strength and determination.

I plant my feet firmly on the mountainside—the ground is black and crinkled like an old man's skin. A vein of red liquid with a black, cracking crust flows down the volcano and it's difficult to find a flat surface where my feet won't slip.

Cory walks next to me, and as I thought, it looks like the fifty pounds he's carrying weighs the same as a toothpick with cotton balls on the sides.

"You had better watch out down here," he says. "I mean, I don't see how you can make it with President Volkov after you. He could send snipers after you, plant bombs, poison..."

"I don't need to hear all the details."

"Sorry, sometimes I get carried away thinking about all the possible hazards. It's an obsession. But seriously, you need to take extra precautions."

I step over a rock. President Volkov just has to be right, and since he says girls can't be in Savage Run, he must make sure I fail so he doesn't look like an idiot.

As we get closer to the volcano, the air turns thicker and hotter and hissing sounds come from the ground. With each step, my legs burn, feeling weaker, and sweat is dripping down my face and chest.

Almost up at the top, I start to become careless about where I tread and with one misstep, I twist my ankle and fall to the ground. The rocks in my bucket go tumbling down the mountain, and the buckets too.

"You all right?" Cory asks.

"I'm fine. Just keep going. I'll be right behind you." Cory reluctantly starts to walk off, but when I assure him again that I'm fine, he moves on.

Arthor, who walks behind me, drops his buckets and catches mine so they don't go tumbling down all the way. He proceeds to fill them with the rocks. I sit for a moment, wondering if I'll be disqualified if I lose any of my rocks.

Would I be required to climb all the way back down to the bottom and get more rocks? There's no way we'll find all of them. I might as well start climbing back down because if I show up with a bucket weighing less than twenty-five pounds, I won't be able to continue. "It's no use," I holler after him, letting my arms fall to the ground. He looks up from where he's searching.

"There are just a few more."

I press my lips together and stare at him for a moment. "No, they'll disqualify both of us if you help me."

"There's no rule that says you'll be disqualified for accepting help."

I move my ankle in a circular motion and it feels like something is stuck inside of it, like it's locked. Arthor continues down the mountain without my approval. After a few minutes he returns with more rocks, but I know he didn't get all of them because one of my buckets is only three quarters of the way full.

"It will have to do," he says.

"No it won't." I stand up and look at the buckets, not placing too much weight on my injured ankle, afraid I might cringe and that he'll notice that I hurt it.

"It will do. No one's going to weigh the buckets up there."

Looking down the mountainside, I see Timothy and Danny climbing up together. And after them comes Johnny and in the far distance there are two other guys I don't know. "Crap."

Arthor turns around and sees Johnny, too.

I pick up the buckets. "You go ahead." I want him to go first so he doesn't see me hobble. I step onto my good leg first, but when I put weight onto my bad ankle, I feel a stabbing pain shoot up my leg. I grit my teeth and hold my breath so that I don't let out a single sound. I only have about twenty feet to go before I reach the top; I have to make it. Grunting and willing myself to walk, I continue onward. My ankle starts to feel swollen in my shoe, the skin pressing against the material. One step more, I tell myself. Just one more. I want to cry out from the pain, but I force the scream back down to where it came from and blow instead. Every step is another one conquered.

Finally reaching the top, I hear some of the participants discussing where to go next. I set the buckets down, glad that the climb is finished.

"Can you believe it?" Arthor says.

"What?"

"The sign says that the entrance to the Caves of Choice is down the volcano. The path is so narrow that only one participant can descend at a time," Arthor says.

Timothy and Danny arrive together and set their buckets down. Danny gives a high five to Cory. Do they know each other?

"I'll go first." Trying to hide the fact that I'm injured, I walk as normally as I can over to the edge of the crater and look down. The boiling sea of magma moves like an aggressive, live creature and heat rises into my face, and feels like it's going to melt my skin and eyes. The cave walls will be hotter than hell and we'll roast alive if we climb down. Surely they can't mean that we have to climb down here? All of us will burn to death and I'm sure President Volkov doesn't want that.

I glance at the sign and it reads:

Next obstacle: Caves of Choice—climb into the red caverns.

The sign mentions multiple caverns. This is only one. "Are there any other caverns on the island?" I ask to anyone listening.

"Playing detective?" Johnny asks, setting down his buckets. There's a second of awkward silence and a series of careful glances.

Johnny's eyebrows sink toward his eyes as he stares at me. Wiping his dripping wet forehead, he slinks toward me.

I swallow—fully aware that with one shove, he could send me into the volcano, but Cory steps in Johnny's path before Johnny reaches me. Johnny forms a fist and punches Cory in the face, sending him to the ground.

"Stop!" I shout—this could end very badly.

But Johnny doesn't stop. Instead, he kicks Cory in the gut and Cory rolls on the ground, grabbing his abdomen, gasping for air. Arthor and Timothy respond right away, immobilizing Johnny by grabbing his arms. Johnny wrings and kicks, spewing out obscenities. Slowly, Cory rises to his feet and I see that he has blood on the side of his mouth. He walks behind Johnny, calm and strong as an oak tree, and slams his fist into the back of Johnny's skull. Johnny drops to the ground unconscious.

"Should we just finish him off?" Timothy says, glancing down into the volcano.

A huge part of me wants that—I'd love to be rid of the threat of Johnny coming after me the rest of the course—and it would be a merciful death—he wouldn't notice a thing—

but I can't find it in myself to kill him. "Let's just leave him here."

"You're way too nice," Timothy says.

"I didn't think you had time to mess with this kind of stuff," I say, quoting what he said last night.

"I thought I'd try it out—being helpful."

Cory interrupts. "We have to keep moving forward. Just leave him here."

I look down the mountainside and see more participants closing in on us and the slight lead we have over the others is diminishing quickly. I peer into the pit again. "If we climb down there, we'll roast alive. There must be some other red caverns somewhere," I say.

"I...I think I saw one down by the shore where I landed," Arthor says. "It was a small cave and the walls were red." He steps over to the edge of the mountain and points. "That way."

One by one, they start to descend the mountain. Everyone except for Arthor and me.

"You're hurt," Arthor whispers.

I shrug my shoulders. "Just a little sprain, that's all."

"If it's so little, why is your left leg swollen?"

I look down and see that he's right; it is swollen. "Shoot." Why now?

"Want a piggy back ride?"

I'll be completely mortified.

"I won't tell anyone about your ankle, I promise."

The last thing I want is for any of the others to see that I'm injured, so they know they have an advantage over me.

I hop onto his back, wrapping my legs around his lean waist, my arms around his shoulders. He smells like a mixture between sweat and the outdoors and the perspiration on his neck and hair glistens in the sun.

Chapter 26

Arthor carries me almost all the way to the caves, gently setting me down by the base of a soaring tree, hiding me behind roots that stretch above my head and reach into the ground like giant veins. Leaning against the smooth bark, I stand on my good foot.

He peeks around the trunk at the red cave. "Looks like there are a number of them and they're crawling in." Turning to me, he says, "You okay to walk?"

"I'll try." I step onto my left foot, and right away, I feel a sharp pain. I grit my teeth, reapply pressure to my wounded leg, and take a step forward. With a little practice, and a lot of determination, I should be able to walk, though not without a limp. Arthor doesn't say anything, only waits patiently while I take another step. It's not easy making the muscles in my face relax.

"You good?" he asks.

"I'm ready."

We head over to the cave's entrance—one of several small holes in the mountain barely large enough to crawl into. I see another guy crawl into the blackness. My throat grows hot and dry.

It looks so easy for the other guy to go into the cave—like he enjoys tight spaces and darkness. I can be that way, can't I? My chest compresses the air out of my lungs and my heart thumps wildly against my ribcage. I have become the girl who was locked up in a trunk when she was five years old, not knowing if she would ever get out.

Trying to ignore my fear, I take three deep breaths and get down on all fours. I feel the damp, leafy earth against my palms and I peer into the cave, noting the hole is no wider than one of my bicycle wheels back home. My chest feels tighter, but still, I walk my hands forward onto the smooth, cold, red surface of the cave's entrance, and stick my head into the cavern. All I see is blackness.

Why am I doing this? I'm crazy. I can't do it. I crawl backwards in retreat, stand up, and limp away from the cave, interlocking my fingers behind my neck.

"Heidi." Arthor follows after me.

"I can't do it. It's too tight—too dark."

He walks backwards right in front of me, reaching his hands to my shoulders and pushes against them so I have to stop.

"Yes, you can," he says.

"What do you know about what I can and can't do?"

"I know that you're strong and brave and caring. And that you won't let an obstacle like this one keep you from your freedom. Or Gemma's."

In a moment of fear, I forgot why I'm doing this in the first place. Gemma. "If the caves were just a little wider, maybe, but they're so tight." I glance back at the hole in the mountain.

He squeezes my shoulders gently. "I have to keep going, Heidi. Every second we wait, someone else might make it to one of those eight cages."

The cages. What am I doing? Will I let one day from my past prevent me from having a life of freedom? I have to be in one of those eight. And I have to finish this course so I can find out for myself if Gemma is still alive. "I'm going in." I limp toward the cave's entrance, pushing my way past two participants, and before anyone's able to object about me sneaking in line, I crawl into the hole. Right away, blackness surrounds me. Normally the darkness combined with the tight space would bother me, but not now. I'm too angry with my father for what he did to me. Too angry with myself for allowing fear to set me back.

Pebbles and dust stick to my palms as I edge forward, and the air smells of mold mixed with sulfur. Within minutes, the cave's walls close in so much that I'm forced down onto my elbows and stomach, slinking forward like a snake. I try not to think about where I am, that I'm inside a tight cave with millions of pounds of rocks and lava looming above me. But the thoughts just creep back in. I grit my teeth and press forward, fighting to ignore the growing tightness in my chest.

I steer my thoughts to other things. Why are these caves called Caves of Choice anyway? It's rather a weird name for a cave. Do I have to choose something? Or maybe the path will divide in several directions, forcing me to decide which path to take, and if I don't take the right one, I'll be lost in here forever. The space around me is getting tighter—I find it impossible to exhale and my hands and arms feel weak and are trembling. I had better think about something else quick.

In an attempt to distract myself, I think back to Nicholas' and my first kiss. I recall the scratchy coats against my back, his soft, wet lips on mine...I didn't even give a second thought to being in a tight closet with him. He made me feel so safe and...calm. Just like Gemma. Just like Ruth.

I speed up so I can be done with this faster, however, soon I'm pushing against a pair of feet.

"Hurry it up!" I yell.

"I'm trying, okay? It's really tight in here."

I inch behind an unknown guy, the smell of dirt, popcorn, and plastic becoming too strong to bear. "Go faster." The walls are pressing away the air around me and my hands are cold and clammy.

"I see a light up ahead," the guy in front of me says.

A light? We've hardly been crawling for ten minutes, fifteen at the most. This can't possibly be the end of this obstacle, can it? There must be something else—I'm sure they wouldn't make this part of the obstacle so easy. Once we progress a little more, I see the light shining beyond the guy ahead of me, too, and I'm so relieved that I let out a laugh. I crawl forward, and finally at the end, I step out and into a large, enclosed cave.

The cave's walls are rust red, and are tinged with green and blue algae. Dozens of clear booths stand in a large circle, and inside the booths, participants are holding a gun, appearing to be shooting at nothing. One of the participants is grabbing his hair and is screaming. Just as his face catches the light, I see tears wetting his cheeks. What would drive him to such despair? The guy ahead of me runs toward one of stalls and enters it. When I step onto my left foot, I clench my teeth and grunt. The pain is still intense, but I can't afford to let anyone else know that I'm injured.

I hear a faint hissing sound, and the air around me turns cloudy. The mist rises to my face and seeps into my nose and mouth, causing me to cough, turning my surroundings blurry. I feel like the back of my skull is falling, and unable to hold my balance, I press my hand to the damp cavern wall, lowering my head so I won't pass out. What's happening to me?

Fortunately, it doesn't take long before the dizziness passes, and once again, I can make out the details of the cave. To my astonishment, there's only one booth left with my name on it— everything else has vanished.

"Hello?" I take a few steps backward, shrinking against the glistening wall. "Is anyone here?" My voice bounces off the rocks and echoes on down the cave.

"Please enter the booth," a female voice announces.

What is this obstacle course about? Cautiously, I walk toward the clear stall, open the door, and step inside. When the door closes behind me, my surroundings change in an instant: I am now in a large rectangular room with light gray walls and white marble floors. In front of me is a floating, square, glass counter with a small red button, and a message. I read it.

1. Once you push the red button, two images will appear in front of you. You will have five minutes to eliminate one of them by shooting it.

2. The image you eliminate will fade away and be replaced with another image.

3. Repeat the cycle.

There are eight rounds total. If you do not finish each round within five minutes, you will be disqualified.

Just as soon as I have finished reading, a silver handgun appears in my fist and my stomach roils as if telling me that this is the most dangerous—the most telling—challenge of them all. What images will be there? What will they be able to tell about me from what I choose to eliminate—and keep?

Reluctantly, I press the button. A red digital clock appears high up on the far wall, displaying ten seconds. Below the clock is a 3D image of my sandals and the quilt my mother made for me. How do they know about my quilt? It doesn't matter; I have to hurry. I aim for and shoot my sandals; though it would be difficult to live without those, I'm not going to eliminate the only thing I have left from my mother.

That was easy enough. When my sandals vanish, up pops an image of my father's trailer. The trailer doesn't mean nearly as much to me as the quilt does, but if I remove the trailer, where will I live? I can live with Gemma's mother so I shoot the old, ugly trailer.

In the trailer's stead, emerges Gemma's mother, Ruth. I shoot the blanket, but this is getting harder—more personal. I feel great. Three shots in less than a minute.

Next appears Arthor. Arthor? What is he doing here? Arthor against Ruth? Who do I choose? How do I choose? Arthor means so much to me, and he's one of the reason's I've made it this far in Savage Run. Why did it have to be him? And why is this a choice? This is ridiculous; that's what it is. It's just a game. It's just a game. But the rules are clear and I have to choose. Ruth or Arthor. Each time I lift my gun to shoot, I lower my hand again. Several times I do this, until the timer flares up red. Ten seconds left of five minutes. The five minutes have flown by all too quickly. It's time to choose. The bottom line is that I can't let Ruth go; she's like a mother to me. I'm so sorry, Arthor. I look around to see if anyone is here, but I'm all alone. Besides, it's just a stupid game anyway. Since I have to choose, I point the gun toward Arthor, hoping he'll never find out that I shot him.

In Arthor's stead appears my father. What is the point of this? Whatever it is, I hate it. Why do they need to know this about me—who I choose? This is abusive; that's what it is. Instead of the physical abuse I've gone through the past few days, now it turns mental. I don't love my father as much as I love Ruth, but he is my father. And though I don't linger on them a lot, there have been moments where he was caring. Like all those times when he repaired my bike, and the time when he gave me my mother's locket. I reach for the place on my chest where it used to hang. He could have kept it for himself—the only thing we had of value. My father's desperate face appears before me. "Heidi, don't do this! I'm sorry I messed up!" He looked so helpless lying there, taking the beating from the Unifers at Culmination Airport. And when Mai asked me if I knew him, I denied him. I hear his voice echo in my ears. "Heidi!" Blood flowing from his nose—the strongest man alive. Now...he might be dead. But there are so many painful memories, too, and it's his fault I'm not able to fully trust any man. A tear rolls down my cheek. My father or Ruth? Ruth is kinder, milder, like a mother to me. The clock is flashing red now. Five seconds. I hate myself for who I am. I aim the gun at my father and pull the trigger. I would never do that in real life, but just the thought of having chosen Ruth over him makes me feel like a traitor. Again.

In my father's place, Nicholas appears. Even before I am able to gasp, every fragment of my being feels like it's being shocked with electrical agony. How do they know about him? Or maybe they don't. Maybe the gas I inhaled earlier is interacting with some part of my brain to uncover the things or the people I care most about. But if that's the case, why did my sandals show up? I study Nicholas, his chestnut hair, his strong nose, his chiseled jawline, his kind, and blue eyes. I hear him saying that a stiff breeze would knock me over. Gemma was dead. And then I remember the magazine incident. I laugh. And he was so sweet when he first danced with me. His fingertips on my collarbone, on my bare back. I hear his deep voice trembling, asking me not to go. His wet lips on mine. His strong, hungry arms. Nicholas makes me feel safe. Ruth makes me feel safe. I've known Ruth for much longer, but the love I feel for her is so different than...do I love Nicholas? It's still so new, and too early to say. Eliminating either of them—I just can't do it. I can't betray Gemma all over again by killing her mother. Wait. This is just a stupid game. I kick the walls with everything I've got. I can't decide. I can't think—the gas must have done something to my brain because my feelings seem exaggerated. The clock lights up red, showing five seconds left. Nicholas or Ruth? Five. I don't know. Four. I won't choose! Three. Two. Despising myself, and not understanding exactly why, I point the gun at Ruth and fire. I

303

watch her vanish into a puff of smoke and it makes me feel like I have committed some unpardonable sin.

As the echo of the gunshot settles, I lean against the counter and swallow again and again to keep the tears from coming. I don't know why these images are making me so emotional—especially because I know they're just a figment of my imagination.

Without yet having seen the next image, I already know who it is: Gemma. I lift my eyes, and as expected, there she is in the very yellow floral dress Ruth made for her eleventh birthday. The rosiness in her cheeks is there and she's smiling as she braids her long, blonde hair. This is in another realm of difficult and I don't know myself well enough to make these kinds of decisions. Or maybe I do, and my hesitancy comes from knowing that the decision was made the very instant I saw Gemma up there. This entire process feels so wrong...so invasive, like the most tender part of me is being violated and used against me, and never before have I despised this program more than now. But even so, I have to choose, and whether I think about it for a second or an hour, my choice will be the same. By choosing her, I can in my own way repay her for what I did. Guilt is a ruthless ruler, and five minutes is way too short to make these kinds of rulings—even for a mind game. Lifting the gun, I point it toward Nicholas and pull the trigger. My heart is like a rock in my chest.

Who's next? There is no one else I care about more than Gemma or Nicholas, is there? Anxiously, I wait for the next person, wondering who it will be. But no person emerges. Only the words 'your freedom.' Panic expands like a demon in my chest. The words take me right back to Culmination when I was running toward the Savage Run registration booth and was forced to make a choice between Gemma and myself.

My gun raised, it vacillates between the words 'your freedom' and Gemma. If I don't have freedom, I have nothing. But Gemma... Instead of making a decision, I want to curl up into a ball and disappear and pass my will over to someone else. And perhaps in this rare instance, it is better to let someone choose for me. Sometimes having a choice is a burden—a curse—and requires a hundred times more than having no choice at all. I bring my hand up to my eyes and sob.

I can't choose.

I'm out.

I withdraw.

I lose.

Defeated, I lower the gun and set it on the counter. I don't understand this inability to choose—especially since I full well recognize that this is the end of it for me. I'll be sent home. Then it hits me; this is exactly what Nicholas was trying to explain: responsibility is a burden. But I refused to listen. Mai's words come back to me, too, and it's like everything I have been through these past few days is all pointing to this one choice. I have to rise to the occasion; be more than who I am. Be braver than ever. Stronger than ever.

And being braver and stronger means that I have to choose—that's the cost of freedom: to not give away my power to anyone else. If Gemma were here, she'd tell me to choose freedom, but what I'd tell her in return is that life is nothing without the ones we love.

Nothing.

Aiming the gun at the words 'your freedom,' I squeeze the trigger, and just as the shot goes off, I'm back in the clear booth, in the red algae cave along with other participants still firing away.

With a heavy heart, I step out of my stall. My foot is still very sore, but having crawled and stood motionless for a while seems to have helped it a bit. As soon as I see others tearing toward the exit sign, I take a deep breath, pull my shoulders back, and shove the entire experience into the back of my mind. There's no time to second-guess my decision—not if I want to be one of the top three.

Chapter 27

I stand in front of the cave's exit—another narrow, black passageway to wriggle through—and every area of my body feels like it's made of rock. I try to inhale and exhale deeply, but with each breath, the suffocating sensation in my chest becomes tighter. Just do it, Heidi. I place my hands on the smooth, warm opening edge, and lean my forehead onto the rock. Why can't I just climb in when I full well know that wasting my time could cost me my spot in the top three? Still, I am unable to make myself move even an inch. I would think that having crawled through another tunnel just like this one earlier would make it easier this time. However, thinking about how the walls closed in on me before, and how dark it was in there, I just know I won't be able to stop the panic from rising within me.

"Heidi!"

I turn around and see Arthor running toward me. For a moment, seeing a familiar, friendly face helps take the edge off my anxiety, but when the image of him vanishing beyond the shot of my gun returns, the muscles in my face involuntarily twitch.

"What's that look?" He stops right next to me and pats me on the back, a patch of sweat darkening the collar of his uniform. He's panting and he has this worried and wild look in his eyes, like something's really bothering him.

"Uh...nothing—just don't like tight spaces, that's all. Are you okay, though? You look like you've been to hell and back."

He blows a couple of times, his face drawing closed. "Still thinking about my choices. Well, best to keep moving. You ready?"

No. I glance into the dim tunnel again and my shoulders go rigid. "Yes."

"Well then, ladies first."

I just can't think about what I'm about to do. If I do, I'll start to hyperventilate again. With a thumping heart and clammy hands wound into fists, I climb into the cavern. The slick, warm rocks press against my palms, and I notice how the dark, warm tunnel smells even more of sulfur. My heart rate increases the farther in I crawl, and as the darkness envelops me, I can't breathe and go to pull back. But Arthor is already behind me.

"I can't do it."

"Yes, you can, Heidi. Just focus on my voice, okay? We'll be okay. This is the easy part."

"For you it is."

"Place one hand in front of the other. That's all you need to do."

I feel his hand around my ankle and he squeezes it gently. "You're doing great, Heidi. One hand in front of the other."

Pausing, I remind myself again why I'm doing this. For Gemma. Yet even with her at the forefront of my thoughts, it takes every morsel of willpower to slide my hand forward. I pick up my knee and pull it toward my hands. The next hand. The next knee. One at a time, I inch forward.

"Good, Heidi. Keep going. A little faster now."

I pick up my pace a little, but thoughts of how I might become forever trapped in this tunnel prevent me from committing one hundred percent.

"The faster you move, the faster we'll be there."

"Okay, okay," I snap impatiently, moving my hands and knees at a faster pace. Mercifully, the rhythm of my movements starts to take over, and I note that the more I focus on what I'm doing, the less anxious I feel.

"What did you have to choose between back there?" Arthor asks.

It takes me a second to recall what I had to choose between. "Things like my sandals and my trailer...Gemma's mother." I'm careful to not bring up that I shot him.

"Really? What was your last one?"

"It was between Gemma and my freedom." Squeezing through a particularly tight area, I grunt. "You?"

"It was between my lover and my freedom." He grunts, too, just as he crawls through the tight space. "So who did you choose?"

"Gemma."

"Really? Over your own freedom?"

"Well...yes. If I don't have those I care about, there's no use in having my freedom, is there?"

He doesn't reply.

"What did you choose?"

"I chose my freedom."

"Oh." My voice sounds flat, but my insides are in turmoil. Obviously, I don't know Arthor as well as I thought I did. All his actions up until now prove that he'd choose his loved ones over freedom or even over his own life.

"What other choices did you have to make?"

Quickly, I reply, "Just some people you don't know."

He pauses for a moment. "You should know that I chose my freedom over my lover because I found out that he cheated on me shortly before I left."

"Oh." Now I feel like a judgmental bigot.

"I thought I had been able to forgive him, but being in the booth, I realized that the hurt sits real deep, you know."

"That's fair."

"I still felt like a scumbag doing it, though."

"Don't," I say. "You deserve someone who will cherish you."

"Thanks, Heidi."

Crawling forward, I notice there is more space between the tunnel's walls and me. We must be getting closer to the end. I take a deep breath. "But don't you think that it was done in a manipulative way? I mean how they forced us to choose like that?"

"Certainly."

After crawling a few more minutes, I see a dim light up ahead and my heart leaps in my chest. "I see light!"

"Finally. I can't wait to be out of here; you stink."

I laugh. "Well, you don't exactly smell like rose petals."

"But I'm downwind to you."

"You insisted," I retort.

The end came much faster than I had anticipated, and it occurs to me that I haven't yet discussed with Arthor how we'll proceed once we get out of here. We should just separate and wish each other well. He's officially my competitor now—and I must see him as such.

"Arthor?"

"Yes."

"I'm just going to run ahead as fast as I can once we reach the end here in a little bit. Good luck out there."

"Okay. Just let me scout out the area first just in case there are any dangerous creatures," he answers.

"Trying to get a head start on me?" I ask, jokingly.

"What?"

I can almost hear the muscles in his jaw tense up.

"You're crazy if that's what you think. Stop being so paranoid; I'm the only friend you have right now and I'm not out to get you like the rest of them."

To say that I'm baffled is an understatement. "I was just joking, Arthor, geez."

"Even when I have nothing I want from you, you still think I'm out to get you. Not everyone is like your father, Heidi."

I stop dead in my tracks, coiling my fingers into fists. "What's gotten into you? Of course I realize that everyone isn't like my father." From the way he reacts, I almost think he's hiding something from me. Maybe he had to shoot me, too, and he's feeling guilty about it.

I continue onward until I get to the end of the passageway, and then pause before I step into the shadowy jungle. Looking up, I have a hard time seeing the tops of some of the trees, and I can only make out a few splotches of the blue sky above, the leaves concealing the rest. Some of their trunks are as wide as four or five lengths of me and the smooth, splotchy bark is covered in moss. There's a constant hum of insects, bird chirps and caws, growling noises, rustling leaves, and squeaking; and bushes, vines, and plants move as if by themselves.

A sharp pain goes through my foot when I first step on it. Standing on my good foot, and circling my injured ankle, I try to loosen it up a bit. I think back to the Opening Ceremony when President Volkov announced that Eastern Republic scientists were hired to recreate dangerous, extinct beasts and various mythological creatures for the O-Region. Sitting in my chair back in the Conference Center, it sounded scary. Now, I don't think there's even a word for how I feel. There's a queasiness that sits in my bones and muscles and blood, screaming for me to crawl back into the hole I came from and quit. Before it's too late. But I can't pull back now.

"Just let me do this for you, Heidi," Arthor says softly, climbing out of the tunnel, brushing the dust off his hands. "You saved my life, remember?"

Why is he acting this way all of a sudden? "Friends don't keep score."

Pulling me into his arms, he says, "True, but I would be honored to do this for you."

Is there something important that he needs to prove to himself in doing this? He did insist on running first during the latter portion of the marathon, too, so maybe he's trying to protect me. "Fine. I'll wait. But if you're not back by thirty seconds, I'm out of here."

"I'm just going to look." He smiles, the sides of his eyes crinkling. "I'll holler once I've scouted out the area."

I watch him vanish behind a large bush and the second I can no longer hear his footsteps, my gut tells me I have made a mistake. But I need to learn to finally trust him. He's done everything for me, and if there's one person I can trust, it must be Arthor. He has proven himself time and again. But we're not part of a team. We're individual participants, competing against each other for the cash prize, and if he were truly my friend, he wouldn't ask me to stay behind. What would we do if we got to the finish line first? Would he let me go ahead of him? Of course he wouldn't. I certainly wouldn't. I need that money to free Gemma. Gemma.

A large shadow passes overhead, causing me to cower down, but by the time I look up, it has disappeared. Did it see me, whatever it was? When a deafening bird-like caw vibrates through the jungle, chills run down my spine. The creature must be gigantic—one of the many dangerous beasts for sure.

It must have been thirty seconds by now, right? Not knowing exactly what to think since Arthor hasn't yet returned, I start limping into the jungle. The ground is covered in roots and mosses, making it even harder to maneuver with my hurt foot, but thankfully the pain isn't unmanageable. I have no idea in which direction to go and after pushing one bush aside, there's always another one waiting to replace it. There are no signs or clues that I can tell, and I don't even see any of the other participants out here yet. But of course, with only a hundred or so of us left, all scattered throughout this vast area, our uniforms blending with the environment, we'll be nearly impossible to spot.

Every achy step I take, I become more furious at Arthor. At least he could have had the decency to just say that we'd separate and not trick me, giving himself a head start. I'm livid with him for messing with my future this way. I thought he was my friend. I would never have done that to him—he knows it—that is why he insisted on going first.

When I push aside the next bush, I enter a small clearing. About twenty feet away, I see Arthor stuck to a large web, grunting and flexing his muscles, and he has blood on the left side of his rib cage. The web is made of chains, and the edges are anchored in the trees and in the ground. In an instant it dawns on me; he didn't abandon me; he was prevented from coming back because he became trapped. A pang of guilt rushes through me.

"Arthor?" I say, limping out from behind a bush. A beam of sunlight streams down upon him, a spotlight from the heavens.

"Heidi."

"What happened?" I ask.

"I set something off...a trap—a strong wind. It blew me onto this..."

I take a step closer. "I want to help you."

"No, stay where you are. If you come any closer you could end up here."

Hundreds of red light beams appear when I take the next step. Undoubtedly, if I touch any of them, I'll set off whatever it is that released the airstreams that blew Arthor onto the web. "I'm going to help you." Without wasting any more time, I look for a way to get to him from above. I locate a tree that has a branch right above him, and head toward it. Maybe if I extend a branch to him, he'll be able to pull himself up.

"Heidi, I'm sorry for leaving you. Forgive me. I...I was trying to get a head start..."

His confession makes me feel like the life has been drained out of me. So he did lie to me.

"I just wanted my parents to be proud of me." He's breathing heavily and his face morphs into a map of sadness. "Ever since they lost Tristan...the strong one...they know I'm different somehow...I thought if I gave them my money...they'd be as proud of me as they were of Tristan." His head falls forward and he sobs.

I could just continue on—leave the traitor here. It's what I should do to him for betraying me. But if I leave, he'll never get free and the man-made beasts that roam this jungle will be attracted by the blood and finish him. There's been enough death to last the century, and if I can help it, I want to stop anyone else from dying. "You owe me big time, Arthor, and once I get you out of here, I'm going to give it to you." I pick up a thick, long branch from the jungle floor, and begin to climb the tree. But before I can climb up even a foot, a hand covers my mouth, and someone pulls me behind the tree. I kick and flail my arms, and scream; the viciousness has started, and I'm one of the first ones who will be killed.

"Shhh...a dragon is scoping out the area." I recognize the voice as Cory's and when I stop resisting him, he lets go. I look up to the sky, and see a huge beast flying above the trees—probably the same one I noticed earlier. The dragon is yellow and has reddish-brown splotches on its body, spikes on its legs, back and head, and brown wings that look like they have claws on the ends. Its head is square with sizeable nostrils, and fan-like gills protrude like branches from its skull. With the flap of its wings, there's a beating sound, and as it roars, it stoops into a clearance, breathing flames right in front of where Arthor hangs, setting the dried branches and twigs on fire. Arthor! Smoke rises to the sky and the smell of burned wood and vegetation breezes past me.

"Is that all you have?" Arthor spews toward the dragon.

The beast roars again, and I cup my hands over my ears to shield them from the piercing sound. My eyes are still glued to my friend's face, and when he looks at me, I reach my arm toward him as two heavy tears roll down my cheeks.

"Cory," I whisper, even though there's hardly anything he can do to save Arthor now.

Cory picks up a large rock from the jungle floor. He places the rock in a makeshift sling made of vines, and hurls it. At first, I think he's aiming for the dragon, but as the rock leaves his hand, I see that it is headed toward Arthor's skull.

I scream at exactly the same time the dragon roars again, my voice being swallowed up by the earsplitting sound. The rock hits Arthor in the center of his forehead just a second before the flames from the dragon's mouth consume him.

A mercy killing.

The dragon seems not to have noticed that it wasn't his flames that killed his victim, rather the rock from Cory's hand.

Cory grabs my hand. "Come—now." He tugs my arm, pulling me with him away from the grove before I can fully wrap my mind around what just happened. I can't see through the tears in my eyes; everything is blurry. I hobble after him for at least ten minutes before he stops by a stream and lets go of my hand, but the smell of flames and the look on Arthor's face just before he died has followed me even here. Kneeling down by the water, Cory cups his hand, scoops some water into it and smells it. He takes a sip and wets the back of his neck and hair. I stand and watch him, unable to move, unable to let go of or fully comprehend what just happened. I want to scream at him for killing my friend, but I can't. I want to cry, but the tears have dried up.

Carrying no sympathy in his eyes—only hardness and determination—he stands up and walks over to me. "Stay present, Heidi. If you want to survive, you can't let what happened back there slow you down. Keep it at a distance. Once you've survived, once you're out of here, there will be time to mourn."

I run my fingers through my hair, clasping the back of my head, and swallow again and again. Breathing fast and hard, I start to feel light-headed and sit down on a rock. Arthor. Gemma. They both sacrificed for me and now one is dead, the other rotting away under the hateful eye of her Master. My desire—my obsession to be free—cost them everything. It's not fair. And though Arthor proved to be a traitor in the end, what really drove him was he didn't have what he should have had his entire life: the freedom that was rightfully his. What lengths we go to—what crazy things we do—to take back what is rightfully ours, and I'm the worst of all, having made everyone else sacrifice for me.

Cory kneels down in front of me.

"This is not your fault," he says.

"It is. And I hardly deserve my freedom. My father was right about me all along. I'm selfish, stupid, and worthless. I'd do anything for myself."

"Is that what Arthor would say?"

"No. But look where my actions got him!"

"Don't believe the ugly. It's not true. The only fatal thing is to give up."

"But..."

"If you can't let go of the past, you'll never be anything but a slave to it. Is that what you want?" His voice is harsh.

"Just leave me alone." I stand up and walk away. He doesn't stop me. I storm through the jungle, whipping away vegetation, pockets of condensation making my hands and the sleeves of my uniform wet. Eight cages. Only eight. I see myself standing in one of them. It's all that keeps me going. Keeps me from stopping to nurse my injured leg. I make my way along the stream; probably the same one Cory just sipped from earlier. Had I not been so upset, I would have thanked him for saving me.

Along the way, I see no sign of the other participants anywhere. It's eerily quiet, and the jungle sounds have died down, too—like the animals know not to come here. Does that mean I'm close? Then I think I see lights in the distance. An obstacle course? The cages? Swerving around the tree to get a better look, I see them. There. Eight shiny ones in a row. And there's not a soul in any of them.

But just as I take my first step toward them, Johnny steps from behind a tree, staring me down, beating a stick in his hand.

Chapter 28

"Nice performance back there," Johnny says.

I look over my shoulder, cursing myself for having run away from Cory. "Cory!" I spin around and sprint in the direction that he vanished. Every time my injured foot collides with the ground, I think I might collapse; my foot hurts so badly. "Cory!" Never mind if the beasts hear me; if Johnny catches me, I'll be dead way before sundown. Running through the jungle, I slap the cool foliage out of my way, but Johnny is too fast and mauls me to the ground.

Breathing heavily into my ear, he says, "Looks like he's gone. Who will protect you now, Imp?"

"Leave me be!" I twist my body beneath his and punch him in the face, but he quickly grabs hold of my wrists and braces my arms across my chest.

"Or what. You'll scream?" He knees me in the side, causing me to wring in pain, and then he swivels me back around onto my stomach and pulls my hands behind my back. "I warned you that this moment would come and just because you're a girl, don't think I'll go any easier on you."

I snatch my arm out of his grip, and elbow him in the nose, but he quickly grabs my wrist again and twists it behind my back so hard that I think he's trying to rip it off. I scream.

"Something you might not know about me, Heidi, is that I would do anything to win the Savage Run; and don't tell me you wouldn't do the same."

"I wouldn't." I kick and scream.

Picking up some vines from the forest floor, he winds them around my wrists and ankles and triple-knots them. "Don't think for a moment I'll let you escape. I have a deal with Pres. And I don't want to disappoint him." Having immobilized me, he stands up. "You say you wouldn't do the same, but I beg to differ. You purchased a fake ID, and registered illegally for the Savage Run. Oh, and I almost forgot—you seduced a registrar who just so happens to be President Volkov's son, and then miraculously, when it's discovered you're a freaking girl, you're still allowed to participate. What's the saying? 'Keep your friends close. Make lovers out of your enemies.' I see what's going on. I have all along."

"I didn't seduce Nicholas..."

"Sure, keep telling yourself that, Imp."

"Listen," I say. "I can see why you might think that, but that's not what happened. And who cares at this point? While we're debating, someone else is running toward the finish line, stealing the victory. You don't want that, do you? We can race together," I suggest. "And at the end, I'll let you pass first. I promise."

"Yeah, right. Is that what you said to Arthor before you threw a boulder at his head and killed him?"

The mention of Arthor's name is like pouring acid on a burn wound. "He...he was going to die anyway." A lump forms in my throat.

"You could have tried to save him."

My bottom lip trembles. "It was a lost cause. I tried—"

"—I think you could have figured out a way. You're good at that."

"Maybe...but there was no time and..." I squint my eyes. "If I could, I would have taken Arthor's place."

His dark eyebrows rise into two sharp peaks. "What a courageous thing to say—after the fact."

No matter what, he's not going to be swayed by anything I have to say, and he's twisting every situation against me.

"Now—what do I do with you?"

"You could let me go."

"Let you go?" He paces back and forth in deep thought. Then out of nowhere, he gives me a swift kick in the stomach.

The force of his foot ramming into my abdomen makes me gasp and cough, as if I might expel a lung.

"Any other suggestions?" When I'm unable to answer, he undoes the vines from around my ankles. "Get up." Jerking my arm, he lifts me to a standing position, and starts to haul me with him into the jungle.

"Where...are you taking me?"

He tugs at my arms so hard that I fall face first into a mudded area. Crouching down beside me, he says, "Do I have to cut your tongue out to get you to shut up?"

I roll over onto my side, the right side of my face covered in grime. "With what, your hands?"

Pulling out a pocketknife, he opens it, and presses it against my cheek. "A present—from Pres. himself," he whispers. "He has guaranteed me Master status—in whatever place I finish—if I finish you off."

"I thought you said you were all about honor and might."

"I am. That's why I agreed to get rid of you." He draws the blade down my cheek hard enough that it pierces the top layer of my skin.

I squeeze my eyes shut. Suddenly I hear voices, and then the rustling of foliage as someone passes a ways away. My eyes pop open. "Help!"

Johnny cups his hand over my mouth and hauls me with him away from the sounds. While he's dragging me, a thought occurs to me. Since I know that Johnny is President Volkov's son, I could use the information to create a wedge between them. He tows me behind him until we reach a wide river. Trees and vines hang like a dome above the white, rushing waves, and the hot air is humid, smelling of flowers and fresh rain. It hurts every time I step onto my injured foot, but determined to not let Johnny know I'm in less than peak condition; I force myself to walk without a limp. He leads me over to a tree. Taking the excess part of the vines secured around my wrists, he ties them to a protruding root.

Johnny makes his way over to the river, and splashes his face with water.

Not having eaten the entire day, my muscles have become depleted from the lack of food and water. I look at the water longingly, but he doesn't offer me any. When he makes his way back over to me, he stomps on my injured foot, smashing it beneath his.

322

Arching my back, I cry out in agony. The pain is so overwhelming I'm convinced he's broken my foot.

"Don't think I didn't notice your limp, Imp."

It takes a while before the worst part of the pain subsides, and I manage to calm my staggering breath. If I weren't bound like an animal, I'd find the heaviest stone I could carry, and smash in his skull. Better yet, I should have dumped him in the volcano when I had the chance.

When I am finally able to open my eyes, I see his knife lying right beside my foot, behind a small rock. My heart feels like it will jump out of my mouth and I look up quickly so I won't draw attention to the weapon. "Why don't you just kill me now? Get it over with so you can claim your money?"

"Oh, I'm just getting warmed up. You see, the most beautiful thing to watch is a little dove fearing for her life, dreading the moment when life ceases to exist. Why would I want to rush such a...delightful process?"

"You're sick; you know that?" As subtly as I can, I stretch my leg out and cover the knife with my foot.

"You say that only because you don't understand what a blessing it is to have complete power over another. Just look at you, Heidi. You're shaking like a leaf, and I am the one who is creating that fear in you. I have become your god."

"You will never be my god."

As if noticing something, Johnny, lifts his chin and stiffens where he stands. "Don't move."

I hear a low growl coming from behind me and I turn my head to look. There, in between the sea of vegetation, I see a saber-toothed tiger moving methodically toward us. "Untie me," I whisper, my chest pounding.

He looks straight at me and shakes his head, mouthing the word 'no.'

If I can just get the knife close enough to my hands, I'll be able to pick it up and cut myself loose. Johnny's gaze shifts back to the beast, and I squeeze my foot to my bottom, dragging the knife with it. Fortunately, Johnny isn't paying attention to me; he's thinking about how he can escape. I pick up the knife and begin to saw at the vines. I nick my wrist, but I don't care; I want to stay alive and a few cuts don't matter at this point. With one final pull, the vine breaks and I'm free. Johnny must have heard the cracking sound as the vine snapped because his eyes whip to mine.

If I can just reach the river the current will carry me away and I'll have a chance at escaping. I shoot to my feet and head toward the water. However, my injured leg buckles beneath the weight of my body and I tumble onto the rocks. Standing up again, I hop forward on one foot, but not a second passes before Johnny lunges at me and shoves me to the watery bank, jamming my head into the shallow water so I can't breathe.

Still clenching the knife in my hand, I kick my arm back, and stab him in the leg. He releases my head and I lift my face out of the water, eager to take a deep breath. With nothing more than a low grunt coming from his lips, Johnny grabs my wrist and pulls it, withdrawing the blade from his thigh. Growling, he yanks my fingers back and the knife falls into a small puddle between the rocks. The moment he releases my wrist, it becomes a competition of who can get to the knife first, but before either of us can reach it, the saber-toothed tiger pounces on Johnny's back. The tiger roars and Johnny screams. The instant I feel Johnny's weight lift off me, I squeeze forward on elbows and knees toward the center of the river. The tiger roars again and again and it's as if Johnny's cries vibrate through my blood. Once I'm up to my neck in the water, I rise to my feet, and hobble against the strong current. Not until I am waist-high in the river and I can no longer hear Johnny's shrieks, do I dare turn around.

Contrary to what I had expected, Johnny isn't lying in a pool of his own blood. He's standing above the saber-toothed tiger, pulling the blade out of the lifeless beast's cranium. When our eyes connect, Johnny shoves the tiger to the side, and heads straight toward me. My chest fills with terror and I immediately swivel around and head deeper into the river.

"Stop!" Johnny yells.

I lift my feet and let the river pull me with it, but just as the current draws me beneath the surface, I realize the river is no friend of mine either. First, my shoulder crashes against a rock, and next, my hip scrapes against a tree or large root. I kick my legs and move my arms, and soon I reach the surface.

I hear a loud roar downstream. A waterfall? I scan ahead, and sure enough, the end of the river is just a few hundred feet away. Fighting to keep my head above water, I look up to see if there are any low-hanging branches or vines to grab hold of that might prevent me from going over the edge. But there's nothing. I do, however, see a large boulder protruding out of the river. If I can just steer myself toward it, I can cling onto it.

Though the rock is heaven-sent, it is approaching all too quickly and the closer I get, the more I begin to worry that I won't be able to control the impact—especially with my injured foot. But there is no time to reconsider. I stretch my good leg out in front of me and when it collides with the rock, I bend my knee and reach my arms around the boulder. The surface is slimy and there's no place to lodge my fingers. Instead, my palms skate across the rock and I continue down the stream. Soon I'm at the edge of the river, peering down to the bottom of the waterfall, and as I tumble over the edge, my head spins.

Chapter 29

I splash into the pool of water and sink all the way to the bottom. When my feet hit the rocks, a surge of pain shoots up my injured leg, causing me to scream out in pain. I push off from the bottom with my right leg and before long, I float to the top and swim to the bank. I crawl out of the water and drag myself onto the muddy rocks, panting for air. But there's no time to rest. I stagger to my right foot and hop over to the side of the waterfall. I press my body and palms against the cold, wet, black rock, and mist sprays on my hands, prickling my skin. I wonder how much time I've lost and how far behind the others I really am. The worst would be if by the time I get to the cages, they are all already filled.

I start to climb up the mountainside, relying heavily on my upper body and right leg, grabbing onto exposed roots and small ledges. Every time I put pressure on my injured foot is like an assault, and I bite my lips until they bleed trying to keep from screaming. The last thing I need is for Johnny to find me and finish the job he started.

It has started to become dark, making it difficult to see where I'm going. The setting sun is no help at all down here below the dome of trees and the only consolation I have is that everyone else is in darkness, too.

Halfway up the mountainside, I reach out my cupped hand, let the water gather into my palm, and drink. The cool liquid meets the hollow feeling in my stomach, but does nothing to stop the incessant gnawing—like my stomach might eat itself.

I continue to climb, and before long, I'm at the top. In the distance, I see light and my heart sinks. With it being dark, and the way the obstacle course glows as a pillar in the darkness, it's almost guaranteed the eight cages have already been taken. But I'm not giving up. I alternate between walking and jogging as I make my way toward the light, only slowing down when I need a break from the pain or as I approach a particularly dark area, afraid Johnny might be lurking around. I'm about halfway to the obstacle course when I feel a sharp pain in my right shoulder, sending me to the ground. I reach behind me and feel the hilt of a knife.

"Wait up, Imp."

His voice works like a shot of adrenaline, and I don't even bother to look back before I spring to my feet and make a run for it. But I can't go as fast as I want because every time my left foot hits the ground, a knife-like jab radiates up my leg, and when I pump my arms, the back of my shoulder feels like it's being ripped apart. I hear Johnny's footsteps behind me, growing louder and louder, and the sound of him slapping foliage away is right at the back of my neck. I keep my eyes fixed forward, letting the bright lights in the near distance pull me to my destination. If I can just make it there. If I can just make it. Trees pass by in a blur as I whack the leaves and vines to the side. My mouth is parched, my shoulder aching, my lungs on fire, my leg throbbing.

Finally I reach the clearing where the obstacle course is set up. I run to the center of the dirt arena and look behind me. Johnny is nowhere to be seen. My eyes whip to the cages, and see that Timothy, Cory, and four other participants are standing in each their own.

"Heidi!" Cory yells when he sees me. "You made it."

Miraculously, two cages are still vacant. Looking behind me once more, I don't see Johnny anywhere. Dashing over to one of the empty cages, I reach to the back of my shoulder and wrap my fingers around the hilt. Crying out, with one quick move, I draw the blade out my flesh, and throw the knife into the jungle.

Timothy makes a whooping sound encouraging me as I limp forward, but just as I am about to enter the cage, he yells, "Watch out!"

Someone grabs me by the arm, jerks me to the side, and slams the entry shut. Johnny. From the corner of my eye, I see another participant emerge from the jungle and he heads toward us.

"Get away from me!" I kick Johnny in the thigh where I stabbed him earlier and he reaches for his leg and screams.

"I'm so gonna kill you." His face is red and spit launches from his mouth as he yells.

I grab onto the top of the cage, lift my legs up and kick him in the abdomen so he goes flying back. Pain stabs through my left foot. Opening the cage, I get in, slam the gate behind me, and lock it.

Johnny sees the other participant heading toward him and he quickly takes the cage next to me. Just as Johnny's cage door shuts, a loud alarm blasts through the jungle and the cages rise slowly, high into the air. I grab onto the shiny, steel bars to steady myself.

"Don't think you're safe yet, Imp."

"Dude, just let her be, man," I hear Timothy yell.

"Shut your bucket or I'll come after you, too!" Johnny retorts.

With a jolt, the cages stop rising. Right in front of me is a long row of monkey bars, and each row is separated from the others by barbed wires. To protect participants from psychopaths like Johnny, I suppose. After the monkey bars there are numerous swinging, burning wrecking balls, and in the far distance, a track.

A woman's voice comes over a speaker. "Ten. Nine. Eight..."

I focus my eyes toward the end of the bars and in an instant all the energy leaves my body. The distance is way farther than my arms will be able to carry me—especially with the gash in my shoulder. Peering down, I see a pit of spikes below the bars, and instinctively, I wipe my sweaty hands on my pants. Maybe this is one of those obstacles where there's a short cut. I search my surroundings for any possible clues, the artificial spotlights from the sides blinding me.

"Good luck," Cory says to me.

I nod back. "You too."

The woman continues. "Three. Two. One."

The doors to the cages swing open and I hop on one leg onto a small, bamboo platform. Rising up onto the ball of my right foot, I reach up and curl my fingers around the first smooth bar. I feel my pulse in my ears.

When I release my foot off the podium so I hang from the bar, a shot of pain tears through my shoulder. I squeeze my lips together and pant through my nose, gripping the bar even harder. I swing from one bar to the next while keeping my eyes fixed on the bars, not forward—I'll only become discouraged about how far I have yet to go. I quickly find a rhythm. One two. One two.

"You'll never make it, Imp." Johnny's right next to me, swinging from bar to bar like it's nothing.

"Shut up." The thought comes to me again that I should tell him who he is. "Do you know that President Volkov is your father?"

"Yeah, right—that's the most ludicrous thing I've ever heard."

"Nicholas made me promise not to tell you, but I thought I'd let you in on the secret. Everyone has a right to know where they came from." I'm moving slower now, and I feel my arms start to tire.

"What a crack load of lies," he yells. "And like you'd tell me for that reason—to help me. Please. Save your breath."

"It's true. Why do you think Nicholas especially invited you to this program? No one else was." I pause for a moment to catch my breath.

"I know what you're doing and it's not going to work."

I'll have to add a little of my own embellishment, so he'll focus on finishing the obstacle course and get his mind off me. "Nicholas says President Volkov did that to make sure you were good enough for him. And if you make it, President Volkov plans to announce to the world who you are."

"Whatever," he scoffs.

But I can hear that his voice isn't as certain as earlier. "Your grandmother knew all along, and she didn't tell you. President Volkov bought her silence." That's a lie. "And if you don't make it, you'll be sent home packing, back to an Advisor life for you." Another lie, but I'll do whatever it takes to get him off my back.

I glance forward and though I've been at it for what seems an unreasonably long time, it doesn't even look like I've made any progress. My arms and hands tremble as they clamp the bars, and my palms burn already. I keep pressing on, but the strength in my upper body is quickly fading and my motivation is dwindling, seeing how far behind the others I am. I press on, slower and slower, the burning in my hands becoming unbearably painful, and I think I feel my first blister pop. Sweat drips in my eyes, making my surroundings blurry.

I feel my fingers slipping, and desperately in need of a break, I swing my legs up and loop them around the outside where there is no barbed wire.

"Can't keep up, huh?" Johnny says. "I'll just hang out here and wait until you fall."

Looking past the monkey bars, up to the deep blue sky, I start to sob. I'm so tired, and being injured practically everywhere—in so much pain—I don't know how I'll make it. But as I look up, an idea pops into my mind. Maybe I can walk or crawl on top of the bars and balance across the beams to the end. Would it be considered cheating? Right now it's my only option. I scoot to the outside of the bars, getting as close as I can.

"What are you doing?" Johnny asks.

I struggle for a while, but I finally manage to loop myself around the railing and crawl up to the top of the bars. Each of the two beams is a mere three inches, but even so, it will be easier and faster for me to crawl across than swing my way forward.

"You're cheating!"

"Too bad you're on the inside, stuck behind the barbed-wires. See you later." Crawling on hands and knees, I soon catch up with the others.

"You little cheat, just wait until I catch up with you!"

I ignore him. When I reach the end of the monkey bars, I climb down to the bamboo podium. The platform lowers to the ground and in front of me are huge, burning, swinging wrecking balls. Of course they had to be on fire. Below the wrecking balls are stakes that stick out from a green scum-covered swamp. It looks like the challenge is to jump from stake to stake while not getting hit by the gigantic flaming balls. Tricky. I check behind me to make sure Johnny isn't near, and he isn't. What luck that I chose the outer rail.

After hopping off from two legs, I land on my right foot on the first stake. I wobble a bit, but manage to maintain my balance by reaching my arms out to the sides, slightly in front of me. Repeating the process, I move ahead a few more stakes until I approach the first blazing ball. Side to side it swings, warming my face and hands with every pass, crackling loudly. I watch the ball carefully, assessing how much time I need to clear the four stakes below it. I have three seconds at most.

With the next swing, and just as the scorching globe passes, I launch off from where I'm standing and hop to the first stake. Keep going—just a few more. I tighten the muscles in my stomach. Once I land on the second stake, the fireball reaches its apex and begins its descent. Two more. With my heart in my head, and just as the lit ball returns, I hop from the third to the fourth one without stopping, the flames licking my backside. That was close—way too close. Just a few inches, and I'd be thrown into the swamp.

"You don't know anything about me," I hear Johnny behind me.

He must be thinking about what I told him. "Just ask Nicholas once we're out of here." Maybe telling him wasn't such a good idea after all. Somehow in the midst of trying to save my life, I hadn't stopped to consider what consequences it would have.

"You're such a liar."

I wish I were. "Johnny, it's the truth. I swear."

He makes this grunting, screaming sound, but I don't look back. The next fireball is coming up and if I am to make it, I have to tune him out completely.

He laughs. "Once I come for you, you'll have no defense. One little push and whoosh, you're a goner!"

I take a few deep breaths, preparing myself for the next wrecking ball. Right as it passes me, I move from stake to stake, moving much quicker than the first time. Easy breezy, I can do this.

Approaching the last round, however, I see that there are two balls in a row, the second ball swinging in the opposite direction from the first one. I can't tell how much space, if any, is between the balls, and to make matters worse, the stakes vary in height and distance. If I don't pause at all, I think I might make it, but one misstep and...if there was ever a time during this round when I needed solid foot holding, it is now. But my foot hurts so bad that even moving it a little causes me to wince in pain. I wind my fingers up so tightly that they go numb.

Just as the ball closest to me passes, I spring to the first stake. Moving on, I jump up to the second one, and grab around the edges of the wood to steady myself. Landing on the third stake, however, it wobbles, and for a split second I lose my balance and am forced to pause. Still standing on the third stake, the wrecking balls have already reached their peaks and are on their way back down. Seeing there's no way I'll clear the second ball on time, I freeze where I stand, desperately hoping there's enough space between the two globes of fire so that I won't get crushed.

Waiting for the wrecking balls to descend, I turn my head sideways, exhale all the air from my lungs and close my eyes. As the balls come barreling down, I just give into the moment. Whatever happens, happens. If this is it, I hope it's quick—I hope Nicholas will find Gemma for me and buy her freedom. I should have asked him to. I think he will. I hope...

Heat is the first thing I notice, followed by intense burning as the flames brush against the right side of my face and abdomen. The sweltering pain is more than I can handle and I cry out in agony. As the balls meet in the middle, I'm crushed between them, and my abdomen and back are seared raw. When the wrecking balls finally pass, I lose balance and fall straight down. But before I hit the swamp, I manage to clutch onto the wooden stake, my numb hands digging into the splinters, my legs clinging to the wooden beam.

My abdomen and back burn, and the right side of my face feels like it's on fire. Opening my eyes, I see I'm a mere foot above the swamp and only five stakes away from the end. I figure that my options are either to climb up the rod or somehow maneuver my way from stake to stake from down here. I decide on the latter because if I climb upward, I'll run into the wrecking balls again.

Then there's a faint laugh above me. Johnny. "Hey, Imp, you stuck?"

He doesn't wait for my answer before moving on, and I wonder if it is because of what I told him earlier. Maybe he wants to prove to President Volkov that he is good enough to be a Master. And the next president. Or maybe he just thinks there's no way I'll get out of this alive.

I peel one of my hands off the wooden rod, detaching it from the splinters that have wedged beneath my skin. Drops of blood fall into the mire below as I reach toward the next stake. Still clinging onto the first post, I lean over, and proceed to push off with my legs to get to the next one. In the transfer, I sink down a few inches, and to stop my decent, I wrap my legs around the stake, squeezing my inner thighs together so hard that they cramp, trying to avoid touching the wood with my burned abdomen. My hands sting something awful, but not nearly as much as my face, stomach and back where the flames scorched my skin.

I wonder if Nicholas will care if I die. If my father will care. Or Gemma's mother. Or Gemma. It's not like I was an especially good person toward any of them, only took what I thought I needed and left them behind. Even Nicholas.

I move onto the next stake, gritting my teeth, stifling screams of pain, red-faced and tearful. I shouldn't cry right now. It will blur my vision and I need all my senses to make it through this part. Any movement sends stabs of pain through my body. Then the nausea comes, and I vomit down the side of the stake, making it even more slippery. How can I make it? The burning wrecking balls are swinging just as eagerly above my head. I haven't seen anyone in some time and I wonder if all the others beside Johnny have died before they even made it here or if they just passed me without me noticing.

I cling to the stake, sliding down a few inches now and then, my legs shaking, and my arms giving out on me. I tell them to clench harder, but they won't listen. I reach for the next stake, and in the transfer, my legs sink into the swamp.

But then, as if the liquid wakes some part of me, something inside of me revolts against the weakness. Mai's words echo in my mind. "You have to be stronger than ever before." This is the moment she was talking about, and though she didn't know exactly when that moment would come, I do. Because this is the moment I want to give up, and I could—easily. Oh, it would be so easy to release my grip. Sink into the swamp and drown. It would be over in a few minutes and there would be no more pain. But this is when I can't give into what's easy. If I give in, Johnny takes the money I could use to set Gemma free. I can't let that jerk win. I can't let him be the victor of this entire program where freedom is the ultimate reward. He hasn't a moral bone in his body. And to think he might be the next president of Newland...

With gritted teeth, I climb up the stake a few more inches, and swing my leg over to the next one. The pain is unbearable, but I force myself to remain conscious, thrusting any thought of giving up out of my mind. Every move is an effort, but I'm not going to let Johnny win. The balls are swooshing behind me now, the crackling noise of the flames a constant reminder of the burns on my face, abdomen and hands. I don't feel like a human being at all, just a partial person, held together by raw stubbornness.

With every single ounce of energy I can muster, I climb upward. My body is trembling violently, but I refuse to give in. I'm so close to the end. If I just climb a little higher, I'll be able to see it. I wrap my forearms around the pole instead of using my palms. It makes it harder, but my legs are strong and I manage to keep most of the pressure there. I reach for the flat surface of the post and climb up to a standing position. I want to cry, want the triumph to register, but I'm not done yet. I hop onto the last post, and landing onto the metal platform at the end, I collapse to the ground.

But knowing how little time I have left—I dig deep and find the strength to stand up. In front of me, at the end of the long track, I see the finish line and there stands Johnny, whooping and jumping, congratulating himself on his triumph. Cory stands there too, pulling something out of his thigh. An arrow? I'm relieved to see that he made it, but who won? And where are the others? I see a body—someone from another city—lying lifeless on the track, facedown with blood coming from his chest, arrows jutting out from his back. He didn't deserve to die this way, not when he was so close to victory. The other four—Timothy included—must have died back in the swamps because surely they would have made it by now.

I, however, still have a chance at third place. I stand up and start limping forward. Just as I'm about to move ahead, I see Timothy zooming by me. No! I push off from the gritty ground, my leg stabbing in pain but I won't let it stop me from sprinting as fast as I can. Then I feel a sharp pain in my upper arm followed by a sharp pain in my calf muscle. Timothy's body vanishes beyond my sight, but I don't slow down. Another sharp pain appears in my abdomen, exactly where Johnny kicked me, and it causes me to fall to the ground, scraping my hands and knees. I gasp, but rise up again, still without taking my eyes off the end.

I limp forward—the pain is unbearable now, and yet another sharp pain hits my thigh. Looking down, I see a small silver arrow. Why are they shooting at us? Haven't they had their fun? Haven't we proven ourselves yet? Anger wells up inside as I hobble forward, commanding my legs to move when all they want to do is quit. Nothing will stop me from finishing this. Nothing. When I'm almost at the end, the tears gone from my eyes, I see Timothy lying on the ground. An arrow is embedded in his head and he lies on his stomach, his cheek resting against the ground. His eyes open and vacant. Oh, Timothy.

I run in third.

Chapter 30

Third! I collapse to the ground onto my side in a fetal position—avoiding lying on my burned skin. Panting, the tears stream down the side of my temple and across the bridge of my nose. It's a silent cry, a barely there moan—I don't have the will for more. Arthor. Gemma. My father. Ruth. Nicholas. All the sacrifices and heartaches and losses that I've endured, now live and breathe inside of me in this very moment. Was it all worth it? For my freedom? I'm too exhausted to weigh that right now. And will President Volkov even let me have my victory? A girl he tried to have killed? As I see it, he has no choice if he wants to keep the support of the Konders' and the other benefactors. But I can never be too certain. If he does, the money I receive will be more than enough to purchase Gemma's freedom. But if he doesn't...it's too terrifying to think about.

I lift my hands to look at them. Inundated with slivers, they're swelling quickly and are bleeding. I touch the right side of my face as lightly as I can, but it stings so badly that I withdraw my hand at once. And when I look at my abdomen, it's a red, round, blistering mess. Lifting my head, I pull out the silver arrows that pierced my body during the sprint, almost too unconscious to feel them.

Cory approaches me and crouches down by my side. His white hair has streaks of blood in it, and his clothes are torn, burned, and caked in dirt. "You look like death. You okay?"

I am too spent to punch him anywhere. "Have you seen what you look like?"

He laughs dryly, offers me his hand and helps me stand up. Carefully, very carefully. "Who won?"

"I did," Cory says, a proud look on his face.

At least there's some comfort in knowing that Johnny wasn't the victor, even though I think there will be a lot more problems moving ahead now that he knows he's the son of President Volkov. I suppose I'll never know if sharing that information with him was what saved my life, but in the end, it was worth the risk. Peering over at Johnny, he looks at me, and he wears a terrifying grin. What's going on in that head of his?

Still afraid that Johnny will come after me, I limp alongside Cory to the UVC station just outside of the track. He offers to help me walk, but I hurt everywhere so it's just as good if I struggle on alone instead of incurring further pain. Just as we're about to get on the capsule, a few other participants run across the finish line—the next round of eight, in which five made it. Their faces are beaming with all sort of emotion—pride, relief, and sadness. Everything I felt and still feel. Though most of them are smiling, some of them fall to the earth and kiss the ground, while others kneel and lift their arms up toward the heavens.

In the distance, past the corpses on the track, I see others swinging on the monkey bars and jumping from stake to stake, avoiding the burning wrecking balls. But way back in the jungle is Arthor—my friend, if they haven't taken his body down already. Tears well up in my eyes and I am incapable of silencing a sob. He almost made it. And he easily could have had I forced him to stay behind with me—had we stayed together. We were stronger as a team. A sudden rush of guilt clenches me when I remember shooting him in the Caves of Choice. Maybe he knew that I did it, and this is why he decided to abandon me. Maybe he was so hurt by what I did he had no other choice but to leave. The only reason I survived is because he helped me—I stood on the shoulders of a giant. I'll never know why he truly decided to do it. Like I'll never know if Gemma would have survived had she come with me. And I still don't know for sure whether or not she's alive. But I will persist until I know.

Back home, my father might be expecting me, waiting for me to show my face so he can tell me what a dishonor I am to the family. Maybe I won't go home. Maybe if President Volkov is set on killing me, I'll have to take Nicholas' offer and flee to the Konders'. But not until I've freed Gemma and her mother.

I follow Cory onto the capsule and sit next to him. Johnny stares at me from the other side, but I'm past caring or reacting to how he treats me. I ease into the harness, but there's no way to prevent my burned back from pressing against the seat and my abdomen from coming in contact with the straps. Soon after, the capsule takes off with a jolt. In a daze of pain and shock, I glare out the window, for the most part unaware of all the trees and mountains that start to pass by. We pass through a tunnel, and the fluorescent blue lights make everyone's faces look like ghouls, the humming sound muffling the whispers and muted laughs.

Slipping in and out of consciousness, I don't know how much time passes before the capsule stops. I peer out the window and see the Newland flag flapping in the wind, and the familiar upside down spin-top structure and shiny metal buildings that make up Volkov Village.

The participants file out of the capsule, and as they step outside, I watch them one by one raising their arms in victory. Cory nods to me as he's about to leave the capsule. "You good?"

"Yeah, just need a minute." Cory leaves and I hear the crowd of representatives cheer for the victor. Sitting here, I try to gather my strength to stand up, but the longer I sit, the weaker I feel. Just one more minute and I think I can gather some strength. But it doesn't come.

After some time, Mai peeks her head in the door. "Heidi?" She rushes to my side, but doesn't touch me, only gasps. I've never seen fear in her eyes until now. "Just lie still. I'll have the paramedics right here."

"Where are we?"

"We're stationed outside of Asolo, Cory's hometown."

"I placed third?" I mumble, not sure if I remember correctly.

"Yes. My brave little girl." Her eyes brim with tears. "We're going to take good care of you."

"Where's..." Just as I'm about to ask where he is, Nicholas enters. I tell my lips to smile, but now even that is asking too much.

"You made it. You placed third."

Hearing him say it, it becomes all the more real. He walks over to me as Mai walks out, and though his expression is reserved, beneath his calm demeanor I sense great alarm.

Mai steps out of the capsule with two men dressed in white scrubs, rolling in a gurney. She keeps turning away, but I can see from here how she keeps whisking her tears away.

"She's severely dehydrated and she's lost a lot of blood," Nicholas says.

The paramedics carefully unfasten my harness and help me onto the bed. On the way to the hospital, Mai drives in a transporter behind us and Nicholas sits in the back of the ambulance with me. The paramedics are hooking me up to all sorts of machines, poking me with needles and sticking devices into my mouth. They're throwing around words like echocardiogram and hypovolemic shock.

"You're going to be fine," Nicholas repeats over and over. "Just fine."

The paramedic must have given me something for the pain because I feel really woozy and the burns don't sting as much. I can't get over how afraid Mai looked when she saw me. Now that I think about it, her face was more than concerned, more than worried about one of her participants. It was as if her eyes carried extreme regret and loss of something that was a not only familiar to her, but a true part of her.

"Can I ask you something?" I say.

"What?" Nicholas says.

"Does Mai...know me from somewhere?"

344

Nicholas folds his hands. "Hmmm. That's a conversation for you and her to have."

So she does know me. But from where? I've ruled out that she is my mother—not that mothers don't leave their children, but what mother would leave a baby with such a cruel man as my father? And then pretend to not know me when we meet again?

"So what happens now is we wait for the results from the Savage Run," Nicholas says.

"Oh—those..."

"The Closing Ceremonies are in two days, and that will give you ample time to recover. You're not considered a Master Citizen until you receive your official certificate and ID, so until then, either I or a Unifer will be staying with you at all times."

"Do you know...did I...?"

"You made it, Heidi. You were in the top three."

"You don't think your father...?"

"He may be a tyrant, but he doesn't lie about everything."

"No, only when it's important," I say more bitterly than I meant.

Nicholas squeezes his lips to a line. "He'll keep his promise because this has to do with money."

"That didn't stop him from trying to kill me off."

"I know what happened to your parachute. And with Johnny." He caresses my hair, probably the only part of me that doesn't hurt. My life, he says, is still in danger from Johnny. And of course I know that. Nicholas thinks that maybe Johnny went off the deep end when chasing me. President Volkov claims he didn't rig my parachute, but Nicholas is almost certain he did. But of course he has to deny it, Nicholas says, because if he doesn't, President Volkov will lose the support of his benefactors. I'm not going to bark up that tree—not until I have made sure Gemma is safe.

"I told Johnny," I admit.

Nicholas's eyes squint for a moment, but then he says, "I'm sure you did it to save your life."

"So you're not mad?"

"All I want is to take you in my arms right now, and the only thing stopping me is that I don't want to hurt you."

I want that too.

Chapter 31

After two days of intensive treatments and several rounds of surgery, Asolo Hospital finally gives me the go ahead, and I'm released into the care of Nicholas. I've soaked in the blue liquid for the past twelve hours, my mind running wild with ideas of what I'll do once I return to Culmination. I won't go home first; I need to hire an advocate the second I step off the aircraft. The most ruthless one in town and I know exactly which one. I delivered blood pressure medicine to him all the time. I don't know his relationship to Master Douglas, but I hope he'll represent me.

My burns are completely gone, the wounds from the arrows healed, but my shoulder still hurts from where Johnny threw his knife into it. And because my foot was broken in three places, the doctor said it would be a few more weeks until I'm completely back to normal and walking without pain.

Once we're seated in the transporter, the doors closed, I remember the very first time I met Nicholas—just shy of ten days ago—and how afraid I was. I'm still afraid now, but for different reasons. And so much has changed. I feel like I know Nicholas, not like I just met him. We've been through so much together, and being partners in crime, as he calls it, makes me feel even more bound to him. I wonder if things will be the same for us now that the stress of the Savage Run, and me surviving it, is gone. The second he reaches over and takes his hand in mine, I know they will.

"Before I forget," I say. "I wanted to tell you that while I was in the Caves of Choice, I finally understood what you meant by saying that sometimes freedom is a burden."

A crinkle appears between his eyebrows. "That's funny."

His comment surprises me. "Why?"

"Because you taught me that responsibility is something I should never again take for granted. And you were right." He lifts my hand to his lips and kisses it. "Heidi. I thought...I thought I would lose you." His voice is trembling.

"Well, you've lived your entire life without me, so I think you'd be just fine."

"But I wasn't really alive before I met you." I give him a smile and he commands the transporter to start.

As if avoiding talking about us, we immediately begin to discuss what our next steps of action will be. It's decided that he will fly with me to Culmination, bringing both of his bodyguards just in case Johnny or President Volkov have any ideas. And we'll hire the advocate with the money I'll receive from having finished third place. As we drive into the Savage Run housing area, Nicholas explains I can either stay with him in his townhome or I can go back to the hole in the floor toilet room. I laugh. Of course I choose his place, though all of a sudden I'm terrified of being alone with him. He drives all the way up to his doorstep.

"Are the others in there?" I ask, eyeing the Nissen hut across the way.

"Yes. Johnny included. I think he felt snubbed when President Volkov didn't invite him to stay elsewhere."

It's too early to tell whether or not that's an indication of what will happen in the future. "It will be interesting to see what happens tonight at the Closing Ceremonies."

"Unfortunately, I know about as much as you do about what's going to happen." He follows me inside the townhome and closes the door behind us. When he comes up behind me and places his hands on my shoulders, I tense up. Does he expect something of me? Maybe I should have gone to my room. I don't know what to tell him because I don't know what I want. There's nothing holding me back now and without the stress of the next obstacle looming in the distance, I feel myself floundering.

"Mai wanted me to give you this."

I turn around and see him holding a white envelope with my name on it. "Where is she?"

"She needed to leave."

I gaze into his blue eyes while taking the letter out of his hands. The letter feels heavy in my hands, like there is something more inside than just paper, and I sense that this is more than just a farewell letter from a registrar.

"I need to make a last visit to the office," he says. "Please, make yourself at home." He walks toward the front door.

It's clear to me that he's giving me room to read the letter by myself, and I'm sure once I read the content of it, I'll be grateful to be alone. But right now I just want to be near him—not alone. Watching him walk away, I wait too long and soon he's out the door.

I sit down at the round kitchen table—the table where just a few days ago we discussed how the four of us remaining would survive the last phase together. I'm the only one left. I remember grabbing Arthor's hand and how Timothy said he couldn't handle being around gays. And what about Danny? I wonder how he died, because I doubt he quit; he doesn't seem like the type of guy. Fighting against my tears, I open the letter. A locket falls onto the table—the locket I gave Sergio, trading it for my freedom. My mother's locket. And though I had suspicions about Mai before, now I know. Of course. I just wasn't ready to see it. Didn't want to see it. How did she get it, though? I inhale deeply and start to read.

Dear Heidi,

I have completed my commitment to Savage Run, but I needed to leave before I had the opportunity to speak with you. You have proved that you are a fearless girl. But now you must be braver and more unwavering than you've ever been, do you hear? Stronger than you ever thought you could be. I'll be thinking of you day and night, praying for you. I love you.

It's the first time those words have ever been spoken to me and all at once the strength and courage I have managed to cling to for the last few hours, days, months, years crumble in my chest. I bring my hands to my eyes and sob quietly for a long time. Drying my tears, I continue to read.

I knew your father was a cruel man, I knew he would abuse, demean, and blame you. But when I left, I had no way to keep you alive. Or safe. At least when you were with him, I knew you'd stay alive. Being a Laborer isn't all bad. There's safety in it. But when the one you love turns against you, life becomes a living nightmare. I couldn't stay with him and be me. And I left you with him because he was the only one who could keep you alive. Nicholas said to me that freedom is more important than being safe; he knows you well. You are your mother's daughter. He is a good man, Heidi, and if he rises to power, this country will finally have the leader it deserves. He needs love, and a good woman by his side—one who believes in freedom, but who also cherishes life, love, friendship. And he's found all that in you. In the Caves of Choice, you proved how much you have grown by choosing to give up freedom for friendship. I wish I were as strong as you, but I have other demons to battle. Maybe one day I can. Maybe never. But I do love you, and I do believe as I said before that everything is the way it should be. I made the right choice and because of it you are alive.

I wish you well, Heidi, and maybe one day we will meet again. But as things are now, please respect and know that though nothing has been discussed, there's nothing more to talk about.

~Mai

Just as I let my hand fall to the table, Nicholas returns. His eyes narrow and he walks over to me. I stand up and curl one arm around his neck and the other around his waist, burying my face in his strong, warm chest. I hear his heartbeat—strong and fast. The top of my head reaches his nose and I feel his warm breaths against my hair, smell his mild cologne.

"Are you okay?"

I cry silently for a while, uncertain of what I'm supposed to be feeling, far less uncertain of what I really am feeling. "She says...there's nothing more...to say." I sniffle

"I know."

"She needs time, I think. She's not really the motherly type. She has fought so hard to get to where she is and she's afraid...maybe...to be—"

"You don't have to defend her to me, Heidi. How she's dealing with this, though it may be all she can manage right now, it isn't right."

No, it isn't. But maybe there are no more words to say because those words would only be angry. Hateful. Bitter. Accusing. Because I do despise how she left with just a letter. And all the years she's been gone, I'll never get them back. Now she's taken away the future, too.

"When my father divorced my mother," Nicholas says. "It was the hardest thing in the world."

I remember reading about it in the news, and it was the talk of Culmination how their relationship ended. And how President Volkov won custody of their nine-year-old son.

"How did you cope?"

"It's probably not what you want to hear, but Mai was there with me, guiding me through it. My second mother. Looking back now, I think she tried to atone for what she did to you, like helping me through troubled times would somehow erase the past. She'll never admit it, of course, but

352

she knows leaving you was wrong. Freedom was more important for her, I suppose. And it still is."

Freedom was more important for her. Than me. Those words are the harshest yet. And I will never again wear her locket.

"But that's where you're different." He looks me in the eyes. "That's why I fell for you from the very beginning. And wanted to be around you." He closes his eyes and exhales, and when he opens them again, I see the fearless young man I first met. "I don't understand this. All I know is that when I'm around you, my life has purpose again. And I just want to be with you."

I give him a smile, and though Mai's letter still hurts, his words are like blue, healing liquid on a sweltering burn. I want to be with him, too. More than be with him—be his. Because of how he cares for me, how he notices my shifting moods, making me feel important. How he makes me feel safe. Home.

He chuckles and suddenly the room seems so much lighter.

"What?"

"I've wanted to call you my girlfriend ever since you pretended to read through that ridiculous magazine on the aircraft." He takes a step closer.

I remember the completely embarrassing moment and the sides of my lips involuntarily curl upward. "That early, huh?"

His eyelids lower, and there's a determination behind them I haven't seen before. "Since then, I haven't been able to get my mind off you." He squeezes my chin between his thumb and index finger, lifting my lips to brush against his.

His nose traces from my cheek to my jaw, and he kisses the side of my neck. "Heidi." His voice is husky and his breath is warm against my skin. My breath trembles. He reaches behind my back and pulls my chest to his as he joins his lips with mine. I rise onto my toes and knit my fingers through his short, course hair while I drag him backward with me. I moan into his mouth and his kiss deepens. He lifts me up onto the table and I wrap my legs around his. I should stop before I can't, but the way he tastes like mint and smells like the outdoors...

I pull him in close and his hands rest on my waist, my hips. Kissing him now is different. Before, I needed strength and release from the fear and tension—to feel safe. Now, I kiss him because I see a future together as partners, not only in crime, but maybe...just maybe in love.

* * *

Nicholas, Johnny, and I drive together over to the Asolo Center. Johnny doesn't say a word the entire way, which I find ten times more disturbing than when he's constantly hurling insults at me. He smirks like he knows something I don't, like he's thinking, "Just you wait, Heidi, because I have two huge cannons up my sleeves."

We approach the Asolo Center. Huh, funny. The oval building looks like a gigantic version of Master Douglas' home with pillars and tons of glass—except for this one is light gray with golden accents around the doors and windows. Outside on the roundabout driveway stands a bald man with a dozen Unifers. At first I think President Volkov is waiting for me and my heart immediately starts pounding.

But the closer we get, the more I think he's waiting for Johnny. The chauffeur stops the transporter and when Johnny steps out, President Volkov greets him with a warm embrace.

"Welcome home, my son," he says.

Nicholas glances at me, but quickly averts his eyes. Just as I step out, President Volkov and Johnny enter the building. Not a word to me. Not a word to Nicholas. There's no doubt what President Volkov will be announcing tonight. I decide right here and now that I am not going to let it bother me, but when I look at Nicholas, his shoulders slumped, his expression empty, my hands wind to fists.

"Are you all right?" I ask, touching his elbow.

The muscles in his jaw tighten.

"I'm sorry."

"It's not your fault. I just think...this is where my actions have led me."

"Oh." I hear the disappointment in my own voice.

Then his eyes flick to mine—angry. "I would have done it again, Heidi. That's not even a question. I just hadn't expected it to happen so abruptly."

We walk in together, hand in hand, and Nicholas escorts me to the seats up on the stage reserved for the top three contenders. I hug Cory and congratulate him on the victory. I wonder if he still plans to work against President Volkov, or if winning the entire thing will make him complacent, content to live out his life in peace. Since I was third and Johnny second, I end up having to sit next to him.

"You going to be okay?" Nicholas asks.

"Nothing you do will spare her from what's to come," Johnny says without looking at either of us.

Back to normal? "Just...just go. I'll be fine." I don't see any weapons and I certainly don't think Johnny or President Volkov will kill me in front of everyone here. This is probably the safest I've been around either of them.

Nicholas nods and makes his way down to the audience. I recognize some of the faces from the benefits, and then I see Nicholas sit down next to Dr. and Mrs. Konders. I smile when they wave.

"Finally believed me, did you?" I ask Johnny.

"Little miss know it all." He scoffs.

Well, that's an improvement from imp. "I'm glad you learned the truth."

"Don't talk to me like you're my equal."

After the blaring Savage Run march, O. J. takes the stage and reads the list of every young man who died in the Savage Run—a staggering nine hundred and seventy-two. When Arthor's name comes up, I let the tears roll down my face without shame. The bodies of the dead were cremated and their ashes scattered at sea. O. J. then reads off the names of those who quit and were sent home, a tone of dishonor in his voice. Seven hundred and seventy-one. When he announces that two hundred and ninety-six participants gained their freedom, the auditorium erupts into applause.

Next, President Volkov takes the stand. "It is my honor to announce the three fastest contenders. But first, I feel I should address the issue of our only female contestant."

It only makes sense that he would bring that up, but it doesn't make it any less uncomfortable for me.

"It was disturbing not only to me, but to many benefactors, to learn that a girl had registered illegally. I am not one to sweep anything under the rug, so if I offend, I am sorry..."

He does plenty of sweeping on other things.

"This course was not intended for females for one reason only. Not because they are weak, or should be submissive, or because they lack anything at all. Women are far more superior to men in many, many regards. Simply because of this." He grips the podium. "Six months from now, another program starts where lower class females between the ages of thirteen through seventeen will brave through obstacle courses for a chance at freedom."

I find Nicholas in the crowd, and his eyes are just as wide as mine. Why haven't I heard about this before now? I feel like a complete idiot. It's becoming difficult to maintain a neutral expression when the muscles in my face want to bend and when I feel as if I need to open my mouth to gasp for air. I think it through for a moment. I made the right choice. Had I known about this and waited six months, Gemma would have been dead by then.

"I promised the world that I was working toward changing the ways of Newland, and I hope you will take this new information as proof that I am a man of my word," President Volkov says.

Why can't he just free everyone? Not have the ranked systems? It's still all about power.

"Cory, Johnny, and Joseph, I mean Heidi," President Volkov says. "Please come here."

Cory stands up first and walks to the podium, followed by Johnny and me, even though in all truthfulness, I'd much rather not be here right now. President Volkov tells us that with our new citizenships come all the rights and privileges to Master status. We can own businesses, go to school, travel wherever we want, vote, run for office, and on and on.

"Heidi, before we hand out the IDs and certificates—"

My chest tightens up.

"I wanted to mention that due to the dishonest nature of your registration, we, the Savage Run board, voted on whether or not you were to receive your freedom."

My stomach drops like a brick, and it's as if the world is shifting beneath my feet. I look at Nicholas, and he's staring at his father like he wants to kill the man.

President Volkov's pale blue eyes peruse the audience. "Fortunately for Heidi, it has been unanimously decided that she will receive her Master status and certificate of freedom."

I didn't realize how tightly I had wound my shoulders until I release them.

Cory receives his ID and certificate first, followed by Johnny and lastly me. I sit back down when Johnny and Cory do.

"The funds of the top three participants will be distributed after the Closing Ceremonies in the green room. Now, before I let O. J. take over and distribute the rest of the IDs and certificates to those who received acceptable scores, I would like to personally congratulate all of you, and I am especially pleased to welcome you into the Master class." He claps, and the audience applauds.

After O. J. reads off and distributes the rest of the IDs and certificates, Nicholas rushes up to me on stage. He scoops me into his arms and swings me around. My laugh gets caught somewhere on its way up because I'm a little shocked that he's being so playful in front of everyone, in front of his father. Then he plants a kiss right on my lips. Pulling back, and looking into my eyes, he says, "Let's go get your money and save Gemma."

We walk down the aisle arm in arm, and I can feel President Volkov's eyes burning in the back of my neck. Johnny's threat to Nicholas lingers in my mind: "Nothing you do will spare her from what's to come."

But clutching my certificate and Master ID in my hands, there's no one who can stop me now.

END OF BOOK 1

SAVAGE RUN 2
Coming Soon

Thank you for reading! If you enjoyed my book, I would be very grateful if you left a review on amazon.com, goodreads.com or on any other site where my books are sold.

CPSIA information can be obtained at www.ICGtesting.com
Printed in the USA
LVOW12s1530100215

426459LV00005B/650/P

9 781505 406375